Dastardly Damsels

edited by Suzie Lockhart

Let the world know:
#IGotMyCLPBook!

Crystal Lake Publishing
www.CrystalLakePub.com

Follow us on Amazon:

WELCOME
TO ANOTHER

CRYSTAL LAKE PUBLISHING
CREATION

I wish to extend my gratitude to each and every author in this book, along with those that submitted stories that were not accepted. I appreciate *all of you*, because you believed in this project before we even had a publisher! I also wish to thank the silent partner that helped with the launch but prefers anonymity.

To Joe Mynhardt, I cannot thank you enough for taking on over 30 Dastardly Damsels, when your plate was already full! Thank you for your patience, listening to me beating your ears with my ideas.

To my four children, always supportive and encouraging as they cheer me on.

Marianne Halbert, thank you for stepping up as my assistant editor, recognizing the enormous size of this anthology! And to Pixie Bruner, Proofreader extraordinaire from Crystal Lake!

I also have numerous friends and family to thank . . . you know who you are!

Table of Contents

Introduction
In the Light We Don't See

SUZIE LOCKHART

Dedicated to Jaidyn Suzanne Lockhart and Brigid Erin Julia Kempton. At only six years old, Brigid passed away from devastating, early-onset Huntington's Disease . . . but in her short time, her beacon illuminated the far corners of our planet.
Jaidyn, my only daughter is Autistic; every day she fights battles of misunderstanding because the Autism Spectrum is both broad and diverse. Two brave girls who have encountered struggles . . . both seen and unseen.

Why am I talking about light we don't see when this is a *horror* anthology? Aren't women who write horror mistresses of the dark?

Well . . . yes and no. We sometimes present ourselves in that fashion because we write in the horror genre, but we are a myriad of diverse writers.

For example, people in my own circle are often stunned when they discover my main writing genre is horror because I am a born-again Christian. But, then again, I don't fit the stereotypical, in-your-face brand of Christianity often displayed in the media. I work with a wide berth of writers, consisting of Wiccans, Atheists, Christians, and everything in-between. And I am honored to work with other female horror writers because many of us are fighting similar stigmas . . . and battles of our own.

I also am often asked why I prefer to manage all-female anthologies. Men that have had serious complaints gave me pause; I had to ask myself that question and give it serious contemplation.

Obviously, I relate to the female gender, because I am female and identify as one. I'm short, only 5'1". I'm often overlooked.

But not when I write or edit. It offers me so much: power over what haunts me, peace through a character, excitement when a story comes together. (Okay, I confess . . . a little stress.) I feel larger than life in those instances.

I have shared experiences with women in the horror genre, and some have become my friends. It's a special bond I can only have through what others of the same sex have experienced. One of my best online friends is an atheist horror writer named Lindsey Goddard. She gave me permission to mention her because she is an open book. It's one of the qualities I admire about her.

We were chatting one day, and she told me about a woman who made it a point to avoid her . . . like she expected to be bitten or something equally horrific. You see, Lindsey has a ton of tattoos and a very goth appearance. She avoided her and missed the light of a person with a sensitive and beautiful soul. That light was a missed opportunity because she wouldn't allow herself to *look* . . . long enough to see it! (Unfortunately, Lindsey had a death in the family during our submission call.)

Sometimes light IS good . . . but not always.

I thought I knew the manner of presentation I wanted to utilize in writing this introduction, and although I'd planned to introduce our readers to the authors that haunt these pages (I'll let the reader be surprised . . .), something my daughter said gave me pause.

I asked her on a whim what *she* thought was in the light we don't see. Her answer stunned me. She said simply, "Evil."

Whoa . . . what?

In one word, she summed it up. Those are the dots I was hoping to connect: light and evil. But her verbalizing it had me heading down the proverbial rabbit hole.

Evil has often been personified as darkness, while goodness or holiness are often used as metaphors for 'the light' . . . but is that truly, well . . . truth?

The first example that obviously pops into my head is mentioned in the Bible, by name only one time: Lucifer. He was once an Angel of 'brightness' known as *The Morning Star*.

I wondered if there were light beings in other cultures that weren't, well . . . good. Hmm.

Yuki-onna is a type of spirit known in Japan as "Yokai". Not someone I'd relish bumping into, as she evokes demons, shapeshifters, and more familiar spirits: ghosts.

Introduction

Quite a number of people believe in ghosts, and some ghosts are considered spirits of unrest who haunt their victims. They are described as translucent beings sporting an unnatural *light*. Words from a favorite song, by Tauren Wells, come to mind:

> ***"A shadow that you thought was the light***
> ***Won't keep away the monsters at night***
> ***That haunt your heart."***

I know a few people who can relate to that. I can.

Although that is your more basic intro into the evils lurking in the 'disguise of light' . . . there is more. There are spectrums of light the human eye cannot see without aide.

Well, that isn't entirely accurate. There are females (only) that have four cones in their eyes as opposed to three. This means they can see more colors on the spectrum! If four eye cones can do that, how many colors are there . . . ?

There is a range of red that cannot be seen with the human eye. During the Vietnam war, goggles were developed (there is speculation it might've been based on Nazi technology) which allowed pilots access to the infrared spectrum. It wasn't the same type as used in equipment today. Those men reported seeing horrific monsters that appeared to also have the ability to also see them! The beings were described as 'demonic' in appearance.

This bodes one to ask, why were the scary creatures also seeing them? They are accessed in that spectrum visually, but are they still . . . out there?

And what's lurking in the ultraviolet range?

Our own bodies give off a light considered an aura, but it disappears when we die. It has been documented that we lose six ounces of weight unaccounted for at death . . . Where does it go?

There are many theories.

But consider something as you read this anthology. Should you be afraid of the dark . . . or is what you cannot see in the light . . . that you should beware of?

Foreword

We all know the trope. From fairytales to Greek mythology, from Gothic fiction to creature features, the young maiden in peril has often been the object that drives forward the story arc of the hero. He would save her by slaying a beast, defeating the enemy, or even just gently planting a mere kiss on her ruby lips. The expectation, of course, was that her love would be his reward.

A virginal maiden enjoying a charmed life finds herself chained to a rock. She is naked, exposed, shivering, and most importantly: utterly helpless. Sprays of seafoam tease her impending doom as her equally hopeless parents clutch each other and sob nearby. Her fate: to be sacrificed to a leviathan encroaching from the ocean depths. But this is not *her* story. She is merely a vehicle, albeit a stunningly beautiful, hopeless, and helpless vehicle, for the tale of the hero. He swoops in to rescue her, vanquishing the monster, and saving her life. Of course, the explicit expectation is that in return for his heroics, she will love him.

An ingenue seeking fame is sacrificed to a giant primate who secrets her deep within an exotic and savage jungle, giving the hero a reason to be— well, heroic. The ingenue's only attributes? She is beautiful. She is helpless. She is in desperate need of rescue. And she will love the hero.

A pure-of-heart princess succumbs to an evil witch's spell and falls into a death-like slumber. She can only be awoken by true love's kiss. Enter the hero and the expectation of love as rightful compensation.

If you're expecting me to describe the woman bound to the train tracks, struggling against her restraints, muffled cries coming from behind the gag in her mouth, I don't need to. You're already picturing the villain twirling his mustache as you read this. So very dastardly. You get the idea. We all know the trope.

Foreword

These are not the stories you'll find within Dastardly Damsels.

I saw the call for submissions for this anthology on Twitter. The title caught my attention immediately. *Dastardly Damsels*. Such a charming contrast. The theme hooked me. "Female or female-identifying authors with stories that include strong elements of horror. Must feature a female symbol of strength." I was familiar with "Killing It Softly" (edited by Suzie Lockhart) and knew the type of talent this project would draw. I couldn't *not* submit a story. After having my story accepted, over a series of conversations, Suzie and I decided the best use of my superpowers would be to assist her in editing the anthology. I withdrew my story, and dove into helping to edit these tales, and what a treat it has been!

As noted, we are all inordinately familiar with the trope of the *damsel in distress*.

But literature, television, and film have introduced stronger, not-so-helpless characters. Women who might be gorgeous or describe themselves as plain, but were remarkable because they were intelligent and brave, and would not be bound by expectations of romantic devotion. This anthology takes things a step further. I imagine some of my favorite characters such as Stephen King's 'Carrie White' and Shirley Jackson's 'Merricat Blackwood' would find themselves very much at home with the dastardly damsels that inhabit these pages.

As I read these stories, what struck me was not only the unremitting talent when it came to the writing styles and the "voice" of each author, but how refreshingly unpredictable these stories are. Whether the protagonist is a human or something else (and, to my delight, these stories include a wide assortment of "something else") they are the ones to fear. The lead characters may find themselves in hopeless situations, but they are far from helpless. Their resolve, ferocity, and drive – whether for self-preservation, protecting another, revenge, or other motivation – is relentless. When strong female characters have agency over their own fate and exercise that agency despite overwhelming odds, I find myself cheering. When they're dastardly because the situation calls for that, I cheer even more.

The authors in this anthology include names you may be familiar with, some may be new to you, but all brought their A-game when it comes to providing you, dear reader, with their unique version of the dastardly damsel. These damsels aren't helpless. They definitely don't need a hero to swoop in to rescue them. These are *their* stories.

They might rescue you; they might inspire you; they might shock you; they might just destroy you. And in return, I predict . . . you *will* love them.

—*Marianne Halbert*
October 2023

Thy Neighbor

NANCY HOLDER

This story is for Leslie Ackel, Mother of Cats.

Brianna pulled her Toyota into the Goodes' driveway and made a sour face as Kelsey got ready to get out.

"I hate this place. It's so creepy," Brianna said.

Kelsey saw a fairly standard two-story stucco house with a tall arched doorway and a brick wishing well in the grassy front yard.

"It's a normal house in Normal Heights," Kelsey replied. "Nicer than most. You don't see a lot of wishing wells."

Brianna huffed. "They probably chose this neighborhood for the irony. These people are not normal."

"They're totally normal. They're just workaholics." Kelsey flopped down the sun visor and checked her eye makeup. She was a freckle-faced blue-eyed blonde. Brianna was the one who always got all the looks when they went to the mall together, dark and mysterious, wafting sexy perfumes with names Kelsey had never heard of.

"They're freaky," Brianna insisted.

"See, I don't get that. They don't seem freaky at all to me."

"Weird. Well, fingers crossed that Three-Three-Three takes a nap. Then call me and we'll avoid the flunkation of calculus."

Kelsey shrugged, raised the sun visor back into position, and gave her friend a little smile. "You know that's not too likely. He never naps."

"Because he's evil."

"Lonely," Kelsey countered. "His parents are never home."

"Because they're out worshiping Satan." Brianna pointed through the windshield. "What the hell is *that*?"

Kelsey followed Brianna's pointed finger. In the center of the brick walk to the arched doorway sat a sort of triangular bundle of sticks. They looked as though they had been tied together by leaves or twine.

"It's a bundle of sticks," she said patiently.

"It's some witchy thing." Brianna shook her head. "I wish you'd quit working for them. No one needs money this badly, not even you. There's a bazillion childcare gigs in the job bank in Mrs. Meyerson's office. San Diego is full of jobs. Go look."

"No one pays as much as these guys," Kelsey said. "College is going to be expensive. And their fridge is a fairyland of food."

"They're paying you well because they're prepping you for sacrifice. They're fattening you up for the slaughter. If you had any sense at all, you'd give it up to Troy. They can only use virgins."

Kelsey mock-pouted as she opened the car door. "You make me sound so blond and naive. I'm not. I'm totally in the know." She wrinkled her nose as she got out. "And seriously, *Troy*? No one is that desperate, not even me."

"Troy's unit could save your life," Brianna replied. She lowered her voice and affected a British accent. "Or your immortal soul." She made the sign of the cross.

"He could give me a disease," she replied and gave Brianna a wave. "I'll walk home," she reminded her. "It's not that far."

"No wonder my mother loves you," Brianna said. "Text me every thirty seconds."

"Drive carefully, Bree," she said. "I mean it."

Brianna nodded and Kelsey waved as Brianna backed out. She hadn't even reached the front door when Three-Three-Three, AKA Jonah, pushed it open, shrieking with joy. They called him Three-Three-Three because he was too little to be Six-Six-Six.

He threw his arms around Kelsey's legs as his mother appeared behind him, looking so young Kelsey wondered how on earth she could be his mother.

"Hi, Kelse," Ms. Goode said. She was wearing a business suit and she was probably off to a meeting. Kelsey knew the Goodes had other sitters, practically around the clock. Both of Three-Three-Three's parents were always coming and going and in the six weeks Kelsey had worked for them, their schedules had never been the same for two days running.

"Listen, I finally saw Mr. Bright and I asked him to give back

Magic's rawhide bone and he won't." She scowled as she fluffed up her hair. "He says that anything that lands in his yard is his."

"Nice," Kelsey said. Mr. Bright was their reclusive next-door neighbor. Ms. Goode had told her that she'd only seen him a handful of times since they'd moved in five years ago.

Ms. Goode grinned. "I hope I can hold him to it. I caught Jonah lobbing the puppy's turds over the fence this morning."

Kelsey cracked up. "That's one way to clean up the yard."

She sighed. "I suppose I should also tell you that my little angel stopped up the guest room toilet with his Legos."

That's why we call him Three-Three-Three, Kelsey thought.

"Let's go see the puppy!" Jonah shrieked, yanking on Kelsey's hand.

"Anyway, so use our bathroom and be careful with anything going over the fence. Because that's the last you'll ever see of it."

"Got it," Kelsey said.

Ms. Goode bent to kiss Jonah, but Jonah grabbed Kelsey's hand and bellowed, "Magic! Magic! Magic!"

Kelsey waved goodbye to Ms. Goode and she and Jonah zoomed into the back yard where the little black Doberman was bounding around with a tennis ball in his mouth. He saw Jonah and yipped, dropping the ball. It bounced and rolled to Kelsey, and she picked it up. The dog sprang up and down like crazy, and she tossed it toward Jonah.

"Catch, Jonah!" she cried, gently lobbing the ball.

The ball slipped through Jonah's fingers. He muttered, "Oops," and scooped it up. Then he trotted over to the fence, grinned at Kelsey, scrabbled onto a white wrought-iron chair planted beside a matching table, and threw the ball as hard as he could over the eight-foot barrier. It just cleared the top.

"Jonah," she protested mildly. "Why did you do that?"

He covered his mouth with both hands and giggled. Then he ran around in a circle making noises like an airplane while poor Magic kept his gaze glued to Kelsey, sitting down and chuffing when no tennis ball was forthcoming.

"Do you have another ball?" she asked the wee terror-boy. He shook his head.

Magic whined.

"I can't believe you bought a can of tennis balls for their *dog*," Brianna said the next day.

"You haven't done much babysitting, have you?" Kelsey said. "Sitters do stuff like this." She tapped the can. "Three bright yellow tennis balls cost two dollars. The goodwill? Priceless."

"Well then, well done, old chap, well done. You are perhaps sneakier than I gave you credit for," Brianna said in a snobby British accent.

"I am often underestimated," Kelsey said, dipping her head.

"He'll have them over the fence in five minutes," Brianna declared.

"He's grown as a person since you met him."

"Six weeks ago? When he *peed on my shoe?*"

"Yeah, well." Kelsey made a "sorry" face. "He's just feisty."

"You got this job to *make* money, not to lose it," Brianna reminded her. "Dogs can catch sticks. Sticks are free." She pointed a finger at Kelsey. "Don't be too soft-hearted."

"Me? Never." She got out of the car and put her hand on the open window. "Drive safely."

"Text me if you get a break."

"Give *me* a break," Kelsey said, and they both smiled ruefully.

Then Brianna's eyes widened, and she jabbed a finger through the windshield. "Witch sticks! Witch sticks!" she said.

Another triangular bundle of twigs lay on the path to the house. Kelsey shrugged.

"It's nothing," she said. "God, Bree."

"They're freaky," Brianna said, and she drove away.

This time one of the other babysitters was on deck; she gave Kelsey the lowdown on all the nefarious things Jonah had done that day.

"So far," she finished. She couldn't get out of there fast enough.

When Kelsey entered the house, she saw why: Jonah had used chocolate syrup—no, Nutella—to finger paint on the sliding glass door that led to the backyard. She examined the brown smears and found his name and some happy faces. And was that a pentagram?

She wrote "333" with her forefinger, then filled a bucket with water and found two sponges. Then she called Jonah in.

4

He protested, of course, he did, and then he bargained.

"If we clean it all up, can we play with Magic for hours and hours?"

She grinned at him. "Sure, buddy."

Jonah got bored and tried to quit more times than Kelsey could keep track of. But they finally got the syrup cleaned up. She showed Jonah the can of tennis balls and encouraged him to make every effort to keep them on their side of the fence. But as if he really was possessed, he tossed them merrily over the fence into Mr. Bright's yard.

As she'd known he would.

The next day, Ms. Goode met her at the door. She was dressed in a black business suit and there was a briefcase in her hand. Her face was drawn, her manner grave. She came out onto the porch and pulled the door closed behind her.

"Mr. Bright died last night," she said quietly.

"Oh," Kelsey said. "That's . . . terrible. How did it happen?"

"It was bad. It looks like he had some kind of stomach bug. He was getting up to go to the kitchen and he had a heart attack. And he fell . . . " She swallowed " . . . into the fireplace."

"Yow," Kelsey said. "Wow."

"I'm not clear how they knew to come. The EMT's, I mean. It was two in the morning and they broke down the door. Jonah slept through the whole thing. But of course, *we* didn't." She waited, and Kelsey nodded, not sure what else to do.

"We hardly knew him, but if Jonah hears about it . . . I mean, it was so gruesome."

Death can be very gruesome, Kelsey thought but didn't say.

"You might wait until he asks," Kelsey said. "He might never know." She thought about saying something then but didn't.

"I see." Ms. Goode nodded as if she were taking notes. "Will you be all right if I leave? I can call and cancel—"

"I'll be fine," Kelsey said, mildly curious about whom Ms. Goode would call and what she would cancel. It didn't matter. After tonight, she would give her notice. "Really."

"Okay." Ms. Goode smiled sadly at her, scooted into the garage, and left.

That afternoon, Three-Three-Three took a nap. In fact, he slept like a log. And would, until full moonrise. Kelsey had arranged it with a triangle of twigs under his bed.

The triangles were charms, which she had created to protect the Goodes from magical fallout. To keep them safe, even as she used their house as the base of her operation. That was why she had taken the job. And that was why, after tonight, she would no longer need it.

She waited for darkness to fall, and the moon to lift, and then she clambered over the fence. In her right hand was the empty tennis ball can. She carried a flashlight in her right, and she clicked it on. She supposed Mr. Bright's relatives would show up fairly soon. Maybe the police were keeping an eye on the house. She needed to do this. She needed, in her way, to make sure that he had paid the ultimate price.

Arnold Bright's yard was a mess, a jungle of dandelions and mustard plants. A rusty rake sat crossed over a wheelbarrow encased in pampas grass and in it, she saw Magic's rawhide bone, perhaps a dozen tennis balls, Nerf balls, baseballs, and lots of Lego pieces. Kept out of spite. Kept because he was mean.

The three tennis balls she had brought for Magic shimmered with very faint green energy. Wisps of smoke rose into the night sky. If she had worked the spell properly, everything would dissipate now that she had completed the hex.

Magic worked in threes. Three balls. Three hexes. Stomach, heart, fire.

Her hand shook a little as she picked up each ball and put it back in the can. They bobbled like trapped birds as she sealed the end with the plastic lid. Jonah had happily tossed them over the fence for her, and so Mr. Bright had received them from the hand of an innocent. That had set the curses in motion.

She murmured an incantation in backwards Latin and if the back door was locked, it wasn't now. It swung open as she approached.

"You're dead, you bastard," she whispered and violated his house. To her surprise, it was clean and orderly, giving no hint of the destruction Mr. Bright had caused. The screaming, weeping, wishing of her parents, and her bargaining.

The plotting, the planning, and the learning.

A spell to find the driver who had hit Mark and left him for dead. A spell to kill him. A spell to send the unrepentant murderer's soul to hell.

She had found Mr. Arnold Bright, who lived next to the Goodes on Leland Street. Now his body was in the morgue, and she was in his house.

But soon he would dwell elsewhere, somewhere horrible, forever.

There was hardly anything in his house—the kitchen counters were barren. There were no pictures on the walls of the family room. Just one easy chair, and a TV. Cursed. Miserable.

Good.

But the next room was busier; there was an old oak dining table piled high with manila folders. She crossed to it and opened the first folder.

Her brother's smiling face stared up at her from a news clipping about the accident—the crime. Hit and run. Unidentified driver, who took off.

All the clippings, collected in folder after folder. She smiled grimly, glad to see that he had been haunted by what he'd done. That was the curse she had learned for the killer of her brother: that he, or she, shouldn't have a moment of peace. In his mind's eye, he'd see the wreck he'd walked away from, the boy whose life he could have saved if he hadn't so callously fled.

"Good," she muttered. "I'm glad."

But the second stack of folders was different: they contained pamphlets from Alcoholics Anonymous about taking everything one day at a time. There was a computer chart that told a story of its own: One Day Sober, One Week, One Month, Ninety Days.

A picture of Jesus and a Bible verse:

For I will forgive their wickedness and will remember their sins no more.

"What the hell?" she muttered.

She slowly sat in the chair Arnold Bright must have sat in. She looked at the clippings, each one. She found part of an email printout:

I have to make amends. It will give the family closure if I come forward.

And an answer:

—Yes, but it will ruin your life if you do. Do other things, great things, and find peace.

Then there were clippings about donations to charities, about an anonymous "good Samaritan" who went around cleaning up trash and performing good deeds. Never identified. Never discovered. What a saint.

Another email:

—I'm so proud of you.

Another answer:

I never dreamed my life would turn around so completely because I did something so wrong. I'm forgiven. I'm happy. Fulfilled.

She clenched her fists and clamped her jaw in fury.

"No," she said, "this is wrong."

The moon blazed full through the window. Three tennis balls to curse him, and a soul to seal the deal.

A weakened, aching, miserable soul.

She had thought it would be his, Mr. Arnold Bright's.

But now . . . she wasn't so sure.

She stared down at her dead brother's happy face. At the emails.

The can of tennis balls wiggled on the table.

She smelled the sulfur. She felt the heat.

The One was standing behind the chair. Her hair stood on end and she began to shake.

She said, "You said that if I served you, you would take the soul of the unrepentant murderer in payment."

There was a chuckle. And then a low, evil voice whispered fire and brimstone and damnation in her ear:

"Let's go."

Moth Girl

Katie Young

For Amber, Liz, and Louise—with all my warped love.

The first relic Emily ever took was a sorry specimen. She had been sitting on a blanket, eating a peanut butter sandwich, cut into small triangles, when a movement in the grass caught her eye. Rolling onto her belly, sandwich forgotten, Emily put her face low to the ground and gently parted the cool grass. A train of soldier ants marched relentlessly through the roots. Emily placed her finger in their midst, and they scattered only to reform their neat line immediately when she lifted it again. Order restored.

She watched them for a while, scurrying with feelers winding around and around, until something extraordinary passed under her nose. A few of the ants bore a strange object on their backs. A dead wasp, black and yellow striped with a crushed stinger and curled up legs. It must have been at least ten times the size of the largest ant, but they hurried along with their burden as though it weighed nothing at all.

Emily reached out a small hand and carefully snatched the wasp up by its wings. She laid it gently on the blanket. The ants scampered to—and fro—for a bit, butting heads and wriggling their antennae in the empty air above them, searching the space where their cargo had been. Emily peered back over her shoulder to find the grown-ups still deep in conversation. She spied a discarded cocktail stick on a waxed paper plate and picked it up. Turning her attention back to the wasp, she poked at it experimentally, but its body remained tightly furled, so she speared its desiccated thorax to the woolen fabric with the sharp little stick. Once it was pinned, she closed her tiny fingers around the base of one wing, avoiding the poisoned stinger, and tugged. To her delight, the wing came off cleanly.

She put it on her tingling palm, cupping slightly lest it should be taken on the breeze, and tilted it toward the light. It looked like a miniature, intricate, lead-paned window. Emily wondered what it would be like to have wings of her own, like a wasp, a bird, or an angel. She pulled the second delicate wing off and wrapped them both in her hankie which she folded and tucked up the sleeve of her sweater. She threw the rest of the wasp back to the ants.

Over the next few months and years, Emily's collection expanded. She harvested the corpses of blue bottles from windowsills and scoured the inside of the glass lamps on the porch for the burnt-up shells of moths. She gathered feathers and trailed dozy crane flies until they dropped so she could rid them of their gossamer appendages.

One day, she even found a dead tree Swallow out in the woods, but her mother made her wrap it in newspaper and put it in the trash before she could devise the best way of removing its pretty, iridescent wings. Emily didn't understand why the bird made her mother squeamish. It wasn't as if she'd killed it herself. She only ever took from things that were already dead.

At sixteen, Emily decided it was a shame to preserve her collection inside of matchboxes wrapped in tissue paper, hidden in drawers. An artistic girl, she began to model tiny bodies out of wire and clay, out of slivers of chicken bone and matchsticks, bound up using her own hair. To each of these creations, she carefully attached the wings of an insect. She made a ring of teensy beings with bright red and yellow ladybird wings. She crafted imps with long dragonfly wings that shimmered with a myriad of colors, like oil on water. She sculpted a creature—a fallen angel—adorning him with the sleek, jet-black wing casing of a stag beetle, and fashioning him a crown from its vicious jaws. It seemed fitting to make something lasting out of these small, impermanent bodies; objects both beautiful and grotesque as they had been in life.

Emily's parents, while unnerved by her macabre little creations, recognized her talent. They stopped confiscating the food scraps she squirreled away from her dinner plate for the bones and swept the husks of bumble bees on her bedside table into the bin.

Over time, she became well-known in the town. People came

from far and wide to photograph her work, and a local art gallery offered Emily an exhibition of her very own. She accepted, and critics and journalists arrived in her sleepy town to meet this mysterious young prodigy. Despite protestations from her father, she eschewed college, preferring to concentrate on her dioramas. By the time she was nineteen, Emily was making a fine living as a renowned artist—with pieces in the Renwick and the Guggenheim.

Emily bought herself a cabin on the outskirts of the woods where she'd spent endless hours hunting for bug and butterfly remnants as a child, favoring the solitude and space over the bustle of the cities she frequented for work. The walls of her home were decorated with glass cases containing swallowtails and death's head moths, Goliath beetles and metallic blue morphos, all staked out, their wings spread and shimmering when they caught the light. Domes and bell jars filled bookshelves, boasting excellent examples of antique taxidermy: hummingbirds and finches, wrens and orioles.

She used one of the bedrooms as her workshop. It had a large, south-facing window which let in plenty of light from dawn until dusk. She'd sit for hours, hunched over her minuscule models, her fingers quick and nimble beneath the magnifying lens as she whittled and threaded and bent and wrapped. She'd hold her breath as she applied minute blobs of glue before the precise placement of the fragile wings, held lightly by sharp-tipped tweezers.

Emily took commissions from private collectors, but mostly she worked on large ensemble pieces. Vast tableaus of warring seraphs, fairy banquets, and goblin trials; warped scenes of mischief and terror which, once in situ, crowds paid to see in droves. The more acclaim she received, the more determined she became to make increasingly ambitious and fantastical pieces.

One warm evening in early summer, Emily sat on her porch drinking a glass of Viognier; a rare indulgence as she usually avoided any substance which might give her steady hands even a slight tremor. As she watched the darkening sky, a large moth flitted up towards the light by her front door. Emily recognized it immediately.

A Luna moth.

She knew that, although not uncommon, the nocturnal moths only lived a week in their adult form, so were rarely seen by the human eye. It circled the lamp outside the cabin, bright green wings fluttering frantically. Emily slowly got to her feet and crept towards it, tipping the dregs of her drink out onto the ground as she went. She watched as the moth landed on the wall in a pool of sodium light, its chartreuse wings beating intermittently. Emily's arm shot out, the large glass fitting over the moth, trapping it against the wall. The panicked creature bounced around inside the confines of the wine glass and finally settled. Emily slid the glass to the edge of the wall and placed her hand flat over the open end. She took the moth into her kitchen and put the glass, still upturned, onto the table.

Then . . . she waited.

Guilt squirmed in her belly as Emily pegged the moth down by its fat, furry body and set to work removing the wings. They were a vibrant absinthe color, rimmed with black, and on each of the four sections was a round marking, which looked like a tiny moon during the middle of an eclipse. At the bottom, each wing swept down into two long tails.

Beautiful.

Emily had never killed before. Her father had once told her that killing a moth, or a butterfly would bring bad luck down upon a person. In some cultures, moths were considered harbingers of death. They were feared and revered. But Emily *needed* those wings. The moth would only have lived for a week at best. Was it really so wrong . . . to steal a few short days when she could immortalize its beauty and share it with the whole world?

The Luna moth's wings became the centerpiece of Emily's latest work; a fae queen dancing in a stone circle by the light of the full moon. Critics agreed it was her best yet. But something had shifted irrevocably inside Emily. Her queen seemed imbued with an extra, indefinable quality, as though the spirit of the moth; its essence, lingered in the peridot sheen of its wings. No more would she make do with tattered remains and found objects. Only perfection would do, and perfection required sacrifice.

Emily made a killing jar, emptying out the dill pickles, rinsing it, and putting a piece of kitchen towel soaked in ethyl acetate in the bottom. Before long, every surface in her home was covered with drying specimens and parts of insects and small animals. Emily caught shrews, mice, voles, frogs, and small birds and boiled their creamy bones clean. She turned their skulls into little chalices, their spines into ladders, their pelts and feathers into diminutive robes.

There was a particular smell in the cottage now. Emily was used to the musty smell of old death. Desiccated husks, dry bones, and teeth, moldering fur and dust. But this new stink was intoxicating. Blood and innards — metallic, elemental, vital.

Sleep became fitful. When she closed her eyes, she saw the Luna moth flapping inside the wine glass and heard the thrumming of its wings. She saw the life leeching out of its wet, black eyes as the fern-like feelers on its head thrashed and drooped. A strange, squeezing sensation gripped Emily's chest. She supposed that it was grief of a kind but, even as the pangs kept her awake, she knew it was only a matter of time before she'd watch something else die so that she could give it a new life.

But if she was ever to sleep through the night again, Emily needed to atone for her deeds. For each life she took, she'd contribute a little something of herself to restore the balance. A lock of hair. A fingernail. A smear of blood. It worked at first. The dreams became less harrowing, and Emily grew more and more prolific.

The first time one of her sculptures moved of its own accord, it startled Emily so much that she urinated a little in her underwear. She was attaching an elf-like creature with the wings of a leafhopper to a saddle, which was to be mounted upon a large tree spider, when the wings twitched. At first, Emily thought she must have exhaled, ruffling them with her breath, but then the wings began to beat in earnest and the thing *flew*. It *flew*. Emily shrieked and locked herself in the bathroom where she stayed for a full hour. When she finally returned to her workshop, everything was still, and the tiny creature was lying motionless on her desk.

The second time came as less of a shock. The third time, she was almost expecting it. After a while, she became used to the occasional flurry of activity. It was actually quite comforting to know that the things she pulled apart and rearranged bore her no ill will. They seemed to enjoy their second incarnations, scuttling and lumbering and fluttering as much as the artificial parts of their new forms would allow. Emily learned to enjoy their company. It was like sharing her home with lots of strange little pets.

Emily became reluctant to share her artwork with the outside world, only selling when she really needed to, and putting more and more of herself into each piece. She was especially proud of her depiction of a tooth fairy. It had the wings of a cabbage white, and carried a little moleskin bag, inside which rested a premolar which Emily had carefully levered out of her own mouth with a dinner knife.

But the raw materials Emily had to give were finite. She found that blood loss and pain were not conducive to creativity. They made her eyesight blurry and her hands tremble. Her mind got all fogged up and she couldn't find her way to conjure up the fantastical images required for new designs.

But a line had been crossed. A door had been opened that could never again be closed. Emily's tiny miracles were a delicate balance of animal and human parts. A pact had been made, and Emily couldn't renege now. For every little life she took, Emily must restore the balance with human ingredients.

It was surprisingly easy the first time. Emily washed and brushed her hair, put on a floaty top, and slicked some pink lipstick on. She drove an hour south of her woods and found a bar—the kind of dive where people went to be anonymous. The sort of place that people whose lives were going well would avoid. She pulled up a stool and ordered a rum and cola. The sugar and caffeine would render her useless for a day or two, but she needed to settle her nerves. Most of the men in the room made her skin crawl. They were either older than her father or looked dirty or smelled bad. She nursed her drink and finally caught sight of a young man shooting pool. He seemed less threatening than the others. Emily slipped from her barstool and moved over to the tables. She watched the man break with a crack and the shiny little balls spin around the green baize at dizzying speed. He looked up, held her gaze, and smiled.

He pawed at her all the way home. He was drunk enough not to ask how much further it was after the first few times. Instead, he turned his attention to feeling Emily's knee through her jeans and trying to nuzzle her neck. Emily kept her eyes on the road and cooed and told him *not long now, Sweetheart.*

She didn't ask his name. She took her clothes off and waited for him to do the same. He looked pale in the gloom of her bedroom, almost luminous like that first moth. He seemed much more fragile now he was naked. Emily poured the man a drink, which he tossed back greedily. She told him to lie on the bed and close his eyes. It didn't take long for the sedative to take effect. Once he was snoring deeply, Emily held a cloth soaked in chloroform over his mouth and nose for several long minutes and waited for the rise and fall of his chest to stop.

She kept his body in an old chest freezer in the outhouse. It made for a strange reliquary. She tried various methods to preserve him, to keep him dry and clean like insects. But she found herself locked in a losing battle with the invisible lifeforms that began to liquify and consume her offering, and soon he was soup and pulp and fruiting bodies.

But Emily persevered. She found smaller segments were easier to maintain than the whole. She kept only what she needed and returned the rest to the earth. Food for the trees. Beetles could strip the flesh from a hand or a foot in no time. Packing in warm sand kept the creeping things at bay. Boiling was unsatisfactory for larger bones. The eyes began to lose their jewel-like colors almost immediately after the heart stopped. Some oils were better than others at keeping the skin supple enough to craft minute leather shoes with. Delicate tattoos could be fashioned into painted canvases or patterned upholstery for miniature thrones and sedan chairs. Hair and teeth were extremely versatile—but she knew that anyway.

Emily became something of a recluse. Her patrons didn't mind. The art world was full of eccentrics, and her unwillingness to leave her home just fueled the collective curiosity of her fans. She got a double-page feature in the New York Times when one of her exhibits featured a tiny drum made from what appeared to be the intermediate phalanx of a human toe.

Her parents, once simultaneously proud of and bewildered by her odd career choice, tried to maintain contact, but their phone calls and visits trailed off after months and years of finding themselves turned away and roundly ignored. Emily didn't much care. She had always felt more at home with the quiet little remains and cadavers she hoarded and repurposed. There was magic to be found in the decadent, fragmented parts of beasts. She had never realized quite how much magic . . . until now.

But something was shifting. The once docile little creations began to bite and sting. Emily would find them on her pillow at night, tiny weapons raised. She heard whispers coming from the cobwebby corners of rooms, the spaces between the floorboards. She found sprinklings of what appeared to be powdery glass in her food and glittering among the sediment in her increasingly frequent glasses of wine. No number of sacrifices seemed to appease the dead things in Emily's cottage.

It took them a long time to check on her, after she had stopped turning in work. Her agent finally raised the alarm when it transpired that Emily hadn't cashed a single check for a full year. It wasn't clear how long she'd been gone, but the interior of her house was cloaked in a layer of dust that suggested months and months of stasis. At first, everyone supposed that she had simply vanished — upped and left one day — but upon closer inspection, it became apparent that Emily was still in the house.

All over the house, in fact.

They found bits of her scattered about every room, jumbled up with her works of art. Fairytale creatures read tiny books bound with vellum made from her skin. Her hair had been spun into a yellow-gold rug for a family of chimeras. The bones of her fingers had been whittled into delicate crockery, and her skull turned into a coach for some skeletal pixies. Her teeth dangled from strands of her loose hair and hung at different lengths from the lintel so that they jingled when a breeze caught them. She had been picked apart with such skill and dexterity that, when news of her death got out, the media speculated that the deranged artist had done much of the deconstruction herself.

But what had happened to the rest of Emily? Who had finished her transformation? And who had buried all those poor boys in the woods around the cottage? The simple fact was, although the house was meticulously searched from top to bottom, no evidence could be found that anyone unaccounted for had ever set foot inside.

There were, however, tracks in the dust that covered every surface of Emily's house. Tiny, perfect paw prints. Scuffs and scrapes. Trails of what could be written off as insect and rodent life. Birds and rats setting up home in the abandoned cabin. If it occurred to anyone involved that the marks seemed a bit too organized, a little too ordered, or too *purposeful*, they never mentioned it. And if anyone thought they heard malicious little laughs and whispers in the rafters, then it must have been the wind rasping through the dry leaves of the woods and whistling through the old window frames.

Just the wind.

Caught Out

ROSE BLACKTHORN

To Geno—my biggest fan and the one who, after reading each of my short stories, invariably says, "And then what happens?"

It's dark out here beneath the starlit sky. The only light is a faint reflection in the treetops from the dive bar on the highway. Jukebox music comes from there too, and the occasional sound of an engine as a car or truck speeds by on its way into town.

I'm wondering now if Billy was just teasing. When he asked me today after school if I'd meet him in the woods between the highway and our little country lane, my heart seized up and my breath caught in my throat. I tried to be cool and act like it was no big deal, even though my lips had gone numb, and my fingertips were tingling. Billy's a year older than me, and he's cute. In a few years, he's like to be downright handsome, and I've had a crush on him as long as I can remember. He talks to me sometimes, sits by me in class, but never gives me any special attention before. However, I have finally reached that age where I'm starting to look more like a woman and less like a little girl, so maybe that's the difference now. My mouth was so dry when he asked, I couldn't even manage to speak, so I just nodded.

"Out by the poplar," he added with the little crooked grin that made my heart start to pound again. "I'll meet you at midnight." When he walked away, he looked back once just to see if I was watching and smiled wide when he saw that I was.

The thing about meeting him at midnight, though . . . that meant sneaking out of the house and stealing down the road and through the woods in the night shadows. I'd have to be extra

18

careful, 'cause if Daddy caught me out, I wouldn't be sitting for a few days.

I'm wearing my best jeans, faded but without any holes or frayed spots. I pulled my hair up with the rhinestone barrette I got from Mama before she passed, letting it hang loose down my back. I know I'm no beauty, but I do have a few things going for me, and my long, thick hair is one of them. I dabbed a tiny bit of Mama's expensive flowery perfume behind my earlobes and on the inside of my wrists, the perfume that's almost all gone now— and there won't be anymore. I checked that Daddy was still in the living room with Uncle John, both men settled in the old lumpy recliners and watching TV while they talked and sipped at bottles of beer. My younger brother Jimmy was asleep in his own closet-sized room, snoring lightly when I poked my head in. I climbed out my bedroom window, quiet as a whisper, and went out into the night, feeling excited and a little scared. As I crept through the woods, I kept thinking about Mama and wondering what she'd say if she could see me right now.

Something moves in the shadows. I see pretty well at night, but I wish I had a flashlight. Or, even more, wished I had a cell phone to use for light. Or to send a text to Billy and find out where he is. No cell phone for me, though. I've asked before, even offered to get a part-time job after school to earn the money for it. Daddy made it clear, and not too kindly.

"You earnin' money, it can go toward the household bills." He'd stood there, slightly slumped in his dirty boots and threadbare shirt, looking twenty years older than his actual forty-five. In the pictures of his and Mama's wedding day, he'd been straight and tall and smiling. Hard to recognize that he's the same man. Losing Mama had been mighty hard on him, as hard as it had been on me and Jimmy. Losing her with no warning just made it worse. "Might be a good idea anyway; we could use the extra cash. But your mama made me promise you wouldn't have to work 'til after graduation. You can do without some expensive gadget, least 'til you're done with school." Then he'd turned away, going to the fridge to grab a beer, and that was the end of that.

The wind's rising now, making the leaves shiver and rustle. More engine sounds from the highway, a lot of them. The bikers I guess, pullin' in or out of the dive bar's gravel parking lot. They've been hanging around town the last two or three weeks, rough-looking men with long hair and beards, dressed in denim and leather and smelling of smoke and whiskey. It's pretty warm tonight, even at this late hour, as Indian summer hangs on through the end of September. Still, I shiver and hug myself, nervous but excited as I wonder what will happen when Billy gets here. I don't have a watch, but I'm pretty sure I've been out here more than half an hour. Much as I want to see how things might go, I'm not gonna wait all night for Billy, regardless of how cute he is. He said to meet at the poplar, and that means only one thing out here. The ancient, giant poplar tree that's so big it made its own little clearing. It stands dozens of feet taller than any other trees in the area, and I'm leaning against its wrinkled bark.

More sounds from the highway. Tires screeching on the pavement, revving engines, voices raised in celebration or anger; it's hard to tell from half a mile away. Something rustles in the underbrush not far from the edge of the clearing, but I can't see anything. Is Billy playing games?

"Billy?" I say it quietly but make my voice firm.

More crackling, furtive sounds. But no reply.

"Billy Sorensen, if that's you, then just say so."

There are strange guttural noises and, for a second, I swear I can see an enormous figure looming in the darkness. My chest tightens and I feel my breath whistling through my constricted throat. Whatever it is, it's not Billy. I'm out here by myself, and nobody knows it except the cute boy who apparently played a joke on me.

There's a burring, scratching noise and a flame appears at the top of a hinged metal lighter. The man holding it lifts the flame to the cigarette clamped between his lips. In the sudden flash of light, I can see the wild hair and heavy face, the leather vest open over the broad pot belly. He takes a long drag on the cigarette, the cherry glowing bright gold, and smoke trickles out of his mouth as he chuckles.

"Ain't you just the sweetest thing." The lighter goes out and for a second, all I can see is the glowing ember at the end of his cigarette. Then other lights appear, cell phone screens, and a couple of flashlights as other men come forward.

"Time to party," one of the others says as he strides out of the shadows and into the narrow clearing around the poplar.

"Boy howdy," another said with a wheezing laugh.

I feel the rough bark of the tree trunk digging into my back through my thin shirt.

"Billy?" I try to yell it, hoping he's close enough to hear, but my heart is pounding so hard in my ears, that I'm not sure if any sound has escaped my throat at all.

"Billy ain't comin'," the first man says with a nasty grin.

I slip around the trunk, turning toward home. I can run through these trees even in the dark, better than these strangers ever could. I'll lose them in the night shadows.

But there are two men there already, blocking my path, and they're all coming closer.

"Your little Billy had some nice things to say about you," another man says, coming close enough to stroke my hair. "He wasn't lyin', neither. Young and sweet, that's what you are."

"Where is he?" My voice is thin and stretched as I try to pull away from the greasy-voiced guy whose fingers trail through my hair. "What did you do to him?"

Grumbling laughter, the smell of cigarette smoke and beer. "He came to the bar, tried to talk us into buying him a bottle for this little date. Once we found out where the meet-up was, we just left him by the back door and headed over. Wanted to make sure you don't get too lonely. He won't be bothering us."

My heart is thudding so fast, lips numb again as adrenaline rushes through my body. My fingertips tingle and itch and an ache in my bones is becoming a burning pain.

"Okay, sweetheart," the first man says as he comes close, pushing away the other man whose fingers tangle in my hair. "It's time to party." The barrette pulls my hair, rhinestones glittering in the uncertain light as it flickers and falls to the ground, disappearing under heavy riding boots.

"Video's rolling," another voice says, and bright light from the cell phone blinds me as it's lifted high to take in the scene.

"Just let me go—" My voice sounds harsh and strange in my own ears, the words slurred with panic and something else. Need, want, maybe even desire.

"What the hell?" The big man with the cigarette still hanging from his lip draws back, nose wrinkled, and teeth bared in something like disgust.

I'd ask them to stop, to have pity, it would only be fair. But it's too late now. Pain claws through my body and blood thrums in my ears. Somewhere far away there is the sound of howling and sharp ripping, tearing noises filling the clearing.

"Holy God!" The man holding the cell phone falls back, his voice coming shrill and loud, a drill in my skull as all my senses explode.

Then there's screaming. So much screaming. The night turns bright and electric, full of the bitter smell of blood.

It's hours later when I finally make it home. My clothes are torn and spattered with blood. The rhinestone barrette is lost somewhere in the clearing around the poplar. I'm exhausted, shivering with fatigue, and my muscles quaking with weakness and over-use. All the lights are on in the house, even the yellow, faded globe by the front door. There are dark silhouettes before the big picture window and even above the scent of blood and dirt, I can smell my daddy's worry.

"Mae!" His voice is harsh, but not loud and he comes to me with what I think is a rifle in one hand. Uncle John waits back by the house with someone else. When the third figure pulls away and follows Daddy toward me, I can see the glint of light on long white hair. It's Granny Ames, my mama's mama.

Daddy stares at me, jaw clenched, and nostrils flared as he takes in my state. He doesn't say anything, but I know he's upset. He looked like this when Mama died.

"That's enough, Jim." Granny's voice is cool and dismissive as she comes to take my arm. "Let's get you inside and cleaned up, girl."

All I want is to sit in a hot bath, close my eyes, and pretend tonight never happened. But there's one thing I have to do first.

"Daddy," I say before Granny leads me away. "Billy."

He nods once, curt and controlled. "Billy's fine. He called tonight, gave me warning about what happened at the bar. Told me where you were. I told him to stay home."

"Enough," Granny said again and pulled me toward the house. "She's her mother's daughter and carries our heritage. You knew this would happen one day; it was just a matter of time." Her arm is around my shoulders, offering her strength and at the same time, not giving me any choice about staying or going. As she guides me up the steps, she adds, "I'll take care of Mae. You take care of that garbage out in the woods."

I wonder if all this woke up Jimmy, or if he managed to sleep through the hubbub, like he did the night Mama never came home.

Uncle John passes us on his way to Daddy and he looks as serious and determined as I've ever seen him. And I see now, before Granny takes me into the house, that it's not rifles but shovels both men are carrying.

Unclean Break

L. E. DANIELS

*For keepers of memory: the brave children, wise women, and bone
collectors all.*

Forget.
They press us to forget,
push us to forget;
encourage our forgetting
by saying they forgot.

No.
Not me.
I can't recall.
You can't possibly
mean me.

If I could
go back and break your arm
defending myself: an unclean break—
you'd remember
always how you got it.

Instead I wait,
steeped in memory,
soaking the waters of Lethe
into a rag meant
just for you.

Unclean Break

I've outlived
my grandmothers
who could not survive
those forgetful
as you.

Now
my house creaks
with unclean breaks,
knitted with sinew of careless
forgetting.

And I have
room enough
to hold everything
and make new things
from your remains.

Time
makes
everything clear:
I'll do the remembering
for both of us now.

Lucille Sings the Blues

H.R. BOLDWOOD

Roy sang the blues as he wiped down his elevator, polishing every delicate dip and swirl of its filigreed cage. He spit-shined the stubborn spot where customers' shoes rubbed against the baseboard. A job done well is a job done once, he mused, staring at the stained rag in his hand. The soft, checkered scrap had once been his favorite flannel shirt, but Roy thought it would be gentle on the aging bones of the elevator. He supposed it was time to replace it, perhaps with one of those microfiber cloths.

Only the best for his Lucille.

Fifty years he'd been the elevator operator at the The Crenshaw, a turn-of-the-century commercial building nestled in the heart of New Orleans, and he'd never had to tinker with Lucille's sound system. All day, every day, she played tunes from the '40s, mostly jazz and the blues—her favorite was the blues, from Ma Rainey to Sippie Wallace—never a skip or a scratch. He had the best job in the world. And singing the blues with Lucille was icing on his cake.

After polishing her brass handrail, he swept and mopped her tiled floor, then switched on the vacuum to fluff the velvet nap on her customers' bench. Roy hadn't noticed Mr. Redmond until the portly general manager pulled back the scissor gate and stepped into the cage. The car dipped, but instantly leveled. Roy turned off the sweeper, and nodded at his boss, making a mental note to call Otis. The old girl's counterweights might need adjustment.

"Morning, Roy."

"Happy Friday, sir."

Redmond ran his finger along the cage's pristine bars, then pointed at the spotless bench. "Wish all our employees were this conscientious." He let his hand glide along the gleaming rail. "This monstrosity's been around since Moses was a child, but you really have a way with her."

Roy turned away, flinching as if he'd been slapped. "My Lucille's a good ol' girl. Dependable as the day is long."

Redmond looked pensive for a moment, then tapped his ring against the rail. "How about stopping by my office for a chat tonight? Around 8:45. There's something I want to discuss."

"Yes, sir. I'll be there—on the dot."

The car bobbled again as Redmond stepped back into the hallway. "See you later, Roy," he said, giving him a little salute. Roy wiped the manager's fingerprints from the freshly polished rail and wondered what he wanted to talk about. Not long ago, Roy had left a suggestion in the box about new flooring for the elevator; maybe that was it.

He left the fourth floor and stopped on three to pick up Lydia McElroy, from Coldwell Banker. "Lobby, please, Roy," she said, stepping into the cage. "Cross your fingers. I've got a showing in Montgomery."

"Ah," Roy said. "Pretty day for it."

"Hold still a second, Roy. You've got something—" She reached over, straightened his collar, and then patted his chest. "There. Can't have you looking rumpled."

Roy's face blazed. "Thanks, Lydia."

Lucille pitched, dropping several inches. Lydia screeched, and spilled to the floor, dropping her armload of files. Roy helped her to her feet. "Oh my gosh, are you alright?" He picked up the documents and handed them to her. "I'm so sorry."

The realtor dusted herself off with a nervous giggle. "No harm done. I'm a bit of a klutz . . . maybe it's a good omen." The car descended smoothly to the first floor, and Lydia scurried into the lobby with a wave. "Wish me luck."

Roy waved back, then closed the doors, and shook his head. "C'mon, girl. She didn't mean no harm. You know I'm yours forever."

Roy all but forgot his meeting with the manager and spent the rest of the day as he always did, chatting up customers, giving out directions, and crooning with Lucille. Their torch song harmonies filtered through the iron bars, filling the building with music from the days of speakeasies and bathtub gin.

At 8:43 p.m., Roy pressed the fourth-floor button. He asked Lucille to wish him well, then stepped into the hallway and followed the tiled floor to the manager's door. Mr. Redmond ushered him inside and showed him to a leather, winged-back chair opposite the cherry executive desk. Grand to the point of gaudy, the room, and the power it implied, made Work-a-day Roy feel small.

"Thanks for coming. I appreciate your time, Roy. Bottled water?" Redmond asked, pointing to his mini fridge. Roy shook his head, and the manager moved behind his desk, pausing reflectively before he sat. "It's no secret we've been tightening our belts around here. No more free coffee in the breakroom, the payroll freeze, and the like."

"Yes, sir. Times are tough."

"That they are." Redmond clicked his pen nervously and shifted his gaze to the floor. "There's no easy way to say this, Roy. I'm afraid we're going to have to let you go. Effective now."

Roy's stomach lurched. Surely, he hadn't heard right. "I'm sorry, what—"

"You haven't done anything wrong," Redmond interjected. "It's a matter of numbers. And frankly, nobody uses elevator operators anymore. They're a thing of the past, along with that wrought iron eyesore you love so much." He rose from his chair and perched on the edge of his desk. "You'll get a full pension, of course. And a 401K—a tidy nest egg for retirement. And lifetime medical. That's rare these . . . "

Roy had stopped listening. He stared at the gold-plated elephant on his boss's desk with its upturned trunk for good luck, lost in resentment and disbelief. How could they? After everything he'd given? This was so unfair, so . . .

"You're 70, Roy. Surely, you've thought about slowing down. Spending your golden years doing what you love."

"But Lucille—"

"She'll be fine, Roy. We'll take good care of her." The manager stood, signaling their meeting had come to an end. "I'm truly sorry; I wish there were something I could do." Speechless, Roy struggled to his feet. He grabbed the corner of the desk to steady himself as he reached to shake Redmond's outstretched hand. "You're the best worker I've ever had," the manager said, walking him to the doorway. "We're sure going to miss you."

Redmond's door closed with a resounding bang. Gutted to his core, Roy lingered in the hallway, twisting the shiny brass buttons of his uniform. He loved his job and the customers. What would he do without them? All the passengers he had transported over the years. Where were they now? he wondered. How had their lives turned out? Did they ever think of him, or his one-of-a-kind Lucille?

Lucille . . . How would he tell her? They'd spent fifty years together. He couldn't leave without telling her. He wanted . . . her blessing. A fool's errand, Roy mused as he tottered down the hallway, shaking his head. Lucille would never understand.

The scent of Murphy's Oil Soap filled Roy's nose as he struck out for the call station. The lemony bouquet reminded him of the everyday smells he would miss. Popcorn, perfume, and the freshly printed ink of a morning paper. He'd never again hear the chaotic chatter of customers, Lucille's cheery ding, or holiday bustle in the lobby.

The rhythmic clack of his shoes against the tiled floor set Roy's mind adrift. Would Lucille share his sense of outrage? Feel the same betrayal? And if so, how would she react? She'd grown downright truculent in her old age.

Like the time Ellen Wasserman from First City Bank raced into the elevator, late for work, and whined, "If this damned contraption moved any slower, I'd go gray before I clocked in." Lucille had inexplicably stopped inches above the lip of the second floor. Ellen had stumbled on her way out the door and broken her femur.

Or the day Suzie from maintenance called Lucille an antique. The car ground to a halt mid-descent, slamming Suzie to the floor, and knocking her unconscious.

Oh, and that time six months or so ago. Betty Ripley from accounting had asked him when they were going to replace Lucille with a 'real' elevator that played 'decent' Muzak. The next day, poor Betty was found dead at the bottom of the elevator shaft.

Accidents.

Or so the investigators had called them. But in the dark corners of Roy's mind, a quiet voice contended that these victims had one thing in common. They'd all pissed the old girl off. Roy stirred from his ruminations and found himself in front of Lucille, finger poised above her call button.

A mechanical whir filled the air. Roy fixated on the call button. He didn't remember pushing it, yet, somehow, she'd known he was there, waiting. The warm strains of Benny Goodman's clarinet greeted him as she glided to a stop.

The scissor gate opened with a melancholy creak. Roy stepped inside and toggled the Stop switch, holding the car on the 4th floor. His conversation with Lucille would require privacy. "Hey, ole' girl," he murmured, stroking her velvet bench. "I got something to talk to you about." The music crackled to a stop. Roy slumped to the bench, feeling weary and beaten. "I have to leave. The manager says it's time . . . time for me to move on. He says nobody uses elevator operators anymore. I guess he thinks we're both just . . . too damned old."

Lucille remained silent. Had she not understood?

He cleared his throat and tried again. "Today's my last day. I came to say goodbye."

The car went dark as the dome light flickered and died. The cables moaned and the cage began to sway. If the cable snapped . . . Roy wiped sweat from his brow. The elevator shimmied, and the control panel lights began to strobe. The cage's sway slowly spiraled to a swing. Roy stood and braced himself, balancing with his legs. He breathed deep and pushed down his fear. Four stories up; they'd never survive a drop.

"C'mon, baby, stop this," he pleaded. "You're gonna kill us both. This isn't my choice. All I've ever wanted was to be with you. You're my girl."

The panel lights stopped flashing, and the swaying cage settled so quickly Roy almost lost his footing. Lucille uttered a long, mournful moan and then fell ominously silent. Had he reached her?

He waited for a sign.

The audio system crackled to life. One of Irving Berlin's show tunes filled the cage. With a heavy heart, Roy pressed the first-floor button, and joined Lucille for one final duet:

Lucille Sings the Blues

"What'll I do
when you
are far away,
and I'm so blue?"
What'll I do?"

When the doors reopened, Roy lingered in the car, wishing it were yesterday, wishing that he could return to work Monday morning as if nothing had changed. He fished Lucille's flannel scrap from his pocket, laid it on her bench, and finished the last few lines of their song before stepping into the lobby.

"Love you, ole' girl," he whispered, latching her wrought iron gate behind him for the last time. "And I always will."

⁂

Mr. Redmond popped a cheese puff into his mouth, then licked his fingers and glanced at his watch: 9:45. The stores had closed nearly an hour ago. The building's tenants would be gone by now, and so too, would Roy. The coast was clear. He could write up Roy's termination Monday morning, and send it to HR with the timecards.

Redmond switched off his desk lamp, and strolled down the hallway, wearing a smile. Roy's paycheck hadn't amounted to much, but less overhead equaled more bonus money in his own pocket. Redmond pushed Lucille's call button several times with his greasy orange fingers, and tapped his foot, waiting for the ancient behemoth to arrive.

Lucille coasted to a perfect stop but dipped mightily as the manager stepped inside. He stifled a gasp and grabbed the cage door for balance. "Fucking rust bucket," he hissed, pounding the first-floor button with his fist.

The dome light exploded. Shards of glass burst through the air, raining down on him like shrapnel, embedding in his face and eyes. The tinny tones of twenties blues warbled from the speakers, blaring in, and then fading out at dizzying intervals. Redmond yanked at the cage door, but the car had begun its descent. Screws that held the control panel in place spun in their holes, worked themselves loose and then screamed across the cage.

The rectangular panel fell away. A jumble of wires tumbled to the floor and snaked across the cage. They wound around Redmond's arms, legs, and neck, strapping him upright in the center of the car. He struggled to free himself, letting out a squeal as an ear-splitting pop sounded above the ceiling of the car. A resounding whip peeled through the air, followed by another, and then another. The cables began to unravel.

Lucille careened downward, then slingshot up the shaft, over and over, again and again. Redmond shrieked as his body whipped against the strands of copper wire, a multitude of tiny ligatures that shredded his skin, layer by layer, sawing through muscle and bone. Lucille catapulted to the top of the shaft and then fell one last time. He was garroted by the wiring as it severed his carotid artery and then sliced through the musculature of his neck. Mr. Redmond's decapitated head flopped onto the velvet bench, and bobbled several times, before rolling onto the blood-soaked floor.

Monday morning, 10:15 a.m.

Roy's fingers fumbled as he pushed the tiny brass buttons of his operator's uniform through their proper holes. After one last glance in the mirror, he raced out his door, jumped into his car, and contemplated the most wonderfully confusing telephone conversation of his life. Not fifteen minutes earlier, Mr. Redmond's assistant, Harry, had called Roy to ask why he wasn't at work.

Roy had sighed. "Maybe you haven't heard. Mr. Redmond—"

"I know." Harry lowered his voice to a whisper. "Isn't it horrible?"

"Isn't . . . what horrible?"

"Redmond . . . The elevator?"

Roy paused.

"Oh, my God! You haven't heard! The elevator malfunctioned Friday night with Redmond inside. Roy, he was . . . decapitated. Security found him Saturday morning on their walk-through. Holy crap! There was blood everywhere. Otis and OSHA were here the whole weekend. Apparently, the cables broke, and the car fell. Simple wear and tear, they're saying. Can you imagine? How the damn thing checked out fine three months ago is anyone's guess."

Roy's stomach roiled. "Oh, my. Oh, I . . . I . . ."

"Otis replaced the cable. The elevator's all cleaned up and good to go. Oh, and I ordered new material for the customer's bench. There was no cleaning that. OSHA wants to ask you a few questions about how the elevator's been handling lately. I told 'em you'd be in any minute."

Roy scraped his jaw up off the floor. "Sure. Just running late. Be right there."

Roy drove to work, rehearsing his answers to the questions OSHA would likely ask. No, sir. She's been handling fine. No hesitation. No electrical malfunctions. Nothing out of the ordinary. Smooth as a baby's behind, sir. No mishaps at all.

He whipped his Malibu into the employee lot, parked, and then sprinted into the building, determined to make the most of his second chance, no matter how it had come about.

Roy strolled through the lobby and waved good morning to his coworkers as usual. After punching in, he chatted with the OSHA inspectors in the HR department, and then headed straight to Lucille. He pressed her call button, but she was already there waiting for him. When she opened her doors, Roy stepped inside, stroked her control panel, and whispered, "What did you do, you naughty girl?"

Lucille's voice crackled through the speakers, belting out a strange new song Roy had never heard:

> "He was a mean man, baby. Filled me full of woe.
> Yeah, that mean ole' Redmond, tryin' to vex my soul.
> Got no time for games, baby. That man, he had to go."

Roy pressed the close-door button and let out a long, deep sigh. "How 'bout we keep that little ditty between us?"

She

GERRI LEEN

I was born in this laboratory. I'm a creature of steel and flame and wet cotton. I woke to pain and she was there.

She looks at me like I should know who she is.

I don't.

I try. I remember nothing. How could I? I was born hours ago, and yet she sits and stares at me, asking me questions I can't answer.

I say I was born . . . and yet to be born is to be a child. I'm not a child. I don't think as a child, or so she says. I don't remember how children think, or speak, or play—play? Do I remember play?

No. She showed me a book, with pictures of children playing. With a doll. A doll with red hair and dressed in green velvet.

But . . . the children in the books were playing with blocks.

"Do I have a doll?"

"It's all right," she says, smiling in a way I don't understand, her hand warm on mine.

Hand—how do I know this word? How do I know how it should feel—cold or warm, soft or hard?

Why does her hand feel so good on mine? Why do I think it should be other places on my body?

"Are you my mother?" The children in the book had a mother.

She laughs. "Oh, heavens, no. I'm not that much older than you. Come see." She leads me down to a looking glass that hangs at the far end of the laboratory. She says I'm beautiful, and I take her word for it. We don't look alike, she with her little glasses and pulled back dark hair. My hair is blonde and wavy and hangs

34

wild around my shoulders. My eyes are green while hers are brown.

Chocolate. I reach out to her reflection and touch her eyes reflected in the glass. "What is chocolate?"

She smiles. "Your favorite."

"My favorite what?"

Her smile dies. "I'll get you some. Soon."

"So, it's something you . . . eat?"

"Or drink. You like to drink it."

I nod, but I don't remember drinking it. I only remember water, just hours ago, when I awoke screaming, my flesh on fire, and she was there, wrapping me in cool, wet cotton, letting me sip water from a cup, murmuring that I was back.

Where did I go? Would one not have to leave to come back?

"I'm thirsty," I whisper, and I hear an echo of that in my mind—have I said that before? I begin to cough and look down at my hand in alarm.

It's fine. Just a hand. Not covered in . . . red.

"Why was it red?"

She makes a face that somehow, I know means she doesn't want to speak of this.

"It was red."

She turns us away from the mirror. "Let's get you some water."

I think I hear her add, "My darling," so I ask, "Am I?"

She turns.

"Your darling?" The words are familiar, like her hand, like the expectation of blood—yes, red is blood. Blood on my hand, on the handkerchiefs, on the bedclothes. "Oh."

She pushes me into a chair, hurries to the pitcher, and pours more water. The sound is so familiar. I close my eyes and feel the soft touch of bedclothes, hear her gentle murmurs as she soothes me.

"You've done this before."

"Yes." She holds the glass for me, and that, too, is familiar. "Always," she whispers. "I will always do this for you."

I wake in a bed this time. She's sitting in a chair by the window, gazing out and the sunshine lights up her hair, giving it a red tinge.

Like the doll. Why do I remember a doll?

She put me to bed in this room last night. Tucked me in and kissed me on the forehead. "Sleep well, my dearest," she said, and then she handed me a glass of water.

Water that tasted strange. But strange in a way that I know.

"You drugged me." I struggle to sit up, and she's at my side in an instant.

"Only because you were fighting sleep, and your body desperately needed to rest. You've been through a lot."

I frown. What could I have possibly been through? I was just born. I look around the room and see a doll sitting on a low dresser. "That—the doll."

She brings it to me. "Do you like it?"

"It's mine," I say this and I know it, somewhere, in the deepest part of me, even though it makes no sense.

She smiles. "Miranda. That's her name."

I touch the doll's red hair and trail my finger along its porcelain cheek. Then I look at her and ask, "What's my name?"

"Isabelle." She says it with such . . . emotion. Heavy and dark, but her eyes are so soft.

"What's your name?"

"Mary." She takes the doll from me. "Let's put this back where it's safe."

"Is it not safe with me?"

"Of course it is," she says gently, but when she puts the doll down, I see that one of its legs flops strangely. She has to fiddle with it to make it sit as it had been. "There, safe as houses."

That saying. She's said it before. I look down at these buttercream-colored sheets, at the coverlet in cornflower blue. The bed is made of some dark wood—ebony, I think, but I have no idea how I know that.

"Let's get you dressed for breakfast. It's a big day today. Your first whole day."

I slip out of bed and let her help me with the complicated clothing. She names each piece as she slips it on me: stockings, drawers, chemise, the corset—how uncomfortable this thing is, and she says she is lacing it loosely—then the bustle, the camisole, and petticoat until, finally, a skirt and bodice. She kneels and puts small boots on my feet, brown to match the ivory and brown pattern of my skirt.

"There. Aren't you a sight for sore eyes?"

I touch her cheek beneath her glasses and check to see if her eyes are indeed sore. They don't appear so, the deep brown—chocolate, yes, that is how I cannot help but think of them—seem happy as far as I can tell, and she laughs.

"I've made all your favorites for breakfast, Isabelle."

"How do you know them?"

"I know everything, dearest." She takes my hands in hers, bends down, and kisses them and my body tingles as if I remember her lips in other places. "I've memorized every detail."

I don't ask how this can be, even though her knowledge seems strange when I myself am not sure of my favorites. I don't ask because she won't give me a straight answer—I know this, if nothing else.

I find her in the laboratory after breakfast. She had left me to wander around the house, and it's huge and somewhat dark. There are no pictures anywhere—no photographs, I mean. There are plenty of paintings scattered around the walls of this place.

Then I wondered how I know what a photograph is. I can picture one, a hazy image of Mary and me, taken . . . when? Is this a memory I have concocted?

She's sitting at a steel table, a white cat lying stretched out before her.

"Is it ill?" I hurry over and feel a pang as I look at it.

"He is." She doesn't stop me from touching the creature, and he sniffs my hand, then rubs his cheek against it.

"What a sweet animal." He lets out a small cry and I lean down. "What is it?" He licks me, his scratchy tongue making me laugh, and I say, "Snow, stop it."

How do I know his name?

I look up at Mary, and she closes her eyes for a moment. "Snow's sick, Isabelle."

"What's wrong with him?"

"He's dying." She pets him gently. "I can fix him. You can help me."

"But he's dying." Dying is dying. Isn't it?

"I can fix it. Now, will you help me?" She's agitated in a way I've not seen before, so I murmur, "Of course."

She picks the cat up, carrying him to a different steel table—the one that I first awoke on. "Hold him while I give him something to calm him."

I pet the cat as he purrs, and I can hear the catch in his breath as he cuddles into me. She motions for me to lay him down and I do, holding him while she injects him with a large needle.

He cries, but then goes still, his eyes half-lidded.

"Snow," Mary says, "I do this for so many reasons, my loyal friend." She reaches under the table and brings up straps that she lays over him, tightening them above his shoulders and hindquarters.

She nods to the next table and hands me a bottle. A roll of cotton lies on the table. "Soak the cotton in this. It is diluted carbolic acid. We will need to cool him once this is done—and relieve his pain."

I put the cotton in a small bowl and pour the liquid over it. The smell is familiar: it was what she wrapped around me when I woke to fiery pain.

"Move back, Isabelle."

I step to the other side of the table and watch as a clear glass covering, like the top of a cake dish, goes over Snow. Mary walks to the wall, pulls down some large switches, and sparks begin to fly inside the glass container.

Snow screams: he moves but not much—clearly whatever she's given him prevents him from getting up, but not from making it known that he's in pain.

I close my eyes, suddenly assailed by the memory. Fire through my whole body. And the pins-and-needles feeling of a limb gone to sleep—only all over, and so many times worse. Pain and pain and pain and then . . . this. This whimpering silence.

"Snow," I say, and my voice comes out as a sob. "Let me help him."

She flips the switches back, the sparks die down, and the clear box lifts off the poor creature. He's moaning, a low, horrible sound.

I think I remember that sound. Did I make that sound?

I grab the bowl, pull out the soaked cotton, and lay it over him, winding it around his body when he ceases to struggle when he lays his head back, and the horrible keening stops. "My dearest boy," I murmur as I work. "All will be well."

I look up and see that Mary is watching me with a look so gentle and full of . . . of what? Is that love?

Is what I feel for Snow love?

Can I feel love? I'm new to this world. I know things I should not, yet I don't know other things, such as why her smile makes me feel safe. Why the touch of her hands as she comes to help me and the feeling of her breath on my hair move me so?

She grasps my shoulder for a moment, then goes and gets a strange contraption that fits into her ears, with a small bell-like thing hanging down from the other end.

"It's a stethoscope." She takes it off and puts it on me, the ear bits sinking slightly in, and she holds the bell against my chest.

I laugh at the sound.

"That's your heart."

She touches my cheek, and I hear my heartbeat become louder and faster. I swallow hard, take the earpieces out, and hand her the thing. She puts it on again and listens to multiple parts of Snow's body, then begins removing the cotton. "Too little of this carbolic acid treatment and he feels the pain. Too much and it will cause him more. It's a balancing act, getting it just right."

She picks the cat up and carries him upstairs, and I follow her. She gestures with her chin to a chaise. "Sit. You can hold him. He'll like that."

I recline in the chaise and hold my hands out. She gives him to me gently, then once we are settled, covers us both with a light blanket. "Rest, my darlings."

"What is love, Mary?" I gaze up at her, and I imagine my heart begins to beat harder again as she leans down and puts her lips against mine, a soft touch, a short one, too.

"This, my dear. This is love." She touches Snow on the forehead, rubbing on the bridge of his nose, and I hear him purr. "He's happy to be back with us."

Back. We all seem to come back. "You said I was back."

"I did say that, Isabelle. You and Snow. Life is very good indeed."

We're outside today, having a picnic. Snow romps around us, chasing birds and stalking squirrels. We laugh as he fails to catch anything, and he tears around us, finally collapsing on the blanket, his chest heaving.

"He's the best company," Mary says, and I smile and pet our white terror.

He licks my hand, then rolls and looks at Mary, as if to say, "You, too."

We both laugh and share a look—a look of pure affection, I think. I know that I don't know this woman well, but deep inside me, I feel so much regard for her. Love, I suppose. She has taken such care of me, her tenderness so dear.

"I love you," I say into the silence, and her expression changes to one of pure joy.

"I love you, too, Isabelle. I always have. I always will."

I pull her to me, and we kiss over our cat, who rolls and kneads my leg as if to say, "I'm still here."

When we pull away, she grins at me. "That was nice." She strokes my face, the feeling bringing up more of the warm feelings. "And I didn't have to make the first move. I very much like that."

I laugh. "I am a wanton woman, clearly."

"You are free and innocent, dearest. You've never been wanton. It is one of the things I love most about you. You love only me."

I frown, and for a moment her look changes to one of wariness and she swallows visibly. "Have I known anyone else?" I ask. Other than the servants who come and go, changing frequently since none of them seem to meet Mary's exacting expectations, we see no one. "Why do we not entertain?"

"Am I not enough for you?" Her tone is light, but her expression isn't.

"I'm just curious. How can you know how I behave—how I am? If I've only just been born?"

She seems to relax. "Character is always apparent."

I pet the cat. "Did you know how he would be when you picked him out?"

"I did." There is something off in her eyes, although her smile is real. "He was the sweetest of the litter. And look at him now. So dear."

"Yes. He is." I offer him some chicken from my plate, and he gobbles it up.

She

"You've eaten so little of your food, Isabelle."

"I'm not hungry." I drink some of the wine she poured us, but it goes down the wrong way, and I begin to cough. A cough that doesn't seem to want to stop.

She watches me with an almost hopeless expression. "It will pass. It will pass." She sounds as if she is trying to convince herself as much as me.

I finally stop coughing and sit, not moving, afraid to set off the fit again.

She reaches out and touches my hand. "I will make you a syrup of honey and whiskey. It is good for coughs."

"So is laudanum." I don't know why I've said this—I'm not sure I even know what laudanum is.

She sighs. "Yes, laudanum's good. But perhaps a bit strong? You just swallowed the wrong way. You don't feel chilled or feverish, do you?"

"No." I smile at her.

"Are you fatigued?"

I laugh. "With you? Never."

She shoos the cat from between us, and he takes off after a bird he has no chance of catching. Then she eases me down and seems to be waiting to see if I'll cough again.

"I'm fine."

She slowly begins to touch my body. "Is it alright if I do this?"

The feeling is new—but also familiar; the touches are the ones I've remembered since my birth. I can feel a slow fire building. "That fever you mentioned . . . ?" I smile.

She laughs. "This one is of an entirely different origin." And then she kisses me, while she continues to run her hands up and down, to the most amazing effect.

My skirt and petticoat are soon up, and I am very noisy as we lie on our blanket. "My," I say, enjoying the trembling ennui that has overcome me. I turn my head to look at her and she's smiling. "Shall I return the flavor?"

"It would be the ladylike thing to do."

I laugh, sure that it would probably not be, but I do it anyway. She's even noisier than I was.

"Darling, are you coming down for dinner?" Mary had found me in my dressing gown, lying on the fainting couch and sipping water. "Are you alright?"

"I had another coughing fit. Perhaps you should make me some of your remedy."

She comes over, settles her hand on my forehead, and frowns. "You're so warm."

"I'm also tired."

Snow comes in, mewling for his dinner, no doubt, but he jumps up on the couch with me and crawls up my legs to my chest to nose me.

"Yes, my love," I say as I stroke his soft fur—does it feel a bit oily? "You'll make me feel all better."

Mary smiles. "I'll bring the food in here. We'll enjoy a little tête-à-tête in our bedroom."

My bedroom has become our bedroom. Ever since the picnic, when she showed me how love could be when it was acted upon, how good we could make each other feel. "Yes, that would be lovely."

She turns, and Snow deserts me for the possibility of dinner. I notice he's moving more slowly and seems to be limping. "Mary?"

She turns back.

"Snow—something's wrong with him."

"He probably jumped down from one of the China cabinets again. You know how intrepid he is. It's his misfortune that the concept of finessing the landing eludes him more often than not."

I laugh. She's right, of course.

Mary and I lie in bed, and I stare over at the doll, Miranda—why did I name her that? But how could I have named her? She's Mary's doll no matter how much I might delude myself that she is mine.

Mary follows my gaze and smiles, slipping from my embrace and getting up to fetch Miranda, to bring her to me. I take her as Mary gets back into bed. She cuddles against me, and I kiss her forehead, then turn back to the doll.

"She's so beautiful." I realize her leg moves strangely because it's been broken. "What happened?"

"She fell." There's something in Mary's voice that makes me think there's more to this story.

She

"Fell?"

"Yes. The maid. Clumsy girl. I let her go, of course."

"You let all of them go. No one stays around here for long."

"I have high expectations for how they'll keep this house. They never seem to share those expectations. I prefer to try again than live with a poor outcome."

I laugh and put the doll between us. "If I had a daughter, I'd name her Miranda."

Mary's look is haunted, but before I can ask why, I begin to cough. She helps me up, and I reach for the handkerchiefs I keep by the bed. Then she gets up and hurries to her room, coming back with laudanum. "Here. This will make it better."

I take the syrup reluctantly. It does make the cough better but leaves me so enervated that all I do is doze. "We should call a doctor."

"I am a doctor, my darling. This is best." She rubs my back as I continue to cough, but the fit calms, as it always seems to with this medicine. "Rest. Lie close to me. I'll look after you. I will always look after you."

✎✎✎✎✎

I lie in bed, sipping the cup of hot chocolate Mary has brought me. Snow lies on the coverlet, his eyes only half focused, his breathing as labored as mine has become.

"He's sick again," I say, and she nods. "Your procedure didn't heal him."

"It did. For a time." She reaches over to pet him, and he presses his head against her hand. "I love him so. I know you don't remember, but he was ours—we got him from a farmer who had a basket of kittens on his wagon. *We* picked Snow out, not just I. He was the sweetest of the litter. He loved us both so much."

I frown. I have no idea what she's talking about. "When did we do this?"

"He's nine now. We got him when he was but a few months old."

"Nine years? We have been together that long—but how? I am . . . I don't remember."

"I know." She pets Snow, and he rolls over slowly, clearly not an easy movement for him, but he seems to want to let her rub his belly. "I'll fix him again. Each time he lasts a little longer."

"But he's only been with us for a few months since you fixed him the first time."

"Not the first time. And when I started working on him, he only lasted days." She meets my eyes. "He seems to remember less and less each time about this place. Has to explore every nook and cranny to learn the smells again. But his essence—his sweetness—that never changes. And he always loves me—us. No matter how much he forgets."

"How many times have you fixed him?"

She looks away, swallows hard, and then says, "Eighty-nine."

I do not doubt her. She has a mind for such details. I meet her eyes and see a sadness in hers, but also an openness that isn't usually there.

I realize she's not hiding anything anymore, and a chill runs through me.

I put the cup back onto the saucer. "And me? You've done it to me before, haven't you? That's why I woke up—was born—on that slab."

She nods.

"Why?" I start to cough again, the racking hurting my sides, and I cough something up into my hand.

Blood. It's blood. Just like I first expected to see.

"You have consumption, my darling. You're dying. You're always dying. But each time I get you back, it lasts a little longer."

Just like Snow. "And do I forget more each time?"

"You do." She reaches over and grasps my hand firmly in hers. "But you always love me. Always. No matter how much you forget. Next time you may forget how you think my eyes look like chocolate. Or how much you love that doll. But you never forget me. Not at your essence. We're destined to be together."

I'm not sure what to say. I gaze down at Snow, then let my eyes go to Miranda, sitting so still, so perfect—except for that leg. Never leaving this room, posed and pretty and . . . a prisoner.

"Mary, you love me. You said so."

"I do love you. I would do anything for you." She lets go of my hand and pets Snow again. "I'll fix him one last time, and he'll be here when you next wake up. But he's the problem, every time. Because I cannot resist bringing him back as many times as he needs it. But I have to resist because he's what tips you off. Makes you question. Makes the days you have between the current waking and the next full of doubt." She leans down, her lips lying on his forehead, and he pushes up into her. "I'll let him go after this last healing, so that I can keep you."

"Me? How much of me is going to be left when you get done? I've lost so much already." I stare at the doll. "Did she really fall?"

"No. You broke her. Early on. When you had almost all your memories and you figured out what I was doing. You were angry with me—compared yourself to her—and threw her across the room. It was lucky that she wasn't more damaged." She studies the doll, biting gently into her lower lip. "I probably need to get rid of her, too."

"Mary. I won't let you do this. I'll leave. You can't bring me back if you can't find me." I start to get up, but the room begins to spin.

"You said that last time, my darling. And the time before that. And the time before that. Once you even managed to get to the stables, but you had forgotten how to saddle your own horse. I caught you before you could leave."

"I'm your prisoner?"

"You're my love."

I stare at her. Her expression hasn't changed, and it's so full of love for me that I reach out to her. "If you love me, then don't do this. It's not what's best for me."

"But it is what's best for *us*." She looks down, her hand still on poor Snow. "And for me."

I feel a terrible lethargy come over me—the chocolate, she has drugged my chocolate—and I see her expression change to one of utmost sorrow. "Let me go," I whisper.

"I'm sorry, Isabelle. But I can't."

I feel her hand on my cheek, her lips pushing lightly on mine, the same kiss as our first one—how many first kisses have we had?

And then the world goes black.

⚬⚭⚮⚯

I was born in this laboratory. I am a creature of steel and flame and wet cotton. I woke to pain, and she was there.

She looks at me like I should know who she is.

I don't.

Matilda's Mourning

DONNA J. W. MUNRO

This story is dedicated to those who mourn. The pain never completely leaves, but you will learn to breathe again intime.

Prolonged mourning is referred to as Queen Victoria's curse.

In most cases, women are the true vessels of grief, but only women with a specific set of skills rise to the heights of funerary perfection.

When Latisha died, Matilda, her twin, and my younger sister, cut off Latisha's golden hair. Alive, it had been a waving wheat field in the soft afternoon sun. In death, Matilda wove it into a knotted lacework tree, covered with a crystal dome, and installed in an iron cage that hung over Latisha's grave; a memorial of her life, beautifying the cold stone that commemorated her death.

Lady Eustine, leader of the lady mourners' brigade, marveled, "We've never seen such fine work done on any mourning sculpture."

Soon, every new resident in the necropolis had a grave festooned with such remembrances . . . though none were as fine as our Latisha's.

The braiding alone had taken Matilda every hour since our sister had died. No sleep. Just thoughts of her childhood, playing in streams and chasing the rabbits in the yard. Weaving flowers into crowns.

Matilda's tears lit the hair from within.

Her gifted fingers made the braided strands finer.

When Uncle Josup passed, a photographer was hired to take portraits of the remains. He was posed in his finest with Latisha,

Mama, and me neatly tucked next to him. His first photo and he'd sat perfectly still. Of course, he had. And of course, Matilda found a way to have that *memento mori* chipped into his headstone, a sculptural frieze as fine as any marble taken from the Parthenon at the London Museum.

And when our father died, Matilda pulled all her gifts together to create the most perfect send-off. The mourners she hired for Father's funeral never sobbed louder than they did for him. They paraded to the family crypt, topped by a weeping angel so beautiful that Mama said the costly artist Matilda chose, and his fine Italian marble, were worth every precious penny. So were the flowers that Matilda arranged in cascades to adorn the ornate, lead-lined casket. The papers hailed it as the funeral of the season, and our family crypt the model of Victorian familial devotion to their beloved dead. Matilda's mourning works drew attendees to the funeral as surely as had father's well-known business prowess and mother's social standing.

After that, she became a sensation.

Matilda's calendar became filled with funerals and death watches, viewings, and wakes. She wore widow's weeds to every event, crying in the corner with such fervency. She took the mementos given by the families and turned them into art that they might display on mantles, atop caskets, or in displays at the crypts for visitors to admire.

She fashioned dolls of rags, made from the clothes that beloved children had died in. She designed delicate jewelry, created from the gold taken from the teeth of fallen lovers. She even carved lily-shaped cameos, using enamel gleaned from maiden aunts' ivory dentures.

Matilda ate and drank so little that her corseted waist began to shrink in on itself, causing her to faint daintily during the graveside funeral sermons she attended. Papers wrote columns of admiring prose about her: she was the angel of Queen's Gate Restful Meadows, the saint of Delmar's Hope Fields, the paragon of Forest Park Cemetery. Good families sought her out, vying for her devotion while they were still alive, as an investment for future funerals.

For a while, Mama worried about Matilda spending so much time serving others—that too much time might pass, and she'd miss out on a good marriage for herself.

"I don't think marriage is for me," Matilda would say, dabbing at her ever-weeping eyes with a cotton hankie wrung so many times its fibers had stretched into an incredible softness. She was a beauteous crier. No red eyes or hectic cheeks. Just a white pallor and two streams of salty sadness, glistening as they fell from her lovely, dark eyes. "To marry and bring a child into the world— only to watch it age, suffer, maybe to die before me— I'd never survive such sadness."

We nodded, each secretly relieved.

Perhaps we should have sent her to a sanitarium for rest, or up north to take the healing waters, but with the strides we'd made socially, we didn't see how we could. Families clamored to have Matilda weave a memory of their dearly departed. She took no money— that would be crass. But Mama and I spent the social capital she earned as if it *was* our family fortune.

I even secured a better marital union than thought possible, mostly because my husband's family wanted access to my sister.

In retrospect, had we been paying more attention to Matilda, and less to what she accomplished each week at the mortuary, the wakes, and the cemeteries, we might have noticed the subtle signs.

Her work designing mourning jewelry became so fine that her lack of tears went unnoticed.

The splendid lily arrangements she designed for wakes outshone the roses that grew on her marbled cheeks.

It was my husband who one day asked, "Has she always worn flowers on her sleeve?"

The sprig of bright color was a sharp contrast against her inky widow's weeds.

Mama and I spoke with Matilda that Sunday after church services had concluded and dinner had been served, but before Matilda set about her work for my husband's favorite uncle's impending death . . . although the old man had the gall to continue hanging on beyond all predictions. We were sure the end had to be near, and with Matilda working exclusively for us, we were confident to stun with our graveside accouterments. Sculptors, seamstresses, and choirs of mourners all had deposits, with instructions so detailed that all we needed was Matilda's final creation and, well . . . Uncle to die.

But she wasn't herself as he was gasping for his last breaths.

"Matilda," I whispered. "What's happened to you?"

Mama flanked me, worried. "You don't seem yourself, child."

"I've been to every event. I've gone to all the memorials and remembrances I've been asked to attend. Nothing's wrong. *Au contraire*. Has anyone complained?"

And she *had* done everything anyone had asked of her, but her odd lightness disrupted the somber air. Works would not replace heart in the business of mourning, and clearly, her heart had changed.

"No, dear, only . . . you're too . . . happy. It's as plain as day. Is there anything you need to tell us?" Mama asked.

We awaited her response with bated breath.

Was it possible she'd fallen in love?

We might be forced to abdicate our control over the mourning of the Saint Louis high society. Widow's weeds and weddings did not mix. Mama and I had spoken of this at length and concluded Matilda had ascended to become our designated gift from God— the same way second sons of Catholic families often became priests—only Matilda served without the vows and vestments. She served in grave marker poems and black lace veils.

If the unthinkable had somehow happened, we would talk her out of love, chase away her man, and keep her focused on her saintly work.

She considered my question, and as she did, I noticed the plumpness of her hand and how life seemed to press back against the black of her dress. Even the somberness of her braids, that only recently pulled her face so severely, now appeared to be a complimentary construction of her sable mane.

"I'm *not* in love if that's what you are worried about." Matilda smoothed the needlepoint death mask of Uncle, that she'd been laboring over for a month. "I do all that is asked of me. But my heart is lighter. I think helping others has healed me. I feel like myself before Latisha died."

That wouldn't do.

Mama and I had discussed this possibility. How our standing meant more than the life of one member. How the family name must continue to rise.

Mama was the clear choice because I would have to bear the children who'd carry on our lineage.

It couldn't be suicide. Suicide was morally and socially unacceptable.

And besides, wouldn't it be more impactful if Matilda *was* involved, somehow?

The next morning, we tried to set it up so that Matilda would use rat poison to sweeten Mama's tea. *Accidentally, of course.* The realization that she'd killed Mama would surely send her into a depression that would last for years and years. Mama and I swooned as we whispered about what she might produce with such a devastating inducement.

The poison box and sugar box looked almost identical. I watched her hand hover over the poison I'd put next to the creamer, but Matilda opted for fresh honey for Mama's tea before returning to knotting a sweet sailboat from the red locks of a boy who'd died at eight from the pox.

Later, Mama tried flinging herself down the grand stairs, but only her bustle caught the top step, slowing her so that all she did was bloody her nose and scrape her cheek. Matilda helped her up, singing a bright song as she did.

Whispers found us. Matilda's joy diluted the glorious, dark effect of Queen Victoria's curse and people were noticing; souring on this ethereal joy that was pushing out her earnest sadness.

I decided to take matters into my own hands.

Mama, Matilda, and I walked the river boardwalk, as ladies did in the afternoon. When we'd made our way to the most dramatic spot where the other ladies might see, I coughed and barked, pretending to be overcome with a fit of madness. I screamed. Scratched my face. My hat tore free, and my hair tumbled down my back like a girl's. Looking delightfully disturbed, I turned and shoved Mama off her feet. Her head struck the bricks with a crack and opened like a walnut, blood, and brain tissue staining her hair, but I knew Matilda would lovingly wash away all the gore before she started knotting and weaving.

Matilda screamed and fell to her knees as I raved and spit, blocking her from helping Mama. I'd fallen across Mama's body, ranting and keening; something Mama and I had worked out ahead of time. Of course, when we whispered over needlepoint, she hadn't been bleeding to death in the gutter, head split and eyes rolling in her sockets . . . but one must soldier on.

The white-coated men from the sanitarium came as the ladies on the boardwalk pulled Matilda into their pitying embrace. She wept with such abandon; I felt certain we'd succeeded. A few months away and I'd come back to a Matilda who'd be mourning forever. Our position would be secured.

They took me away to treat my hysteria. After bloodletting, and other treatments much too delicate to mention, my husband brought me home a cured woman.

I'd done it.

He was proud of my efforts. Our reputation for being eccentric grew, naturally; but eccentric, when combined with skills that couldn't be replicated, would always be forgiven. And Mama's funeral was everything she'd ever dreamed of, resplendent with every expression of Matilda's funerary gifts. Her widow's weeds glowed against her saintly, pale skin and black-rimmed eyes.

She wept those pretty tears constantly.

Even when she slept.

But when the mourners left and I tucked her in so she'd be ready for the next day's funeral games, she whispered in my ear, "You can't keep me this way forever."

I fussed with her covers and tutted about her black gown thrown in a pile in the corner, ignoring her declaration. I pulled the curtains over the tall windows and rang for servants to fan the flames of the fire.

"You can't keep me this way," Matilda said again from the nest of covers I'd tucked her under. And she might be right. Who would I have to kill next to maintain her delectable grief? Who did she even have left to mourn?

And then, even as the tears ran down her face, she smiled.

How discordant is a holy smile when it blooms across a stricken face! The mismatch of sad eyes and curving lips slithered through me as no chill could. She slid from the covers; padding toward me in her black nightdress, eyes brimming with a strange countenance that didn't fit on the plains of Matilda's mourning face.

Hope. They shone bright with hope.

"All that's left for me to mourn is you," she said, pulling a silver knitting needle from the depths of her sleeve. "Just you, and then I'll be able to be happy again."

As she lunged at me, my only hope was that my funeral would be legendary in Saint Louis society and that our family crypt would shine one last time with Matilda's resplendent mourning.

The Hollow Tree

NEMMA WOLLENFANG

It is quick. I'll give you that. You don't hesitate or draw it out. Stealth is your ally as you slip up behind me while I chop peppers in the kitchen, place your hands around my neck, and . . .

One, quick, SNAP!

After that first searing flash of pain, there is nothing. I don't feel the knife fall from my fingers. I don't feel my body slump in a graceless heap. I don't feel. Glassy eyes observe as you calmly switch off the hob, turn the water off boil, and lay out a length of black plastic.

You prepared; it seems. My diligent husband, ever the pragmatist.

It is only as you drag my limp weight through the backyard that a semblance of 'me' begins to return. It comes in degrees. Like waking from a deep sleep. I hear the scrape of tarp over grass, I smell the musk of damp earth, and I recognize your huff of exertion with every tug. At the same time, I am not a part of it, just some spectral observer, as intangible as air. Aware but unfeeling. There is nothing left *to* feel; no pulsing heart, no breath. Only dim apathy. Flesh falls away, the world expands below. Unsheathed, I rise up. Float like a balloon.

The hollow oak at the periphery of our land is where you take my body; the one at the border of the forest that's gnarled and knotted, stooped like an old crone, and ancient as time itself. It hides the evidence well; an encompassing ring of bark that conceals all you store inside from prying eyes— the mottling skin, the broken bones, shielded from the world.

From my strange new vantage point, I see more than I ever have. More than I ever wished to. You don't even dig a hole. Apparently, I'm not worth the effort. All you do is cram and stomp. I don't want to see this; watch my body brutalized.

Then, wiping your hands, you return to our house to finish your beer.

Something snags. A hook, a thread, an anchor to what lies below. And there I stay—tethered, somehow— to that lifeless cadaver. An incorporeal being with no fleshly boundaries to divide me from the air. Hazy, immobile, uncaring. Floating. All I can do is watch the stars dim overhead as the sun chases away the moon. How can one watch without the use of eyes? Those are the body's apparatus. With easy detachment, apparently. I even watch as you take away a suitcase of my belongings the next day and remove my car. I watch as you call work to tell them I'm sick. I watch as time rolls by. Nothing changes. Everything continues on, seamlessly. As if I was nothing more than a blip. Had my presence meant so little?

Work doesn't even quibble over my absence. Which makes me wonder . . . How will the plants in my lab survive? Will anyone tend them? My work area was secluded, a room at the building's rear. I always preferred it that way, but now . . . none of the technicians will venture in there. No one will notice as they shrivel and crisp, deprived of water. My poor fern, an *Osmunda claytoniana*, in the window with the sun's full blast, will be the first to go. I spent my entire career battling my way up, fighting for my doctorate, scraping for that professorship, championing the Amazon. *Desperate* to help plants, save the planet. To reach a position where I could make a difference. How utterly naive. In the end, I couldn't even save myself.

Around me, the birches seem to wilt in commiseration. I always did relate better to vegetation than people. Perhaps that's why I didn't see you for what you are—parasitic, strangling ivy.

Neighbors *do* start to wonder after a while. I hear their whispers. And eventually, some come by.

"Violet's left me," you say. "Gone to her mother's." You even manage a few tears, reptilian though they are. With such heartfelt anguish, with your pain on display, none doubt your sincerity. There isn't even an investigation. What a sly, canny creature you are. Believable. Slithering your way around each query with such faultless precision . . .

. . . while all the bones of my body are picked clean of every wet sliver of flesh.

People may not know what you placed in this tree, but the worms do, and the beetles, and the flies. Little rodents gnaw, tiny teeth chipping into bone. Crows strip away sloughing muscle, while songbirds pilfer tangles of hair to line their nests. And the creeping roots of the oak seek out and pry apart a rapidly hollowing torso to envelop the decaying heart within.

But that's okay; their embraces mean more than yours ever did. They are welcoming, an acceptance of sorts, into their fold. Knowing that my matter cycles on brings a semblance of peace. One that may have coaxed whatever phantom remains of me to drift away into oblivion . . .

If not for *her*. Alis.

She's exuberant, she's spry. Bursting with energy. Those elfin features, that pixie-cut hair, those big, bright eyes. So childlike . . . Her appearance jars me back; seeing her smile as she clutches your arm. You lead her under the porch and into our house.

I learn a lot, listening in—about her humdrum background, her non-existent social life. Clearly, no one has ever charmed her like you have.

In some ways, she's a lot like me. Only less shy.

More of my previous self stirs. I begin to . . . care. Care about who she is, her doe-like innocence, her lack of family. Care about why you brought her home, what it means.

From an unknown reserve, I find the strength to follow the thread back down. To watch. And wait. There's no mention of a previous wife and you don't take long to propose. You're married for three months—less than we were—before I start to notice a change. Small things, oddities *I* disregarded before—a tic in your cheek whenever she laughs, a twitch of your fingers whenever she calls you "Pookie." Like there's an irritant beneath your skin, an itch that cannot be scratched. It builds, and eventually, it overwhelms. From within the tree, I have to watch that hellish night play out again; a helpless observer of the poor girl's terror, because she sees you coming—she recognizes the darkness in your eyes.

I strain towards her with fingers of air, no longer apathetic but crackling with the need to stop you! But I'm impotent in my nothingness, as weak as a newborn. Weaker, with no body. That does not stop me from trying. From pushing and pushing, goaded on by her cries.

"Please don't! Stop this!"

That's when I feel it, the faintest brush. Connecting life . . . Ivy vines. *Hedera helix.*

The name dances out from the remnants of my subconscious. Known, ingrained. Their tiny roots plaster the outer bark of my tree in pin-prick strips. There's strength in them, in all the surrounding foliage. A network of it. Untapped but ripe for the taking. I can feel it, touch it, *use* it . . . I think. Knowledge unfurls like a fern leaf, my botanical side re-emerging. I understand how they function, how they're *designed*. I remember. Every stringy fiber and flexing tuber are as familiar to me as my own hands. I stretch . . . edging outward. My essence fills a leaf bud, moves in it. Can I move in the roots of the oak too? It takes effort, sheer will, but yes, I can. And I know Oaks, I've studied *Quercus robur*. Their root systems spread far and wide, branching secretly in all directions, including the one that matters most. They reach all the way to our house, to her. Unfortunately, the discovery comes too late.

"I'll tell anyone who asks that we weren't a good match," you say when it's done. "That you were just someone I met on the rebound. We broke up. Perfectly understandable."

You toss her into the lake, because perhaps on some unacknowledged level, you sense that the tree is no longer yours to trespass upon. Perhaps you don't want her within my reach—no solace for us, no companionship, even in death. Or perhaps you just like somewhere fresh.

Whatever the reason, it does not matter, because the roots of the hollow oak reach even there, burrowing, peeking through the cloudy silt of the lakebed, and waving in the water. I can feel them, now I know what to feel for, tangling with the waxy greenery—the water lilies and the algae, the cattails, and the pondweeds. *Nymphaea, Spirogyra, Typha, Lemna.* Every plant is linked, and I experiment with my newfound extremities by winnowing down the branching lines. Slow at first, then fast. Learning them, making them my own as I go. From dry dirt rhizomes to slimy filamentous masses. Until I reach her. Beneath the cooling hunks of meat, deep inside, something still remains. She's a quivering, curled-up ball of nictitating energy, half burnt out. I touch her, and she knows me then, your second wife. Once the shock and the panic subside, we embrace in what limited way we can. Twin souls, united within the lakebed.

I take her from you and make her my sister. And as we commune the fear mellows, sloughing away from her like a shed husk. The water swirls, filling her body, saturating her skin, embracing her too, as the watery flora sways and pricks at her with tiny tubers.

It is then that she understands: she is far from alone.

Mother Nature is a dark goddess who protects Her own.

You have a type. I've seen how you select us now. The third bride shares so many of our attributes: the ink-black hair, the dark eyes, the sweet smile. What you don't count on is her wit.

This one has a sharp mind, and she sees straight through you, right to the raw truth.

Rose is . . . unexpected.

Why she married you is a mystery. Your charm, perhaps? A whirlwind romance? It had to be something blinding, a moment of madness, because she's too strong-willed for you—a lawyer. Not your usual meek and subservient type. This time you chose imperfectly. Alis and I smile at your expense, our humor a brush of wind against the windows. But with the way she's starting to ask questions, I can hazard a guess you won't be married much longer.

You'll be thrice the widower yet.

It happens on a Tuesday night. You approach her from behind, once she's drowsy from two glasses of merlot. She fights, you don't expect that. The shock on your face is clear. For a moment we brace . . . When her nails tear rivulets down your cheeks, Alis is certain she will win.

Then you grab the bottle and bring it down with force.

It's a sad day when she joins our ranks.

This time, you try opting for fire. Making a leafy pyre in the guise of yard-burning. As her flesh burns the odor is horrific. You douse the fire and dig a hole, then shove her charred remains into the ground.

By the time the sun crests the horizon, all that remains is glittering black leaf ash, which you spread with a shovel over her freshly-covered grave—a site you chose beneath the briar on the eastern lawn, the farthest spot from the oak and the lake, and after you're done you chuckle as you sniff the roses. Her namesake. Fury, not fear, bristles in those scarlet petals and needle-tipped thorns. Yet she is as powerless as we are now, deprived of any means of vengeance.

All Alis and I can do is reach out in mute consolation—the flora a tether between us all.

This time when the neighbors query, you tell them she ran off with a work colleague.

No one questions you. Blind acceptance.

I wonder how many more excuses there will be before someone takes notice.

Knowledge is power, as they say. And I share what I know with my sister-brides. Showing them with thought alone how to move, how to navigate these new forms. Within our wilderness we stretch ourselves, pushing ever further. We sway in grasses, we tangle in roots, we furl and unfurl in delicate fronds. Slowly learning, *mastering* control.

There's a lantern by Rose's briar; its bracket is nailed to the outer brick wall. You light it now, every night. For some reason, you've taken to keeping the garden illuminated at all hours—as if sight in the darkness provides a measure of assurance.

Does it?

Do you fear what you cannot see?

Its orange glow attracts moths; seemingly innocuous, ultimately deadly. In a way, it's like you. You were our flame; you drew us in. We were the poor gregarious creatures who unwittingly singed our own wings in your vicious fire . . . and fell.

All the while you blaze on.

Nemma Wollenfang

There's a fourth. Her name is Hope.

It's a cruel joke, that name. As if she has any when wed to you.

Does she know? What you did to us? Is that why this one hides inside? Why she never ventures out to our neglected grove? Perhaps not. Perhaps she's just not the outdoors type. Or perhaps you steer her away. I see you looking, thinking. There's a growing nervousness in your eyes, taking hold like roots, burrowing and anchoring deep. It started when the insects fell silent. Do you sense us? Lingering out here?

Do you feel the ire entrenched within the bark of my oak? Do you feel the fury simmering beneath Rose's briar? Do you feel the cool wrath that laps the shores of Alis's lake?

I think you do.

I think you try to ignore it . . .

Madness, I imagine you tell yourself. It's madness to fear the dead.

One night I come close, in pollen, hitchhiking within the banks of fog that crests against the bricks of our house, a mute caress against our windows. The warmth within is such a contradiction to the arctic chill outside, and the scene I see is one of domestic bliss. On the sofa, you drape your arm around her as she snuggles into your side, content to lounge before the crackling hearth while you watch TV. It's so cozy, so familiar. You did the same with me. And Alis. And Rose.

I stick to the glass, leaving invisible streaks in the dew. You have no idea I'm there, but that's fine. It's not you whom I've come to see. She's perfect—all bright-eyed grace and bubbling laughter— absolutely *exquisite*. A delightful, happy creature. Innocent to the extreme.

Rain falls, making tiny tracks down the pane—tears I can no longer cry.

Because I know—to the very depths of my being—that you will destroy her too.

Hope has a brother, a twin. One who clearly cares about her.

"There's something about him that I don't like," he says as soon as he has her alone.

"You don't like any of my men, Hector." She laughs. "You never have."

"That's because they're always sleazebags," he mutters. They are on the back porch, basking in the sunset while you fetch refreshments. After checking it's safe, he whispers, "But there *is* something about him, something off. It's in the eyes . . . I've spoken to the neighbors. Do you know what they said? That all of his previous wives have gone *missing*."

That riles her, she grows defensive. "That's rubbish, they left him!"

"Are you sure?"

"He loves me," she says quietly.

"Come home," he begs.

Neither reaches a compromise before you return with their drinks.

⁂

None of us had any close friends or caring relatives—no one to raise a red flag when we vanished. I wonder now if that was intentional. If you chose us because of it.

Hope has her brother, though. Did you know about him before you wed her? Or was he an unexpected complication? Perhaps his presence will make you leerier.

⁂

The signs start again. The tic is back, the twitches in your behavior ever-present. Sometimes you snap at her for the simplest of things—burning dinner, dropping the mail.

The time is coming, I can feel it. We *all* can. And I think, to an extent, she does too. Even if she tries to ignore it.

You don't venture out here anymore. Alis is certain it's because you're afraid. Perhaps you are. Within our green realm, we sister-brides flourish. We coil and writhe, spanning every nuance of plant life. From leaf vein to new sapling to fungal spore. We stretch ourselves far and wide. The yard is ours now. The wild place we've claimed: encouraged its growth, nurtured its chaos, made it our wilderness . . . vast, bleak, and forbidden. Wind and earth, rain and wood—we're a part of them as much as they are a part of us. Our connection is intangible, something that goes beyond flesh, blood, and bone, down to the raw essence of life and being. I love them completely, more than I ever . . . well, the realization has dawned that I never truly loved you. You were never for me. I see that now. I was lonely and weak, that's how you trapped me.

No longer. I'm strong and supported and my place is with them. As I think it was always meant to be.

The bark of the oak, its roots, and its leaves, are my domain now. As much as the water and reeds are a part of Alis, and the ashes and briar are a part of Rose. She can even reach the lantern now, mingling with its flame, frolicking amongst the sparks. Perhaps it was the manner of her death and disposal, but the way she communes with the fire is almost familial.

There's power in numbers. The three of us are different now. Changed from the meek little wives you knew us to be. With our bodies gone, we've evolved, adapted. Grown stronger, taken on new shapes and forms. Like larvae shedding the confines of cocoons to find wings. Now that Mother Earth has had Her way with us, we have become visceral, feral as a pack of wolves. Dark in ways even your twisted mind couldn't possibly comprehend.

No longer do we just have movement within the foliage, we have command.

Of our own emerald army.

Our minds are unfettered, our earthly bonds unbound. All we know, we've passed to each other. Every seed of information has blossomed in our minds. And perhaps now, together, we finally have the strength to accomplish what none of us ever managed alone.

⁂

We all know you now. We know you well.

It's no surprise when you turn on her. What sets you off none of us can tell. What we do know is, she escapes your clutches long enough to reach the garden.

She fumbles with her phone, fingers clumsy with fright. Eventually, she must succeed because a crackly voice answers over the line. "Hello, Hope? You there?"

"Hector, he's . . . I need . . . Help me!"

The call alerts you, and you find her quickly, cowering beside the briars.

With a scream, she drops the phone, and it clatters to the ground.

"Hope?" The voice on the other end crackles. "What's happening? Hope?!"

You snag her arm, dragging her up, and a tornado of thorns scours your face, unleashed from the briars Rose now commands. *Rosa kordesii*, those hybrid perennials, have the sharpest thorns. Now *you* feel their sting. Throwing up your arms as a shield, you release Hope and fall back against the lantern. Again, Rose attacks. Lashing out with fingers of fire, clawing your face as she did once before. Through our connection, I can taste her glee, and feel her vicious thrill. Her abject jubilance is one we share!

It doesn't last. She can't hold you. Swaying and cursing you tear away.

You stumble to the lake to douse your face in the freezing water . . . which swells up, engulfing you. A tidal force shoves itself into your throat as pondweeds tangle about your wrists and ankles. You lurch back, spluttering and coughing, uncomprehending.

And Alis hisses as you break free of her grip too.

Perhaps you're blinded by your anger and the fresh burns and the inexplicable icy assault. Perhaps you just cannot see anything beyond your sopping-wet hair. Whatever the case, your one target is still her. Nothing else seems to matter.

She's like a fawn before a hunter, all doe-eyed and defenseless with her tear-streaked face. Too fragile for all this.

When you stalk her way, she bolts, seeking shelter inside the hollow oak. *My* oak.

My strong and noble *Quercus robur*.

Her legs tangle and she falls—straight into what's left of me.

One hand crunches through the brittle sternum, splintering ribs. There's little flesh left now but what remains is sticky with rot, the bones beneath stark white. Even in the gloom, she knows what she sees; I can tell by the way her tiny gasps turn to whines. Frantically, she wipes her hand in the dirt, vainly trying to rid it of my clinging decay.

But she's safe here, better protected than out there.

Because this place is *mine*.

Half-blind you follow her. With grasping hands and rage clouding your mind, you charge headfirst through the tall grass and untamed weeds—*Urtica, Rumex, Plantago*—into the depths of my herbaceous lair.

Big mistake. Huge.

They're only the precursors, an intricately laid web of stationary sentinels, and I am the spider that waits at the heart of them.

Their General and Commander.

It's easy to order them to snag an ankle, it's easy to drop you down. At first, you don't even notice, clawing at the dead leaves and uncontrolled grasses, too intent on reaching her. By the time you understand exactly what is happening, it's too late. I already have a hold.

Then, it's only a matter of binding . . .

Alis and Rose winnow towards me via roots and leaves and grass blades, to add their strength too, ensuring you don't escape. When one vine snaps, two more rise to replace it.

Taraxacum, Agrostis, Trifolium, dandelion, bent grass, clover . . . we call on them all. Every plant we have ever known. Our collective, deadly arsenal of whipping flora.

If we let you go it won't end. You'll travel somewhere new, start again. With new girls, new wives, new unsuspecting playthings. Another and another and another. The heinous cycle will continue. We can't let that happen. Not again. It's already gone on far too long.

Dandelions tighten, clovers constrict, nettles sting. Barbs of other thorny perennials dig into your skin, gaining purchase and drawing blood. Finally, you panic and cry out.

But no one's coming to help you.

In the end, it's quick. I give you that one mercy, same as you gave me. I don't hesitate or draw it out. Stealth is *my* ally now as I crawl up along you, in rhizomes and creepers and curl around your hips, your torso, your neck, and . . . One, quick, *SNAP!*

Instant stillness. All fighting stops.

Your weight droops within our grasp.

But we're not through yet. We command our roots to break the soil, to crack open the earth, and in a shower of grit, they rise like living hairs. Our vines and branches willow down in curling spirals to join them. And like a mannequin on strings, we winch you up.

The Hollow Tree

Your fourth wife wavers before you, gaping mutely as she totters in the grass, eyes glassy and uncomprehending.

In the distance, there's the roar of a car engine, and the screech of wheels. A door slams.

"Hope? *HOPE?!*" Her twin comes running. Skidding around onto the back lawn, he sees the grisliness of it all—the agitated flames, the frothing lake, the roots and branches still leisurely winding. It takes some time, but eventually, he grasps her arm. "Come away, Sis . . . "

They leave you there, to your fate, strung up by unforgiving ivy, with only the wind to accompany you as you sway, limp and lifeless, up in the hollow tree.

You won't join us, within the earth.

No. You're destined for a much darker place, where oblivion would seem like a kindness.

Turn Around, Bright Eyes

RIE SHERIDAN ROSE

This story is for Newell, who I would willingly follow anywhere—even to Hell and back.

"Oh, my gods! What in Hades is he *doing* here? I thought I was done with him!" Her hands shook as she read the message the courier sprite had given her.

"What's wrong, Reesie?" Pandora asked, reaching across the picnic blanket for more ambrosia. It was a perfect day for a picnic, the sun beaming down in welcome warmth with a touch of a breeze riffling the leaves and grasses. The four friends had decided to take advantage of the fact to get together for lunch. Bread, cheese, and a great deal of wine had already been disposed of, and now they were down to the fruit and sweets.

"It's my ex! He's conned his way down here and convinced Hades to give him permission to 'rescue' me. I bet he charmed Sephie into persuading the king. He's always had a silver tongue, especially with the ladies." She waved the messenger sprite away, biting her lip in consternation.

"Is this the bard you were telling us about?" Andromache asked, popping another pomegranate seed into her mouth.

"Yeah . . . Orpheus. He was fun at first, and I really did love him when I married him . . . but we were starting to grow apart, he just didn't know it yet. When Aristaeus propositioned me, I tried to escape from both of them. That's when the snake bit me."

"How is your ankle doing, by the way?" Medusa pushed up her sunglasses self-consciously. "Sometimes the wild ones get a bit feisty," she apologized, and the snakes writhing on her head hissed

64

in agreement. She ran a soothing hand over the serpentine knot, and they settled at once.

"Don't worry about it, Meddie. You can't hold yourself responsible for every serpent in all the realms." Eurydice threw her arms out in a gesture that encompassed the rolling fields and gently flowing river surrounding them. "Besides, I love it here! Who wouldn't? It's gorgeous—and I have made wonderful new friends." She beamed at the other women. "I wouldn't trade you three for a thousand Orpheuses."

"It is lovely here, isn't it?" sighed Pandora contentedly, stretching out on the grass with a peach in her hand. "Absolute perfection."

"Eurydice!" A male voice shattered the peaceful stillness.

"Gods . . . " she groaned, burying her face in her hands. "He's going to ruin everything."

Medusa put a finger to the bow of her sunglasses. "You want me to . . . ?" Her voice trailed off.

Eurydice shook her head, patting the Gorgon's arm. "No, thanks. I do appreciate the offer, but then we'd be stuck with a statue of him forever, and I don't need that constant reminder of my own stupidity. I just want him gone!"

Pandora shrugged. "Statues can be broken, y'know . . . "

"Since when have you gone gangsta?" Eurydice said with a laugh. "No. I don't think Hades would look kindly on that. He's really into statuary. Destroying one on purpose would really irritate him. He might kick me down to Asphodel—or worse! I don't want to take that chance."

Andromache's face grew fierce. "Do you want us to take care of him? I know what it's like to have to hide behind a loveless marriage. I think I still have one of Hector's swords somewhere . . . "

"Beloved!" The call was closer this time.

"No, sweetie. That would only make things worse. After all, then he'd be dead, and he could stay legitimately—and *you* might end up in the Fields of Punishment." A shudder ran through her at the thought of being stuck with him for eternity. "I couldn't bear that. I'll figure out some way to get rid of him." Eurydice pushed reluctantly to her feet. "I better go talk to him. See you girls later."

"We'll grab dinner," Pandora offered. "I know you'll be back by then."

"Sounds good."

Andromache stood and gave her a fierce hug. "Just in case he talks you into leaving, it's been a pleasure knowing you," she whispered, eyes glistening with tears.

"Don't worry, Andi. I'll be back. I promise you that." She pasted a brittle smile on her face and turned to head off the young man striding confidently across the waving grass.

He was a handsome specimen, if a bit smirky. His hands played absently across the strings of a golden lyre, sending ripples of melody through the morning air.

"Why are you here, Orf?" she asked, cutting him off before he could disturb the picnickers further.

His hands flew to cover his eyes, and then he spun to face away from her. "Good news, my darling! I have convinced the iron-hearted king of Tartarus to release you from the cold chains of death and allow you to return, with me, to the world of the living. Isn't that wonderful news?"

"That's hardly fair, is it? Why should I get preferential treatment? I mean, I did *die*, after all . . . "

"I know! And I have been heartbroken ever since. My song of woe has melted the icy core of Hades, and he will allow us to depart this wasteland together, to live once more as man and wife—"

"Have you looked at this place?" she asked. *Was he really that clueless?* "It's a paradise! I was honored to find myself in the Elysian Fields. It's the highest tribute a soul can receive. Why should I want to return to a two-room hovel when I have all of this?"

"My brave girl . . . " he cooed. "Always trying to make the best of a bad situation. That's why I love you so. Now, come. His only condition is that I must lead you forth from this torment without turning to gaze upon your beauty."

"That's the dumbest condition I've ever heard. Wouldn't it make more sense for *me* to lead *you* out? Since you don't live here and might get lost on the way to the surface?"

"This was his one request of me, and I will follow his injunction to the letter."

"What if I won't go?" she asked.

"Then, I suppose, I would have no choice but to drown myself in yon river and stay here at your side."

"You do know that's the Lethe, right?"

"Oh. Well, then I'd think of some other way to remain with you."

Her mind raced. If she didn't go with him, he really was likely to get lost and be wandering about the Elysian Fields for eternity. She didn't want *that* to happen for damn sure. "Fine. I'll follow you."

After all, there *was* a way out of this. All she had to do was get him to turn around. That shouldn't be too hard. The hard part had always been getting him to leave her alone for five minutes at a time.

"Then come, beloved, let us away!"

"After you," she said dryly. She turned and waved goodbye to her friends.

Pandora gave her a thumbs up, while Medusa crossed her fingers—and snakes—and Andromache blew her a kiss. Each had reacted in their own sweet way—Pandora, always hopeful; Medusa, hedging her bets with luck; and her beloved Andromache . . . reminding her of what she had to lose.

"I'll be back," she mouthed, then turned back to follow Orpheus.

They walked in silence for a while before she let out the best breathy whine she could muster. "Orf . . . can we stop for a minute? I'm sooo tired."

"We must push on, my sweet! We will rest at the top of the trail. There's a lovely little glade just outside the entrance to this hell." His back remained squarely in her sights as he began to strum the lyre again.

Gods, she hated that thing. Yeah, he played it well—with a skill it was said even his parents envied—but he played it constantly.

All. The. Damn. Time!

At least it was a nice day for walking. Though it was usually pleasant in the Fields, sometimes there were storms. With her luck history, today it should be raining fire. Thankfully, that wasn't the case.

After about half a mile further, clouds began to veil the sun, and the breeze gained strength. Maybe she'd—mentally—spoken too soon. The perfect Elysian day was beginning to devolve around her. It reflected the change in her mood.

She tried again to persuade him to turn. "Y'know, hon . . . Hades and Sephie have been really good to me ever since I arrived. It seems kinda rude to leave without saying goodbye. Do you think we could drop by the palace on the way out, so I could properly thank them for their hospitality?"

The music crashed to a halt with a jarring chord; it was surprising he didn't break a string. The sky darkened, along with his visibly worsening mood. Eurydice saw it reflected in the tight set of his shoulders.

"Hospitality?" he growled. "Are you crazy? They've kept you here in this gilded prison . . . away from me for an eternity now! No, I will not give them the satisfaction."

She'd known that would get to him . . . but he still didn't turn around. *Stubborn ass.*

He drew himself together with a deep breath. "Come, beloved. We have quite a distance to go."

Maybe she could get Andromache or one of the other girls to follow him in her place. Then it wouldn't matter if he turned around or not—she wouldn't be the one following him. If she tried that, though, it was quite likely Hades would rebuke her for the attempt to circumvent the rules and make her start over on the challenge, to be fair to Orpheus. Men. They always stuck together.

She looked around in desperation. Eurydice recognized this infernal part of the realm. They were getting close to Tartarus. At least, that was what she remembered . . . but her memory wasn't as good as it used to be. She'd managed to avoid more than a sip from the Lethe, but it had been enough to blur her remembrances somewhat.

The lovely green trees and lush grass of Elysium were replaced by skeletal branches stretching over sere wastes. Howls of torment broke through the silence between them as they skirted the Fields of Punishment. Fires flickered in the distance, and the stench of burning flesh permeated the air.

Wasn't Cerberus's kennel somewhere around here? Orpheus had always nattered on about wanting a dog. Maybe she could use that to her advantage.

Weird she remembered that. Were her memories getting stronger the closer they got to the surface? If so, put her down for a pint of Lethe water when she got back to the girls!

"Orf, sweetie, I'd really like to say goodbye to Cerberus. I know you don't want to waste any time in conversation, but surely, we can spare enough to pat that good doggie on his heads. Can we? Please?"

"I'm sure they will be fine. The hounds were guarding the gates as I entered, and understood the urgency of my errand when I passed them on the way in."

"But you know how dogs are—they get upset if you don't let them know every detail of your life. Surely it would be worth the delay . . . "

"You are a tender-hearted woman, my love—but we can't afford to stop. I explained it all to them before, and they ushered me on my way. I found them very intelligent and articulate. Especially Josh."

"Josh?"

"The middle head. They introduced themselves as Phil, Josh, and Raven. Cerberus is the family name."

"I see." The information took her aback. In all the time she'd been here, she had never even considered the beast might be capable of speech. He—or they, apparently—was just the guard at the gate. This was something to think about moving forward. If there was a forward.

"I still think it's rude not to say goodbye, but you are the one under the compulsion." *Another plan bites the dust.*

The definitive taint of sulfur had replaced the scent of jasmine and lavender she had become accustomed to. They were closer to the Fields of Punishment than she'd realized. Wasted and withered bodies hung from some of the branches they passed—several still moaning piteously, retaining a spark of life despite the torments they'd had to endure.

Eurydice shivered. She'd been lucky to wind up in Elysium, where she'd met her friends and carved herself a worthwhile existence. She did *not* want to risk reassignment.

Piercing cries of agony rose from the tormented dead now, as the sky boiled with clouds above them. Their pain tore at her heart.

"Orpheus . . . could you spare a moment to play for the dead over there in Tartarus? I am certain those poor tortured souls would be eternally grateful."

"I will not be swayed from my mission, dearest, though it is admirable of you to think of those less fortunate. A clever ploy, but I will not be moved."

"I'm not trying to—" Well, not at that precise moment. She truly *had* been thinking of the damned, wanting to relieve just a bit of their misery, but she could see his suspicions were so roused that he would see trickery in every word she uttered.

They walked on in silence—except for the soothing strains of the lyre. He just couldn't help himself. Maybe the melody would be carried on the now keening wind and provide a touch of comfort to the sufferers.

The path was climbing now, and she found herself hard-pressed to keep up. It was black as night, making footing treacherous.

All the sitting around eating and chatting with the girls had caught up to her. When she got back—*if* she got back—she'd have to start a dancercise class or something.

She studied Orpheus through the gathering gloom as they walked. He *was* a fine specimen of male. He had Apollo's golden curls and toned muscles, and his mother's musical talents. Eurydice had thought the world began and ended with him when they'd met . . . but that was long ago now.

Seemed like forever.

The more time they'd spent together, the more she'd come to realize his less impressive aspects—like the fiery temper, and the egotism. It was always his way or not at all. He had tried to mold her into the wife he wanted, curbing her wild Nymph nature with chains of propriety.

Eventually, she'd grown resentful.

By contrast, Pandora and her other friends looked up to her. She was often the instigator of their adventures. The day's picnic, for example, had been her idea. She loved the freedom she'd discovered in the Elysian Fields, and she didn't relish the idea of giving it up for anyone—*especially Orpheus.*

"I can see the gate!" he cried excitedly. "Look, beloved. We shall soon step aboard Charon's ferry. From there, it is mere steps to the egress."

A towering gate wrought with fantastical shapes stood at the head of the rise. It stood ajar—no doubt Orpheus's doing. She had little time left.

"Did you say we have to take the ferry back across the Styx? I have no coin. Money is unnecessary on this side of the river."

"Don't worry, my darling girl. I have enough for both of us."

Of course, he did. He'd thought of everything. She was going to be stuck leaving, and the thought brought tears to her eyes.

She'd never felt as at home as she did here. Mortal women had been intimidated by her beauty, and the Nymphs were all such hedonists that she couldn't even carry on a conversation with them. Here . . . She was a part of something. She and her friends helped ease newcomers into the routines of their new circumstances. She and Andi were thinking of setting-up house together.

There had to be a way to make him look at her!

They stepped through the gate, and the oily black waters of the Styx slithered before them. The ferry was currently across the river.

"Ho, Ferryman!" called Orpheus. "We have need of your services."

The tall gaunt figure of Charon rose from the stern of the ferry and began poling it toward them with slow, deliberate strokes.

Orpheus cupped his hands around his mouth. "We are in rather a hurry, my good man. Could you speed it up a little?"

Charon continued his snail-like progress.

She could almost see the smoke beginning to pour out of Orpheus's ears. He was never one to take perceived slights lightly—and ignoring his desires was *always* perceived as a slight. He was almost angry enough to make a mistake. Maybe there was some of Pandora's hope left yet . . .

The ferry bumped against the bank, and Orpheus hurried aboard, slapping two coins into the ferryman's outstretched palm. She could swear a slight wince crossed Charon's impassive features.

Orpheus moved to the stern, staring at the far bank with arms crossed over his chest. He looked like a petulant child.

Charon extended a helping hand to her, and she took a step toward the gently rocking ferry. An odd sensation assaulted her senses—as if the boat knew she shouldn't be there. She fully agreed.

She reached to take the extended hand then snatched hers back, straightening her shoulders and standing firm. "No. I can't do it. I just can't."

With an eloquent shrug, Charon turned to take up his pole again.

"Eurydice," growled Orpheus coldly, "get in the boat."

"No."

The final leg of their journey stretched before them; a rising path—perhaps a quarter league in length—led to a tunnel mouth beyond the Styx. Daylight from beyond spilled through the channel to play upon the threshold. She fancied she caught the scent of the sea upon the breeze. Oceanus was mere steps beyond that cavern.

"We are home free now, my dearest!" Orpheus called impatiently. "Tonight, we will feast in our own home."

"*This* is my home!"

Lightning crashed overhead, jarring ribbons of cold, blue light streaking across the sky to the timpani of thunder. Even at its worst, her world was beautiful. She had found joy here, and she would not leave it.

"Eurydice, I am becoming tired of your games! We have no time for this nonsense," he shouted angrily, forgetting himself in the heat of the moment.

He whirled around to face her.

Eurydice grinned triumphantly. "Thank you! I'll see you when I see you . . . hopefully never!"

Turning on her heel, she fled away from the Styx, ignoring Orpheus and his bellows of outrage behind her—their strident echoes reverberating until she was well past the Fields of Punishment.

She knew Hades would not be persuaded to give him a second try. At least for now, she was free to do as she pleased.

It was time to see if the girls would keep their promise of dinner. She could do with a flagon of nectar.

The Roxy Special

ROWAN HILL

To all my horror ladies, Jill, Kenzie, Demi, Sarah, Janine, and many others I admire and think of as I write a good final girl.

Roxy

The Groom-to-be had a perfect right hook he knew exactly where to aim on a woman's body. Roxy's fingers probed the ribs he had viscously punched. Nothing felt broken, at least not the kind of broken to puncture her lung. But she could move, and the pain was tolerable. She looked down at the real problem: the small hunting knife lodged in her upper thigh.

The red-sequin thong barely covering her crotch rubbed against the wooden handle with a pearl inlay. In the faint slivers of light entering through the floorboard's gaps, she studied her wound. It stung like hell, but she was lucky. The Best Man's errant stab as he fell caught the fatty part of her inner thigh. The part that jiggled when she gave lap dances. The part men usually liked . . . never stabbed.

She pulled it out carefully, millimeters at a time, biting her lip so hard she tasted the copper of blood. Relief swelled when she saw blood weep, but not spurt from the wound. No arteries. No muscles. Damn lucky.

Roxy turned the blade over, slowly examining it. A beautiful drop-point hunting knife with an ornate, customized handle, and a belt clip thoughtfully placed on the opposite side. There was a smooth curve to the knife, making it appear like an extension of your hand. Someone loved this blade. Five tally marks were purposefully carved into the base. Roxy ran her finger over them, a small grin forming on her lips. She was about to study them closer when the frantic shouts from below grew louder, and a bright light flashed through the attic's floorboards before Roxy heard a female groan.

Destiny.

Distributing her weight evenly, Roxy moved forward, bear-crawling away from the secret hatch she'd used for her escape earlier. She leaned down, peering between the gaps in the floor in order to see better. In one of the many rooms of the privately rented lodge, Roxy watched two groomsmen drag Destiny's prostrate body into the sparsely furnished room, unceremoniously dropping her beside the bed.

Roxy's throat tightened, and she fought the urge to vomit when she saw that Destiny's chest had several large punctures digging deep into flesh and rib bone. Her nipples were still covered by the green pasties with tassels, now stained a dirty crimson. Bruises marred her lovely, seductive face and blood streamed from the corners of her lips, which she opened and closed with fishlike, frantic gasps, trying desperately to breathe.

Her attention was diverted by one of the groomsmen being helped into the room and laid *gently* onto the bed. Roxy recognized the man named Carter, mostly for the icepick she'd punched deep into his lower shoulder, hoping to catch an artery. He groaned pathetically as the Groom and Second Groomsman released him.

"*FUCK!*" the Groom shouted, his voice raspy as his hands gripped his scalp, while the Second Groomsman inspected the ice pick wound of their comrade.

"Carter, she got you good, bro, right through the bone. It's like she knew where to stab. I don't think we should take this thing out ourselves."

A deep, angry growl erupted, and the tall, strapping figure of the Best Man, Duke stalked into the room. The biggest man had both women's purses, which he tossed next to Destiny's body.

Shit.

Roxy had thought he was a hunk right up until he stabbed her while falling to his knees from her uppercut.

"She has my knife . . . " he growled.

"Fuck your knife, man. Where the fuck *is* she? I mean, there she was in the hallway, and then suddenly she wasn't. Did she run up here, to the second floor?" The Second Groomsman's voice was a few octaves too high. The Groom stopped pacing, turning to face the three other men.

"None of the door alarms have gone off. This place is big . . . but not big enough to hide a wounded stripper. I've got the car keys, and you locked up tight after we all came together, right, Duke?" he asked, and Duke nodded solemnly.

"She's inside here, somewhere. Unless she kicks out a window, there's no way out. And the stripper's car keys were in her purse." He dangled them from one beefy finger.

Hopefully dying, the wounded Groomsman coughed blood, "That bitch, I'm gonna—"

The Groom cut him off. "You're gonna do shit, asshole. You're the one who got us into this mess! You and your goddamn choking fetish." He waved a hand towards Destiny, lying on the floor, exsanguinating over her own Fendi purse. "Crazy Carter strikes again, huh? Couldn't let me have just one normal night? You had to take it too far, then you freaked out when she said "No." and fought back?"

"I don't think Roxy is some ordinary stripper," Carter muttered, the second groomsman dabbing the blood around the ice pick on his friend.

Hidden above her attackers, Roxy tensed, waiting, her muscles tightening between her shoulders.

Duke, who had sat and was leaning over his knees on the bedside, erected himself. His nose had bled profusely, dripping down his cupid bow, over his full lips and strong chin to stain his white Tommy Bahama shirt. "What do you mean?"

"When she was giving me my dance, I saw a tat on her nape, like, below her hairline. She had some strange scars, above a snake. It was curling around some really girly writing. I only caught it for a second, because she started grinding on me and then my brain fritzed . . . "

"So, what did it *say*, Eli?"

"I think it said 'Semper Fidelis.'"

Duke expelled air in a loud sigh, and Roxy silently cursed the up-do she wore that was best for pole dancing. He chuckled, then shot to his feet, walked over to Eli, and smacked his head.

"Do you know what that means, asshole?! It means she was a

Marine!" He went to the doorway and yelled, "You a fucking *Marine*, ROXY?!"

The angry shout echoed down the hallway and throughout that portion of the hunting lodge, designed specifically for men's retreats. Miles from the nearest town in the desolate, inhospitable New Mexico desert that undoubtedly crawled with coyotes and rattlesnakes. Duke turned back to face the others, rubbing his hands together, smearing Roxy's and his own blood between them.

"No, nononononono . . . but that makes sense. I've never had a chick punch me like that, let alone esca—" his mouth suddenly clamped shut and the Groom frowned, shaking his head.

"Well, before Duke stabbed her, I'm sure I cracked a rib. She's probably hiding in a cupboard somewhere, hoping we go outside and look for her. It's three of us against one chick."

Duke crossed the room, his thick boot toeing into Destiny's ribs, and Roxy felt ashamed that she'd found him attractive when they first met; she had even considered taking him upstairs later for a freebie.

"Yo, stripper."

Destiny, slack on the floor, didn't respond. Duke nudged her harder, closer to a kick, and Roxy's fists tightened, her knuckles whitening against her own bloodstained hands. "Hey, bitch . . . wake the fuck up!"

The kick retrieved Destiny from death's brink; her eyes fluttered open, and she sputtered, releasing a bloody cough. Duke crouched beside her, his muscular back straining against the fitted white shirt.

"That other stripper, Roxy; she serve?"

A strange, garbled noise came from Destiny—her cackles were muted, and Roxy realized she was laughing at Duke. Bubbles of blood rolled from her mouth as she told him, "You guys are fuuuuuccccked."

His open palm smacked Destiny hard enough for her face to jerk aside before he pinched her chin to face him again. The hit stunned the dying woman; her eyes were wide and alert.

"Tell me." He calmly demanded. Roxy shivered involuntarily as the deep timbre of his voice filled the small room.

Fear had overwhelmed the lethargy of death on Destiny's face, and she began to stutter. "She . . . she doesn't like t-talking about it. Roxy . . . she's smart. Tough."

Silence in the room dragged out until the Groom said, frustrated, "That's it? She's smart and tough?"

Destiny nodded before a bloody cough burst from her lips. Duke exhaled and lifted a leg, straddling her body while his hands came to her face, gentle and slow. Almost lovingly.

"What aren't you telling me, stripper?"

Destiny sobbed before whimpering, "Went to Navy and . . . Almost became a SEAL."

"Huh. Guess she couldn't handle the training."

Roxy's entire body tensed as she waited.

She watched as Destiny shook her head, biting her lip. "No. She . . . beast at the gym. S-she couldn't pass . . . psych."

"Why?" he murmured, his fingers calmly pressing into her face.

Roxy thought she saw a corner of Destiny's lips turn up, her courage rearing. "Liked killing . . . assholes . . . like you too much." With that, Destiny spat blood onto Duke's face.

Roxy realized Destiny probably knew she was dying, but it still felt as if her heart was being squeezed as she watched the scene below; she was familiar with Duke's technique as fingers from one hand pinched Destiny's nose, and the other palm covered her mouth.

Her eyes widened, frantic. Her slender fingers grasped his stronger hands, trying to pry them away as her whole body convulsed from the lack of air. Spiked heels fruitlessly kicked the floor while he held her down, expertly, the motions natural to him.

Practiced.

Hot tears stung Roxy's eyes, and her forehead pressed against the rough wood, silently crying as the fight left Destiny. After another moment of weak struggling, Destiny was dead. Duke's hands left her blood-caked face and he stood, before wiping her spittle from his own.

Destiny's glazed eyes stared up at the log-plank ceiling, and Roxy felt them burning through the wood, demanding vengeance. To some, Destiny was nothing more than a stripper and part-time prostitute; but to Roxy, she'd been a friend.

And friends avenged one another.

The smoldering fire spread, throbbing through her veins. An old, seasoned flame with the familiar pull of wanting justice . . . and these men had gotten away with too much already.

Lifting to her fingertips, Roxy slunk soundlessly away from the scene below and across the attic, back to the trap door, recalling what she knew of the lodge's layout from the brief tour these arrogant men had given. A back stairwell led up to the second floor, the first floor overlooking the main. The warren of interlocking rooms.

She knew exactly where the electric panel would be.

From what she had learned, she ranked them from least to most dangerous. Her gut and honed intuition sang to her now, thrumming a familiar rhythm as she gripped the knife that had been used to stab her. The weight in her palm was reassuring.

Did they want a little fun? Roxy was pretty good at providing men with 'fun.'

Duke

The others in the room were quiet, intently watching Duke as he suffocated the stripper. He had stiffened with a semi as she'd taken her last breath, and then he noticed Carter, Sam's burgeoning psycho brother still with an icepick in his shoulder, enthralled as his own auto-erotica fantasies played out, witnessing the scene on the floor.

Instead of acknowledging their attention, he reached for the non designer purse, a deep desire to learn more about Roxy. The others shook off their stupor and began planning while he searched her things. He flipped through the cards in her wallet until he found one in particular—her Military ID card.

He stood and read it in the light, slightly impressed, certainly aroused; the card showed *Roxanne* had left the Marines, then Navy, over three years ago.

"Well, it's true," Duke said.

Sam, the Groom, ran a hand through his short hair, newly trimmed for his upcoming wedding. "Shit," he said, then began directing everyone. His voice was still raspy from Roxy's punch to his throat that sent him to his knees. When she discovered them cleaning up Carter's mistakes, her ferocity and fists had taken them by surprise in the tight confines of the first-floor hallway, and then she quickly bolted in the opposite direction.

"Eli, check the basement. There's that unfinished portion that's just dirt and the start of the frame, where she could hide behind a wall. It's big down there. Duke, you're on the main and first floor, it's the biggest, but she's not gonna hide behind a couch or kitchen table. Check *every* room, every bed, every closet, every fucking cupboard. Let's move, before she changes her mind and runs for it."

Duke remained silent, thinking, fingering the photo on the card, smearing Destiny's blood over Roxy's little portrait. Thought over what he would do if stuck with four men who had just killed a friend, given him a leg wound, and there was no escape from a house deep in the dry desert. Certainly not run.

"Duke? Are you listening? Please say you didn't snort any of that shit yet!"

He was ready to answer and take charge of the situation when all the lights flicked off. She must've found the breaker box.

"Fuck!" Sam whispered as Eli shot up from the bed.

Down the hallway, the thumping rhythm of the 80's synth-pop song, 'You Spin Me Round' began playing at a deafening volume. It filled the house, cramming its empty spaces and reverberating off the interior polished wooden walls and floors. An insistent thump to scatter their thoughts.

Before he could stop him, Eli, whom Duke always thought of as soft, turned on the flashlight from his cell phone and bravely ran from the room, heading toward the back stairwell that would take him to the basement.

The rented lodge could sleep twenty comfortably. But that wasn't why Duke chose it for Sam's stag night. It was the isolation. The size and privacy to do whatever the hell you wanted was thrilling. Now even more so.

Sam quickly followed his future brother-in-law, starting to check and clear rooms, not understanding the darkness and loud music was intentionally disruptive. Not comprehending what they were up against. Duke looked back to Carter, propped up on the bed, sitting in the moonlight. Blood coursed a black river down his shirt from the ice pick. The two shared a glance before Carter fell back onto the bed.

Duke looked at the half-buried, protruding ice pick. Roxy had missed his lung, but the way the blood pulsed from the wound, he would bet she clipped the artery in his arm. Carter would be dead by morning.

He left the room, listening to Sam throw open closets and tipping beds in panic before descending the stairway to the first-floor balcony, to try and think over what he recalled.

Darkness and aggressive, loud music. Guerilla warfare 101. Disorient, divide, and conquer; that definitely was some *'Art of War'* shit, right there. A minute later, Sam joined him at the interior balcony overlooking the large open space of the main floor. It was still dark except for moonlight streaming through the wall of windows overlooking the flat desert, which turned silver in the night. The loud, repetitive chorus continued blaring from the stripper's portable, hidden speakers.

Sam leaned to Duke's ear. "Let's get downstairs, I bet she is hiding somewhere in that game room . . . lots of nooks and crannies."

Duke was nodding when movement on the darkened floor below caught his eye. His hand shot out, grabbing Sam's shirt and holding him still. He followed Duke's gaze to the far side of the room, where the balcony continued around and the front entrance of the basement stairs began, a black ingress leading beneath the floor.

There was nothing for a moment and Duke started to think he imagined the movement before a flickering light appeared from the black stairwell. A second later, Eli ascended, his phone's flashlight in his hand. He topped the stairs and saw his two friends on the other side of the enormous main room. He shook his head, and that's when Duke saw it. Beneath the balcony floor, hanging over half of the main floor, something moved above Eli's head, and Duke's fingers curled tighter around Sam's shirt to make sure he was looking. Using loud music and darkness as a cloak, the lithe body of Roxanne Demarco lowered out of the plank above the balcony, clinging to the exposed logs.

She slowly unfurled; a beautiful, carnivorous flower blooming open until her entire, stretched-out physique hung from her grip. Still dressed in her sequined bra and panty set, it reflected the moonlight and sparkled. Duke spied blackness dripping from her thigh as she dropped lithely to the ground. Right behind Eli.

Duke was entranced; enthralled watching the sinewy, leonine movements of the stripper in the shadows, radiating danger and, along with it, a new level of eroticism he had never known. His heart thumped in time with the music. Sam, however, wasn't bewitched and screamed Eli's name, straining to be heard across the distance and over the synth.

He was too late.

A firm hand palmed Eli's forehead from behind as another slid across his throat, the motion fast, familiar as it moved quickly across. A black line spread across Eli's lower neck, thickening as it ran down his shirt like spilled ink. She had used Duke's knife to cut Eli's throat.

Eli dropped to the floor in a heap, revealing Roxy. Her chest huffed with exertion, breasts proudly on display in that salacious bra. Standing tall, she locked eyes with Duke, a sliver of lunar light slicing across her face, and she blew him a kiss before sprinting below the balcony and out of sight.

The song ended and silence enveloped the house, the tread of her footsteps already gone. Stunned, Sam and Duke watched Eli's body twitch, an inky pool of blood spreading across the floor.

Finally, Duke broke their stunned silence.

"Bro, I think I'm in love."

Sam swatted his hands away. *"WHAT THE FUCK!?"* He began pacing the length of the balcony, an annoying habit. Duke leaned over the railing and watched Eli's final moments as he twitched in his own lifeblood. Sam wrenched his shoulder back. "What the hell, man? Why aren't you taking care of this? Why aren't you fired up?!"

"I'm thinking."

"Thinking?! Fuck thinking, man! Goddamn Einstein . . . that was my new brother-in-law! You remember how much dick I had to suck when Chrissy's father took care of that hit-and-run last year? *FIX this!*"

Duke turned, flexing muscles that had grown stiff from inactivity. He stood, staring down at Sam. "This isn't like other times. Those other girls weren't shit. Weak, running through the woods like they could just stay quiet and give us the slip. This girl, this *woman*, is experienced."

Sam grasped at Duke's collar, panic creasing his forehead. "You're an ex-Green Beret! One who avoided a court martial for some seriously fucked-up, Apocalypse-Now-type shit. Get your balls together and take care of this psychotic stripper!"

Duke breathed deeply, remembering his childhood friend always freaked out on trips if something didn't go as planned, if a woman surprised them. But more than that, Duke didn't want to admit it, but he wanted to see this game of cat and mouse play out. This was more exciting, more stimulating than any other night he'd ever planned. "Sam, you don't get it. This isn't just another one of our hunts; I think this is more like . . . a battle royale. Somebody isn't leaving. We gotta be smart."

Sam nearly retorted with angry criticism before he was interrupted by another loud sound. The house security alarm. A long, cacophonic wail, punctuated by a robotic voice from a control panel downstairs, repeating, "Game-room-window breach."

They exhaled in unison.

"Well shit, I guess one of us is definitely leaving," Duke finished.

⁂

Roxy

The alarm abruptly ceased and from the shadows of the foosball table, Roxy smirked, watching the two men run into the room and straight across to the broken picture window. The gap between the sill and the remaining jagged glass was just enough for a thin woman to slip out. The men kicked more glass away to immediately scan the quiet desert outside.

Shrouded by darkness, she inched closer, listening to their loud, frustrated voices.

"Fuck, I guess this *is* another hunt. I did not see that coming tonight . . . I thought for sure she would—"

"Okay. Okay okay," Sam interrupted. "You're faster, man. She's gotta be heading for the road, right? You chase her on foot, and I'll get the car. Moon's pretty bright out so she might be easy to spot. We're three miles away from anything, so she'll probably hug the dirt road, but not be too close."

"You catch her first, just start honking. Don't try shit. She's still got my knife and apparently knows how to use it."

Roxy's fingers tightened around his pretty blade.

Duke used his elbow to break more glass, and Sam remained, leaning out. Roxy listened as the heavy footsteps of the Best Man slowly faded.

As predicted, the lesser threat was now left alone. Easy pickings.

Roxy stood from her crouch and padded barefoot across the game room to stand behind the Groom, who was still staring out the window as he fumbled for his car keys. Sweat beaded the back of his neck, and he reeked of musk and fear. He finally turned, his hand still in his pocket jiggling a key as Roxy's fist came out again, punching his larynx in the exact same spot she'd hit before.

His mouth gaped open, his voice gravelly and dry as he tried to holler. The glorious expression of shock on his face left a moment later, however, when he threw a wild right jab to her face. Instead of ducking, Roxy stepped around and into him, letting his outstretched arm pass by her head, while hers swung up and hooked around it.

Her sinewy body twisted behind his shoulder and pulled his arm back. Roxy quickly adjusted his wrist to twist his entire arm, and he grunted. She had stunned him with the pain in his throat, but not enough to make her feel in control, so she kicked out his knees and sent him to the floor, his arm bending further.

Locked in tight, snug as a bug.

"So, this was lovely. *Really*. Thank you. I've always wondered just how fucked-up a bachelor party could get. And this? Superb."

The Groom rasped out something crude, and she smacked the back of his head. Unclipping it from the side of her panties, she held out the folded knife, so he saw it in his peripheral as the ornate handle caught the moonlight. The pearl inlay gleamed, highlighting those five engraved marks.

"They mean what I think?"

The Groom didn't respond, stubbornly quiet, so Roxy lifted his curled elbow higher, feeling the strain of his bone until she heard a creak. A hoarse cry came from his throat, uttering a single, garbled word. "Yes!"

Her free hand grasped his scalp, his hair soft through her fingers as she made him look up.

"How does he do it?" she purred.

His reply was immediate, his croaky voice laced with a hint of shame. "H-he takes them out for a . . . fun night. B-before setting them loose and . . . you know."

"Well, romance isn't dead until your date is, huh?"

The Groom's other arm flung around, trying to elbow her hip and break her hold on his arm. She smacked his head again as if he were a bad puppy. "Now cut that out. And what about you? You getting some pre-marriage action?"

"No. I just . . . watch. A-and . . . help."

Roxy sighed, feeling disappointed in men everywhere. She unfolded the knife with one hand in a practiced motion. "So . . . you're a watcher, huh?"

Duke

Duke knew they had been fooled within ten minutes of running through the cold desert night. The half-moon was too bright, too clear for him not to be able to see a half-naked female bounding through the landscape. Also, Sam's car hadn't driven down the parallel road. Which meant he found her inside . . . *or she found him.* His adrenaline spiked with anticipation as he ran up the driveway. Ten minutes out, ten minutes back. That was a lot of time for busy hands.

The house was still dark; the garage door was locked and closed. But a spark of blue light burst over the small, frosted window beside the front door, and he paused mid-stride, tentatively reaching for its handle. He pulled on it, surprised when it opened.

He entered the front hallway leading into the large, open space where colorful lights rapidly flashed in blues and violets, in opposition to slow, sensual synth music now drifting from the speakers. Duke trod warily, the lights growing brighter as he approached the main room.

He was struck still, blood pulsing through him as the rotating, mechanical disco ball at the front of the stage spun wildly to illuminate the room.

An agile body circled the stripper pole, swirling around its metal in sync with the hypnotic rhythm of the song, lights sparkling off those red sequins like an erotic carousel.

Roxy.

Her calf and thigh clutched the bar as she climbed near the top, where she planked her body straight before twirling as she slid down. Her curly hair spilled out, and across the distance, she locked eyes with him and winked playfully before continuing her captivating routine.

She seemed unconcerned with his presence, spinning in full circles, holding the pole between her thighs, leaving smears of blood as a macabre lubricant on the shiny chrome. Her taut body spun, faster and faster, the swirl of lights flashing over her flesh.

Duke walked forward in a daze, engrossed, his eyes lingering on her muscles flexing beneath the strobing light.

A chair waited for him, thoughtfully placed directly in front of the platform, and he sat slowly, his thoughts fogged by lustful haze, not immediately noticing the chair beside him as he watched her red sequins sparkle. Roxy moved like a flame in zero gravity. Lithe and supple. Unbound.

Defiant.

She thrust, spread, then grabbed and pulled her body as it caressed the pole until sweat shone on her brow. Her eyes flickered to him occasionally, as she moved and gyrated her hips, the alluring movements making Duke's blood surge. His heart again thumped against his ribs.

The crotch of his pants strained against his growing erection.

Something fell, and clattered to the hardwood floor, and still mesmerized, Duke's eyes glanced away from Venus on her pole. Another man sat in another chair, watching Roxy's lewd, bloody performance. It was the ice pick, previously stuck out from his chest, and in silhouette, Duke could see it had been punched through to his back. Blood dripped off the tip. The figure was slumped back in the chair, eyes blank.

He returned to Roxy, a magnet pulling his eyes. She had left the pole and was walking towards him in long, swaying strides . . . like a lioness sauntering through the grass. A long stain of blood glistened over her strong thighs, all the way down to her foot, adding to her eroticism and carnality. Dancing and bleeding, she was the most alive thing he had ever seen.

She was unarmed, though he wasn't sure he would have noticed, in any case. The way her hips moved, the shoulders, her arms reaching behind her own back, thrusting her breasts out. She was at the edge of her platform, smiling like they shared a secret, his gaze glued to the dimple on her cheek. With a bent knee, she leaped the short distance between them to straddle his lap, landing against the erection in his jeans. Duke's open palms instinctively clasped her hips as she landed; she was heavier than he anticipated.

He grunted from the brief, sharp pain, but couldn't stop his grin as the two finally came face to face. Her skin was warm beneath his hands, their groins separated only by fabric.

"I'm guessing you were no simple marksman, huh, *Roxanne?*"

She shook her head, hair falling over her face as she answered. "Naw, I was something more like a . . . cleaner."

"Like with mops and brooms?" he chuckled.

Roxy's laugh was as clear as a church bell, "No, not like that. More like cleaning up *human* trash." Her index finger grazed his chin, then pointed towards the other men.

Dead.

Eli was seated the farthest, and Duke inhaled as he saw Sam. His face was slack, dead from the hole in his head, one eye missing. Pain seared in his heart seeing his friend dead. So many dead friends over one dead stripper.

He turned back; she wore a wide smile, and with her hair flipped to one side, the blue light displayed the scars of carved tally marks behind her ear. Scars she'd given herself, just like the ones on his knife.

At least fifteen. He clasped her neck in his wide palm, rubbing the area with the pad of his thumb, struggling to summon enough breath to laugh.

"Huh, I no longer think I'm in love. I fucking know it. I knew we were the same. Yin for my *yang.*" Duke could kill her right now. Just dig his thumb into the soft hollow behind her ear. Push it as deep as possible until he hit something worthwhile. But she was growing heavier, and his chest felt strained.

Roxy ground against him and all thoughts of killing her were driven away, in favor of more primal urges. She whispered low to him. and Duke could barely breathe at her erotic transformation.

"You didn't think you were the only one who missed it, right? The thrill of holding a knife, a gun . . . a life in your hands. I'm just not stupid enough to leave my body count *on* my body—physical evidence."

Suddenly he coughed, a spray of blood hitting Roxy's chest. He looked down, and the source of his discomfort became obvious; his own knife had been expertly slid between his fifth and sixth rib, below his pectoral, where there were few nerves.

Deep in his lungs.

He coughed again, wheezing, straining for air as Roxy's relaxed body suddenly clenched around him, holding him tight to lean forward and kiss him in a smothering embrace. Covering his lips with her soft ones. Before he could think of his fingers breaking her soft flesh, she slammed their bodies together, pushing his knife fatally deeper.

Duke went taut with pain and howled into her open mouth, blood filling his lungs until it reached his orifices, pleading to be let out. And Roxy was holding him down. Smothering him.

An animal cornered; Duke went berserk. He pushed her away, punched her ribs, and tore at her hair. But she wouldn't budge, and her legs clenched around him as if they were anacondas. Grasping her ass, he stood, frantically attempting to break her hold. His movements were wild, jerky. Roxy clung like a blanket—a feral, oppressive, weighted blanket. Her hands held his head, mashing their faces together while he tried to reach between them for his knife. His fingers were slow, fumbling because they were too cold. His movements became sluggish as his knees gave out, and they fell to the floor together. Roxy's supple body still clung, her strong thighs planted in a firm straddle, her lips still kissing him, her tongue still filling his mouth to combine with his suffocating blood.

Roxy's eyes were hooded through his sleepy gaze as she pulled back; Duke's were still full of lust and pleasure. Even as death knocked, he savored every moment of their shared embrace.

Her movements were expert.

Practiced.

It was a hell of a show, he thought, *if he had to go down . . .*

Her hair was now draped over the other side of her neck, revealing three fresh, pink cuts.

"Always room for one more," Roxy whispered, placing his hand on her scars, before yanking the knife out, and ripping it across his torso in one final, swift movement.

Return Policy

CLAIRE DAVON

Dedicated, with thanks, to all the amazing women in my life! You have shown me the true meaning of friendship and I cherish you every day.

"No way!"

Walter sprawled in the lunchroom's uncomfortable plastic chair; his legs splayed like a newborn colt. "Way," he said, and grinned, a smile full of teeth and trouble.

I gave him a skeptical look as the original speaker, Bram, shook his head.

"You're full of shit," Bram said, and Walter's smile widened.

"Dude, I saw it. For myself." He gestured to the remaining tables. "He was bleeding like crazy. Don't go upstairs. They're going to have to pay someone extra to clean it up."

My eyes went to where Rich would be sitting, but his chair was empty. To the left was the small clique of Indian IT folks; the ones who were based locally, and not in India. They chattered among themselves in whatever language they spoke, ignoring the remainder of the tables.

A new person joined the group a few weeks ago.

To my surprise, it was a woman.

Up until now, the Indian contingent had been exclusively male, but then this overweight woman had appeared and became one of their group. We had been introduced, but I'd forgotten her name—Jora or Jazz or something. Jyestha, that was it. Difficult to remember.

She sat amongst the dusky-faced men, not saying anything, dressed in a blue and red sari with a white line and dot on her forehead. Her braided hair wound around her head in an intricate pattern.

I only interacted with her in meetings, and so far, she hadn't said much. I turned my attention back to Bram, who was talking again.

"He's had some whack-ass shit happen to him lately."

Walter waved off Bram's words as if they were flies.

"Dude, it was totally splatter-city. Add it to all the bizarre crap that's happened. He's got bad karma or something. Crazy."

"Pics or it didn't happen," Bram said, casting an apologetic look at Rose, the other woman at the table. She had dated Rich for a little under a year, up until a week ago. A mutual friend had set them up. Rich said it had been unexpected, that she had just dumped him out of nowhere.

It had made for some uncomfortable silences recently.

The Indian table took no notice of us, speaking in that other language that none of us understood. I had just a little knowledge of their languages but thought it might be Hindi. Or perhaps Tamil. I didn't have a clue. I'd been working with the Information Technology group and dealing with my share of folks from India. Perhaps it would be courteous of me to learn the language they spoke.

"You don't want pics of that. Texas Chainsaw stuff. Then there's his office. There's nothing in there."

I discovered later that nothing had been an overstatement. The computer was still in there, as well as various equipment that came standard with all of our desks. It was the tchotchkes that were gone. Rich had worked here for years and acquired a lot of swag during his tenure . . . or used to.

"Nope," Walter said, and although his tone had turned somber, I noted an edge of glee behind it. "All of it, all the crap that the company gave out. Every time he came back, more was gone."

I shook my head. It was ridiculous. There was a coordinator right outside Rich's office. If people had been stealing his paraphernalia, someone would have seen it.

I cleared my throat. "Stuff doesn't just vanish, Walter," I said, giving him a stern look.

"I'm telling you, Rebecca, *his* stuff *did*." He gave me his most earnest Boy Scout look, and even crossed an X over his chest.

"What, it just floated away . . . like on a cloud?" Bram spoke again.

Walter scoffed.

A low titter of laughter drew my attention to the Indians again. None of them were looking our way, but I had the distinct impression they were listening. That would have been unusual. They were insular, if polite, but barely acknowledged our presence in the small room. They existed unto themselves, a contingent of a foreign country under our company's banner.

"No, dude, remember? Rich said it just vanished. Like, he had to take a personal day last week because shit was missing from his house when he came back from his weekend trip to Vegas. Cops couldn't find anything."

I looked again at the table of Indians. They were chattering amongst themselves, appearing to not pay us any attention . . . but maybe they were.

I couldn't see the woman, Jyestha, who seemed to have disappeared into the throng of men. Since she got there, they had been oddly protective of her, something I wouldn't have expected from their group.

We had been none too kind to them. I had hoped over time our relationship would improve, but subtle differences constantly surfaced. Things like they always pointed with their middle finger, not knowing it was rude here. Add to that their thick accents and Indian English sayings like the word "prepone" to mean the opposite of "postpone" meant they were proving a challenge to integrate.

"Christ, you guys were there. You heard him raving. Talking all sorts of crap. Thieves. Thieves everywhere. At home and here." He glanced where the other group sat, a look of unease on his face.

We all looked at the spot where Rich would normally be. We all had our designated "seats," and it felt weird that he wasn't in his usual chair, the one with the missing slat in the plastic spine.

We had been hearing the stories for almost two weeks prior. First, it was his favorite pen, a ballpoint with a taco on top that he'd gotten from a company event on Cinco de Mayo. Pens were easy to lose, we all said, and that was the end of that conversation.

Then it was a miniature clock tower of Big Ben that a former girlfriend had given him when she had visited London, back when they had been together. That one was a little stranger, but the janitorial staff had been known to take things.

The theft at home hadn't been the first instance of things going missing there, either. His best sneakers, a Christmas gift from his mother, had vanished. He insisted he knew right where he'd left them, but Rich's house was a terminal mess. We'd thought it likely he had thrown them into a corner and would find them eventually, if he ever bothered to clean.

It was a bit weird, but nothing to get freaked out about. People lose things all the time. It was just bad luck.

I wondered how the Indians were reacting to Rich's plight. Of all of us, he had been the worst to them. He had mocked their Indian English words, at first behind their backs, and then to their faces, all in a *so-called* joking manner. He moved our lunch table when the Indians had started coming into the room, shifting to a table as far away as possible in that small space.

He had been as rude as he could get away with in meetings, often asking Akarsh and Ziya to repeat themselves.

Jyestha's arrival had only made his behavior worse. She was a quiet, unassuming woman, and her obvious, traditional Indian dress and manner only seemed to fuel his fire. She rarely spoke, which had made Rich try harder to get her to talk. When she did, with her thick accent, he had curled his lip. *"Speak clearer,"* he would say. *"How can we get anything done if we can't recognize what you're saying?"* While he hadn't said much to me, I knew that he had said terrible things behind closed doors.

Some of his opinions had purposely been said where the Indians could hear him; stuff about taking jobs from others— meaning Americans—and how they should be grateful for the gifts they were given. He had said this once in the hallway, as I had been walking by with several of their group, on our way to a meeting.

That had prompted a response from Ziya, an easygoing slender man, who had fixed Rich with a piercing look.

"Have you earned all the gifts you have received?" he had asked, a chilly undercurrent in his voice.

I remembered how Rich had blustered, his face reddening at the direct confrontation. Apparently, Ziya was supposed to be seen and not heard, instead of commenting on Rich's insults.

"Damn right," Rich had said, pointing to his chest. "I worked hard to get to where I am."

Ziya's dark eyes had fixed on him. "You do not appreciate what you have been given," he'd said and walked away.

Things took a stranger turn after Rich came home from the

Vegas trip. Up until that point, everything was explainable; but when he got home, his apartment was missing . . . stuff. A vase from his parents that he had stuck plastic flowers in. The flat-screen TV his brother had given him for his 30th birthday. His dining room chairs, but not the table. There were holes in odd, random places, where thieves had taken non-valuable items, and left the better ones. A gold chain that his grandmother had gifted him when he graduated from college did qualify as something valuable, but it was one of the few things of real value missing, other than the TV.

His car was stolen yesterday, and Rich had flipped out. It was yet to be recovered. We had to admit it was all bizarre but couldn't point to any particular cause. *Bad luck?* It could only be that.

Then today, in front of his office, this . . . event . . . happened. Now we weren't so sure it was random.

"Have you heard anything from the hospital?"

Walter shook his head. "I'm checking on Facebook. Nothing yet. They'll message me when they have info."

It had only been a few hours since Rich collapsed, clutching his middle back. He occasionally complained of pain there, after a liver transplant three years ago. Untreated Hepatitis B had turned into liver cancer and damaged that organ beyond repair. His brother donated a piece of his liver to him. Lately, Rich had been complaining of feeling ill. Transplants were hard and they took a toll. Then he cried out and fell, screaming in pain. Blood was seeping through his shirt. That was weird. Nobody wanted to touch him, due to Hepatitis, so 911 was called. That's what we were all told. We saw him strapped to the gurney, shouting incoherently as the paramedics wheeled him away.

It cast a pall over our lunch proceedings, although we all tried to joke as normal. We kept away from the other group. We didn't think they'd be sorry it happened. Since we arrived at noon, they hadn't mentioned it. I was sure they were aware of his absence; his sniggering comments over the past few weeks, even ignored, had left no doubt of his presence.

He had been a jerk for sure, but the Indians didn't seem to do more than express mild annoyance at Rich's remarks. For that matter, neither did we.

I looked over but didn't see Jyestha.

Ziya stood up and looked right at me. I thought I glimpsed

Jyestha's sari vanishing around the corner, but it was hard to be sure. The remaining Indians stood and shuffled their feet as he approached our table.

"Anything from Rich's brother?" Bram was asking Walter, who shook his head.

"Last I heard he was going to be out of surgery soon. He'll let us know."

"Rebecca," Ziya said, and I smiled at him. He did not smile in return. He held my gaze for a beat too long and then gestured to where I had last seen Jyestha's sari.

"We were not expecting it to go so far. You Americans have so many things. We had wondered," he said, not meeting my eyes. "What would happen if your gifts were taken away?"

I stared at him, not comprehending.

"We should have known better. Jyestha is a vengeful goddess."

A bad feeling started low in my gut, and I had to look away from him.

"What's done is done and cannot be changed." His accented voice was grave, his face serious. He paused. "I do not think," another pause, "I do not think it will happen to you. Who is to say? The ways of gods are mysterious. Step carefully." He turned and exited the room, his words hanging in the air between us.

"They're taking Rich to post-op," Walter said after a beep from his phone alerted all of us to a message.

I looked down at my phone, thumbing over to the search box. 'Jyestha,' I typed in with no real idea of what to expect. Several search results came up. Jyestha in Vedic astrology. Jyestha as a month in the Hindu calendar. I focused on the other entries, the ones related to a Hindu goddess of . . . misfortune? I pulled up the encyclopedia. It didn't give me much, just told me about a goddess of bad luck and misfortune. One who was associated with sinners, and other things considered unclean.

Indian goddess of bad luck and misfortune? I reviewed what I knew of the chubby woman. She had been so quiet in meetings that I had no fix on her other than her accent and the brightly colored garment she wore. It occurred to me now that she had worn the same one every time these past two weeks.

Two weeks. Rich's trouble had started then. They couldn't be connected. It was ridiculous. There was no such thing as a goddess. This was the modern age. It was just nonsense.

Walter shouted, a cry of dismay. "No fucking way," he was saying into the phone. We all stopped what we were doing and looked at him. His face drained of color, and he stared at us.

"T-that can't happen."

His eyes rounded as his face slackened, widening into a classic look of someone horror-struck. I couldn't pick out much from the tinny voice on the other line, but it sounded as though the other person was shouting. I was fairly certain I heard "impossible" and "screwed up," among more colorful phrases.

Walter pressed the end button and gazed blankly at his phone. We had gathered around him in a loose semi-circle, sometime over the last-minute closing ranks around the table. The lunchroom was deserted except for us.

Bram spoke first. "Walter? What happened?"

Walter was pale, his complexion decidedly green. It was as if whatever he had heard had made him physically ill.

"They asked him if he woke up in a bathtub, which is fucking ridiculous," Walter said as we all waited expectantly. "They can't figure out how he even got to work. They're saying it's not possible, but they ran X-rays and then went in. It happened."

"Walter," Bram repeated, his tone sharper. "What happened?"

Walter's green tinge faded until he was so pale, that he was the color of parchment paper. He looked up but seemed to not see Bram.

"His liver. He's got no liver. His fucking liver is gone."

Bram made a retching sound, and it was my turn to lose color in my face. No liver?

I turned to look at where Ziya and the others had left, and the sari-clad woman before them. I did not think we would see her again. An old phrase popped into my head, *Indian Giver*. Or in this case, the reverse. I thought about the missing items in his office, in his home, and now in him. All of them were gifts.

What had Ziya said? *'What would happen if your gifts were taken away?'* All of them, from the mundane to the necessary. If it continued, could it extend further, to his education, his upbringing, even his genes? Was life considered a gift to an Indian goddess of misfortune?

It was critical I found out.

As we looked from one to the other, Bram's phone fell from his grasp, hit the edge of the table, and vanished.

Dark Moon Devoted

JEZZY WOLFE

To anyone who has ever been made to feel weak or insignificant . . . YOU are everything.

"Where the soil bleeds, you will be redressed."

Thalia repeated the instructions just loud enough to share with whatever hovered in the air around her as she studied the path in front of her. The earth was soft, damp with the remnants of an afternoon drizzle, and worn from the passage of those who came before. Except for gnarled roots intermittently disrupting the surface, the track twisted clearly through a dense growth of shrubs and trees. They loomed at either side like misshapen beasts under the cloaks of Kudzu and Virginia Creeper.

No blood yet, though. The sanctuary waited somewhere down that lush corridor, but how far ahead, she did not know. Her partner said she would find it sometime before midnight if she kept a steady gait and didn't veer off-course. She could make out the crescent of fire resting just over the foliage of sleepy maples, oaks, and hemlocks. The sky above swirled molten rivers of red and orange into the impending autumn cobalt of night. She shifted the velvet backpack on her shoulders and pushed forward, quickening her pace.

Inez instructed Thalia to leave all of her devices locked in the car. The signals they emitted could interfere with the ritual. The trail was easy to find and easier to follow if one knew what to look for, so her GPS was unnecessary. They studied for weeks, waiting for this night, and planned for the rituals to be performed in tandem from separate locations at a quarter past midnight. Inez stayed at the apothecary, in the back room under Thalia's apartment, in a spot beneath Allie's bedroom. A consecrated key was placed on the center of Allie's mattress, left with a prayer given by Inez and Thalia together, earlier in the afternoon.

Thalia pushed everything else from her mind as she followed the passage that grew darker, enshrined with evening shadows falling from the trees and foliage lurking in the distance. The rush of her pulse in her ears muffled the sounds any other creatures might be making around her, a great benefit that prevented her from being too spooked to proceed. She had never been this alone, this isolated, on any hike she had taken before, and the effect was a bit unsettling. She passed no hikers on the trail leading out and spied only glimpses of distant birds and a couple of squirrels as the trail led farther away from the popular destinations within the nature reserve.

Even if she encountered an uncomfortable stranger on the trail, she could not back out. This was too important. Failure would not be permissible.

If she didn't perform, she would let down Inez.

If she didn't succeed, she would let down Allie.

Tears burned the corners of her eyes, and she wiped them away with angry hands. *Be strong,* she scolded. *You cannot be weak now.*

Hours passed as she continued, and the moon was overhead now, the silver face watching her move among higher grasses that now flanked the trail. The faint whisper of a laugh tangled in her hair. A warm breeze wound around her legs and arms and pulled her onward, leading her toward an obstruction of overgrowth on the path, which seemed to writhe in anticipation. She must certainly be getting close now.

Pushing through the thick copse of reeds, she stepped into a clearing, the space well illuminated by the full moon above, outlining each surface with a thread of silver. The ground squished beneath her shoes, and she tested it with her weight. Dark liquid puddled around the toe of her sneaker. She bent down and touched her fingers to the puddle. It was unexpectedly warm and viscous and coated her fingertips in sticky deep crimson. It smelled of copper and clay.

This is the place.

In the center of the clearing sat a large slate stone, its top flat and nearly level. Tall torches of woven willow and bamboo flanked each end. Their tops were black with char, though it did not appear that anyone had been there in a month, at least. Maybe longer.

At the outer perimeter of the clearing, she removed her shoes and socks. The ceremony required she be barefoot during its execution. The ground oozed between her toes as she approached the earthly altar.

Thalia brushed dead leaves and twigs from its surface. Once completely cleared, she rested her backpack on it and removed the contents inside. She positioned everything intentionally—a black pillar candle, a silver flask, an ornate chalice, a small blade with a carved bone handle, an incense burner and dragon's blood incense cone, and various offerings. The chalice was to hold the merlot in the flask, which she poured and placed to her right. She moved the black candle to the center of the slate altar and set the cone on the burner at her left. The offerings—grapes, feathers, garlic cloves, and oak leaves—were then arranged in small piles around the black candle.

To the altar, she added two more final offerings. The first, a palm-sized piece of selenite, tumbled and polished to a soft shine. It glowed in the moonlight. The second would be the most crucial element, though. She pulled a folded red silk scarf from the backpack and opened it gently.

Inside lay an old skeleton key, recently consecrated, its bow wrapped in silk thread and strands of Allie's hair they had found in a hairbrush. She placed it in front of the black candle.

She fished a box of wooden matchsticks from the bottom of the bag and deposited the empty sack on a rock by her feet. Striking the first match, she lit the incense, filling the air above the altar with a familiar, earthy musk. She closed her eyes and inhaled the smoke deeply.

She struck a second match to light the black candle, and as the wick caught flame, the torch tops beside the altar erupted in balls of fire that danced against the black sky. She startled and jumped . . . she had not been prepared for self-igniting torches. They burned of their own volition, wild and dangerous, yet remained contained. Thalia exhaled a long breath, closed her eyes again, and counted to eight, before beginning the ceremony.

She memorized everything she needed to say and do. There would be a call to the goddess with a blood offering, prayer, and wine. She knew the prayer forward and backward, so the performance gave her no trepidation. The change in the air in the torchlight, though, quickened her pulse. Everything felt heavier . . . the wind, and then the absence of it, the warm soaked ground saturating her feet, the unshakeable sensation of being watched from the shadows around the clearing. As if, at any moment, a throng of creatures would emerge and capture her. Followed by the ticklish sensation of something winding up her bare legs and around her waist.

Inez did warn her about the distractions. How they would try to delay her. How she needed to ignore them and perform the ceremony *no matter* what happened around her. Or to her.

Ready to begin, she picked up the blade and pushed the razor edge against the palm of her right hand. With steady motion she pulled it across her skin and scored it, drawing a path of blood over her flesh. She winced at the burning sting that shot through her.

Balling her upturned palm, she called to the moon, "Oh Goddess, Hekate, hear my plea. Show me favor." As she recited the prayer, she held her fist over the black candle, allowing her blood to drip into the quivering fire and melting wax. It sizzled but did not extinguish the flame. As she neared the end of the prayer, she lifted the chalice above her head.

" . . . unto you, I have sworn my oaths. Hear my pleas, oh Goddess." As the last words faded, she brought the chalice to her lips and drank until she had consumed every drop of the merlot. She closed her eyes, tilted her head back, and with both hands turned palms up, counted the pulse in her ears until she reached 526. Without a watch or phone, she relied on her internal clock to gauge 8 minutes and 46 seconds. It was the trickiest part of the ritual.

After that timed pause, she passed first her right palm over the candle flame, and then, her left. The wind picked up, scattering the leaves, and lifting the feathers off the altar, then stilled abruptly.

The sanctuary suffocated under a blanket of silence, the only sound left being the hiss of torch flames. Then the hiss became something more, something new, something *other*. It became the call of a snake moving across the altar, its onyx scales almost blending with the dark stone slab beneath, slithering between the piles of offerings as it approached her. Fixated on the intruder, Thalia held out her bloody palm and allowed its tongue to flick across the cut. She should have been scared—she was terrified of snakes. Now, she stood unwilling to move as the creature slid over her hand, winding its body around her wrist, and moved up her arm, towards her chest. It left a trace of tingling across her flesh, preternatural electricity that emanated from its belly as it wound around her.

The heavy blanket of silence lifted, and the screams of manic birds perched in the trees around the temple defiled the calm. She shivered from an icy wind that circled the space around the altar, frozen by the noise, and the feel of the serpent keeping her captive to that moment. She stood planted in place, the bottoms of her bare feet rooting in the bloody soil beneath her, eyes locked on the torch flames that danced high into the night. The balls of fire were the last thing she remembered seeing as she faded into the warm black of unconsciousness.

A glass of ice water in her hands woke her, the cold condensation shaking her from sleep. Inez was leaning over her, face unreadable in the dim light. Thalia found herself on the couch, leaning back into the soft cushions.

"Drink, *bebé*," said Inez, "You're dehydrated."

Thalia started to speak, but her throat felt rubbed raw, and she coughed instead. She sipped the water, allowing it to slip slowly through the pain, cutting rivulets of relief into the sandpaper coating her esophagus. She finished most of the glass before trying to talk again.

"Where did you find me?" She could only manage a rough whisper.

"I didn't. You came back a few minutes ago. You don't remember?"

Thalia shook her head.

Inez retreated to the kitchen and came back with a damp rag, and dabbed Thalia's temples with it, before laying it across her forehead.

"What time is it?" Her vision was too blurry to make out the time on the clock by the television.

"8:46."

Thalia sat up, alarmed. "Seriously?"

Inez smiled a soft expression that seemed to relay her reaction. "It's okay, *cariña*. You're safe. She brought you back." She ran a cool palm over Thalia's forehead and leaned in to press a soft kiss to her lips. "This is what we wanted."

Thalia's eyes stung, and she finished the glass of water, hoping to staunch the rise of tears. "Has there been any news?"

Inez sighed. "No. None yet. But soon."

"You sure about that?"

"It worked. I know this. We will hear something soon." Inez took the glass to the kitchen and returned with a granola bar, which she offered to Thalia. "One of us should head up there, though."

"I'll go, *mi amor*," Thalia said. She accepted the offering and pushed herself off the couch. Her legs were weaker than she expected, and her calves screamed. She braced them against the couch for a moment before trying to walk. "Shit. Did I dance my way home, or what?"

Inez chuckled. "You may well have flown." She placed a hand on Thalia's back to steady her and guided her to the bedroom at the end of the short hall, past Allie's empty room.

Thalia could not bring herself to look in the doorway.

Inez led her to the edge of their bed, and pulled her in, her arms wrapping Thalia's waist. Her voice was soft in a way that always left her weak and useless. "The ceremony doesn't officially end until the final consecration."

"Is that what we're calling it now?" Thalia grinned as Inez drew her down, the tossed bed sheets cradling them.

⁂

The sterile corridors made Thalia uneasy, the eggshell walls were as cold as winter gray in the ugly fluorescent lighting. Despite her hurried pace, the nurse's station barely grew closer. She imagined the hall stretched before her like pulled taffy, and the faster she walked, the longer it grew. Her legs were still weak from last night's ritual and Inez's attention, but she ignored the sore muscles as she moved on autopilot. Her eyes locked on the destination—a room just beyond the nurse's station.

No one looked up from the desk as she passed them. She rounded the desk, slipped into the room unnoticed, and closed the door behind her, leaning her back against it.

The young girl in the bed lay mottled with angry purple bruises and bandaged almost beyond recognition. Black curls tumbled from under the right side of the gauze wrapping her head. They taped a tube under her nose, with another larger tube positioned in her mouth and down her throat. Wires from various monitors that flanked the bed disappeared under the gown the nurses had put her in. The clothes she wore had been cut free, and Thalia took them home that horrific day, unable to part with anything that touched her daughter. The shredded garments were still in a plastic bag on the floor in Thalia's room.

She took the seat waiting by Allie's bed, almost afraid to touch her, worried that even the lightest pass of her fingers on Allie's arm might inflict further pain. The little girl didn't flinch, didn't move. Her chest rose and fell from the machines forcing air in and out of her lungs, but it was not Allie's breath. Thalia lowered her head and made a silent plea.

A short knock interrupted the chaos of noisy life support, and Thalia mumbled a 'yes' before the door opened.

"Good morning, Ms. Harmin. I trust you got some rest?" Dr. Bristow was a good enough doctor, but his refusal to use her hyphenated surname irritated her.

"Harmin-Garcia," she corrected.

"Oh, yes, sorry." He cleared his throat. "We got back Allie's latest scans. Unfortunately, there does not appear to be any change. We picked up no detection of brain activity. By now, I had hoped to see some evidence of recovery."

"There will be," Thalia whispered.

"It may be time to start considering if this is the life you want for her," he said. "It's an ugly topic, I know, and I am not expecting you to give me an answer right now, or even today. But without any sign of activity, the prospects of her making a significant recovery lessen daily."

She could not look at him, just shook her head.

He made notes, checked the numbers on her blood pressure and oxygen levels, and tapped the bag of fluid connected to Allie's IV. "I will send in the nurse to change this out. She hasn't had anything for pain in the last 8 hours, so I will order some morphine, as well. At least she is comfortable. I just wish I had better news at this time."

He placed a hand on her shoulder, an awkward gesture meant

to comfort her, not noticing that she shrugged him off before he left her alone.

Thalia took Allie's hand in her own and stared at the delicate fingers half the size of hers, at the downy hairs that sprinkled the back of her hand and traveled up her arm. Her fingers gave a small twitch against Thalia's palm, an involuntary muscle spasm. She leaned forward to kiss her baby's fingers and squeezed her eyes shut, repeating another desperate prayer.

Allie turned nine less than two weeks before Donald Marks ran his Mercedes over her bicycle as she was crossing the street, only a block from their apartment. The street was technically in a residential area, which had a 25-mph speed limit, but that block held old businesses that outlived the rezoning, so most motorists ignored the signs and took the street too fast. Allie was not the first child struck by a speeding car along that stretch.

Mr. Marks' attorney argued that "while he was speeding, he was not doing so recklessly, as the reports indicated he was only going 37 mph at impact". He also argued that she rode directly in front of his car.

Of course, he had a previous DUI conviction, and his blood alcohol level that day was .18, so the semantics of 'reckless' driving seemed irrelevant to Thalia. He could have been driving at 23 mph, and it would be reckless. Not to mention, Allie was using the crosswalk next to a 'children playing' sign.

The past month and a half had passed like a nightmare. The doctors waited patiently for Thalia and Inez to decide when to remove their child's life support. Thalia could not wrap her head around the idea that Allie's life would end there, just like that. Was she truly fated to nine short years? In a moment, the laughter, that light voice that brightened their world, fell silent for good.

Thalia could *not* let go of her. They were both destroyed by the very idea. They had one card left to play, and they played it. As Thalia held her daughter's lifeless hand, she worried it wouldn't work. At the least, that bastard deserved punishment. Real, unequivocal agony. She saw his smug, barely penitent face in the photos that had made the news, and she wished him only pain.

Somehow.

Her phone buzzed in her pocket, and she pulled her hands free to answer it. A picture of Inez and Allie lit up the screen. "Hey. What's up?"

Inez's voice on the other end sounded taut. Edgy. Thalia knew it had to be bad.

"Just heard from Ladley." Ladley was their attorney, a shrewd woman with decades of winning cases and getting stiff sentences, hence why they retained her. "Check this out . . . *DUI felony*. He wouldn't get more than five years, though she doesn't think they will hit him with more than two, plus a $2500 fine. Not including whatever we can get for restitution in the civil case, I mean." Her voice broke off.

Thalia sat in stunned silence for a moment, before finding her voice. "What happened to that 20-year judgment?"

"A DUI felony doesn't carry that. They wouldn't sentence him to a 20-year term unless it was manslaughter," Inez's voice cracked in Thalia's ear.

"But . . . the doctor said she is not going to recover. And he is a repeat offender. I thought they would push for a harder sentence."

A sigh echoed through the phone. "Yeah, so did I."

"So now what?" Thalia felt numb, too shocked to be angry.

"We wait and see, *bebé*," Inez said, her voice stronger. "We were told to wait twenty-four hours and see what happens. We knew this wouldn't be immediate."

Thalia nodded, a pointless gesture since Inez couldn't see her. "Well, yeah . . . "

"Why don't we get dinner at Bay Breakers tonight? I don't think I wanna be stirring at home while we wait," Inez said.

"Sounds like a plan," Thalia replied.

Customers at the apothecary interrupted their conversation, so Thalia promised to be home after the shop closed and ended the call.

She studied Allie's face, hoping for even the slightest flutter of her eyes.

No sign of life. Just the whoosh of mechanical breath and a symphony of beeping monitors.

♒♒♒

They sat in a booth in a corner, nursing drinks in the noisy haze of the crowded bar. Thalia craved thick red wine, a choice she usually only made by necessity. She'd had two glasses of Syrah as Inez sipped on her single vodka tonic. She felt guilty that she could not seem to get enough to drown out the rushing in her ears. Inez chastised her lightly about her consumption, but she barely heard her.

The evening found her particularly tense, her hands trembling so badly at dinner earlier that she dropped her fork several times. It came from out of nowhere, this sudden case of nerves. She tried a brief calming meditation and burned some sage, to no avail. She could not stop shaking. Her head filled with the sound of her pulse, her vision blurred, and everything smelled thick with Dragon's Blood, smoke, and garlic cloves.

She kept one hand near her pocket, where she tucked the key she'd swiped off Allie's bed earlier. Inez did not realize she took it. She didn't know why, either, other than a voice she didn't recognize told her to bring it. She obeyed without question, even though she was certain she had hallucinated the episode. She also had the key from the ritual she performed in the temple, as well as the key Inez used for her ceremony at the shop. She slid her hand into her pocket and wrapped it around the keys. Their cold rigidity pressed into her fingers.

Three keys for the three faces of Hekate. *Oh Goddess . . .*

She closed her eyes and heard the prayer in her head, whispered by the unfamiliar voice from earlier. The voice was terrifying and beautiful at the same time, loud and silent, and distinctly feminine. The whisper became chanting, then became a song, and even though her eyes stayed closed, she could see *her* approaching, emerging from rolling smoke. Her arms and legs were long and slim, and she carried a burning torch in each hand. Her skin glowed pale like silvery marble, and her eyes and hair were black obsidian, the latter which danced over her shoulders and across her breasts as if snakes hid in each tendril. Thalia reached out to touch a strand of the writhing hair, expecting a slithering reptile to lash out at her.

It was soft in her fingers, pulsing with breath. Alive. The Goddess smiled and sang louder, as her torch flames shot higher and brighter. Thalia buried her hands in the silken dark tendrils.

At that moment, she found herself standing in front of the slate altar of the temple, under the midnight sky, the moon and stars bathing everything in shadows and silver. The fear that should have gripped her was replaced by an electrified calm that coursed through her veins, turning her body into a circuit of energy she had never experienced before.

"What the hell? Where am I?" A man faced her from the other side of the altar. He demanded answers, but she only smiled, silent. She recognized Mr. Marks from his pictures and the few occasions they sat in the same courtrooms. *She* brought him to her. "Who are you?"

In an instant, she was standing next to him, close enough to smell the whisky on his breath. She grinned again, but this smile no longer belonged to her. It stretched her skin wide, revealing rows of jagged points where her teeth should be. She should have felt pain from the pull on her cheeks, but she felt nothing. Only numb.

Thalia was no longer in her body. She watched herself with the man who shook and sputtered in fear at a face that looked progressively less like her in the moonlight. She looked down but saw only the ground below. She was a spirit cast out of her vessel, watching a new inhabitant play with her prey. The torches jumped with balls of fire that hissed above their heads.

"*Mi corazón*, what are you doing?" A soft voice tore her gaze from the action at the altar.

Inez stood at the entrance of the temple, a combination of horror and worry clouding her face. She was not looking at the altar, either . . . her eyes were locked on Thalia's, in the place her spirit hovered. *How does she see me?*

The Goddess reached forward and traced Thalia's fingers over Donald's face, down his neck, across his shoulders, and down his chest. He sputtered and continued to demand answers, but she said nothing. Just raked her fingers down his legs and back up again. Smiled her twisted grin. Stepped back. The ground trembled around them.

A scream so savage it could have torn from an animal's throat pierced the air. He began to shake, then convulse, his body electrocuted by invisible wires. Smoke trailed from the cuffs and collar of his shirt, out of the legs of his slacks, and poured out of his shoes. The currents coaxed blood from his eyes, ears, nose, and mouth, along with the foam and bile that built in his throat. His shirt shredded under invisible hands, and the women watched in shock from the periphery as his skin began to char and blacken, and then split open. Bright red rents seeped blood in rivers that fell in cascades to the ground.

The bloody soil of the sanctuary drank each drop of Mr. Marks like a sponge until his shredded skin fell from his exsanguinated frame. He stood like a sculpted écorché in the silver light of the dark moon, a smoldering statue of musculature and bone. Both eye sockets were empty, tongue shriveled like a salted slug. Human jerky.

The bloody soil consumed that last bit of him, too.

The Goddess began to sing again, this song a lullaby, which coaxed Thalia from the shadows. As terrified as she should have been, she trusted her.

Then she was back in her body, weak, trembling, and feverish. The Goddess was disappearing into the smoke. She reached into her pocket and removed the keys, laying them upon the slate altar. She barely managed to whisper, "I am your servant, oh Goddess," before collapsing into Inez's arms.

⁂

Inez held Thalia's hand tightly as they made their way to Allie's hospital room. The satisfaction of knowing that Donald Marks finally paid for his crime was darkened by reality.

But their little girl still showed no signs of coming back . . .

It was time to make that decision. Dr. Bristow and two nurses waited as they signed the final papers. Thalia tried to keep herself composed for Inez's sake.

Inez was the strong one, though. She locked her arm around Thalia's waist and whispered to her that it was the right thing to do. "It is time to set her free, mi *corazón*. She will be fine."

Thalia broke.

Dr. Bristow turned off the breathing machine and the IV, and everyone stood in silence as the pump slowed and stopped. No more forced breathing. Just the sound of Thalia's sobs and the slight beat of the heart monitor.

The faint scent of incense filled the room, stirred in by a sudden breeze.

Allie opened her eyes.

A Veil of Darkness in Tower Nigh

MARY GENEVIEVE FORTIER

This poem is dedicated to my Mom (Mary Ellen) who gifted me the Love of words—
my Brother Don, who inspired an endless thirst for knowledge.
Together, they instilled the essence of that which moves me—Music. Our three-part harmony resonates in every note I still sing and the cadence dances within each poem I pen.

A Damsel Fair
   Say the townsfolk, lest
I pray thee of this
   Do not jest

Though, some by swear
   Oh yes, believe
For they ne'er dare
   Nor least deceive

That Damsel be most fair
   Though by my very, daily breath
Without reserve, on thine own death
Fair Maiden, Nay!
   She not be
'Tis Evil dwells
   I implore of thee

Mary Genevieve Fortier

In guise of beauty
By blindest eye
A veil of darkness
          In tower nigh

Said Damsel cross'd tyme afar
In tower high, where say the stars
Lay black'nd 'neath an ancient power
Within that dark, ungodly tower

Imprison'd, lay shelter'd—bound
So deep the forest, so not be found
There, heedfully hidden
               And drear dire where
Nay man nor beast

Wouldst find her there
Distressed was she?
          I thinkst she naught
Shelter'd away
          Wherest tyme forgot

Deep this forest, wherest dead things play
Ere light escapes
          All life decays

In guise of beauty
By blindest eye
A veil of darkness
          In tower nigh

Legend speak, oh Maiden fair
Adorn'd a beauty
               Fiery red hair
Mask'd those eyes
               A piercing blue
Entrance by sorcery,
               Say thus, "they do"

A Veil of Darkness in Tower Nigh

Perched as she
        A caged, frail bird
In tower keep
        Speaks nary a word

Awaits, say he
        A most unfortunate one
A traveler lost,
        Stray weary
            Alone
To stumble quite near
        Awak'n what sleeps
In tower most high
        In this tower keep

Oh, Damsel Fair
Though she be naught
Hath wait, restrain
The soul she sought
    Be ever near
   'Tis certain, she
    The taste of fear
    She kneweth be

The sound a thunderous, beating heart
Bares her hunger
Strained lips part
Whence anxious, extempore
        Riddled chant
Turn'd a ravenous, prodigious rant

In guise of beauty
By blindest eye
A veil of darkness
        In tower nigh

He treads the bramble
Through the brush
Aware its silent, unholy hush

In search a place
He doth knoweth not
Wandering mindless
Whence tyme forgot

Deep, the dark'nd
Wicked wood
There, yon tower
In shadow, stood

Shroud of darkness
Cloak'nd black
Spilleth as rain
Upon his back

Distant cries
          Upfill his head
Scream defiant
          Winds of dread
As doth a dagger
          Plung'd 'neath thy breast
So to his knees
          He plummeth fast

Upturn'd his face
          In skyward prayer
Gazeth in terror
          Yon tower there

Where be the sacred?
          Thou shouldest be
Within its stead
          Some sorcery
A wizardry at hand, be must!
For thine eyes spill tears of ghostly dust

Whereupon a melody
Float from tower nigh
Trickle drops, insanity
An aire about to die

A Veil of Darkness in Tower Nigh

Thus, harken wicked whispers
Carried on in song
Kisseth thine ears to lureth
Yea, to lureth him so wrong

Cloudeth thy judgement
Though feet they doth move
Helpless a power unknowest to prove

There 'neath the tower wall
       Our traveler stoodeth still
Withoutest will to move at all
       Withoutest *any* will

The eerie tune
       Where it cometh again
From above the tower nigh
There reciteth, some ancient chant- begin
As this traveler began to fly

Nay, not so as a raven's wing
So swiftly, wing'ed flight
He soared upon a voice doth sing
Carried upward towardst the night

Upward, towardst the Maiden Fair
Upward, passed her scarlet hair
Upward, towardst his own nightmare
Upward, now within her lair

In guise of beauty
By blindest eye
A veil of darkness
       In tower nigh

There sat this Damsel, oh so fair
Fingers slender, combed red hair
Pined, she did beweep
Distemperate, beweep

Subtle was his movement
Thus it verily caught her eye
Her expression turn'd amusement
As thus beauty revealeth her lie

Lamenting became a cackle
Nay beauty, now a crone
Backed him into shackles
'Gainst his deathly throne of stone

Whereupon a howling
Beget death's final cry
'Neath her breath, a growling
As this traveler doth die

Tearing flesh with nails, she rips
    Whilst his heart she devours
Warm blood she doth sip

Triumphant in grim cause
Blood bolstered locks with claws
The Maiden began to cleave
His bloodied hair to hers she weaves

    Legend spake oh Maiden Fair
    Adorn'd a beauty
        Fiery, red hair . . .

In guise of beauty
By blindest eye
A veil of darkness
    In tower nigh

In Dire Straits

ALISHA RATH

For my mother, Anna; my honorary mother, Kismet; and forever my children, Jada and Cian

For the first time in her lengthy career, she was nervous about entering this old truck. The cancer-riddled body of the pickup reminded her of her God-fearing parents. Daddy drove the same model of Chevy. She felt like maybe she should, but did not, force a smile when he handed her the steaming coffee. She brought the cup to her face with shaking hands and inhaled the aroma. When the steam rose and moistened her nose and upper lip, the corners of her mouth turned upward slightly.

"You've made the right choice Darlin'," he said, tossing a smoke into her lap. He shifted the truck into gear and began driving out of the derelict, vacant alleyway where they always met.

"I hope so." She meant it.

Although the evening was hot and humid, she could not shake the deep chill within her bones. She had an overwhelming need to right all her wrongs, for the sake of Mama and dear Daddy. She hadn't seen them in years, but in the decade since she'd been home last, she had never forgotten every backroad and pathway through the thicket to their hobby farm.

He pulled into the lot of the decrepit and suffering motel. Neon letters erratically flickering, barely signaling 'vacancy'.

"Number 38, there." She pointed a quivering finger to a dark corner of the motel lot.

As he parked, he scanned the area. When he spotted the homeless man sleeping between the vending machine and the trash can, he pulled his cap down and turned off the ignition. "Quickly now. Beth is waiting at home with a hot meal." He hit a switch, unlocking the doors.

"Yes, Sir." She hopped out of the truck, rushing to her room. All her possessions fit into a large, tattered duffel bag with faded pink leopard-print fabric. She wondered how she had been so fortunate to receive such a blessing, as this kind man, who offered her saving from addiction and the streets.

"You make sure you keep this our secret. I don't have room for the rest of them girls. They're not special like you, Sweetkins. They can't be saved." He had said that the first time she met him. She hadn't even been working the corner that night but getting food from a gas station near the motel. There he was, sitting in his truck in the alley next to the abandoned building; she had mistaken him for Daddy, at first.

She tossed her bag into the back of the truck, and as she climbed in, she forced a genuine smile through the violent tremors of withdrawal. She imagined Beth greeting her with a warm smile and a hot plate of fried chicken . . . and maybe even some sweet potatoes. There was no way she could eat, but the smell of the food would make her feel at home. She was ready to quit the dope, ready to be the daughter Mama and Daddy deserved.

When they left the city limits, she rolled down her window and stuck her face out to feel the breeze, savoring the scent of nature, green pastures, even manure.

"Keep your head inside this truck, Sweetkins. Duck down like we talked about."

"Right, sorry." She rolled the window back up, pulling her hood over her head while leaning into the armrest on the door. Daddy used to call her Sweetkins when she was a girl.

"Did you tell anyone where you were going? Or that you were going with me?" he asked, squinting as high beams passed on the opposite highway.

"Don't worry." She lit the cigarette and said, "Nobody even knows who you are."

"That's a good girl." He smacked the brim of his hat forward so all she could see was his nose and mouth.

She understood that he was only trying to protect his reputation, as so he should with the likes of her. If she was an embarrassment to Mama and Daddy, then she certainly was to everyone else.

They pulled up to his house where a single light illuminated the porch. Boisterous barking came from inside. This was not the place she had envisioned. The lawn was unkempt with ivy covering most of the house. Looking out the truck's window, she could make out a barn, but no neighbors.

"Beth like to cook in the dark?" She chuckled, trying to push away any fear.

He exited the truck without saying a word and walked to the house. Reluctantly, she followed, clutching her bag to her chest. He ushered her into the house where she was greeted by a putrid smell. She turned to the sound of several locks, clicking behind her.

A Rottweiler barreled to her feet and barked at her defensively.

"Shut up Beth!" The sharp tone of his voice made her body tense, ceasing the withdrawal shakes.

Too afraid to turn around, she stared at the shadows of furniture in front of her. The smell, that rancid smell burned her nostrils and evoked bile to churn up into her esophagus.

"Are you scared?" he whispered into her ear from behind. She couldn't speak, she couldn't move; the shakes returned more violent than before. "You should be." His words cut into her soul as his moist, warm breath met the back of her neck.

She dropped her bag and hugged herself, unable to control her audible, shuddering whimpers. Beth attacked the bag, and the dog's low throaty growls saturated by gargling saliva, tore through the fabric.

The man she thought was going to save her grabbed the back of the neck, his other hand grabbing a fistful of her hair as he dragged her down the corridor. She screamed and cried, kicking and trying to claw his face, but he had no trouble overpowering her. He dragged her into a dark room, and she could feel the flooring change from wood to carpet as they entered before he roughly released her, and she crawled pathetically into a corner, weeping hysterically. He walked towards her, laughing maniacally with a raised fist. She used her arms to block the impending blow as he delivered his bony fist into her forearm and cheekbone. The other fist drove into her stomach. He punched, kicked, clawed and even bit her for what felt like hours. She could hardly hear her own cries, because one of her eardrums ruptured during the assault.

She awoke the next day to shards of light escaping between boards nailed over a window, illuminating the room enough for her to make out some of the damage done to her body. She could barely open her eyes, and when she brought her fingers to her face, she felt the puffiness of inflammation under her skin. Pain pulsated through her entire body. It hurt too much to even cry. Dark splotches of blood stained the walls and carpet. She was quite aware, even with her limited vision, that the brown and burgundy stains were not blood solely from her *own* body.

She lay in a fetal position, wincing as she laid her face into the blood-crusted carpet and began to accept her fate. She was going to die; she did not know when, or what horrors awaited, but she was going to die.

"He's got you, but he ain't got **you**," a hoarse, woman's voice whispered. She lifted her head, searching the room for the voice. She noticed a closet with sliding doors nearby. She lifted herself to her knees and then began to vomit violently. She felt feverish, cold sweat enveloping her with chills circulating throughout her body. When she was done vomiting, she wiped the bile from her mouth and crawled to the closet. A sour smell became prominent and upon sliding the door of the closet open, where she came face to face with the decomposing corpse of a woman.

The body was swollen, eyes and tongue protruding grotesquely from sockets and mouth. She backed away, terrified and sliding her butt through the bile she had just hurled. She dry-heaved, this time nothing to expel . . . even though she felt as if her eyes might dislodge from the pressure.

She didn't hear the room door open; she was too busy heaving her hollowed-out bruised guts up into her lap.

"I see you've met your predecessor." His voice reverberated through her body. He chuckled and crouched down in front of her as she lay on her side, covering her face with her knees pulled into her chest. He pushed away her hands and lifted her chin, overlooking his handiwork with a smirking grimace. "I know they say beauty is in the eye of the beholder," he said softly caressing her cheek, "but goddamn! You've got miles of bad road, enough to scare a buzzard off a gut pile!" He stood and kicked his steel-toe boot into her stomach. "Get up, time to eat."

She followed him out of the room and immediately they entered the kitchen. Flies swarmed around moldy dishes littering the counters; dirt and grime painted every surface. The smell was not as bad as the corpse in the closet, although equally detesting.

"I may have lied." He chuckled again as he pulled a can of wet dog food from the fridge. "Beth doesn't have a warm meal, but it's a meal nonetheless." He opened the can and forked out brown chunks into a steel tin. "The China is out of commission, I'm afraid, so you and Beth will have to share this dish."

He tossed the dish to the floor. She noticed her bag and belongings scattered in shreds as Beth dashed down the hall. "She don't like to share, so you best get what you can, while you can." She could feel beads of sweat lining her forehead and upper lip, her body ached, and her stomach twisted.

"Now!" He kicked one of her knees, making her fall to the floor. She landed on her side, scaring Beth, and causing the dog to snap its jaws and growl aggressively. Defeated, she lifted herself to her hands and knees. Beth looked from the broken woman in front of her, then to her food dish, and began to eat. "Get in there!" he threatened, raising his foot.

Fearful of meeting his boot again, she crawled closer to the bowl and Beth stopped eating, looking at her with a sideways glance. The dog's lips curled, exposing sharp canines. Trembling, she reached for the bowl. Beth snapped at her hand, warm saliva landing on her face. She quickly retracted her arm and felt the metal tip dig into her ribs, causing her to pitch forward into the dog. She screamed, tucking herself into a ball as Beth's sharp teeth painfully pierced the skin on her shoulder and arm, in a quick series of snarling bites.

Her good ear was pressed to the floor, so all she could hear was distorted, disdainful mumbles while the captor repeatedly kicked into the side of her body. Pain shot up her spine and sparked into her neck. She felt Beth's jaws clamp onto her forearm, and she shook it aggressively as hot agony throbbed throughout.

"Please!" she screamed desperately over and over, her own voice sounding as if she were underwater. Eventually, she was lifted from the kitchen floor by her hair; Beth growled and snapped at her thigh. Blood trickled coldly down her arm and leg as she gasped for air.

"You're a filthy mess," he spat in revulsion. He dragged her through the tattered remains of her belongings near a staircase and into a bathroom. Dark burgundy handprints slid down the tile wall of the bathtub—smears she could only guess belonged to the woman in the closet. He threw her against the toilet and reached down to turn the shower on. She held her knees into her chest, then buried her face in her thighs. The excruciating pain coursing through her body made her wish she was dead. "Even the hottest water couldn't cleanse your sinful soul."

She felt wisps of hot steam against her shins and lifted her head enough to see the water streaming out of the shower head. She looked at the sinewy man standing above her, his face contorted with so much disgust that she barely recognized him. There were no traces of the soft and kind expressions he had exuded to deceive her. Inviting hands now balled into white-knuckled fists, slouching shoulders expanded with seething inhalations, and thin lips that once exposed a warm smile were now curled in a grimace, exposing rotting yellow teeth.

He crouched in front of her until they were at eye level. "If yer a good girl and do whatever yer told, you won't end up like the last whore in the closet."

Tears welled and she nodded desperately. "Please," she sobbed. "Please, I'll do anything you want! Please don't make me go in there!"

"Oh, Sweetkins." A glimmer of the man she'd known briefly appeared, but just as quickly disappeared with a scowl. "You need to be cleansed; this shower will barely touch the surface. It will take a lot more than some hot water." He stood. "Now get up and get in. If you don't make me drag yer ass in, then maybe I'll give ya' a towel."

His wide grey eyes watched intently as she stood slowly, her body trembling as he exposed a menacing smile. She looked at the filthy tub, the smears blurred by the steam, and began to lift the bottom of her shirt when he swatted her hand away in disgust.

"Yer clothes are as foul as the tarnished skin the good Lord gave ya'." He nudged her toward the tub. "It's okay to scream, God Almighty will acknowledge the effort."

She took a step towards the shower, the hot steam burned against the open wounds on her skin. She looked back to him and could see his patience was wearing thin. If she had a chance for survival, or if her death was impending, either way, she would have to suffer. She stepped into the back of the tub and winced as the water hit her feet; she inched forward and wailed as the water scalded her body. She tucked her chin down and let the burning water run over her head. Her body convulsed with pain, and she threw herself against the tile wall, slipping and landing on her back. It felt like hot razors pricked her skin, even through her clothing.

"I can't!" she wailed, within moments of meeting the floor of the searing hot ceramic tub. "Please, I can't," she choked as the water entered her mouth and burned her lungs and esophagus.

He stood watching and leaned into the steam, revealing the sadistic smile she was becoming accustomed to. Scrambling to her knees, there was no other option than to let the boiling, liquid torture run over her back with her face tucked into her lap. He turned the faucet knob and the hot water slowly dissipated and became a freezing stream. She lifted her face into the soothing cold spray of the shower and opened her mouth, satiating her thirst. Eventually, she was so numb her skin felt rubbery, and she was shivering, certainly with lips blue. He turned the water off and walked out of the bathroom, leaving the door ajar. She stared at the open doorway and considered an opportunity for escape until she remembered the sound of the locks.

"This is a test," she heard the hoarse woman whisper through the walls.

A few moments later he returned with an old dirty towel.

"My apologies, laundry day was yesterday. As you know, I was a little busy. The Lord's work holds priority." He tossed her the towel. "As promised, one towel for good behavior. I'm pleased. Yer off to a better start than that last whore."

The towel was crusted with blood, and the hardened fibers scraped against her skin as she tried to dry herself, remaining crouched in the tub. Her skin was as red as a lobster's and still warm to the touch. She prayed blisters wouldn't form, but when she saw her feet, she had her doubts.

⁂

Many days passed while she sat in her room . . . or rather, her prison. Staring at a leather-bound Bible, she reflected on her last interaction with her captor, poking at a large water-filled blister on her foot.

"Is your name even Boone?" she had asked one evening after he'd directed her to wash his feet with her hair while he read a newspaper.

"As sure as yer a whore," he'd replied while turning a page.

"Why are you doing this to me?" She wrung out her hair and dipped it into a soapy bucket next to the one his feet rested in.

"I offered you salvation. You accepted. The Lord works in mysterious ways, Sweetkins. Time to hush now, yer interruptin' my reading!"

The crank was officially out of her system; the first time she'd been clean in over a decade. Yet if Boone had left some dope and a pipe in her vicinity, she would suffer punishment in order to smoke it. Anything would be better than living the daily torture she endured.

Wet chunks of dog food for meals, she had finally earned her own dish. Scalding showers led into ice baths; her skin was littered with blisters and boils. She was sure a majority of her ribs were broken, as well as her nose and a few toes. He never tried to touch her sexually, only with malice.

Beth was even becoming accustomed to her presence, only snarling, or biting when she received a beating. Beatings that came out of nowhere, for no reason. She realized if she stood a little too tall or spoke too loudly, she would be struck by a bony fist or steel-tipped boot.

"You keep pickin' at them boils and you're gonna lose what little of that pretty skin ya' got left," the hoarse closet woman's voice called out.

She looked to the closet; Boone had referred to the corpse as Ivy. She and Ivy had begun having regular conversations when Boone was out of earshot.

"Shut up, Ivy. Mind your own damn business." She poked at a large boil and watched it ripple.

Ivy was beginning to leak out bodily fluids through her orifices, and one warm night when the smell was particularly repugnant, she tried to close the closet door, but it hit Ivy's forearm making the skin snap like a water balloon. Black and yellow liquid spewed out of the wound onto the carpet, draining from the swollen arm until the lingering skin looked like a purple lasagna noodle.

"You should be trying to find a way to escape," Ivy hissed.

"You don't think I haven't tried? This place is locked up tighter than Fort Knox. And besides, he ain't ever gonna leave long enough to have enough time to get out. Even if I figured something out." She decided to abandon her boil and lay back on the floor, spreading her arms out and running her fingertips along the crusty, stained carpet.

"Maybe there's a loose board blocking one of them windows?" Ivy's voice echoed all around her.

She had looked over the heavy pallet boards barricading the windows before. When she saw fingernails embedded, she decided to save herself the added torture and agony. Curiosity eventually got the best of her, so she started with the first window. Each board was tightly fitted to the next and there was no room for her to wedge more than the tips of her fingers in between. The nails were fastened securely into the wood.

She checked the next window and found one board where the nail head was slightly bent.

"You got a hammer in that rotting carcass of yours, Ivy?" She flicked her nail against the edge of the protruding nail head.

"I just might if you use your imagination, Sweetkins." Ivy exhaled in a low moan.

She looked to the closet where Ivy lay, looking like a soggy, bloated mannequin melting into the carpet. She tried her best to keep her distance from the corpse, the sour stench intensifying with each passing hot and humid day. She walked to the closet and stood over Ivy grimacing. Stepping into the puddle drained from Ivy's arm, she noticed remnants of the drainage, still damp and sticky. She winced and threw her hands onto the upper shelf in the closet, searching for anything. All she found were thick layers of greasy dust, now transferred to her skin. She reached further, standing on the tips of her toes, when her knee pushed into the soft exterior of Ivy's putrefied body. She looked down and noticed something red peeking out from beneath Ivy, between her backside and the wall of the closet.

She was nervous to touch the corpse. Even though she spoke to Ivy's spirit often, the body in the room with her was nothing more than a terrifying, inanimate object now. A constant reminder of the fate she was likely to meet.

"Not unless you take your fate into your own hands." Ivy interrupted her thoughts.

"Yeah, because you did such a good job with that," she hissed, leaning in, sheepishly pushing Ivy's hair aside to reveal a picture.

She pulled the crumpled photo out and brought it into a ray of sunlight streaming between the boards nailed to the window.

The photo was of herself!

It had been taken one Christmas morning, when she was a child, clutching a new porcelain doll. Bloody fingerprints smeared the surface of the glossy memento. Immediately her insides twisted, and she could taste the dog chow coming up, bile burning in her throat. The photo she held in her hands was the same photo Mama had kept on her dresser, at home.

Her hands began to shake, and the room began to spin.

Had Boone been to her house? Had he hurt Mama or Daddy? She hugged the photo to her chest and sank to her knees, weeping silently. She was forced to acknowledge all her decisions in life that had led to exactly where she was at, in this moment. She had told Boone all about her childhood home, which backroad trail to take, leading to the farm—and exactly how to find them.

She ran to the door, beating her fists against the wood and screaming, "You monster! You sonofabitch! Where are my parents?!"

Beth barked aggressively and scratched from the other side of the door, then she heard the heavy footsteps making their way down the stairs. She didn't care—he could beat her—she wanted him to kill her.

"Boone!" she shrieked, pounding, and kicking the door as hard as she could. She heard him walk up to the door, as Beth continued to bark at her cries, but he did not enter. Instead, when her knuckles were bloodied and her toenails bruised, she sank to the floor and wept into the carpet.

"You done havin' a tantrum?" She could hear the flick of a lighter. "All that hootin' n' hollerin'.' I have half a mind to burn this house to the ground with you in it."

"Please," she sobbed. "Please just tell me if my parents are okay."

"They haven't been okay since the moment you decided to smoke them drugs and sell your body and soul to the Devil."

"Where did you get this picture?!" She bent over, the photo in her fist.

"Yer Mama practically shoved it in my pocket." He chuckled.

"Liar!" She screamed as loud as she could, her voice cracking, making her choke and cough.

"You're not being a very good girl, Sweetkins," he taunted from behind the door.

"Kill me! I don't care! Kill me!!" She spat at the door.

He laughed for a while as she wept, then walked away. She heard his boots thud slowly from step to step, back up the stairs.

She cried herself to sleep clutching the photograph and when she awoke the room was dark. Her throat was dry, and her stomach twisted and gurgled. She ignored the hunger pains and prayed for God, or the Devil, to take her. Anything to relieve her from being present in this horrific, earthly plane that burdened her existence.

By the next day, she was choking from dehydration. Her throat was so parched it cut her esophagus to swallow air. She considered drinking her own urine, she had heard about people doing that to survive. She reminded herself she didn't want to survive and deserved to suffer if any harm had come to her parents. She rolled across the carpet until she was facing Ivy from a foot away.

"Why aren't you talking to me?" She stared at Ivy's blackening flesh.

"You've givin' up, Sweetkins? What's there left to say?" She stared at Ivy's lips, half expecting her jutting tongue to suck back in between her lips and start speaking. Instead, it was the same hoarse whisper echoing around her. "Don't you think you should try and find out if your parents are okay? Maybe they need help; maybe you're the only one who can save them." Ivy's voice sounded soothing.

She thought about Ivy's words and sighed. "Tell me what to do."

"Creek is risin' honey. Time to work with what you got."

"I ain't got nothin'!" Her voice quivered, on the verge of tears once more.

"Can't never could." Ivy replicated Mama's voice, speaking a phrase Mama had often used.

She sat up and squinted at the body; it must have been a rainy day because no sunrays streamed between the boards. She looked at the wound she had inflicted, the one which drained Ivy's arm. The skin had curled back and dried up, revealing the bone in her forearm. A bone was a sturdy product. Her mind scrambled; she could try using a bone to pry off a couple of boards. Heck, it could probably break the window too. Prying the boards would be too loud; she would need to get the nails out and that way, she could lightly put them back in without raising Boone's suspicion.

He would notice if she took the bone from Ivy's arm, had already made a comment about the mess she was making, specifically saying, "Ya' best be more careful with your roommate there, you'll be livin' with her filth for a while. The same way the rest of society has been livin' with yours."

"Ribs are easily broken, not so easily seen." Ivy's voice raised the hairs on the back of her neck and arms.

"He'd know, he'd know for sure," she whispered to the corpse, imagining her guts spilling all over the rug in front of her, if she attempted to retrieve a rib.

She looked at her childhood photo and thought for a moment, then knew what she needed to do. She took her shirt off and tied it around her face like a bandana, leaving only her eyes exposed. She crouched over Ivy and leaned in over the body's backside. Even with her shirt pressed against her nostrils, the stench made her eyes water. She carefully lifted Ivy's shirt, exposing her puffy, mottled back.

"Jesus, help me," she muttered under her breath as she pushed fingertips into the skin of the corpse's back.

The muscles were stiff from rigor mortis, but she found she could move them around beneath the skin easily enough as if they were stones beneath a blanket. When she pushed one of the back muscles down with considerable force, it tore loose, taking skin with it. It peeled open like a grape being split. Dark, liquid sludge oozed from the wound, and the putrid smell made her jump back, gasping. She gagged, panting heavily for a moment.

She clenched her teeth and took a deep breath before leaning over the seeping cadaver. Black coagulated blood ran down Ivy's back and settled thickly between the closet floor and wall. She leaned against the wall of the closet and squatted over the body. Her makeshift scent guard did little to thwart the increasingly foul stench. She let out a silent gag, took a deep breath, and slowly penetrated the opening of Ivy's back with the tips of her fingers. Ivy's remaining blood felt like pudding. She pushed her hand further into the muck until she felt the hard texture of bones. Gently feeling around, she grasped her hand around a rib bone. She looked to Ivy's bulging, rotting face, and winced. Turning her face away to take a deep breath and blow it out before continuing, she tugged at the rib gently with the irrational fear Ivy would leap to life and scream in pain.

"You best give it a better effort," Ivy whispered in her ear. Damn, sometimes she sounded just like Mama.

She tightened her grip on the slippery bone and yanked hard, feeling and hearing a sickening snap. She quickly removed her dripping forearm from the body and stared at the sopping bone in front of her. She found an area of soiled rug in the room to wipe her arm, and the bone clean. Once satisfied, she hurried to a corner behind the door and dry-heaved for several minutes.

Hungry, and shaking, it was the first time she felt hope. She retrieved the bone and took it to the protruding nail.

"This is too blunt!" she whispered angrily, scraping the bone against the nail head.

"Shave it," Ivy responded.

"And how do you suggest I do that?"

"Usin' your teeth is likely your best bet." Ivy's voice was a hiss.

She grimaced. No way in hell was she puttin' that fetid bone near her mouth, no offense to Ivy.

Ivy spat, "You keep wastin' time and maybe the next girl will be smart enough to put your acrid remains in her mouth."

The next girl.

If she didn't get out of this place, there *would* be a next girl, and she may never know what became of dear Mama and poor Daddy. She had to try.

She put the smallest end of the rib against her bottom molars and began rubbing the bone back and forth against her teeth. The scraping of teeth to bone made her skin prickle and her neck chill. She even tried to bite at it, but it was too hard to penetrate.

She heard early morning birds chirping before she decided to rest. The bone felt thinner, but it was grinding down the enamel of her molars as well. Years of drug abuse had dilapidated her teeth. She tore up the corner of the carpet, jagged slivers from the flooring beneath stabbing under her nails. Tucking the bone into the crevice, she prayed it would be unnoticeable.

She awoke with her back pressed against the wall beneath the window. Her entire body was saturated in sweat—another hot Louisiana day. Her tongue felt like a Velcro strip as she peeled it from the top of her mouth and choked. She was weak, barely able to roll herself over to face the door. She tried to rise to her knees but collapsed.

She needed water. She hadn't urinated since the afternoon before and still had no urge. Laying on her stomach, she slid herself to the door, clawing at the carpet and using her toes to propel herself forward.

Laying in front of the door, she weakly scratched at the bottom until Beth came. She could see Beth's nose and claws digging at the door. The dog barked a few times and whined, and then the heavy steps came and stood in front of the door.

"Boone," her voice cracked as she continued her pathetic scraping against the door. "Please," she whimpered hoarsely, "I'll be good. I'll be a good girl, please Boone, I promise."

Boone opened the door slowly and stood over her, sneering at the scent which greeted him, and at the wretched pile of her on the floor.

"I was gonna let yer ass rot in here." He sighed and looked to Beth, panting at his feet. "Maybe I'm gettin' soft."

Boone walked into the kitchen where she could see him grab a soiled cup from the counter. As soon as the tap turned on, she could feel her body jolt with life. She struggled to sit on her knees, feeling as if she would weep if her body had enough hydration to produce tears. The water was yellow, and residue from the previous drink danced in the liquid as he held the glass in front of her face. Her hands shook and her tongue throbbed. He smiled wickedly as he handed her the glass, then pulled it away just before she could grab it.

"I do spoil you." He let out that evil laugh of his before finally giving her the glass.

She drank ravenously, water spilling out the corners of her mouth, the cool sensation running down her esophagus and into her stomach both refreshing and relieving.

"Heck, this room is beginin' to make this whole house unbearable." He covered his nose and mouth with his forearm. "Yer getting yer friend out of this house today. Don't think about gettin' any smart ideas, because I can bury the both of ya' in the same grave. No matter to me." He watched her carefully for a moment, observing her reaction.

Out of this house, *today*. The words she focused on; perhaps an opportunity to escape would be easier than she had thought.

When Boone was satisfied the woman in front of him was completely broken, he left her sitting on her knees in the doorway.

Beth watched her intently, panting and looking from her to the corpse. When he returned, he held a thick leather studded collar and a leash.

"Time to go outside, fresh air will do ya' good." He strapped the collar around her neck tightly and clipped the leash. She barely made it to her feet as he half-dragged her through the kitchen and out the back door through a mudroom.

The sunlight burned her eyes, the sting penetrating their very sockets and making her head throb. The backyard was heavily overgrown with grass, weeds, and saplings standing a couple of feet high. Directly outside the door, he attached her leash to another leash connected to a clothesline. The clothesline ran to a shed about fifty feet away. He clicked his tongue and kicked the back of her heel, forcing her to walk through the wet and overgrown terrain barefoot while he whistled.

"Barrow is in the shed. Go get it. I'll be waitin' here." He lit a cigarette and stood watching.

Her knees buckled and the wet grass made the skin on her legs itch; still, she savored the opportunity to inhale fresh air. She opened a squeaky door to a rotting woodshed where daylight illuminated a blood-soaked wheelbarrow. She stared at the wheelbarrow, then turned to look at Boone. He was forty feet away watching her intently with the cigarette hanging out of his mouth.

She could unclip herself from the leash and take off right now. Her hands were free, she could easily remove the collar and run, run for her life. If she did, and she was unsuccessful with her escape, she would surely die.

"C'mon now!" he hollered impatiently.

She leaned into the shed to grab the wheelbarrow, but the slack wasn't long enough. She practically hung herself, choking to the point she felt pressure behind her eyes while trying to grab the wheelbarrow handles.

She exited the shed gagging and coughing, heart racing and a flurry of emotions running rampant because she decided not to free herself.

A muffled noise interrupted her choking, and she stopped walking. Turning to her right, she noticed a red-skinned woman who appeared to be standing on her knees in the grass. A thick, rusted chain hung heavily around her neck. The chain links clanged, grinding together as the woman reached out to her. The woman's skin was badly burnt, and her face was covered in dried blood. Her mouth was open, desperately blubbering with wide, frightened eyes.

She let go of the handles of the wheelbarrow. Moving closer, she realized who she was looking at. It was Mama, and her tongue had been gruesomely removed.

"Mama," she uttered quietly, standing still.

"Surprise! It's a family reunion!" Boone slapped his knee, damn near dropping the cigarette from his mouth as he chuckled.

She sprinted forward, straining the clothesline until it propelled her back into the wheelbarrow, and she landed on her ass.

"Mama!" She wailed, reaching for her. Mama hoarsely blubbered back, inaudibly, then released a primitive scream that made sharp pinpricks run down her spine.

"I hope yer happy, Sweetkins." Boone stood beside her now, a firm hand pressed on her shoulder. "She is a sinner as much as you, raisin' a bastard like you to sow the oats of the Devil."

"Please!" She wept, turning to face Boone. "Please, let her go. I will do anything you want, anything! I swear, please let her go!"

The corners of Boone's lips curled upwards making his sun-weathered skin crease into a million tiny wrinkles, stretching across his face with his sinister grin. "It's too late for that now, Sweetkins." His smile faded into a smug smirk. "Ivy's ripenin' by the second . . . better get a move on."

She hastily picked up the wheelbarrow and pushed it to the house. If she obeyed, maybe he would oblige her by setting Mama free. Boone followed and unhooked her from the lead. The wheelbarrow caught on to the door frame as she attempted to push it through.

"Tilt the goddamn thing!" Boone barked from behind her.

She fastened her grip with sweaty palms and tilted the barrow, pushing it through as quickly as she could to her room. The doorway was smaller, there was no way the barrow was going to fit. In a panic, she climbed over the barrow, leaving it parked in the doorway.

She barely caught her breath before she hooked her arms beneath Ivy's and attempted to drag her across the floor. She could feel Ivy's skin split beneath her grip. She was only able to drag her a couple of feet before she realized she had a portion of Ivy's scalp stuck to the side of her sweaty face. She threw the sticky mass of hair to the floor and jumped back, crying out.

Boone stood in the doorway laughing hysterically. "She done spooked ya' good, girl."

The smell was nauseatingly prominent now, after being exposed to fresh air. She found herself gagging again on her hands and knees, in front of Ivy's body.

"Good Lord, Sweetkins. Yer makin' a bloody mess." He leaned against the doorframe. "No pun intended!" He slapped at his knees, keeling over in another bout of maniacal laughter.

The room began spinning and she vomited what little water she had consumed. Defeated, she collapsed face-first into her vomit and sobbed uncontrollably. She barely noticed Boone's boots in front of her but jolted backward abruptly, finding his face was in front of hers.

"I tell ya what," he whispered. "You get this mess up and outta here real quick-like, and I will let ya' give yer dear ole' mama a glass of water."

She continued to whimper, searching his eyes for an ounce of sincerity.

"Sound fair?" He took a deep breath, then grimaced from the smell.

She nodded and climbed to her feet, wiping wet, matted hair from her eyes and the sides of her face. Boone returned to his post outside the doorway, leaning against the wall. With great effort, she managed to slide Ivy's body into the wheelbarrow, leaving black, sludge-stained drag marks across the carpet. Ivy lay face down with arms outstretched, clothes heavily saturated in coagulated blood.

She was bone weary, panting, and feeling nauseous and dizzy. Her head throbbed with every effort exerted to lift the sopping, stiff body into the barrow. She propped Ivy's body first onto the side, then attempted to lift her legs to swivel her body around and in. It worked, but as she pushed Ivy's legs into the barrow, the lip of the barrow pulled her shirt up and chunks of muscle, blood, and tissue spilled out of her back from the opening she had created when retrieving the rib bone.

"All of her! All of her in that barrow!" Boone's tone was harsh as he backed away from the rotting corpse . . . *but he hadn't noticed what had caused the gruesome sight.*

She didn't realize she was sobbing and whimpering throughout the entire process, as she scooped up Ivy's innards into cupped hands and slopped them beside the body. She struggled significantly to snap Ivy's limbs, so they fit into the barrow.

Her mouth was dry from the work, and she made choking sounds as she pushed the barrow to the back door. When she had to tilt the wheelbarrow to get through the back door, Ivy spilled out onto the grass. Boone attached her to the lead and watched as she struggled once more to return the body to its carrier.

"Get the shovel out the shed and dig a hole as close as you can to yer mama over there." Boone lit another cigarette. "Better yet, dig two."

"Please," she trembled before walking to the shed. "I need some water." She stared at his feet.

"Go on now." Boone ignored her request.

She moved sluggishly to the shed, swallowing hard and licking her dry tongue along the inside of her mouth, searching for saliva. When she returned with a shovel, to the spot where she had bungee-d herself on the clothesline, attempting to run to her mother, Boone appeared holding a glass of water.

After ravenously downing the water, she spent what seemed like hours digging up the long, weedy grass and earth. The sun was setting by the time she finished the two four-foot-deep holes Boone had demanded.

Her joints throbbed and the blisters on her palms bled.

All the while, Boone stood by patiently monitoring her every move, smoking cigarettes, and wearing a contented smirk on his face. Sporadically, he would read verses from a pocket Bible he kept in his shirt.

Dumping the body and replacing the dirt on top was relatively easy; ignoring Mama's unintelligible cries was impossible.

"Come, let's have some dinner, then we will go and fix yer mama up." Boone tugged at her leash, leading her to the house.

She and Beth sat on the floor of the kitchen, patiently anticipating the sound of chunky, wet dog food sloshing into bowls.

Boone held both dishes in his hands and looked from her to Beth approvingly. "Good girls," he said, tossing the dishes to the ground.

She crunched the grit from dirt on her hands along with the foul chow, shoving it into her mouth ravenously.

Boone filled a glass of water. "I'll allow, just this once, for you to share some of yer dinner with yer mama."

She stared at her almost empty dish. She took the glass from Boone and stood with her bowl.

He let her out the back door, holding onto her leash tightly, leading her to her mama.

Mama lay in the grass, managing to prop herself on her knees and back away in fear, sobbing as they approached. It pained her to see Mama so ragged, just as she was unrecognizable.

Her skin was red and blistering and her ears were charred from the multiple sunburns. Tears and sweat had washed away most of the crusted blood from her mouth, but remnants of the stains ran in crevices along her chest and covered her shirt.

Mama scooted back, shaking uncontrollably as she approached with the water and food.

"It's okay Mama," her voice cracked as she released tears. "It's me, your baby. Please, you need this."

She squatted to Mama's level and handed her the glass and tin bowl. Mama eyed her suspiciously and stared at the offering with an expression of disgust. Mama grabbed the glass with both hands and drank as ravenously as she, herself, had earlier. She could see the stump of Mama's tongue waving back and forth through the glass, the water turning a milky red as it entered her mouth.

When Mama finished with the water, she offered the tin bowl. Mama sat upright with a disdained look. She peered into the bowl grimacing, then slapped the dish out of her hands.

"She's feisty, that one, ain't she?" Boone chortled from behind her.

"Mama, please." She picked up the bowl and scooped the dog chow back in, offering it again.

Mama released a harsh scream and slapped the dish out of her hands, then lunged for her. It happened so quickly, and now Mama had both hands around her neck, squeezing tightly.

"Ma-ma." She tried to push her off, but Mama squeezed tighter.

Stars began appearing in her vision, and she wondered why Boone hadn't pulled Mama off by now.

"Ain't this poetic?" She heard Boone's voice above her.

Her eyes felt as if they were bulging from their sockets, and she no longer had the energy to try to push Mama off. Mama stared into her eyes with a maddening rage, focusing all her weight into her grip. She stopped pushing into Mama's chest, letting her arms fall to the side.

It was time she gave up. She didn't understand why she was being attacked but knew she deserved it.

She felt something hard being placed in her right hand. Her vision was blurry and blackening, and instinctively she swung the object at Mama's face. Mama's grip loosened but she remained hovered over her. She gasped for air, feeling warm liquid pouring over her face and chest. As her vision cleared, she noticed the large gash in Mama's throat. The menacing look remained on Mama's face, but she gurgled as blood spewed out.

She looked at the object in her hand, a gardening spade.

Then she looked up behind her and saw Boone, with a satisfied sneer on his face. "I told ya' you'd need two graves."

Mama collapsed on top of her, all the weight bearing down on her chest while warm blood gushed across her. She let out a cry of anguish after Mama rolled off to the side, laying face first in the grass.

She stared blankly at the evening sky above her.

Sobbing, she wiped the blood from her face and neck and pulled herself into a fetal position before she reached the point of hysterics.

"Why?" she asked, voice filled with angst. "Why her, Boone?" She tore grass from the ground and clutched it to her chest.

Boone let her weep for a while, watching silently before he nudged her with his boot. "Two holes. Fill 'em."

The day was breaking before she finished covering the holes with dirt. The smell of Ivy didn't even bother her. But the sight of Mama . . . laying in the dirt, mouth agape and bloodied. Well, that made her stomach turn and her heart palpitate in such a way she thought death might be imminent.

Boone put her in her room, soiled and with her collar still on. Ivy's reek had dissipated considerably, but she hardly noticed, flashbacks haunting her.

"She never had a chance, Sweetkins," Ivy whispered.

"Go away," she muttered under her breath, face pressed into the carpet.

"You can still fix this, Sweetkins. You bring justice for me and your mama, maybe even your daddy. You can fix it."

She turned her face outward, staring at the place where she'd hidden Ivy's rib bone. She sluggishly pulled the bone from beneath the carpet and rubbed it against her molars in her catatonic state. The room was bright when she pierced the side of her tongue. The pain jolted her, and she realized the few inches of bone she scraped against her teeth was now pointed, and quite sharp. The taste of blood was becoming too familiar, she thought as she poked the sharp end at the tip of her finger until her eyelids felt heavy. She returned the bone to its hiding spot and eventually fell asleep.

When she awoke, the room was dark. A glass of water sat on the floor beside the door. She pulled herself up and scrambled to the glass, tasting copper from dried blood on her lips. She didn't notice the door was slightly ajar until she heard Beth panting in the hall. She set the glass down, crawling on hands and knees, she peered out the doorway, eyes now adjusting to the darkness. Beth looked at her but appeared resigned to her presence. A familiar sound pierced the quiet—whistling—exactly as if it came from Daddy's own lips. An old tune Daddy had often whistled.

"Dear Daddy is alive and well. And it don't look like that door was meant to be left open." Ivy's voice slithered up the back of her neck.

She knew her opportunity was now, but uncertain for what. Her body was so sore, her mind was exhausted, and her throat was endlessly parched. The footsteps above put her mind on alert as she listened intently. The steps rummaged from one room before stopping inside the next.

"Your window is closing," Ivy warned.

She was on the verge of tears; terror froze every muscle in her body even as her heart rapidly thumped inside her chest. Grabbing the bone from its hiding place, she shakily crawled to the doorway. She peeked around the doorway again. This time, Beth stopped panting and looked at her inquisitively.

With a trembling hand, she held the bone out. Beth only stared, until she grew impatient and waved the bone back and forth.

"Come Beth" she whispered. "Good girl, come on now."

Beth rose to her feet, The nails on her paws clacking loudly against the hardwood floors. She scooted back into the room, kicking the door open with one of her feet. Beth came in cautiously, smelling the carpet, and stopped. She continued to beckon her, but the dog was wary.

"Good girl, come on now." She placed the bone on the floor a foot in front of her, sitting back on her heels.

Beth approached the bone, nose to the ground, and eyes on her. When the dog opened her mouth to pick up the bone, she lunged forward, trying to grab it before Beth could. Beth growled and snapped her jaws, piercing her forearm. White hot pain flooded up into her shoulder as she tried to muffle her own scream. Beth shook her head from side to side, throwing her around and starting to drag her towards the door. She grabbed the bone and stabbed it into Beth's face, pushing hard with her palm deep into the dog's head until it released its grip and fell to the floor.

When she noticed how audible her breathing and whimpering were, she cupped her hands around her mouth and nose. She winced at the muscles contracting from putting pressure on her face. She looked to her forearm to see flesh ripped open, blood gushing from the wound.

Thudding steps above made her leap into action. She reluctantly pulled the bone out of Beth's eye, the sound sickening, like pulling a stick out of wet mud.

She rose to her feet, legs shaking violently as she stepped out the doorway. A deafening scream reverberated throughout the house.

"Daddy," she murmured, swaying from side to side as her face contorted in anguish.

She ran in the direction of the scream and paused at the old wooden steps, covered in glinting shattered glass. She clutched the bone in her right hand, her left hand dripping blood off her fingertips from her wound. She crept up the stairs, pressing her feet into broken glass. Pain was irrelevant now with the adrenaline fueling her. She walked boldly, quietly up each step, letting the glass sink into and pierce the bottom of her feet.

The screaming stopped and she heard Boone's awful laughter. Reaching the top of the stairs, she pressed herself against a wall and scaled to the closest room. She heard Boone cough as he flicked his lighter, and smelled the cigarette smoke.

"Beth!" Boone's throaty voice shook her entire body.

Before she could react, Boone was rounding the corner to the stairs, calling for his dog again. He stood right beside her as she stared at him in terror.

A cigarette hanging out the corner of his mouth, he noticed her in his peripheral. "What the—"

He reached out to grab her, but she charged forward, stabbing the bone into his side. He lost his balance, and grabbed her wounded arm, fingers digging through the tissue to the bone. She let out a wail as they both tumbled down the steps. She rolled over the top of him, then his body landed on top of hers, glass piercing various parts of her body until they reached the bottom.

Her head smashed against the railing, making her vision blur. When her senses returned, she saw Boone holding his side, curled up on the floor.

"Daddy," she slurred as she scrambled to her feet and up the stairs.

When she entered the room, she saw Daddy lying on his back, blankets and sheets tangled around his body illuminated by moonlight. Daddy's lips were blue, and when she grabbed his arm—it was cold.

"No, no, no! Daddy, no!" Heartbroken, she sobbed while pushing on his chest.

She remembered taking a first-aid course when she was younger, something she had protested but Mama and dear Daddy had insisted. She pinched his nose. lifted his chin, and brought her mouth to his. Before she could blow air into his lungs, something crawled into her mouth.

Taken aback, she spit the entity onto Daddy's chest. A large black beetle spun slightly on its back, legs shuffling wildly.

"Oh Sweetkins, you've really gone and done it now." Boone's voice was as thunderous as his steps as he climbed the stairs, boots crunching the glass.

She lifted her hand, believing the bone would magically appear. She looked to the ground and quickly scanned the room, but could find nothing that would suffice as a weapon.

She dropped to the ground and rolled under the bed. She cupped her hands around her mouth and silently wept at her impending demise. Boone's feet emerged and she inched further beneath the bed. Boone walked towards the bed, his boots mere inches from her face. She stared at his steel toes and held her breath.

"C'mon Sweetkins. Ain't no use in hidin'. Yer bed is made, yer grave is sealed." Boone sat on the bed next to Daddy's body.

As he turned his heels towards her, something caught her eye beneath the bed next to the nightstand. She slowly reached out and carefully lifted the object off the floor. It was Daddy's straight razor, crusted in blood, likely the tool used to extract Mama's tongue. She defensively gripped the blade, and angrily thrust it into the back of Boone's leg. She tore through the jeans and boot, leaving a deep and jagged wound.

Boone hollered and his legs flew up. She pulled herself out from under the bed quickly and stood over Boone, who now lay on top of Daddy, clutching his ankle and moaning in agony.

For the first time in her life, she felt empowered. She stood over Boone, wretched and moaning in pain. She could see the fear in his eyes, etched in every crease of his sadistic face.

She realized after a moment she was screaming. She couldn't hear her own cries, but her vocal cords vibrated and her throat hurt. Every emotion she had been harboring throughout her entire, miserable life was surfacing through an adrenalized shriek.

Fury fueled her now.

She climbed on top of Boone, straddling his chest and using her left hand to cup his chin. She pushed his head right beside Daddy's and jammed the blade of the straight razor through his lips. He screamed as the blade scraped against his teeth, pushing into his tongue.

Swiveling the knife, she cut out his tongue and used the same hand still holding the blade to shove it down his throat. Boone choked and gasped, groaning inaudibly as Mama had in her final moments.

She screamed into his face again, feeling the sides of her mouth froth with saliva as she pushed both thumbs through Boone's eyeballs.

After she gouged his eyes, she sat back on his chest and watched as he grasped at his empty sockets and torn lips with trembling hands.

She took her time with the blade, enjoying the sounds of suffering he produced while sawing at his neck until his head was practically removed.

Boone made no more sounds, and his blood darkened the sheets, trickling over top of Daddy. She threw her head back and took in a deep breath, her body vibrating with adrenaline. She slowly pushed herself off of Boone, then stood over him and her daddy. Dear Daddy, stiff beneath the mangled monster.

"You're free now," Ivy whispered.

In Dire Straights

A warm breeze caressed her face from the window making her wounds sting and ache. She smiled.

She felt free.

She walked slowly down the stairs, unfeeling the glass gouging her feet. She sauntered in a hypnotic state to the kitchen and drank for several minutes from the tap. She walked to her old room, Beth's limp body lying in a pool of blood on the soiled carpet.

Then she went out and stared for several moments at the mounds of dirt covering dear Mama and Ivy's torn remains. The quiet was deafening.

"I'm sorry Mama," she said solemnly before turning to walk away.

She found a pack of smokes on the dash of Boone's truck and lit one before firing up the engine. She noted her blood-stained fingers, but her mission was not yet over.

When she finally entered the police department, she was greeted by a handful of stunned stares. No doubt one of the most gruesome spectacles to ever enter the precinct.

She looked to the left and saw one of the girls she worked the corner with; Ginger, sitting in cuffs on a bench.

"Sugar?" Ginger uttered in astonishment.

5 days later . . .

"Chief," Detective Delaney said, throwing a stack of papers onto Chief William Decuir's desk. "You're not going to believe this shit."

Chief Decuir looked up and set his pen down. "This must be the Holly Boutin case?"

"AKA Sugar, you got that right." Detective Delaney took a seat. "What a mess."

"How's the poor girl doing?" Chief Decuir rubbed at his temples.

"You ain't gonna be feelin' so sorry for her once you read them coroner's reports." Detective Delaney appeared slightly bemused.

"Spit it out while I read it over." Chief Decuir picked up the paperwork.

"So, you know how we couldn't find this Boone individual's body?" Detective Delaney leaned in. "I don't think the son of a bitch even exists."

Chief Decuir stopped reading the documents and listened intently.

"The truck is registered to an Olivia Comeaux, AKA street name Ivy. After Ginger identified Holly, Ginger said Ivy was taking Holly to see her parents, who had just moved."

Chief Decuir crinkled his nose. "And . . . ?"

"Ivy is the other body we dug out with Mrs. Boutin, Holly's mother. Coroner's report says Ivy was the first to die, then the father, then mom was chained up and tortured in the yard." Detective Delaney lowered his voice, as if speaking cursed words.

"So, no Boone? She said she killed him, up by her daddy's body." Chief Decuir started chewing on a pen, a habit he only partook in when stressed.

"There's no Boone, Chief. Flip to the back." Detective Delaney flipped through the pages and brought up diagrams of the autopsies. "The tongue being removed, head practically severed, body all ripped to shit . . . that was all done postmortem to her father, Mr. Boutin."

"What in God's will . . . " Chief Decuir muttered to himself, reading over the report.

"Psych eval is stating she had some kind of methamphetamine psychosis. Like schizophrenia or something. Fuckin' junkie murdered her friend and parents, thinking it was an imaginary captor." Detective Delaney sat back in his seat and shook his head. "Fucked-up part is, she had no drugs in her system, whatsoever. Tox came back clean."

"You do enough of that shit, and it don't matter if you're clean. Your brain gets fried." Chief Decuir tried to let it all sink in. He had sat in the interrogation room with Holly and had listened to her entire story. "And the dog?"

"No dog. Coroner said the bite wounds were self-inflicted. Inconsistent with any kind of animal."

Detective Delaney grimaced. "We're booking her this afternoon. Just wanted to give you a heads-up, because the media is still going crazy."

"Ah, hell." Chief Decuir spat to the side. The two men sat in silence, both reflecting on the recent revelations concerning the most horrific event to ever touch their careers. Then the chief said, "Maybe this will be the best anti-drug campaign the county's ever had."

Revenge is . . .

Yvonne Mason

This story is dedicated to all those teachers who said I couldn't write so many years ago. You told me I couldn't, so I did.

As she wiped the blood from the corner of her mouth, she promised herself this would be the last time. For years she took the beatings, the verbal abuse, and the mental torment. But tonight, something in her died. Was it her emotions, or her ability to love . . .

Or was she just finally over all of it?

As she tasted the copper of the seeping blood, her taste buds were warm and alive. She felt as if she was feeding a starving child . . . could not seem to get enough. Her eyes followed as he walked toward the shower, and she smiled.

She didn't dare let him see that smile, knew what would happen if he did. He would start the beatings all over again.

No, she would bide her time, keeping her newfound smile locked inside. There was an old saying that came to mind. "Revenge is best served on a plate cold." Well, *cold it would be.* Already the wheels in her head were churning; all the planning, and how it might play out, beginning to formulate and gel.

He thought he'd won, as always. Well, let him think that. In all reality, it would give her the upper hand.

She heard the shower running and quietly made her way to the kitchen. First, a cup of tea, which always soothed her mind and soul. She knew his patterns well. Once the beatings were over, which for him amounted to intimacy, he went to sleep. And when he slept . . . it was the sleep of the dead. He would not move until morning.

Oh, what a night this would be.

The tea kettle whistled, and she absently poured the water into her cup. Steam rose to her face and warmed it.

After placing the kettle back on the stove, she sat down and began to methodically plan her revenge, one step at a time.

Years ago, a therapist had caught on to the abuse and offered good advice . . . on making plans to leave.

The first step she took was starting her own bank accounts in a different town, with all the statements going to a PO Box. Naturally, he never would've suspected. To date, she had squirreled away enough money to disappear forever. Next, she opened a safe deposit box, to store photos documenting her injuries and a diary of dates, for the evidence she would need when the time came. She also kept an updated passport and a few pieces of precious jewelry in that box.

In the back of her mind, she knew she could not last much longer. So, her final step, in the last year, was to keep a stashed suitcase filled with clothes concealed in the trunk of her car—which she always kept filled with gas. There was also a change of clothes hidden in the garage that could be grabbed, to put on quickly, along with a wig. She had covered all the bases, she thought.

Now it was time.

She would put the plan into motion and see if it would work.

Sipping her tea, she again composed the letter to the newspaper in her head; she would leave no paper trail.

When the shower finally stopped, she knew he was headed to bed. In thirty minutes, he would be out. He had become predictable.

She put her hand underneath the table and grabbed the keys to her car and the large envelope she had taped there days earlier. She had known the beating was going to happen. She always knew. Taking the keys, she slowly made her way to the back door.

This had been one of those nights he forgot to close the garage door, because he came home in a foul mood, focused on using his own wife as the punching bag for his anger. Tonight, that would work in her favor. The back door opened soundlessly—she had kept the hinges and the knob oiled, so it could not be heard. Silently, she slipped out, and then into the garage where she quickly changed her clothes. Grabbing the extra set of keys kept hidden in plain sight, minus the one for the trunk, she quickly walked the two blocks to her car, gassed and ready to go. She hid her car a week ago, as things became progressively worse. When her husband asked where her car was, she told him a story he would believe; that it was in the shop getting serviced. Although he was a stickler for his vehicle, always being in top-notch shape, he enjoyed isolating her.

When she arrived at her car, she made sure all was secure before getting in and heading to her safe house. Once there, she would book the flight to her destination. The first thing tomorrow morning, she would retrieve her belongings from the bank.

Yes, her revenge would be served on a plate *very cold.*

Upon arriving at her safe place, she showered and fell into bed, sleeping fitfully. The next morning with her flight booked, she made her way to the bank and cleaned out the safety deposit box, along with everything in her secret account, which she closed. She made her way to the airport and parked in the long-term parking area. She knew he would never think to look there. She had already removed the GPS tracking device and left it in the garbage can at the house they had both shared. Her lips curved upwards, and she chuckled, wondering about what he would think once he started looking for her.

It was several hours later when her hometown paper received an email from an unknown source.

The email read: *"Councilman, Mr. Roger Coleman, who is up for reelection to be charged with spousal abuse, money laundering, adultery, and bribery."* The email went on to show evidence of all those accusations—including photos of the spousal abuse, the accepting of bribes, including screenshots of the person who bribed him . . . who happened to be the Governor's aide. There were also videos, containing conversations about how money was laundered through his company; and finally, photos and recorded conversations with his mistress, who was the wife of the local Mob Don. The email also stated that it would disappear in one hour once opened—if it was not read or saved.

The editor immediately saved it and printed out all the information. Opening his door, he called in his top reporter.

Here read this," he said, handing over the damning evidence. "What do you know about this guy?"

"Nothing," he replied. "He has always appeared to keep his nose clean."

"Jack, I need you to follow up. Find out what you can, and let's get this on the news today. This is good stuff. Call your gal that does . . . what's it called? Ah, video—no, image forensics. Ask her to make certain nothing has been altered."

"Sir, what about the source? Is it credible?"

He sat without speaking for a long moment. "Son, in my opinion very credible, but I must keep it anonymous. We cannot allow the name to get out there. It could put our source in danger, and things could get ugly."

Jack nodded in understanding as he thought, "*She finally did it.*"

Jack immediately went to work—calling in favors, twisting arms, and even making subtle threats, when necessary. Everything checked out, so he wrote the story and sent it to his editor.

When it broke, the Internet lit up like a firestorm; the phones in the newsroom rang like bells. It reminded Jack of the saying, "Send not for whom the bells toll, it tolls for thee."

They tolled indeed for Mr. Roger Coleman, a city councilman up for re-election who was now under investigation for all the above crimes. During Jack's fact-gathering mission, he found that the same information had been sent to a detective friend, who had eagerly jumped on it. Apparently, Councilman Coleman had been under investigation for a while . . . but until that incriminating email broke, he had covered his tracks too well.

Jack stood outside, observing the scene when the authorities came to Coleman's house to arrest him, surrounded by cameras flashing and videos rolling. He was there to hear threats hurled at everyone within hearing distance, including the man's absent wife. He watched the live newscast from their station that evening and smiled. *What a story.* He knew just how his editor got the scoop, but he would take that knowledge to his grave. For now, he would simply take the moment, and live it.

She also watched the broadcast from her undisclosed location. She had received the divorce papers via her attorney, signed them, and immediately sent them back. He was probably furious; she knew he'd expected a devoted wife who would stand by him. Ha!

What he didn't know . . . is that she would be a witness for the prosecution. Although she could not wait to see the look on his face when it all came out at trial; inside lurked a remnant of that familiar fear.

The day of the trial was one of the most perfect days she ever remembered. As she entered the courtroom, she was surrounded by two bodyguards hired by the prosecutor. When her former spouse saw her, he was so visibly livid that the judge promised to have him handcuffed and shackled if he didn't sit down and behave. If looks could have killed, she would have been dead, as she testified, maintaining in a clear strong voice. Even his attorney could not shake her airtight testimony. When the prosecutor presented all the evidence, his face turned blood red and he mouthed to her, "You are dead."

At first, she flinched, but as she realized he was going away for a long, long time, her lips curled into a smile. That set him over the edge. Jumping up from his seat he called her every name he could think of—none of them good. His verbal threats angered the judge, who had him shackled, and flanked by two court-appointed deputies. Nothing his attorney advised would calm him down. She watched the jurors' faces as this show of madness continued. He was done.

A hand touched her shoulder, and she turned to see a familiar-looking man, who had been sitting behind her. He was stone-faced, but paying close attention to the antics of her now ex-husband. Something clicked in her brain, and she gave him a slight nod. He averted his gaze, glanced briefly her way. and nodded back.

As her ex-husband continued his tirade, the Judge had him removed and placed in a holding room with a camera, along with the deputies, to continue the trial. His attorney tried to get a continuance, since his client was so distraught, claiming he was unable to help with his own defense. The Judge overruled, reminding the attorney that his client was, indeed, in complete control of his faculties, and charged him with Contempt of Court. The trial continued, and the verdict was handed down.

Guilty on all counts.

She watched the morning news to hear the results of the sentencing phase. There would be no appeal. Cameras followed as he was led from the courtroom to the prison van. He had been convicted, publicly shamed, lost all of his assets . . . and was going to prison for so many years he would be an old man when he got out. Sipping her coffee, she smiled and toasted him.

Remember the first time you ever hit me? Remember when I said, "Revenge is best served on a plate cold?" You laughed and said I would never go against you because I needed you more than you needed me. My dear, never allow your ego to be bigger than your common sense. Your Achilles heel is the fact that you thought you were smarter than everyone else. That you were untouchable. Enjoy your new digs. Thanks for the memories. You taught me how to not only survive. but to thrive. Oh, and the money is not so bad either.

She hadn't realized she'd spoken the words out loud until Jack's cell phone made her startle as it alerted him to a new message, and he switched the news channel to another report, a new breaking story. She gave him a questioning look.

He nodded to the large flat screen. "Just watch. There is a new ending to your story."

"We have just learned that former Councilman Roger Coleman, who was only recently convicted on multiple charges and sentenced to thirty years in prison, has died. His body was found in his cell, and he was unresponsive. We will follow up as we know more."

She pondered whether it had been murder or suicide. Either way: *Revenge is . . .*

Too Close to the Edge

ROSALIND PLACE

My fist in the small of your back. It won't take much pressure. Just enough. It will be the shock of it that will tip you forward . . .

I was at the lake only last week. You remember the lake. How Eva loved that place! The last time she and I were there together, she was recording an album. You can hear a mourning dove on one of the tracks. I've been back countless times since she died, and the doves are always there. Or so it seems. Perhaps it's just her I hear, calling me, reminding me to pay attention.

I have lost count of how many times I have stood on this station platform waiting. It's a short commute to the hospital but the schedule isn't always accurate, so I have to get an early train because it is always busy and always running behind. You can't be late for a shift at the ER, and I like to have a coffee beforehand.

That day, I was doing what I always do—reading the newspaper on my phone—trying to keep some distance from all those other commuters trundling into the city every weekday morning. The platform was too crowded, there was too much noise and movement, so I buried myself in the news on my phone and let everything swirl around me.

I might never have seen you. I might never have noticed you standing there.

I was trying to keep my heart rate at a reasonable level, so I wasn't paying attention. I felt the rush of adrenaline and the tightness in my chest before I even realized what I'd heard.

It was a cough, a single cough.

How did I even hear it amidst all the hubbub? I looked up but saw only a gray, immovable wall of raincoats. It might all have ended then and there except it started to pour. The wall started to wobble and move as people popped open their umbrellas and a gap appeared ahead of me.

I only saw your back. You stood there, right at the front of the crowd, looking as you always did—as if you owned everyone and everything around you. You were standing on the yellow lines, much too close to the edge of the platform, and I swear I could hear your voice coming back to me over all these years. *Careful is for nobodies, Eva! You wanna be a nobody?*

You think you've come to terms with the past and then, suddenly it's there right in front of you and the memories are so clear that they take your breath away.

It was the first time I met you. I was a student nurse in another city and hadn't been home for some time. Eva had been going out with you for a while by then, but I'd only ever heard about you on the telephone. *A lovely man,* she told me. *So supportive and caring. These last few months have been the best of my life. I've been writing music again. How quickly things can change!* And she sounded genuinely happy. It was such a relief to hear the excitement in her voice. She had been so down and so lonely.

All the good dishes were laid out on the dining room table. *A celebratory dinner*, Mum said. Eva came up to me and gave me a big sisterly hug and I was so glad to see her. It didn't even register at first that we were celebrating an engagement. You stepped forward, smiling, extending your hand, and I felt something shift. By the end of the evening, I knew. It was the way you looked at her and the way you looked at me.

A cough. A single cough

Such an innocuous sound. Why did I even look up? And I wasn't absolutely sure at first, just a rush of anxiety looking at someone's back, watching them reach into the side pocket of their coat for a tissue as they started to cough again. People edged away from you, and it gave me the chance to move up a little and look more closely.

No one else stands like you or moves like you. It's hard to imagine that you could get such a mundane thing as a cold. You had a fever too. I could see it when you took off your hat, wiped your forehead with your sleeve. I could see that you're starting to lose your hair. I was close enough to you by the time the train finally arrived, to see the broken veins in your cheeks, the soft bulge of your stomach, the hitch in your step as you moved forward. You weren't as strong or as fit as you used to be.

The impatient crowd started to move. I let them all pass while I tried to slow my breathing. I lost sight of you. The train screeched to a halt and as the crowd rushed forward, I saw you again, pushing your way past the passengers getting off.

I couldn't get on the train. I was a cliché, standing there frozen.

It was on the day you left on your honeymoon. We were all standing on the platform of the old train station, that long narrow platform. Eva was wearing a pale green summer dress and a beautiful straw hat. She kept walking away from everyone to look down the tracks and I remember thinking, *What are you doing Eva? Why can't you see who he is?*

It was a hot summer's day and for some odd reason, you were wearing a suit. The train pulled up and you bent towards Eva in an old-fashioned gesture, extending your arm as if guiding her onto the train. She jumped up the stairs ahead of you, holding onto her straw hat, waving back, and smiling.

You looked back too. You looked directly at me. You didn't even bother to smile. *She's mine now.*

I'm very good at compartmentalizing. You must be in my profession. By the time the next train pulled into the station, I had put you out of my mind.

It wasn't until the ride home that I allowed myself to think about you again. I'd half convinced myself, by then, that it wasn't you I'd seen. After all, why would you come back here, to this small town, where you could be seen, and recognized?

But then I had to remind myself that the worst of what you did wasn't technically a crime. Your picture wasn't in the paper. You were never named as Eva's murderer. My sister took her own life. That's what they told me that day, over the telephone, as I stood in the hospital corridor, people brushing past me, the known world starting its slow collapse to nothing.

Except it wasn't her life she took that day; by then her life was no longer hers. It belonged to you, was taken by you, and destroyed by you.

Careful is for nobodies. The things you said to her. The way you twisted and turned everything until she couldn't trust anything she thought or did. Until she couldn't trust anyone, not even herself.

She seemed so genuinely happy at first that I thought I must have misread you. I'd moved further away by then. I had a new job in a new city, a new life. Still, we talked often, as we always had, my little sister and I. They were good times for both of us. I loved my work, and her career was on the upswing. She had regular bookings now—had been invited to play at a regional festival.

It's going to be okay, I thought. I still don't know if I even noticed those first hints of uncertainty in her voice; the first time I heard her say no to something she would have jumped at in the past.

Well, you know I've always wanted children, and this must come first. I can't do both. I can't tour while I'm pregnant. I can't raise a child on the road. Having a family is far more important than music.

But music is who you are Eva. You can adjust things. It doesn't have to be one or the other. Or is that him speaking?

You won't even use his name! Of course, it isn't him! This is my decision. He said he'll support whatever I want to do, and I want this, for both of us. You don't know me anymore. You don't know what's important to me. No, you never knew me. I've only just come to understand that.

Your words in her mouth. How easily you separated us. There were fewer phone calls. I was hurt and angry and I looked away.

She was pregnant and then she wasn't and then she was pregnant again. It's what brought me back—that second miscarriage. It's what brought me to see exactly what kind of a person you were. It's what brought me to understand, as I got off the train that day and headed for home, that I couldn't stand on that platform again, see you there again, and do nothing about it.

At first, they were just fantasies, vengeful fantasies. I told myself it was a one-time thing, seeing you. It wouldn't happen again. I told myself there was no point to revenge. It wouldn't bring her back and it wouldn't help me. You weren't there the next day or the day after. My schedule shifted to afternoons then nights. I convinced myself I must have been mistaken. It was unresolved grief. I had simply imagined it was you.

My first day back on mornings, I wasn't thinking about you at all. It was a Saturday. There weren't any crowds. You were standing in exactly the same spot, right at the front, feet on the yellow line and, oddly, I wasn't shocked to see you there. I wasn't overcome with anxiety, in fact, quite the opposite. I remember taking a deep, easy breath as my body relaxed. I followed you into the train car, stood in front of you. You were busy on your phone the whole trip into the city, only glanced up once when someone sat down next to you, brushing against you as they moved. It wasn't until you stood up and reached for the pole that I saw the wedding ring on your finger.

That day at the hospital, the day I saw my sister for the last time, you were sitting in a chair in her room, looking bored, leafing through a magazine. You didn't say anything the entire time I was there, only got up when I moved to put on my coat. You followed me out into the hall.

I'm an ER nurse. I see it all the time. The wife with the broken arm, the broken rib, the broken spirit, a loving husband by her side. I see it in how gently dismissive they can be, how they do all the talking, and how they never leave the room. They know that I don't believe them, or suspect it, anyway. And they know that there's absolutely nothing anyone can do about it until their spell is broken.

I stood in the hallway that day and listened to you trying to explain everything away, knowing there was nothing I could do. You didn't even bother to come up with an original excuse. *She fell down the stairs. She hasn't been herself lately. She wanted the baby so much but she wouldn't take care of herself. I told her over and over again, but she wouldn't listen.*

I am powerless, I thought then.

I'm not powerless anymore.

I've watched you, week after week, standing there, too close to the edge. I've rehearsed it over and over again in my mind and I know no one will suspect me. It will take the slightest pressure, enough to put you off balance. I'll reach out to save you, but I'll be too late. The crowd will vouch for me. They'll see only that I tried to save you.

Another rainy day. Another crowded platform. I move carefully forward until I am standing behind you, so close I can smell the wet wool of your coat. My fist in the small of your back. I feel your body tense as you start to fall.

Someone screams. It must be some kind of instinctive reaction. I reach for you, and I am not pretending. I grab your coat; I've always been strong. I have you in my arms in an instant. I pull you back from the edge and as soon as you find your footing, you turn toward me and push me away. I fall backward at the same instant you collapse.

What a nasty tumble it is, too. Yours, that is, not mine. Your head hits the cement with quite a crack. I am on my feet immediately. People move back as I start first aid. They see that I know what I'm doing.

I am furious. My heart is racing and my hands shake. *I didn't prepare well enough*, I think as I bend over you, pretending to take your pulse. *What made me think it would be that easy? Why didn't I think it through?* I take off my coat and cover you, kneel beside you trying to bring my breathing back to normal. I hear the faint wail of the sirens growing louder and suddenly find myself wanting to laugh out loud. You're missing all the drama and you always enjoyed being the center of attention.

Before I know it, the paramedics are there, in front of us. As they strap you onto the stretcher and I stand up, the crowd parts, and suddenly everyone begins to applaud. People come up to me, pat me on the back, treat me like a hero.

I have just saved your life. Little me, an off-duty ER nurse, who just happened to be there, standing behind you when you fell, has saved your life.

I watch the ambulance turn a slow circle and leave. The sirens wail again and then fade to nothing. I speak briefly to a police officer who is obviously in a rush to be somewhere else.

The platform is empty. The train has come and gone without me noticing. I sit down on one of the sodden benches, ignoring the wet seat. I close my eyes.

Eva and I are playing the game she always won.

She arranges everything on the table: a pen, a knife, a pebble, a shell, a piece of candy, a playing card, a puzzle piece, a bit of candle, and a little toy. I look at the pieces before Eva shouts. Stop!

She covers the pieces with an old cloth and pushes the blank paper toward me. I remember some, struggle to get the order right. I am frustrated and don't want to be stuck there, humoring my little sister.

"It's a stupid game!" I shout, pushing everything off the table and Eva starts to cry. She kneels on the floor collecting the pieces and then she stops crying and stands up.

All you had to do, she says, looking straight at me, was pay attention.

I wasn't then, when I could have done something to stop it, but I am now.

I understand perfectly what has happened. I have just discovered how difficult it can be to kill someone, that's all. It isn't too late. It isn't too late for me to find the peace I need. It was my good luck that someone screamed. It wouldn't have been enough, you see.

It wouldn't have been enough. You would never have known that it was me, Eva's big sister, who pushed you, who stood on the platform, smiling down at you as you fell.

I need you to see who it is, killing you.

I hear the click of the numbers changing on the announcement board in front of me. The next train is due in five minutes. It's going to be early today.

I'll have plenty of time to prepare on the train, time to rehearse my plan. I really don't need that long, though. They'll have taken you to the nearest hospital, after all.

My hospital.

Even if I am a little late it won't matter. I'll be there soon enough.

I'll be there when you wake up.

Excisor

RUE KARNEY

For KR, who knows all my secrets and loves me anyway.

The window shuddered in its frame. I clutched the sheet up to my neck as silver light flickered, cutting through the dark.

"Kaya! Wake up!" I jumped out of bed. "Someone's at the window."

"Mnnh." Kaya rolled onto her side, and mumbled, "Go back t'sleep, Edin."

A thud, a crack, and then glass shattered over the floor.

Kaya screamed. I grabbed her arm, dragging her into the bathroom and locking the door behind us. On the other side, claws skittered across the timber floorboards. A bird chirped, followed by three short, sharp squeals. Hard thuds against the floor, five, six times. Then, silence.

They're here. I buried the thought, replaced it with another. *No panicking before facts.* I forced a deep breath down into my belly. *Focus on facts.* For months I'd worked a dull cashier's job in this city of millions, keeping my head down, unnoticed and anonymous, and done nothing to attract attention.

Well . . . Maybe one thing.

I dug my fingernails into my palms as if that would slow my pounding heart.

Kaya reached behind the shower curtain at the end of the bathtub and pulled out a broom. She handed me the toilet brush.

"What am I supposed to do with this?" Fear made me feel giddy. "Flush whoever is out there down the toilet?" I brandished the brush like a dagger. "Defend yourself, you piece of shit!" I hissed at the door.

Kaya clapped her hand over her mouth, and we leaned against the bathroom wall, our shoulders and chests shaking with laughter.

"Here." She grabbed a couple of oversized t-shirts from the laundry basket and threw one at me. "Best not to mount an attack while naked," she said, winking.

The t-shirt held the whole world of her as I pulled it over my head, its fabric soft against my skin, a heady perfume consisting of her deodorant and sweat; a world easy to lose myself in.

Kaya, brave in her ignorance, gripped the broom like a spear. "Let's go." She flung open the door without hesitation.

Wind whistled through the small apartment, and pages of a magazine fluttered on the coffee table. Kaya moved, stepping as softly as a cat into the living room, with me by her side, and flipped the light switch.

"Ugh!" She grimaced at the sight; in the corner, an arc of blood splattered the white-painted wall. Wings flapped and a black feather drifted to the floor.

I stepped in front, trying to shield her view, but Kaya peeped over my shoulder. "Is that a bird attacking a rat?" She covered her mouth and nose with her hand. "That is seriously disgusting."

The butcher bird tilted its black-feathered head towards us, its knowing eye a diamond of glittering malice. It picked at the rat's spilled guts, pulling blue-grey entrails out of the bloodied mess of stomach. The Shiraz we'd drank with our dinner burned sour in the back of my throat.

"This shit is too weird," Kaya said. "A bird smashes a window to get in and then it finds a rat to kill. How did I *not* notice a rat in this tiny apartment?"

"Yeah, weird." I clenched the toilet brush in my fist, an absurd symbol of the situation that might be about to unfold, praying silently for a miracle. "I'll clean up the dead rat and get rid of the bird if you want to deal with the bedroom."

"Suits me," Kaya said. "The rubber gloves and disinfectant are under the sink."

I made each tiny task an escape: the wet-fish cold of pulling on rubber gloves, the sweet-acrid scent released from pouring disinfectant, the hiss of bubbles rising up as hot water swirled into the bucket. I slow-stepped across the room, heel-toe, heel-toe, watching as the butcher bird cocked its head towards me. A worm-like intestine glistened in its black-tipped beak. My head spun with the smell of meat and blood, and the bucket slipped from my hand and dropped to the floor, slopping water over the sides. A trickle of rat's blood turned from red to pink as it seeped across the timber floorboards.

The bird sang three discordant notes and hopped closer, predator to prey.

Kaya stuck her head through the bedroom door. "Haven't you got rid of that bird yet?"

"You go back to bed. I'll have it sorted out in a minute," I said.

"Don't be long." She blew me a kiss.

The bird picked at the rat's bones, keeping one eye fixed on me.

"Shoo, shoo." I opened the apartment's front door and pushed the bird with my foot.

It flapped up and around and trilled a mocking laugh. I swiped at it with my forearm and pushed it out, stepping onto the landing to watch as it flapped its wings before descending the dark stairwell. Seconds passed while I waited, wanting to ensure it was gone before I allowed myself a deep breath, my shoulders slumping with relief.

No danger at all. Just a bizarre coincidence.

I turned to go back inside the apartment, yearning to join Kaya in her warm bed, but the apartment door had clicked shut.

I twisted the handle to discover it had automatically locked behind me.

The floor juddered beneath me, and my stomach dropped. Darkness, thick as fur, enveloped me. Wings flapped against my ear and sharp claws scraped across my scalp. A piercing squawk, then a beak stabbed at my cheek, drawing blood. Rage surged through me, and I snatched at the bird and tried to crush its fragile ribcage between my bare palms. My blood chilled at the curse of its silenced heartbeat before the alien glow broke through the gloom.

Shit.

Panic shoved its fist into my belly. One split second of blind stupidity, that was all it took.

"Kaya! Open up!" I banged on the door. "Kaya!"

I shouldered the door and pain ripped through my bones. The glow evolved into a hulking shadow. In desperation, I charged towards it, as if that could stop the phenomenon my reckless anger had unleashed, but an unseen force shoved me back. I cowered against the door as the leathered-skinned entity filled the space.

Armored feathers sprouted from its back and its beak curved, sharp as a talon. Spreading its wings, the creature opened its beak and a corpse flower stench rose from its spiked tongue. Round silver eyes glittered as they regarded me . . . its prize.

The stench of death flooded my tastebuds.

The apartment door abruptly swung open, and Kaya pulled me inside, slamming the heavy timber door shut behind us. I fell against it, panting, my heart pounding, the truth of who I was simmering beneath my skin.

Kaya stared at me. "What the hell was that thing?"

"Nothing, I—" I covered my mouth and forced back a retch. My past had crashed into my present, and they were colliding . . . coming for me.

With immense effort, I stood and gathered the jagged pieces of myself together.

"Babe, whatever that was—whatever is going on—just tell me," Kaya said, putting a hand on my shoulder as the promise of a future together began to shatter.

The creature threw its body against the door, shaking the frame. A piece of timber split.

"I'm calling the cops," Kaya said, pulling out her phone.

"Wait." All adrenaline and lizard brain, I raced into the kitchen and grabbed a cleaver and a boning knife from the rack.

Kaya took the cleaver and weighed it in her hand. "There is some seriously crazy shit happening around you, Edin. You sure you're not cursed?"

"It's not a curse. It's a game." The voice came from inside the apartment.

Kaya screamed.

My blood froze.

No! No! No! No! Noise roared inside my head.

In the blood-spattered corner, the mess of split carcass and exposed bone from the rat had gathered itself up into something *other*. A long-limbed creature, sharp-clawed with a dark, greasy pelt, looked down its pointed nose and bared its curved, rat teeth into a heinous grin.

The boning knife in my hand clattered to the floor. Weapons were useless against a creature that could incarnate from a pile of gutted fur and bones.

"It's a game." It leaned against the door and pounded it in an offbeat rhythm to the thumps from the other side.

"Shut up and give up, Hollard!" Picking at a crust of blood on the matted fur, it turned to us and said, "Ha! He thought he'd won. As usual, he'd counted his Earth-things before they fought back."

The knocking stopped. The rat creature planted itself on the sofa, resting its claws on a red cushion, surveying the room like an interested buyer. "I'm sorry, I've failed to introduce myself." It proffered a paw. "Beaufort's the name."

Kaya raised her cleaver. I grabbed her free arm and squeezed it.

Stop, careful. You don't know what you're dealing with! Of course, I couldn't say that out loud. Not yet . . .

Beaufort shrugged and dropped its paw. "Don't you want to know what game we are playing?" It picked up a used mug from the coffee table and sniffed, as if it was an exotic delicacy, then vanished from the sofa.

"It's a scavenger hunt." Beaufort's voice resonated from every corner of the room. "And you, my dear, are on the hunting list."

Kaya pressed her arm against mine. Our hands entwined and a shiver rippled through us, one to the other.

"In fact, you are number one, Excisor! And I daresay, I'll get bonus points for your companion."

Excisor. The poisonous label that I'd tried to run from leached back into my bloodstream. "I have nothing to offer you," I said, trying to keep my voice steady.

"Ah, such sweet modesty." Beaufort appeared in a cloud of sewer breath and encircled me, the precious prize. "Your skill is legendary throughout all realms."

"What . . . skill?" Kaya dropped my hand and backed away, looking at me like an intruder in her home. "Edin, what's it . . . he, talking about?"

"Not sharing your secrets, my dear?" Beaufort tut-tutted. "For shame. Dishonesty is the unhappiest policy."

"You're making a mistake," I lied. "I'm not an Excisor. I'm not whoever you think—"

Beaufort cut me off, faking a yawn as he inspected his claws. "How tedious your denials are becoming."

A crash sounded from behind. I grabbed Kaya, pushed her into the bathroom, and locked us inside as Hollard barreled through the apartment toward Beaufort.

"What are those things?" Kaya pressed her back into the door, her dark eyes narrowed with suspicion. "What *are* you?"

"Stay calm while I figure this out." I reached for her, but she shoved my hand away.

"You're not laying a fingernail on me until you tell me exactly who and *what* you are." Her mouth trembled in distress, and my heart ached.

Before Kaya, I'd never spent more than two months in any one place on Earth. I fed, clothed, and sheltered myself with minimal human contact, because anonymity guaranteed a safe life. Then one day, she walked into that café, and her smile upended my world. I resisted, of course. Her laugh, her cheeky wink, the smudge of chocolate at the corner of her lips when she drank a cappuccino, her offer of movie tickets, and drinks at the local bar to see a cool new band; I refused it all, until the day I didn't. The day, six weeks ago, I chose not to leave this town.

Day after day, I lied to myself while love filled my body and soul, beaming out a starry carpet of pheromones direct to Bledworld. In retrospect, I might as well have shaved my head and painted a target on it.

"I promise I'll explain after we escape." I checked around the bathroom. "Can we squeeze through that window?"

"I don't know! I've never tried to *escape from my own bathroom* before." Kaya pressed her knuckles into her eyes. "Fuck, this is crazy."

From the edge of the tub, I pushed open the single small window and checked outside. The chilled air smacked my face, a reality check. We were two stories up and there was no drainpipe, no ladder, and no way to get ourselves over to the neighbor's balcony.

"Well?"

"Not gonna work." My mind wrestled with thoughts of what to do, hopeless prayers against the inevitable.

Maybe if . . . I could . . . they might . . .

All dead ends. The selfish choice I'd made six weeks ago had snookered us both.

"I'm sorry." I stepped down from the edge of the bathtub.

"What are—"

Her body jerked as I pressed my palm flat against her forehead and summoned her memories into me. They trickled at first, mundane things such as putting the kettle on and brushing her teeth. I winced at the memory of her climbing into bed a few hours ago, then dug deeper. Moved beyond the dross to find the gems that could appease the Bledworld hunters. They were particular about what they prized—births, deaths, first love, first heartbreak— they craved deep connections, the memories that would not fade with time. Most of all they desired fear. Suffocating, thick, gray, worming through bones kind of fear, their blind lust for it our one chance at survival.

Kaya's body began to tremble, and goosebumps prickled on her arms. I was getting closer, although to what, I did not know. Even as my apprehension grew, I dug deeper into her flood of memories: first day of high school, a thrilling roller coaster ride, a slice of her grandma's hot apple pie with ice cream melting on top.

Closer. Deeper.

Sweat slicked Kaya's forehead, and bracing her body, I pushed harder against her feverish skin. If I lost my grip now, she'd be stuck in the in-between, lost and broken.

Shrill squeals came from outside the door as the battle between the hunters began reaching its peak. Soon, the victor would come to claim us. It didn't matter who won. Each had their own particular brand of cruelty—although I imagined Hollard's straightforward violence might be easier to suffer than Beaufort's faux society manners and lethal cunning.

Kaya gasped for breath, her eyes rolled back, and only the whites could be seen, though they were tinged with broken red blood vessels.

A sour odor oozed from her pores.

Almost there.

I delved deeper, already regretting what I might find.

Beneath her skin, the memory bulged like a tumor—a greasy grey slug, and with it a putrid smell. A dank, abandoned house smell. *Dark. Hidden. Cold.* A tremor rolled through Kaya's body and into mine as I clung onto her limp form, and my tenuous hold of that memory, pinching its edge, drawing it toward me.

From the kitchen came a crash, a thump, and another squeal. I shielded my mind to block the noise. There was no time for anything except the slow, excruciating extraction of Kaya's memory. Tears rolled down my face as she whimpered; a distressed child, and though the agony of the memory barbed me with its poisonous tips, I continued excising it.

It was the only way . . .

Exciser

The keening wail that burst from her mouth burrowed into my bones as the memory slid from her body. I clutched it, trapped it in my hand while I lowered her listless form carefully to the floor.

When I uncurled my fingers, the rotten-teeth stench of the memory tainted the air and coated my tongue: a memory as simple and awful as any nighttime terror, when the darkness is a vampire's cloak, and the space under the bed a monster's cave.

Heart thudding.

Breath stopping.

A paralyzing freefall into fear, sweat-drenched and all-consuming. A voice too afraid to call out, because there would be no answer, because hope was dead, buried, and gone. The memory in the palm of my hand held all these things.

And now . . . Kaya's most painful memory held me.

The door opened.

Hollard stared at the plump morsel of dread that arched and writhed on my palm and opened its beak. The wreck of Beaufort dropped to the floor with a skull crunch.

I offered up the memory to Hollard.

Sweat trickled from my armpits as the creature's head bobbed towards the prize with shuttering translucent eyelids.

I edged closer.

Beak gawping, it flicked its tongue, spikes bristling with inhuman salaciousness.

I raised my palm, heartbeat throbbing in my throat as it bent forward, closer, closer.

Its tongue lashed at the memory slug, impaled and inhaled it. The monster's eyes lolled in ecstasy as it swooned under the memory's power.

At that very moment, I thrust my hands into Hollard's chest. Armored feathers quivered as my knuckles kneaded into the leathery skin, digging deeper, deeper; peeling back layers to reveal the small bird within. Matter fizzled and dissolved; a flutter, a trill, and the butcher bird burst out in a wild flapping of grey, black, and white feathers. I slapped it quickly between my palms, wrenched open a bottom drawer with my toes, threw the bird in, and slammed it shut.

I heard Kaya groan. She sat up, groggy, her eyes bruises against her pale face. "What did you do to me?"

Inside the drawer, the bird squawked and scrabbled its claws against the jumble of mascaras, lipsticks, eye shadows, and perfumes. Soon it would gather enough strength to push its way out.

On the floor, a faint but perceptible pulse could be detected inside the rat's furred chest. It emitted a low gurgle, squeezing bloodied breath through its windpipe.

"I'll explain later. First, I need to deal with these hunters . . . while I can."

"How?"

I hesitated. "It might be better if you close your eyes."

"No." Her jaw was set hard. "I want to see."

"I don't want —"

"Do it."

"Promise you won't—"

"Do it." She spoke through gritted teeth.

"I need to be naked."

"Whatever, Edin."

I turned my back and stripped.

Kaya's disdain chilled my bare skin.

I swallowed my shame and focused on my toes, wiggling them one by one until they moved in a wave-like sequence, then continued the movement into my feet, up my ankles, calves and knees, my thighs, hips, belly and breasts, my shoulders, neck, and finally, my face. The micro-movements of my muscles didn't hurt, though I struggled to find the right rhythm to separate my outer coating from the fresh skin beneath.

Eyes shut, I shifted my focus inward, to the ripple of muscle and flesh, expanding the air in the cells that separated the old from the new. Kaya's face penetrated my mind's eye, grimacing with disgust, and my grip on the cells faltered. I pushed the image away.

Any moment now she'd be throwing me out of her apartment and her life, anyway. And I would honor her wishes, absolutely, after I finished this task because the only way to make sure Hollard and Beaufort went back to Bledworld was to wrap them in the skin I'd shed.

My final one.

I clenched and unclenched, shrugged, wriggled, and wormed until the final vestiges of my old skin detached and dropped to the floor.

Kaya gasped. Her breath quickened.

Light and energy emanated from my body. A faint scent of petrichor drifted from my pores and my new skin, shiny and clean, sealed my flesh—my shed-self lay on the tiles, empty as a ghost. I shook it out and smoothed it with my hands.

"I have to wrap the hunters in this while they're still in their small animal forms." I didn't dare raise my eyes.

"Do what you have to," Kaya said.

From the drawer, the bird screeched. I gestured towards it. "It'll fly out as soon as I open the draw. I need you to be backup if I don't catch it. Grab it with both hands and hold on tight."

"Fine." Kaya pushed the bathroom door shut and crouched against it, hands out front.

I pulled open the drawer. The bird flew at my face and jabbed its beak above my eyebrow. "Shit!"

Kaya swung her hand through the air and smacked the bird to the floor. I covered it with my shed skin and knelt on it. It beat its wings and jabbed its beak at my knee, but the skin held fast.

"Ugh!" Kaya picked up the rat with fingers pincered and threw it. It squealed as it bounced off my shed skin and skidded onto the tiles. When I made a grab for it, its blood-slicked fur slipped around the fresh skin on my palm. I gripped it tighter and shoved it in the old skin with the bird, wrapping them up in the substance that was no more a part of me than shorn hair on a salon floor, rolling and kneading until both creatures blended and meshed, transforming into a doughy substance.

Neither rat nor bird, Beaufort nor Hollard; just pliant, organic matter.

Between my new-skin hands, I squeezed and compressed the mound until it resembled the grey slug of memory I'd pulled from Kaya's mind. I dropped it into the toilet, slammed the lid, and flushed.

"That's it?" Kaya looked at me, fear and wonder mixed in her eyes. "You just flush them down the toilet?"

"Yeah, that's it." A shudder rippled through my body. "Sorry, I need a minute."

I squeezed my fists and pressed them into my thighs. The bathroom tiles chilled the fresh soles of my feet and ice crept into the marrow of my bones. I leaned forward, breathed out, and shook my hands, arms, and shoulders loose.

And when I looked up, Kaya was gone.

For a moment, I couldn't breathe.

I splashed water on my face and washed my hands, soaped, and scrubbed from the tips of my fingernails to my wrists, cursing the remains of my foes that swirled through the sewer pipes for their destruction of the simple life, the simple love, I had dared to covet.

In the mirror, my face held a faint glow, a remnant of my new state. Some kept their final shed skin as a holy relic, preserved, framed, and displayed; a keepsake of the moment when they were most beautiful.

I'd never intended to do that. I was glad to be rid of my last shed skin, happy to be in my final adult form in this world where I would be nothing special, just another post-human doing their best to get by each day. Back in Bledworld, being an Excisor had marked and confined me. Here on Earth, I was insignificant, a nobody, and that . . . made me free.

"All done?" Kaya's reflection appeared behind me, in the mirror.

"Yes." My hands trembled as I rinsed them under water again and turned off the tap.

"They won't be back?"

"No." I wrapped a towel around myself.

"Don't cover yourself. You're beautiful, all shiny like a newly minted coin."

My face tingled with embarrassment.

"Come into the living room. I've made tea and I want to hear this story, whatever the hell it might be."

"You're not kicking me out?"

"I didn't say that. You've been hiding who you are from me, but we've only known each other six weeks. There's stuff about me I haven't told *you* yet." She reached out her hand. "Come on, let's talk."

Her hand in mine was a soft cotton glove. I held it tight and prayed that I could keep her safe from the alien worlds that crept through the shadows and cracks of this one.

In the bowels of the building, the pipes rumbled.

Full Moon Mother

KAY LESLIE REEVES

This poem is dedicated to my two dastardly daughters. Love them both to bits.

Last night I looked up at the moon
And knew the time had come
Things would alter very soon.
Yesterday she was our Mum
Singing, as she rearranged
The plates upon the rack.
This morning she is changed.
She didn't hug me back.
No smile lights up her face.
No loving greeting on her lips,
Her features slightly out of place
Claws on her fingertips
Her apron's where it always hangs
But no lunch, packed in a tin.
Her teeth are growing into fangs
There's dribble on her chin.

The rosy cheeks have whiskers stiff
Her hair is growing wild
She licks her chops and looks as if
I'm dinner, not her child.

Unafraid

SUZANNE REYNOLDS-ALPERT

For Ari, Ethan, and Asherah—thank you for allowing me to be the weirdo I am and loving me nonetheless.

Year after year, I stood in front of the Yule bonfire; threw my pinecones, and made my wishes. *Help me to find the right job* or *help me to be a successful writer* or *help me be more likeable.* But there was always the constant—*help me get rid of my fear.*

I've lived my life timid; shy, unassuming, average. Afraid to draw negative attention. As a child, I was scared of the *gringas* who taunted me because my mother cleaned houses and I didn't have a father. As a teen, I was afraid of the popular kids who made fun of my second-hand clothes. Now, I'm afraid of the stories I want to tell—they are mostly grim and dark and I wonder what that says about me . . . what people will think of me if they know I conjure such bleakness.

December 21st

The solstice celebration—Yule—began like every other, with the usual coven members and guests spread out in a messy circle around the blazing bonfire. The evening was clear and windless and a waxing, almost-full moon shone among a few glittering stars.

Beside me, Michelle (who insisted everyone call her by her Magickal name, "EarthStar") held the basket of pinecones the children collected. She was five feet two inches of barely contained

164

energy, gray-haired, with a riot of wrinkles across her pale skin. She wore a red *sari* and several colorful scarves; a red *bindi* adorned her forehead. She rejected suggestions by the younger coven members that wearing a *bindi* was cultural appropriation. Her feet were bare despite the lingering patches of icy snow. She considered herself the matriarch of our coven and dispelled her wisdom frequently, loudly, and with little regard for whether the listener wanted it or not.

"Let me tell you, Valeria, in my day, we'd be *at least* half-naked. Skyclad—that's the way to do ritual." EarthStar swept her hands at the scene before us and several pinecones tumbled out of the basket. "Even the children would be naked! Now, everyone's so *worried* all the time. So P.C." She nodded meaningfully at a girl of about seven or eight years, encased in a parka. "That girl must be *sweating* under all those clothes." I was saved when someone called, "EarthStar! What's the name of that herbal tea you were telling me about?" and she rushed off to be indispensable.

The bonfire threw off noticeable warmth, and I swung one side of my cape over my shoulder as Dave filled the void left by EarthStar. I liked Dave—he was a truly nice person. Handsome, tall and slim, quiet and thoughtful. He ran drumming circles and was the resident *djembe* expert. I'd had a secret crush on him until he brought his then-boyfriend to an Equinox event. At least it was easier to talk to him now, without my stammering like an idiot. I'd even shared with him my hope of being a successful writer.

"We're really operating on pagan time here, eh?" he said.

"As usual." I grinned at him. The ritual should have started twenty minutes ago.

He adjusted the shoulder strap attached to his *djembe*. "How's the writing going?"

I chuckled. "The usual—not good. I had a bad case of writer's block this summer and fall—I think I told you that? —mostly due to my *abuela* being sick. I worried about her a lot, and then it was hard when she died." I stole a glance at the ceremonial altar several feet away from the bonfire and at my *Abuela*'s statue of the Vodou *loa* Erzulie that I'd placed there to honor her. "Other than that . . . " I shrugged. "Some rejections, but I did place a poem with an online literary magazine."

"Have you written any more of your opus?" he asked, referring to my horror-novel-in-progress, a Shirley Jackson-esque exploration of a small New England town (or, at least that's what I hoped it would become.) He smiled down at me with his soft brown eyes. They crinkled in the corners, which I found cute.

"No—I'm pretty stuck. It's a pretty horrific story, and . . . I don't know . . . what will people think? My mother would freak out if her church friends knew I wrote stuff like that. And my perfect sister . . . " I rolled my eyes and made the sign of the cross on myself, making Dave laugh. My sister had "married well," as my mother liked to say. Which means her husband has money.

Across the fire Ray and his wife, Amy—my best friend—were calling everyone to attention. EarthStar walked around the circle, staring critically at the attendees, strips of paper clutched in her age-spotted hands, judging whether they were worthy to call in one of the cardinal directions or have another key part in the ritual.

It was your typical pagan Yule celebration here in the (mostly) white Boston suburbs.

⚮⚮⚮

A half-hour later the ritual was almost complete. EarthStar had just graced us with a channeled message—she claimed the goddess spoke through her on the Sabbats. Most of the coven believed her. I'm naturally more skeptical. Not because I'm a nonbeliever—I'd chosen to be neo-pagan rather than a practicing Catholic like my mother and sister. Choosing this religion has been my only rebellion, the only thing that has marked me as more-than-average. So naturally my family knew nothing about it.

I liked to imagine I could someday be like *Abuela,* whose mother had been part Haitian. *Abuela* had been a dynamic, natural leader who'd openly practiced a unique mixture of Mexican-infused Catholicism sprinkled with Vodou rituals. Unlike her, unfortunately, I'm an introvert and riddled with insecurities. But through her, I learned that focused intention—bolstered by energy and the right tools—could affect change.

We'd come to my favorite part of the solstice ritual—the pinecone spell. I was standing next to Amy at this point, who was keeping a wary eye out for her two kids. I didn't see Amy much anymore, so we'd whisper-chatted throughout the ritual to catch up.

"Is your intention going to be something to help with your writing?" she whispered.

I held up my pinecone, thumb running up and down the rough surface.

"Of course," I whispered back, smiling even though a flitter of unease ran through my stomach. "It's got to work one of these years, right?"

"You just have to believe in yourself, Val," Amy said. "Stop having a chip on your shoulder and thinking you're not as good as everyone else in your writing groups just because they have more education. Or, you know, you *could* just give up this whole pipe dream, find some nice guy, and get married like me."

I tried to laugh. "I need to *talk* to guys without feeling like I want to throw up before I can find one to marry. Besides, I'm more interested in writing than marrying right now."

"Maybe, you know, that's the problem? That horror stuff you like to read and write . . . it turns guys off. I prefer to stay focused on positivity myself—but . . . I guess the gods and goddesses move us all in our own ways."

Across the circle, EarthStar and Ray clapped their hands to get everyone's attention. "Okay!" EarthStar yelled. "Now, you will throw your pinecones in the ceremonial fire; as you do, state your intentions for all to hear. What changes or energies do you want to bring forth in the coming year?"

Ray strained to speak as loudly as EarthStar over the crackling fire and boisterous children outside the circle. "You have all been blessed by this sacred ritual, in the ways of our ancestors."

Gazing up at the nearly full moon, I had the thought that many of *my* ancestors had been doing blood sacrifices and gods-knew-what-else at an Aztec temple.

"I'll start," EarthStar offered, unsurprisingly. "And we can go clockwise from there." She held her pinecone up to her heart and squeezed her eyes closed. "I wish the divine feminine reassert her dominance to bring balance and correct the evils of patriarchy." She tossed her pinecone.

Ray readied his own offering to the flames. "I wish for more peace in my home, and that my family be happy and healthy." Beside me, Amy bristled.

As my turn neared, anxiety rippled through me. Would it work this time? Would this be the year I would stop caring so much about what other people thought of me so that I could start doing—and writing—what I really wanted?

Somewhere in my mind, I heard a strangely accented, feminine-sounding voice. *Poor Valeria, always so concerned with everyone's opinions.*

Without thinking, I responded to the unseen voice: *It's not been easy for me, raised by a single mother among rich white kids. Never enough money to do everything I wanted.*

The scent of floral perfume wafted around me. My gut twisted. Narrowing my eyes, I scanned the circle, looking for the voice, my hand tightening around the pinecone. It bit painfully into my palm, but I ignored it.

I heard Amy beside me: "I wish to be more appreciated for all I do for my family." She sounded aggravated as she tossed her cone to the bonfire. I wrinkled my nose against the pungent floral fragrance and turned to ask Amy about the perfumy smell. But her four-year-old daughter was tugging on her cape and demanding to be picked up.

"Your turn," Dave bent to whisper in my ear. I wanted to ask him if he smelled it, too, but the thought of delaying the ritual helped me refocus on my intention . . .

That's when I caught a figure—no, a suggestion of a figure—writhing and dancing in the flames. My heart thumped as I thought, *the Yule god, he is here!* My vision swam as I beheld the sacrificial sun god—he who dies at Yule each year and is reborn to bring light back into the world—he who, she believed, was later co-opted by the Christians and rebranded as Christ.

But the fiery image shifted. I saw the suggestion of Jesus—the white Jesus depicted in paintings and the stations of the cross in my mother's Catholic church!

The figure morphed yet again, and a tingle of fear or excitement shot through me as a new form took shape. It slithered like a snake as it rose from the body of the flames, head growing and swaying. Long, sharp teeth protruded from its mouth and its snout elongated toward me. Spikes sprouted behind its head; a whip-like tail similarly adorned with spikes flashed toward me from the flames . . .

"Val!" Amy poked me in the ribs with her elbow and whispered urgently. "You've been standing there, for like, thirty seconds doing nothing. You're holding things up!"

Mortified, I loosened my grip on the pinecone clutched in my hand. A prickly bit had cut the soft skin near the center of my palm.

The fire cast enough light for me to see the dark stain of blood it elicited.

Stating my intention, I felt unnaturally sure and clear: "Make me lose my fear!" My voice reverberated in the air around me. I tossed my cone, wondering if it was only my imagination when that snake-shaped flame caught the cone in its mouth.

A brisk wind whipped up. A strong gust singled me out, twisting like a mini tornado and blowing my hair in all directions. I closed my eyes against the torrent and opened them only when I felt the squall abate. At the altar, the wind lifted *Abuela*'s statue of Erzulie into the dancing tongues of the bonfire. I cried out in shock, but there was no way to save it.

There are certain things all women know. Things we learn from an early age; things we're taught *not* to do. Don't get into your car or walk alone at night without being aware of your surroundings. Don't get together with a man you've met online unless you're in a public place.

But the day after the ritual . . . I broke several common-sense rules.

December 22nd

It was a cold Saturday night and I'd agreed to meet some work friends in Boston. Unlike me, they lived in the city—most of them have better educations and higher incomes and could afford to.

I took the commuter rail to South Station. After disembarking, I bundled up and headed to the Seaport District. As I crossed the bridge, a cold wind assailed me, reminiscent of the biting and sentient-feeling squall from the ritual the previous night. Remembering it, I chilled further. I stepped up my pace, keeping my gaze on the far side of the bridge as I hurried along.

Up ahead, three men walked toward me. *Gringos*. Even from a distance of thirty yards or so, I could see the men were drunk. They were loud and stumbling into each other.

I'm a short woman, barely five-foot-four. Loud, intoxicated

men in groups can be dangerous to a woman walking alone. Especially a small woman who doesn't look entirely "white."

Yet, the expected spike of healthy fear did not shoot through me. I didn't have the urge to alter my steps or cross the street. Even though they noticed me, I wasn't afraid. Even as the distance closed between us and one called for me to accompany them to a "party," I remained calm and unhurried.

"Heyyyy, little lady . . . " one of the men drawled. They looked younger than my own twenty-five years. The one who'd spoken wore a well-loved Red Sox cap and his jacket was unzipped despite the cold. I could smell alcohol wafting off them.

I rolled my eyes and kept walking. "Leave me alone, pricks," I said.

A hand grasped my arm, and I was pulled off balance, crashing into the one who held me. He wore a dark grey sweatshirt with the hood up. "We just wanna talk, is all," he said. "Be nice."

I should have been terrified. Twenty-five years of conditioning should have had me quivering, fearing for my safety.

But instead, I looked up at grey hoodie, meeting his uneven gaze as I pried his fingers from my arm, digging into his flesh with my fingernails. "I. Don't. Want. To. Be. Nicccccc." I hissed, punctuating each word with venom as the wind howled and snatched the cap off his friend's head.

The now-hatless man made an uncomfortable, nervous sound as he glanced from his cap sailing away back to me. The third one frowned as his eyes raked over me. Something unreadable crossed his face. "Come on guys," he muttered. "She's probably, like, a dyke or something."

"Yeahhh . . . " Grey hoodie backed up a step, rubbing the hand where I'd left bloody crescents. "This dyke isn't worth it."

"Whatever." I stepped around them and continued toward the new trendy bar where I was meeting my colleagues. I shook out the arm that jerk had grabbed and didn't even think to look back.

As I reached the far end of the bridge, I realized my actions had been uncharacteristically brave.

Unafraid

December 23rd

I spent a low-key Sunday at home, nursing a hangover. I'd called *Mamá* to tell her I was sick and wouldn't accompany her to church. Instead, I took a bath—something I rarely did—and added a healthy dose of pungent floral bath salts someone had given me, which I'd never been inclined to use.

Later in the day, I set my laptop on my battered kitchen table and fleshed out a pivotal scene from my novel outline: A woman is lost in the woods, wondering what was real, what was supernatural, and what was in her head. On a whim, I went off-outline and added a few paragraphs about her being bitten by a snake. The words flowed; my writer's block was gone. It felt wonderful!

The following day would bring about more changes.

December 24th

I waited for the morning commuter train, sipping home-brewed coffee from my travel mug and hopping from foot to foot to keep warm. It was about twenty-three degrees outside, and I could see my breath. Since it was Christmas Eve, the crowd was lighter than usual.

A familiar *ding ding ding!* announced the train.

Someone down the platform screamed.

Heads snapped in unison. Some people were running. News spread up through the crowd. "A girl was down on the tracks."

"She says she wants to kill herself!" someone yelled frantically.

Without thinking, I ran toward the ruckus, pushing people out of the way. The platform rattled as the train approached. The crowd was looking down and yelling. Some people were calling 911; others were using their phones to take videos.

I thrust my mug into someone's hands, dropped my backpack, and ripped off my coat.

I jumped—the eight feet down to the tracks.

My right ankle twisted, and a stabbing pain shot up my calf. A teenage girl was sprawled across a track. Her hair was a mess and mascara ringed her red eyes. She clutched a phone in one hand.

Gritting my teeth as I put weight on my throbbing ankle, I hobbled over to her. "We have to get out of here!" I grabbed her arm. "You're going to get hit by the train!"

"I want to diiiiiiie—" she moaned. At least I think that's what she said. The *ding ding ding* was loud. And the screaming—people up on the platform kept screaming.

I yanked her up and pushed her toward the platform where people reached down, ready to grab us. "You're coming *now*!"

"No! He broke up with me! Fuck him! I don't want to live —" A glance down the tracks showed the train taking the last bend, passenger cars curving behind it like a giant serpent. It appeared to be slowing, but at its current speed, it would hit us . . .

I was not afraid.

A biting wind howled along the tracks. I hurled the sobbing, unwilling girl in front of me and into the grasping hands of onlookers. Arms pulled me up as the train screeched and stopped with a hard jerk about ten yards past where the girl had been. My face scratched on the rough pavement as I was hauled up, and once on the platform, I rolled onto my back, breathing heavily. I was scraped and my ankle was sore, but I was otherwise okay.

"Are you crazy?" A woman shouted at me. "Fuck, you're brave as hell but crazy!"

I had no response. Because that's when I realized what must have happened. Impossible . . . but . . .

⁂

It really happened. I'd lost my fear. Hours later I was on the train home, staring out the window at the rising full moon, thinking about the girl I'd saved. The previous hours had been a blur, answering police questions, having paramedics tend my scrapes and wrap my ankle, and having my photo taken by reporters and Instagrammers.

Lost in my thoughts, I was only vaguely aware that the train had stopped to unload passengers. I felt someone take the seat next to me.

"Penny for your thoughts?"

I turned. A handsome *gringo* smiled at me. I guessed he was forty-ish; he was dressed in a nice suit.

"Excuse me?"

"You know . . . 'Penny for your thoughts'? It's a stupid expression . . . but you look like you have a lot on your mind."

"Oh . . . yes. And yes, I do."

"You're the woman from this morning," he said, a smile growing as he looked at me with very nice blue eyes. "That was some real brave stuff, saving that girl. And, I have to say, pretty badass . . . " He scanned me down to my waist, then back up. His hand shot out. "My name's Steve. I've noticed you before. Nice to meet you."

I shook his hand. "Val. Nice to meet you, too."

"So, what do you do for work, Val?"

"I'm an admin assistant at Paulson & Associates. You?"

"Finance. At Putnam."

A heady floral scent tickled my nose as I did something I'd never done in my life: "So, Steve in finance at Putnam. I see you don't have a wedding ring, and assuming you have no urgent business for Christmas Eve, care to grab a drink when we get off the train? I've had quite a week." I reached out and fingered his red tie, wrapping it around my hand and letting it slither through my fingers.

❧❧❧❧❧

December 25th

I kicked Steve out around 1 a.m. I'd had too much wine and the best sex of my life. Actually, it was the most uninhibited I'd ever been, how I'd demanded my own pleasure.

I was drinking a glass of water at 1:15 when my phone buzzed—a text from Steve. *When can I see you again? You are amazing.* I chuckled and put the phone down without replying. Instead, I went to the refrigerator and grabbed a beer. I was still drunk, but it wasn't like I had to work the next day. I popped the can and snuggled into my favorite end of the couch, turning the TV on.

The 1950s version of **A Christmas Carol** played. I sipped my beer and tucked my legs under me, trying to get comfortable. But the movie didn't capture my attention.

Outside, the wind howled and icy snow pinged against the window panes.

I carried my beer to the kitchen table, taking the seat in front of my laptop. I opened it and waited for it to wake up. Restless, I stood and grabbed my phone. Ignoring Steve's message, I texted Amy: *You're not going to believe what happened to me.* Sometimes Amy has insomnia. Besides, she might still be up doing the Santa thing for her kids.

I brought the phone back to the table and took another sip of beer as I sat. I clicked on the file with my novel draft, scrolling to the last chapter I'd written. Instead of rereading it, I thought about the last few days. The solstice ritual. My wish. All the strange and brave and wonderful and scary things I'd done.

I'm not afraid anymore, I thought. *I can do whatever I want and not be scared.*

I stood again and paced back and forth in my small kitchen, thinking, wincing at my sore right ankle still wrapped in an ace bandage. What was different about this solstice, this year? *Abuela* had died, and I'd brought one of her statues. A statue of a Vodou *loa*.

And there was that voice. And the shape in the flames. How it looked like the Yule god, then Jesus—until it wasn't—it became that snake-like thing. There was the perfumy scent that had been following me. And my pinecone; it had cut my hand and I'd thrown it, spotted with my blood, into a ritual bonfire. The statue of Erzulie had gone into the flames, too, carried by the wind, *almost as if the wind wanted it to go in.*

I shook my head. Too weird. I was a neo-pagan; I practiced magick. But something this big? This level of magick was make-believe. *Or was it?*

Because . . . here I was. Without fear. Not just without the fear blocking my writing, but without fear of *anything*.

My phone buzzed. Amy, responding to my message. *What up?*

I texted: *Can I call you?*

She replied: *OK let me go downstairs. I'll call u.*

My phone rang a minute later. I pressed the green button and said, "I think magick is real."

"Well, duh."

"No, I'm not talking about the spells we've done that got us love or jobs or whatever. I mean . . . like, it can work *big*."

"Val, you sure you didn't bang your head today?" Amy laughed.

"I mean it . . . my intention at Solstice was 'to lose my fear' . . . only I meant my writing. And being braver, generally. But now . . . I'm not afraid. Of like, anything."

Amy was silent for several seconds. "So, that thing this morning, jumping down onto the train tracks . . . I mean, it sorta didn't seem like you."

"Right? And there's more. The night after the ritual, I practically went berserk on these guys who were harassing me. Three of them, against me, and I stood up to them. And they were afraid of *me* by the end."

"Whoa . . . really?"

"Yea. And there's *more*-more. I, um, picked up a guy on the train on the way home today. We went out for drinks and I invited him back to my place and we hooked-up." Then added under my breath, "A few times."

"Oh, shit, *you*?!"

"Yea. And I don't care. I feel like . . . like nothing can hurt me. Like I'm invincible."

"Val, this is bad. Really bad. Let me wake up Ray, and we should call EarthStar . . . she knows more about this stuff than anyone."

A groan rumbled out of my mouth. "Not her."

"Like I said, Val, EarthStar knows more about magick than anyone. She's done rituals with both Starhawk and Margot Adler." I heard the adoration in her voice and rolled my eyes. "We're coming over."

The three arrived at my apartment forty minutes later, shaking flakes of snow from their hair and coats. "Who's watching your kids?" I asked Ray, who entered first. He glanced at the skimpy tank top and shorts I'd thrown on after Steve left and raised an eyebrow.

Amy stepped around him. "Eh, they're asleep. Ray's mom is there. If they heard any noises, we'll tell them it was Santa. Nice 'war wounds', by the way," she said, pointing to the scratched cheek I'd gotten that morning.

Now that they'd arrived, I realized how much the three annoyed me. But I tried to be nice and relayed the past few days' events as we sat at my kitchen table.

As I spoke, EarthStar watched me closely, eyes narrowed and mouth frowning. She was the first to speak once I'd finished. "I knew I felt the presence of forces greater than usual the night of the ritual," she said.

"See?" Amy turned and touched my arm. "I told you EarthStar would help." She didn't seem to notice that EarthStar hadn't promised she *could* help. My irritation upped a notch. I stood to grab the emergency cigarettes I'd hidden in an upper cupboard. I'd quit several years ago but kept a pack around in a sealed bag . . . just in case.

This was one of those cases.

I found a small glass to use as an ashtray and lit up, sitting back down. Amy frowned and backed her chair away.

"So, *Michelle*, it's great you noticed something different that night, but what should I *do* about it?"

Her face turned pink, her wrinkles becoming more pronounced when she frowned at me. "Call me EarthStar," she said.

"Whatever," I said, drawing on my cigarette.

Her eyes narrowed further, becoming slits as she leaned across the table. "The spirits—or whatever they are—are angry."

"Uh-huh. And you know this how?"

"Val!" Amy reprimanded me sharply.

I rolled my eyes. "Heaven forbid I don't show *the matriarch* the proper deference."

"Did the spell make you unafraid or turn you into a bitch?" Ray asked, leaning back in his chair and folding his arms across his chest.

"Maybe you should shut up and be more concerned about keeping your wife happy," I snapped back at him.

"Enough!" EarthStar banged both fists on the table. "Valeria, you are clearly not afraid to say whatever you want, and you don't give a rat's ass what people think. This is serious. You cannot go through life like this! Now focus and tell us everything you did and thought about at the ritual."

❧❧❧❧❧

A couple hours later, an exhausted Ray and Amy went home. It was almost five a.m., and their kids would be waking up soon.

Michelle—EarthStar—stayed. She'd brought her favorite Tarot deck and other divination tools. and set up an elaborate Tarot spread once the others left. She concluded that her original assumption was correct, that I had displeased some gods or ancestral spirits or something. For the first time since I'd known her, EarthStar looked scared.

I tried to be concerned. But I didn't feel it. "What's the worst that can happen?" I asked.

She sipped some coffee I'd brewed and squinted at me over the brim. She put the cup down gently. "Your behavior has already become erratic. You are not only doing things that are unsafe, but you are pissing people off." She grimaced. "We need to figure out how to reverse the spell."

What she didn't know was that I'd decided about an hour ago that I was going to finish my novel before reversing the spell. "So, you'll go and research that?" I wanted her gone.

She squinted at me again. "I need to do a scrying, then I think I'll have the information I need," she said, reaching into her battered tote bag and pulling out a velvet pouch.

As she set up the scrying materials, I sighed and checked my phone. Another text from Steve. One from my mother, confirming that she'd received a text I sent earlier about not being able to make it to my sister's house for Christmas Day because I was still feeling sick and had hurt my ankle. *I hope you feel like yourself again soon*, it ended. I grinned at the irony. I liked feeling the way I did right now. Powerful. Uninhibited. Like I could accomplish anything.

"Here." EarthStar patted the battered top of my second-hand table. She'd propped up a metal mirror. Magickal symbols were painted on the one-inch-thick edge with what looked like nail polish. The mirror was surrounded by herbs and flanked by two candles. As she fussed with her tools, I inspected my hands. The annoying wart I'd had on my left index finger for over two years caught my attention. I'd been thinking about going to the doctor to have it removed, but it was expensive and not covered by insurance. I hated the damn thing and found it embarrassing. I grasped at the base of the wart with my fingernails and ripped it off. It hurt, but I was happy it was gone. I limped to the sink to throw the wart down the drain and wrap paper towels around my bloody finger.

"Val, come back and take my hands," EarthStar instructed. I played along, thinking the sooner she got done, the sooner she would leave.

She glanced at my paper towel-wrapped finger and the red bloom forming but didn't say anything. Her hands were cool and dry, the skin thin like parchment. She closed her eyes. "Gaia, mother of all, hear us. Set up your guardians at the watchtowers to protect us as we scry and aim to see the spirits or gods your daughter, Valeria, has displeased." When she reopened her eyes, they had an unfocused look as she gazed at the mirror. "You who appeared to Val during the Yule ritual, show yourself," she whispered.

I watched her face absently as she scryed, my attention focused inwardly on the plot of my novel. I needed to write a romance scene—a sex scene, really—and it was one of the things I'd been stuck on. I almost laughed out loud as I thought about how I'd been afraid of what my mother would think if I wrote a sex scene! Speaking of sex . . . I glanced toward my phone on the counter next to the sink. I should text Steve and see if he could come back over tonight . . .

As if on cue, my phone dinged. I sprang from my chair to retrieve it, ripping my hands free from her grasp. Unfortunately, it was my sister. Her kids must be awake and wading through their presents.

Mom says u r still sick, it read, *but even before that, hasn't seen much of u. It's your job to keep an eye on her since u don't have a family . . . like I do.*

I texted back: *I've been busy. And sick.* Blood covered most of the paper towels I'd wrapped around my finger, so I balled them up and replaced them with new ones.

My phone dinged again. *That's no excuse.*

I typed back. *You should visit her more, you're her favorite anyway.*

Then I opened Steve's last text: *You are the sexiest woman I've ever met.*

I replied: *Get out of whatever X-mas stuff you have and meet me back here at noon.* As I sent the text, the now-familiar flowery smell wafted past me. Michelle made a noise like a hiss, and I turned around.

Her eyes were wide and terrified as she stared into the mirror, her mouth gaping. She made the hissing sound again, then gagged before slowly saying, "Val. Come. Here. Right. Now."

I just wanted to get on with my new, unafraid life. Time to kick her out. I sat and said, "Listen, Michelle . . ."

Then I saw her face—really saw her face.

It was ashen, as though something was draining her blood. Her eyes were huge and wet; her mouth a round "o." She reached for me, never taking her eyes off the mirror.

"You insulted the gods," she whispered. "You pitted them against each other. They are furious."

I sighed. "I have no idea what that means."

"You don't know who you are—you don't know what you stand for—so you don't know who to pray to. You offer sacrifices to the pagan gods; ask them to bless your spells but sit in a Catholic church with your mother. Disrespect the magic of the Vodou *loa*; offer your blood to the Feathered Serpent of Mesoamerica and awaken him in a circle meant for others . . . " She made a choking sound again. "They are fighting, now . . . you've provoked very ancient powers . . . I feel . . . I think . . . they are telling me . . . they will only be satisfied when blood is spilled." She choked once again before vomiting across my table.

I jumped from my seat, wincing as pain encircled my ankle. "Gross!"

Michelle looked up, a dribble of vomit clinging to her chin. "Val . . . I can take this away. Turn you back to normal."

"I don't *want* to go back. I *like* feeling this way. I can do anything!"

She stared at me, her face hardening and lips pursed. She grabbed the edge of the table and sprang up with surprising agility. She pointed a finger at me, the joint swollen and red. "You are a child—a child who has done nothing and deserves nothing. I studied with the greatest pagan leaders of our time! I studied transcendental meditation and ceremonial magick. I know more than you'd learn in three lifetimes!"

I laughed. "Are you kidding me? You're a bitter old woman who relies on the kindness of people unwilling to stand up to her. You are a *joke*."

"That's not true!" she screamed back. "The coven respects me!"

Someone from elsewhere in the apartment building banged on a wall or floor and yelled "Shut up!"

I laughed again. "Hear that, *Michelle*? You should just shut the fuck up."

"You don't deserve this power!" she screamed. "You don't deserve it, so *I'm* taking it!" She scrambled around the table, eyes wild, hands balled into fists, vomit still clinging to her chin.

"You and what army; you useless, pathetic old woman?"

She shrieked and flung herself at me, but her tantrum was inconsequential. I captured her hands in mine as she tried to claw at my face.

"I'll kill you, kill you! Then that power will be mine!"

That made me furious. "You're not taking anything from me! I'll decide when I'm done being unafraid!" I pushed her—hard. She fell on her back, onto the worn, stained carpet denoting the start of my living room. She made a *whoosh* sound as the air was knocked out of her.

At least she wasn't screaming.

I straddled her chest, preventing her from catching her breath. She was red-faced and livid. I pinned her arms under my knees. I unwound the blood-stained paper towels from my finger and shoved them in her mouth. "Try screaming now."

The floral perfume hovered closely around me as I placed my hands on her throat, fingers wrapping around the pale skin for several minutes, squeezing like a snake, ignoring the ache in my hands. I watched her face grow reddish-purple, watched her eyes bulge, and then she convulsed. The smell of urine filled the air.

I carefully got up from Michelle's body, glanced at the clock, and went to take a shower. Steve had told me where he lived. Maybe I could surprise him.

⁂

Since I didn't own a car, I retrieved Michelle's keys from her tote bag on my way out the door. I'd have to tell the police she was there at some point. Or maybe I could make up some story? Maybe pin it on Amy? It wasn't like she'd been a great friend to me the past few years. Or ever, really.

The old Toyota sputtered in the cold. The wind blew hard, making it veer slightly. Under my coat, I had on a thong and a sexy, floral bra. On a whim, I'd grabbed a bracelet I hardly ever wore—a thick, silver bangle in the likeness of a snake—and put it on. I'd also applied bright red lipstick. *Steve will die when he sees me,* I thought.

There were not many cars on the road—it was Christmas morning and still early. I thought about being with Steve again and couldn't wait to get to him. I increased my pressure on the gas pedal.

Unafraid

Buildings blurred in my peripheral vision as I sped toward Steve's condo. Another squall had blown up and huge white snowflakes splattered the windshield. I groped for the wiper blade control, racing through a red light at an intersection.

The road curved serpentine up ahead, and I pressed the brakes to make the first turn in time. The wind howled as the brakes locked on a patch of ice or snow, and the car went skidding . . .

I wasn't afraid, as the car spun around and around making me dizzy. I wasn't afraid, as the seatbelt yanked tightly across my chest, taking away my breath. I wasn't afraid, as the car hurtled toward a brick wall, and crashed; or when glass shards bit into my face and the airbag deployed.

As my neck snapped and excruciating pain flooded my body, as white light exploded in my head and bones crunched as they broke, as I smelled perfume surrounding me and remembered *Abuela* . . . I was weirdly happy to have lived—albeit briefly—without fear.

And as my final thought filled my mind: *I guess I'll find out what happens when you die—*

I remained unafraid.

Silver Strands

PATRICIA MILLER

This story is dedicated to my family—biological and otherwise—who provided me with support, encouragement, and a love for the written word. You're amazing!

Gentle Reader, this is a tale about a seamstress, a Malignant Force, and a purple ballgown. Let us first introduce you to the seamstress, Tamia—a simple woman of simple means who tried to do her best every day, and that was enough for her clients—brides brimming with love at approaching nuptials, expectant parents joyful for a christening, young men and women filled with excitement in anticipation of their first formal dress party. Every garment she sewed was imbued with those feelings, carrying with them her wishes for happiness and good fortune.

Her clothes were easy to wear, although the designs often hid a complexity of construction not obvious to the casual observer. The tailoring was precisely executed to highlight a client's best features and draw attention away from any perceived flaws.

She didn't disguise those flaws. Tamia wasn't one for over-tight corsets, stays, or padding; but a less generous bosom was easily overlooked when the shoulders were so gracefully presented. And no one paid attention to fuller waistlines when the eyes were drawn instead to curvaceous hips. She wanted her clients to present their best of themselves, in an authentic garment, as opposed to an artificial, fantasy version that later remained untouched, in the back of their wardrobes. Tamia wasn't rich or famous, and she didn't need to be. Content in the small village she loved, and the valley surrounding it, the occasional trip to the nearby port for cloth or notions was all the adventure she desired.

Tamia's tiny village was in a small Prefecture ruled by Governor Delor Vontelis, who had inherited the role from her father. There were whispered rumors that Delor might have helped speed up his journey to the other side of the veil.

Governor Vontelis . . . is the Malignant Force previously mentioned.

The Governor had many names and titles, including the Magistrate of Windale and the Arbiter of Peace and Justice for the State of Mangrave. She also encouraged effusive salutations such as "Your Worship", "She Who Rivals the Sun", "Your Benevolent Excellency", and—from the lips of the latest unfortunate seamstress headed to the scaffold— "You demon spawn of Satan; You ugly, fat cow; You unholy bitch."

That particular seamstress had made several errors in judgment, which had led to her untimely demise, including the creation of a one-of-a-kind ballgown. Governor Vontelis had worn that ballgown the night before, and unfortunately, it was the exact shade as the host's favorite hunting dog. The host's young son, a precocious four-year-old, had commented on the similarity in that piercing tone only achievable by children of that age, and the comment carried throughout the large gathering.

Some credit should be given to the Governor for not punishing the lad or her host; although one must admit that her anger at the seamstress so enraged her that she forgot about them until after the hanging. She had, however, managed to kick the dog on her way out of the room.

It could also be said the seamstress' dying words were incorrect, for while the governor might indeed have been an unholy demon spawn of Satan, she was also beautiful and slender as a reed.

It should now be evident, Gentle Reader, that Governor Vontelis was not well-liked. In fact, had not the punishment for saying so been fatal to the speaker, one could say she was hated and feared by everyone under her rule. Taxes were burdensome, laws were arbitrarily and injudiciously applied, and she could be as capricious as Spring weather or as vicious as a frozen North wind. No one knew what action might find them in a court— favored one day and a condemned prisoner the next. Needless to say, those who had never been brought to her attention tried their best to keep it that way.

At present, persons trying their damnedest to remain out of sight were the Prefecture's other designers and dressmakers. The latest seamstress had been the third such sent to the gallows in the past six months, and none who remained alive cared to be next. Some fled to the countryside; others departed the Prefecture for backbreaking but stable employment in the textile mills of Remora. Three took the emperor's coin and signed on as sailmakers to the exploration fleet, leaving the Empire behind for places unknown.

The vacancies left a sudden gap in the Prefecture's economy. Luxury fabrics were not sold because no one was around to sew them. No one dared host a party because guests had nothing new to wear—Governor Vontelis had a near-photographic memory and found the sight of a recycled gown or waistcoat insulting.

Weddings became intimate family affairs, with only an entry in court documents serving as notice they had taken place at all. Caterers had no clients, musicians with previously full calendars suddenly found themselves free from engagements, and large numbers of house servants were quietly disbursed into the legions of the recently unemployed, now milling restlessly about within the city's walls.

In the midst of this looming disaster, a child was born. The birth, in itself, is insignificant in our tale—other than to the parents who had awaited the aforementioned birth for months—well before the recent purge of specialists from the local fashion industry. The baby's father had been doing his level best to keep his head on his shoulders, but couldn't help crowing a little over the news that his wife was, at last, increasing with their first child.

It was unfortunate that he mentioned his great personal achievement within earshot of Governor Vontelis who congratulated him, leaving him in the awkward position of replying in a way that would not leave his future heir an orphan. He said the first thing that came to mind—he asked her to serve as Godmother.

It should have been safe, that request, for she'd always turned down similar requests before. She considered such appeals encroaching. Perhaps it was the phase of the moon, the crisp fall air, a misfired synapse in her brain; what it was, we cannot say. But to everyone's surprise, including hers, she said yes—then promptly forgot both the invitation and her response to it for the next six months.

The long and bitter weariness of Winter, with its dearth of entertainment, led to a wet and anxious Spring. The governor was bored, and boredom led to unfortunate situations, including the forced retirement of the Arch Prelate for mentioning the mantle of stars overhead during his annual address dedicated to the Equinox. Mantles reminded the governor of cloaks, and cloaks brought to mind the gowns worn under them, and well, one thing led to another, and the former Arch Prelate found himself banished to a hermitage, perched on a cluster of rocks jutting out of an inland sea, well beyond the faithful he served.

The Arch Prelate was lucky.

The governor had decided to execute the Captain of the Horse Guards (his armor was too shiny), the Master of the Hunt (she was having difficulty letting go of the hunting dog incident), four undergardeners (because of the annoying snick made by their pruning shears), and then she banished every cat from the castle . . . because one had the audacity to snag a drapery panel with its claws. Clearly, the governor had too much time on her hands.

It was late in the day, just on the sweltering edge of Summer. The Privy Council had spent much of it listening to Governor Vontelis debating herself concerning the advisability of implementing the death penalty for anyone caught singing, humming, or playing off-key (she had perfect pitch). Her side of her own argument was winning. In a moment of sheer desperation, a gentleman on the court reminded Her Serenity of the forgotten offer from the father-to-be, who had not been present that day to hush the idiot. He'd been home, instead, privately celebrating with his wife who had safely delivered their own son.

Thankfully, someone preferring to remain nameless and blameless, successfully headed the governor off with the possibility of a diversion. She was intrigued, overwhelmingly bored, or grasping at straws.

She would attend the christening.

The event was utterly unremarkable. Most who attended were thankful it didn't call for a new wardrobe, for tradition dictated they wear items handed down or passed along, from beloved family or friends, as a blessing of happiness and well-being for the new family. Her Benevolent Excellency was wearing a wedding gown (she already had four).

One of the guests wore an outfit which simply radiated benevolent goodwill towards the newborn child. The workmanship was remarkable in the eyes of Governor Vontelis, starved as she was for fashion; naturally, she inquired after the maker of such a gown. The guest had no option but to tell her.

And so, our humble seamstress, Tamia was summoned to the palace.

Tamia momentarily considered declining the governor's offer, but as it was delivered by four guards and a carriage; she had no recourse other than to accept the invitation and accompany them to the governor's residence. The letter—such forceful handwriting! —had described the need for a spectacular ball gown, 'the likes of which had never been seen before.' The governor proceeded to dictate what supplies and tools could and could not accompany the seamstress to the palace. Tamia usually sourced her own trims and fabrics, but the Governor wanted no provincial lace or weaving anywhere near her garment.

Tamia fretted over this. She understood the drape and hand of her own chosen materials and cloth but had no way of knowing the origin or behavior of the supplies to be provided.

In the end, she packed her large workbasket of sewing notions and a small satchel of clothes for herself, selecting the dullest pieces she owned. Perhaps their lack of color would convince Governor Vontelis to send her back home.

The trip to the capital took three days. Tamia used the time to make preliminary sketches of fantastical gowns from the furthest edges of her imagination. She drew gowns with long trains, billowing skirts, and corseted waistlines. She filled pages with every variation she could think of—with and without sleeves, deep backs, a modest décolletage, a daring off-the-shoulder drape. Tamia considered every variation, but in the end, it did not matter what she drew, for the choice of fabric would dictate the most suitable design.

Tamia was ushered in to meet The Magnificent Presence on a bright sunny day less than a week after the christening. A mournful hush followed her steps down the long corridors of power. The few courtiers she saw wore sad smiles. It did not bode well for a successful outcome of the commission awaiting our simple seamstress.

Governor Delor Vontelis was not impressed with the squab of a female before her. Gray on gray on gray was her first impression of Tamia, and she rarely gave anyone a chance to make a second impression. Still, there was something about the clever cut of the dull gray skirt which caught her eye. The flare of the collar, the turn of the cuff . . . for as much as Tamia dressed to unimpress, the quality of her work shone through.

How unfortunate for Tamia.

Our story's Malignant Force stepped down from the elegant chair that had been installed on a platform on one end of her receiving hall— 'twas not a throne, although she wished it to be. She had the loftiest ambitions, the governor, and thought practicing such a regal gesture might bring her one step closer to realizing her fondest desire.

She led Tamia to a sunny chamber nearby; the room held more fabric than any warehouse Tamia had ever visited. Tall rolls of silks, satins, velvet, and brocades surrounded her, along with bolts of taffeta and toile. There were bundles of lace and ribbons, crystals, spangles, spools of silk threads for sewing, and more thread wrapped in precious metal for couched embroidery. In the center of the room were three dress forms standing in splendid isolation. Governor Vontelis had no time available for anything but the final fitting.

Behind the dress forms were a dozen terror-stricken men and women. Assistants, Her Worship told Tamia, specializing in cutting, pressing, and embroidery. Tamia tried to smile, but the oppressive weight of the room's contents was overwhelming, as was its color. Tamia realized almost immediately that her commission might well bring her close to treason, for every inch of yardage was purple. She had an eye for shades and hue. She could see the finest gradient on the spectrum, but to anyone who did not have that eye, that expensive fabric was Imperial Amaranthine. They varied by only a single drop or two of dye, but the rule dictating who wore what color was etched firmly in stone. No wonder the assistants looked terrified. If anyone reported this egregious violation to Her Empress, well . . . it just didn't bear thinking of!

Tamia set down her basket and pulled out her sketchpad, only to have it pushed aside. She had already designed the gown, the governor stated, even down to the embroidered motifs to be scattered on the full skirt. She wanted three versions made—one of each, using satin, silk, and velvet. The dresses were to be completed, down to the last stitch of a gryphon's feathered wing, twenty-six days hence.

Tamia needed only to draft the appropriate pattern. She cast a critical eye over the sketches and saw they were professionally done. She would have considered the design a remarkable achievement for the governor . . . if she hadn't recognized them as reprints of a gown worn by the Emperor's late wife, just months before her unexpected demise.

Treason loomed ever closer . . .

It would be dull, Gentle Reader, to have a detailed account of the seamstress and her fearful minions over those twenty-six days, would it not? There is no need to recount every cut, every missed stitch, every tear shed as they worked into the wee hours. You do not need detailed descriptions of the crippling care exercised by those who embroidered mythical beasts, dancing on twisted silver strands across lengths of satin, silk, and velvet, nor the blinding drudgery of attaching hundreds—nay, thousands—of tiny crystals and diamonds at each intersection. The construction of the bodices alone would curtail anyone's insomnia.

You need only remember that, unlike Tamia's usual commissions of gowns and waistcoats made with feelings of hope and joy, these designs were fabricated with sentiments of desperation and fear. Every yard of fabric, ribbon, and trim arrived in that room already tinged with greed and sorrow, for much of it had been pillaged by the governor's private fleet of privateers—pardon—custom vessels. It is sufficient to let you know that despite the appalling working conditions, the dresses were completed in a timely manner for the governor's scheduled fittings.

Except for one sleeve. A small detail, a minor slip of the facing on the velvet gown had Tamia slide a pin in place and slip in a stitch to hold it fast. She cut the thread just as Your Benevolent Excellency, Governor Delor Vontelis entered the room to pass judgment over their labor. Tamia sent the others out of the room (and out of the castle; she feared for their safety if the dresses were not up to snuff). She lifted the linen coverings from the other two dress forms.

Her Worship dismissed the silk one immediately—she didn't approve of the grape tone cast by the candles. The satin gown was disregarded after a quick walk around the dress. Something about the gathering on the back, she said. All three dresses were made to the same specifications, so Tamia held little hope the velvet gown would be acceptable.

There was no time to make another; the ball celebrating the anniversary of the governor's ascension was scheduled for that very evening. The fact that Delor Vontelis assumed those duties on the day of her father's untimely death did not escape notice, but no one had been bold enough to raise any objection. The purple (not Imperial Amaranthine) velvet gown was the last available option . . . for both women.

There were long moments of examination, ponderous breaths, a sigh that could signal resignation or relief from Her Dark Beneficence. Finally, a nod of approval. Tamia helped Governor Vontelis out of the clothes she wore, removed the velvet creation from the dress form, and slipped it over the governor's head.

The fit was flawless after the corseted bodice was laced up in the back. The embroidery truly danced among the overfull skirt's many gathers. The governor spun in front of the mirrors arranged along the wall. The flare of the skirt, the glitter of diamond and crystal was precisely the effect she had desired.

She truly felt like an Empress. She certainly looked like one. She gave her arms a slight twist and felt a prick.

Tamia instantly understood the flinch. She rushed to remove the offending object, fearing for her life. However, as much as Governor Vontelis liked the gown, she had suffered the indignity of a pin touching her flesh, piercing her flesh.

Tamia's hands shook with dismay as she cautiously pulled it clear of the velvet.

For a moment, Our Malignant Force contemplated consigning Tamia to the same scaffold that had claimed the life of her three predecessors, but the gown was utterly magnificent, and the little gray nonentity had managed to replicate it three times. Upon consideration that her services might again prove useful, Tamia was dismissed with a snap of the Governor's fingers, and so the seamstress quietly followed the same path out of the castle as the assistants before her.

Another snap brought a lackey with three jewelry cases.

Shall I bore you with the two hours Delor Vontelis spent picking out just the right jewels to set off her face and figure? I shall not.

I will, however, tell you that the parure she settled on was fabricated from another successful looting, this one from the grave of a warrior princess from long ago. A brilliant arrangement of diamonds and purple sapphires, dripping in cascading tiers across and down her artfully enhanced bosom. There were matching earrings, bracelets, and a diadem.

Whatever you are imagining, add twice as many jewels to it and you might come close. It was completely inappropriate for a person of her station, but she no longer cared. She was living her dream that night, rehearsing for a time when she danced at court as an empress. She may have also had a hand in the events which led to the current emperor's widower status, but speculation into that misfortune is hardly germane to our tale, so we shall leave those such musings to your imagination, as well.

Her entrance was all she hoped it to be—gasps following the governor's every step. That many of the gasps were of stunned dismay did not register with Our Malignant Force, who was oblivious that the crowd thought she'd crossed that fine line between magnificent, and treasonous. She only viewed her reflection in a thousand panes of glass, lit by ten thousand candles, gazed upon in awe and trepidation by her entire court.

Of course, it wasn't a *real* court; there was only one true imperial court, and the Emperor was strict on imperial perquisites and privileges. Some miniscule part of the Governess understood this, but most of her mind dismissed it as semantics.

She signaled the musicians to play and selected a partner she knew had his fair share of grace. She hadn't gone through all this trouble to open the ball dancing with some clumsy fool.

Silver Strands

Patient and Gentle Reader, you have been wondering all this time, haven't you? You have pondered the course of this narrative, trying to determine when the darkness arrives, the terror strikes, the chills, the blood, and the horror emerges to engage your senses. Perhaps you have smiled at the kind and well-meaning Tamia, chuckled at the ludicrous behavior displayed by Delor . . . *Bringer of Gray Despair*.

But not all tales are shrouded in shadow from the first page. Not all tales are tragedies from Act 1, Scene 1. Some even bring a story forward with ease, soothing the reader into accepting the gradually rising path until they are suddenly at the very precipice. This is one of those stories, now teetering on the edge of a finely honed knife or, in this particular instance, on the sharp end of a pin.

The pin. The pin which, in her haste to wear the treasonous garment, pricked the skin of Her Exalted Worship, and drew forth a single drop of blood. And that single drop, minute though it was, clung to the point of Tamia's pin, and in turn passed through the fine purple velvet, so close in shade to Imperial Amaranthine. That drop, spurred on by the pain and suffering of those who fabricated the strands on which it found itself, traveled among the warp and weft, merged with the mystical motifs so emblematic of its wearer. The spirit of the artist—for there was no denying Tamia was an artist—had infused the silver embroidery with her fear, her pain, and her sorrow. And her feelings merged in turn with those of the other artisans who crippled their hands, their backs, and their eyesight to produce the cascade of hippogriffs, gryphons, and wyverns now flaring gracefully with every turn Delor Vontelis took on the dance floor.

The crowd blinked and struggled to clear their vision, for surely it must be an illusion from too much champagne, or from the candlelight illuminating the fine beadwork, making the patterns appear to move. Surely the hippogriffs did not unfurl their wings, the gryphons did not rear on hind legs and open wide their razor-sharp beaks, wyverns were not skulking upward with clawed wings outstretched toward the governor's vulnerably exposed, dazzling décolletage, dripping in jewels stolen from desecrated tombs.

Surely, the tracings which linked the beasts were not taking on the appearance of real webs, nor were the studded, diamond-eyed spiders emerging from the silken knots within their center.

Guests cautiously backed away.

Our Malignant Force was oblivious; all she was aware of was being the center of attention, as she had decreed she would be. If she noticed the widening gap between her and the other revelers, she would have considered it her due, for all eyes should be focused on her. She did not realize the eyes actually on her belonged to beasts that were slowly encroaching, slowly creeping toward the vessel pumping that vital fluid tasted through one small, solitary drop of blood.

And they wanted more. They wanted it all.

The figure of the dance brought her partner close, close enough to sense the beasts writhing against their chains, bound only by a few fragile threads keeping them from their feast. He panicked and changed the dance, for in such a state of terror, he could think only of escape. He spun her out and away from his arms . . . and fled.

So did the others. The ballroom became a mad rush through crowded doorways, a discordant echo chamber reverberating with bows drawn against strings held by nerveless fingers, horns blown from mouths parched dry with fear. The piccoloist dropped her instrument first, then the flutist, and finally, the oboist. The musicians had an easier path out—the stage exit was hidden from the guests— and through it, they all ran, without being trampled by the high-born guests now pushing and shoving their way out of the ballroom.

Delor didn't hear the music fall silent; she didn't see the fleeing guests. She was still spinning, twirling, lost in her haze of euphoria. She only heard the cheering crowd at her coronation, vision clouded by her dream of someday ruling the entire empire, not just this backwater Prefecture.

Governor Vontelis didn't feel the first rasp of a claw along her jawline, or the first flick of wyvern tail scoring her breast. What she did feel—at last—were the spiders. They had escaped from their embroidered webs, and in breaking those bonds had freed the rest of the deadly menagerie. Those spiders, their diamond-studded eyes glistening in the candlelight, swarming up from the long, full skirt, up the bodice, up the sleeves.

The velvet's luxurious pile did nothing to slow their advance. Indeed, they found better purchase within its dense nap.

Silver Strands

The governor's whirling feet slowed, stumbled, stopped. She made one last turn; abruptly aware she was alone in the vast candlelit ballroom. Alone that is, except for the deadly beasts silently stalking her. The spiders drew forth their own silver strands and began to weave an unbreakable web, catching her now flailing arms in glittering loops and binding them to her side. The wyverns took flight, carrying more spidery silk around and around her voluminous skirts until her legs were held fast. The gryphons put their beaks and claws to use at her hair, raking sharp talons through her scalp. The diadem fell, rolled under a chair toppled during the stampede of guests making their panicked exits moments before. The earrings were ripped from bloodied ears. The crystal-clear diamonds of her necklace, once so brilliant, now better-resembled rubies.

Through it all, she screamed. The guards heard the cries but did not respond, for there was no Captain to give the order. Our Malignant Force had ordered him hung months earlier. The servants heard, but they saw what happened to the undergardeners, whose snicking pruning shears had sounded their doom. No one was inclined to risk their own necks to engage with whatever was tearing at hers. As the beasts gouged, stung, and thrashed away at Delor Vontelis, the few remaining, terrified occupants huddled close in the kitchen.

Of course, that last bit is nonsense. Forgive me, for I cannot misrepresent what really happened at the end. The servants were not huddled in fear, the guards were not rudderless without a hand at the helm. In truth, they were all gathered in the kitchen, sipping on champagne, and feasting on the luxurious dishes prepared for the supper interval.

It was really quite splendid.

While they drank, they waited for the screams to fade into silence, and then they waited until morning, then the next morning, and then the following week. In the meantime, the beasts flayed the velvet to shreds, then flayed the skin underneath. One by one, the wyverns, gryphons, and hippogriffs sought vengeance for their creators.

And then the spiders ate her.

Tell Me About Your Fourth Wife

ALEX T. SINGER

To Valerie, who walked with me on Rue Delphine many times, and made it back to tell the tale.

The honeymooners landed at Charles de Gaulle Airport at 3 AM, well before sunrise. They took the train into Paris, watching the dark of the French countryside roll by. The shadows from the hills loomed far; the light from the station stop loomed near. She put her head on his shoulder and smiled. By the time they surfaced at the Île de la Cité metro stop, dawn began to creep over the line of buildings. Still, they moved with little concern as they walked along the river. They pressed their shoulders together in the cool December air, so close that only her reflection could be seen in the river below.

They'd had a Christmas wedding, and now they would have a New Year's honeymoon. Swinging their arms like children, their bags banged behind them on the uneven cobblestones of the old sidewalks.

"Does it bother you? The river?" she asked.

"It's beautiful," he answered because it was true.

Their little boutique hotel was located on Rue Delphine, with rustic orange carpet throughout and fresh chocolate pastries waiting for them in the lobby. They checked in, claimed the heavy, jangling room key, and then dragged their bags up a set of tight, winding stairs.

He did not like elevators; they reminded him of coffins. It was a small corner room with a huge bed, overlooking a little courtyard, complete with a Christmas tree. Awaiting the happy couple was a gift of complimentary champagne and glasses, sitting on the nightstand.

She closed the blinds, and together they fell on the bed, with her resting on top of him. Her skin and hair were thick with sweat from the trek, but he did not mind.

"I stink," she laughed.

"You smell alive," he said, touching her rumpled hair.

She wanted to take a bath, and he waited for the sound of water to stop before joining her, much to her delight.

"Tell me about your first wife," she said as they emerged, dripping and flushed. She never minded talking about other women in bed, a fact he loved about her.

"Alright," he said. "It was during the First Crusade. She lived in the principality of Antioch, a widowed Syrian woman with two children. She ran an inn for general travelers. No one questioned her virtue, or her capabilities for management. The inn had originally belonged to her late husband, and it had flourished after his death because she treated her guests well. She had an elderly mother and sickly sister who assisted her in keeping the quarters clean. One evening, three guests were turned away for drinking on the premises, and they took issue with her rule. They confronted her later that night when she had gone into town to fetch medicine for her sister. I heard the commotion from down the road, and when I arrived, she was clutching a knife, one man down and two advancing. She very much did not wish to die."

"Bastards," she said. "Did you kill them?"

"They never bothered her again," he said, and they smiled at each other. By then, it was past dawn. He yawned, tired; but she found herself terribly hungry. She left him wrapped up in sheets.

Squashed buildings appeared blue in the morning light, but the city smelled like dirty water and winter. She wandered the streets for an hour, taking in the fresh wind over the old rot of the alleys, occasionally checking her phone for directions.

She bought some bread and cheese from a deli two blocks down, along with a small silver knife from a kitchen store located in one of the courtyard squares. On the way back, she bought a block of beef tips from a grocery store, along with some napkins.

Upon arriving back at their hotel, she took the food to their room and then used the knife to cut the bread and cheese, before slicing the raw meat. Blood welled up between the fibers.

"Hungry?" she asked, munching on her bread and cheese as her husband awoke, mid-morning.

"Famished," he admitted sheepishly, staring at her knife.

They ate together on the bed. They laid out a napkin for the crumbs. He ate the beef tips with his fingers, sucking each carefully, looking only mildly embarrassed at the mess when he was done.

"Tell me about your second wife," she asked, watching him eat. After washing the knife, she cut herself another piece of bread. Something about watching him eat always made her hungrier, and she made certain to let him know.

He smiled, sucking on one of his reddened fingers, and loving her even more.

"Alright," he said, wiping his hands with a napkin. "She was the young mistress of an Italian banker, in Rome during the tenure of Pope Leo X. The banker was often a guest at His Holiness' great parties, and she, through his connections, secured steady work as a serving girl for these events. One evening, they held a banquet on a great barge, which was to run up and down the Arno while they drank and celebrated their Christianity. I noticed her bringing food to the Pope himself. She was diligent about her work; and, although she looked exhausted, she was still very beautiful. Food was served on golden plates and as part of the show, they threw those plates overboard, to show their devotion to God. But her lover had grown tired of her and hoped to throw her overboard along with the dishes. So, his wife would never learn about her. So he could absolve himself of his sin."

"And you saved her?" she asked softly.

"The banker chose to throw himself over instead," he said. "I suppose he had a change of heart."

She laughed and kissed him. The juice from the meat tasted like salt. After sunset, they left the cheese and the knife on their bed stand and went out for dinner in one of the restaurants along the river. She ordered a three-course meal: snails, wine-drenched beef, crème brûlée. He ordered wine.

"Hope you don't mind watching me stuff my face," she said.

"It's entertaining," he admitted. When they returned to the room, she was drunk and laughing.

"Tell me," she gasped, stumbling through the door. "Tell me about your third wife."

"Are you sure?" he asked, eyebrows raised as he scooped her into his arms.

"Yes," she said breathlessly. "Yes, yes, yes."

"Alright," he said, helping her to bed. "She was the daughter of a very wealthy, but very evil, man. This man owned a restaurant, where many people came to make shady agreements. This young woman worked as the hostess at this restaurant. She liked her work but did not like what came with it. She knew whenever someone reserved the table in the back and to the left, it meant that those guests would be dead within a month. One evening a young man came with a reservation for three. He had a conversation with her while waiting for his group. She enjoyed his company, but when the other guests arrived, they sat at that table in the back. The woman . . . She'd had enough, of her father and his games, so she slipped the guest a note in his menu. He read it before the appetizers were served. By morning, there were two bodies in the river, but neither were his. He came again the next night. He knew it would be dangerous, but he wanted to see her again. She'd had such a nice smile."

"Charmer," she teased. "What happened to the evil man? The one who owned the restaurant."

"He died suddenly. It was very sad, but not unexpected. Heart attack. Very sad for her, I'm sure."

"I doubt they were close," she said.

Her laughter suddenly faded. He had not meant to chase it away, so he frowned and leaned over. She let him make it up to her. He made it up to her for a few hours, after which she gasped and fumbled for the bread still on the nightstand. She'd worked up quite an appetite.

"You like rescuing girls in trouble," she said.

"I appreciate . . . survivors," he said. "Life is a remarkable thing. I like when people fight for it. I like it when they fight, and fight, right up until the end. It reminds me of what it means to be alive. It reminds me how . . . How it felt to live."

"But didn't those women grow old?" she asked. "If you took good care of them, they must've gotten old. They must've gotten tired."

"They died fighting for life," he said, with a sad smile. "And for that, I will remember them always. Their lives sustained me. Their lives reminded me how to be human. Their lives gave me a heart, a heart which is now yours."

At dawn, the woman took a walk. She walked out to the river, to watch the sunrise over Notre Dame, pink light on the old gray rocks. She walked back, breathing in the cold air, swallowing every breath, feeling the shiver in her lungs: wet and real, but smelling vaguely of rot. A lot of things died in the river, after all.

She bought a fresh loaf of bread from the grocer. She sat down next to her beloved and ran her hand up his chest. It did not rise and fall as he slept. It did not rise at all.

"So," she said. "Your heart's mine, huh?"

"Mm?" he said, eyes fluttering. His beautiful, pale eyes. Like marbles. Like glass. Empty and ageless.

She took the breadknife off the nightstand. She stabbed it into his chest in one swift motion. Black blood welled around the handle. The metal of it hissed and seared against his clammy flesh. His eyes flew open. He made a noise.

"W-what," he cried. He reached for her, clawed at her, but the silver did its work. His hands touched her shoulders, then fell. The muscles in his neck strained, but his head fell back across the bed. She took one of the champagne glasses from the nightstand. The blood that filled it was black and old.

It would make for a decent toast.

"Forget being human," she said, touching the glass to her red, curving lips. "Being you seems way more interesting. I think I'd like to live as long as you. I think it sounds like fun."

She held the cup aloft. "To your fourth wife— She intends to fight a little while more."

The Gladiatrix

AELTH FAYE

To Lois McMaster Bujold, for showing me that some of the best stories rely on dystopian principles.

Ista heard the roar of the crowds as she ran into the arena. She slipped on a puddle of blood and caught herself on one hand, her sword coming dangerously close to her head. But this was no time to slow down and act cautiously—she needed to intimidate her opponent quickly to win this match.

She was strong, as women went, but this time she was up against a male gladiator whose name was well known . . . Argent. In fact, everyone knew his name. He had been famous before she'd fought her first match, and that scared Ista because it meant that he had won every match he'd fought for the last five years, at *least*.

Her stomach rumbled, a reminder that she had to win. It'd been two weeks since her previous match, and the opponent had been a small-sized female. Gladiators were expected to subsist on their prey, and unfortunately, Ista was no exception.

She came to an abrupt stop, bracing her feet and lifting her sword and dagger in a defensive position, eyes skimming her opponent. He was a few inches taller and rippling with muscle.

Her stomach thought he was a great opponent. Every other part of her didn't.

Thoughts of hunger or fear were beside the point, right now. All that mattered was beating him; that had to be her focus.

Ista had noted Argent's hair was gray at the temples, a sign that age might be taking its toll on him, and he slightly favored one leg; good, weak points she could take advantage of. His weapons of choice were a mace and shield. Presumably, he would be slower, but if he got in a single blow—even a glancing one—she would be knocked down. So, she would have to rely on her speed.

Her attire was made not only for speed but for crowd appeal. Like all gladiators, what she wore was decided on by her owner, and as a woman, she was expected to look sexy. But since her strong points were speed and flexibility, wearing little armor was an asset. The engraved bronze brassiere added nothing for defense, but it didn't slow her down, either. Her mid-thigh, chainmail skirt allowed freedom of movement, yet also offered an area to take a sword cut, if necessary. Her bronze arm guards, of course, were her preferred way to deflect a cut, but the more options the better.

Her opponent was covered by a full breastplate and wore a scale-mail skirt down to his knees. It bulged a little oddly, meaning that Argent had cushioning underneath, to prevent bruising. The benefit for Ista was that it would slow down the older gladiator even more. Yes, speed and agility were definitely going to be the best strategy.

The din of the crowds grew louder, reminding her that she couldn't just stand still. One of them had to strike first, and since it didn't appear likely to be him, it was going to be up to her.

Ista stalked up to him slowly on the balls of her feet. She feinted left, right, and then lunged. His shield came up and she threw herself instantly into a backwards roll. As expected, he swung his mace into the space where she would have been standing, had she not anticipated his move.

She rolled to her feet and took a defensive stance again, brain working furiously to figure out the best way to get through *his* defenses. She was going to have to lunge immediately after he swung, that much was obvious, except there was barely a second between his swing and when he brought his shield up for cover. Any misjudgment, allowing him an opportunity to knock her sword away with his mace, would put her in trouble. If he managed to break it, there was no chance of winning, as getting a dagger through his shield was impossible. She also had her hairpin, decorative enough to look harmless, but sharpened to a needle point. However, that was her last-ditch, emergency weapon . . . one she'd never had to use, and hoped she never would.

She stalked around him, watching him turn as he seemed to contemplate any better plan than a full-on attack. As her body moved, a part of her mind started to wander.

How had things turned out like this?

Her mother had been a concubine for Duke Terence, making Ista, presumably, the daughter of a duke, though she'd never dared confirm that with her mother. Duke Terence had been poisoned, passing the position to his son, Duke Trenton. The new duke had accused his father's concubines and wives of planning the poisoning. All were then sold as slaves, except for Ista's mother and Duke Terence's first wife, both of whom had been impaled by the front gates, an example for anyone who dared question his authority or ponder murder.

Ista had been fifteen at the time, with a womanly figure and a temper that matched her red hair. The first man she'd been sold to, had decided that she wasn't worth the fight after attempts to deflower her had ended with a broken nose and wrist.

Between being sold to her second master and arriving at his castle, Ista taught herself to pick locks. Rumors had circulated that her second master liked to chain women up before having his way with them. When the rumors proved true, Ista used her new skills to escape the chains . . . then castrated him herself. She had escaped the estate grounds but had been caught before reaching the port.

Her red hair was uncommon, and that, combined with her curvaceous figure, proved her too valuable of a commodity to waste by execution, even after committing such a crime. However, it also easily identified her.

Four more men had bought her; two had succeeded in their attempts, only to discover that they quickly tired of a woman smart enough to know when she had no chance, thus avoiding giving them the pleasure of the feistiness they'd desired. Both had then sold her in disgust, claiming to have been misled by the seller.

After that, someone savvy enough to see an opportunity everyone else had overlooked, purchased her. Duchess Chroma had been smart enough to give her a few months' worth of training before sending her into the arena. Ista would never have chosen to be a gladiator, but she quickly discovered a fierce joy in defeating opponents who'd underestimated her strength and her wits.

And Ista discovered the truth in what was often said; once you've tasted human flesh, you can never go back.

In her first few matches with men, she had played the timid female, scurrying away from them, offering only weak swings until they let their guard down. But as soon as the crowds knew her name—greeting her with chants of '*The Gladiatrix*'—that deception no longer worked.

It was inevitable she would eventually lose a match, so she'd already begun work hatching an escape plan. She knew the guard rotation through the slave dungeon by heart, and knowing how to pick locks was mastered, however, getting through the main gate would require help from at least one more person. Ista had once considered trying to recruit a fellow gladiator, owned by the duchess, but the only time she'd ever met another slave whose skills and confidence she'd had faith in . . . he had been sent to the arena and never come back.

Withdrawing from her reverie, she shook off outside thoughts and focused on fighting in the arena to survive the day, thereby gaining enough nourishment to survive a few more weeks while continuing to make plans for the impossible.

Hunger was hindering her battle with the man now advancing on her. Since no better plan presented itself, she went with her usual technique and launched into a sprint.

Argent froze for a second; time enough to get close and throw herself into a roll, slicing under his shield as she passed beneath him. He was wearing leather and bronze boots, but her sword glanced above them, under his scaled skirt, and came away bloodied.

She rolled back onto her feet and lunged again, but he had quickly recovered, and she was met with his shield and descending mace. She blocked the mace with her sword, not trying to stop it, just slowing it enough that she could roll away. She prayed that her sword wouldn't break under the onslaught, but its blade of watered steel remained strong and unbent.

To an uneducated onlooker or even a trained eye, the fight appeared to be a series of lunges and last-second dodges by the Gladiatrix, while Argent methodically continued sweeping strokes with his mace. Ista could see blood sprinkling onto the sand, however, dripping from her sword to suggest that Argent was taking damage at a steady rate.

Eventually, Argent staggered, and that's when the Gladiatrix swooped in. She kicked the inside of his elbow, numbing his arm and causing him to drop the heavy mace. But then his shield came around, trapping her against his chest, pinning her arms.

She struggled, but it was pointless.

"We can both survive this," Argent hissed in her ear.

For a half-second, she froze. And, to her surprise, he didn't take advantage of her shock. Instead, he just continued whispering.

"Let me pretend to kill you. I know the guard rotation and we can escape from my cell. But I can't do it by myself. I need another person."

That sounded surprisingly like the speech she had rehearsed in case she found anyone worthy of pairing up with. But there was one main problem with his plan.

"How do I know you aren't just saying this so that I'll collapse and let you kill me in earnest?"

"My word is my honor."

She scoffed. "No such thing on the battlefield. How about this: you pretend to be dead, and we escape from my cell. I know the guard rotation too and can pick the lock on my cell door in under a minute."

"Too many unknown variables."

"I could say the same about your plan," she reminded him. "Besides, I'm starving. I can't go much longer without food. I need your meat."

He gave a low chuckle. "I have seven fresh rats under my chainmail. You can have three."

"Why not all seven and you?"

He hesitated, long enough for her to break free. But he had said enough. Now she was reluctant to kill him, as he would be a good choice for a partner. Neither of them was badly injured from the combat. Both had years of experience . . . and both had apparently been planning an escape. Yes, he might indeed be the perfect partner.

They danced around each other, both wary but unwilling to make the first move. The crowd booed over the lack of action, and Ista knew that she had to decide. If the crowd became too angry and bored, another gladiator could be sent into the arena, one who was fresh and thereby had an advantage over both of them.

"Drop your shield and I'll kill you painlessly," she shouted.

He bared his teeth and shook his head. She charged at him, but she merely tapped his shield with her sword as she went by. She came up from her roll, but then, suddenly, her arms were trapped at her sides.

"Hit me over the head with my shield. Don't hit the temple," Argent warned her.

Then, as she struggled futilely in his grasp, he let go, stumbling backwards as if she'd kicked him. She ran for his shield, which he had dropped when he grabbed her. Picking it up, she slammed it down on the top of his head.

He dropped like a rock.

She stood over him for a long moment, seeing the very faintest signs of breath and considering whether to just kill him while he was down. But she could always kill him later in the safety of her cell, if he went back on his word or proved useless. The odds of finding another escape route, however, were slim.

Thankfully, gladiators weren't expected to mutilate the bodies of their opponents, since everyone knew meat kept better with fewer cuts on it. So, Ista simply raised her arms in victory and walked around the edge of the arena, drinking in the applause of the audience.

She stripped off his breastplate, and picked up Argent's arms, then dragged him backwards towards her cell. Although panting from exertion by the time she reached it, Ista did not want to raise suspicion, so she stuffed him in the cold box in the corner, but left the lid propped slightly open.

After a moment's thought, she opened it back up and rummaged around. Sure enough, Argent did indeed have fresh rat carcasses tied under his chain mail. She helped herself to three, ignoring the hiss of annoyance she heard. Stringy and warm, they edged on gamey, but her hunger made up for all of that. She could feel strength returning to her as she tore into each one.

Night fell and the transport carrying her cage finally arrived back at Duchess Chroma's estate. It was off-loaded into the dungeons and then Ista was left in peace. She hauled open the cold box again and updated Argent on the situation.

"You ready to take off now?" he asked.

She thought about it for a moment, then shrugged. If she was going to do it, she might as well do it now—when it was dark, and everyone was tired from the match. No one would expect any gladiator to attempt a breakout now.

After checking the timing and mentally mapping out the guards, she nodded her head and strapped on her weapons. In less than thirty seconds, the lock on her cage was picked open. She grinned at the thought it was less than the minute she had boasted about. She hated turning her back on Argent but knew a certain amount of trust was necessary, and it made sense to go first because she knew the guard schedule and the labyrinth of hallways.

She'd only walked these hallways twice before; all the other times her cage had been wheeled in and out. She wasn't quite sure why they bothered to wheel her in with all the turns plainly visible but questioning that right now would be counterproductive. Instead, she concentrated on walking silently.

Would any of the other gladiators rat her out if they noticed her walking about freely? She didn't want to find out tonight.

The two arrived safely at the guard station, having avoided one guard passing by in their area by hiding in the cold box of an empty cage. She gestured to Argent, reminding him of their plan before slipping inside. Taking the first guard by surprise, she managed to slice his throat before the second one noticed. But as soon as he did, the guard yelled and grabbed for his gun. Right before he could target her, she wove and ran out the door. She slipped Argent her knife and he plunged it into the second guard's side, and Ista helped herself to his gun. She also chopped off his pointer finger to use for the fingerprint scanner on the gun. Ista wasn't sure how long a dead finger would continue to work, but hopefully, she would only need it for a few hours.

She headed back inside the guard station and saw Argent glaring at the array of buttons and switches. He said, "Don't suppose you know how to open the gate? These are coded differently from my own master's guard station."

That was an odd thing to say. Ista had never been inside the guard station as a gladiator. The only reason she knew how to work them was from her keen memory. As a child, even children of concubines were allowed mostly free range of their fathers' estates.

Then her eye glimpsed a pile of bones. She blinked as she took in what she was seeing. A tentative nudge with her foot rolled them apart, enough to get a good look. And despite being a gladiator who subsisted from human flesh, she was disgusted. Because although she was used to seeing human bones, many of these were smaller. It appeared that the guards were not just feasting on people but on children. She tried to focus on the important thing—escaping—but she struggled to shake off the disgust and horror.

"Well?" Argent interrupted.

She forced herself to snap out of it and studied the switches for a few moments. Soon enough, the pattern was clear to her. She didn't admit to Argent that she could read the coded controls either, she said that her decision was based on the worn patterns on the switches and their placement. One of the levers for the doors had to be convenient to access while watching a video feed, so that told her which bank of switches contained one. Audio switches looked different from physical controls, cutting out another swath of options.

She pointed out one lever to Argent, halfway across the room, and grabbed an identical one near the video feed. They pulled them in unison, and Ista was relieved when the feed showed the gate going up. She'd felt certain it was the right combination, but it was nice to have confirmation. Unfortunately, there was a crackle from the speaker, and someone asked why the gate was opening. Ista gestured to Argent. She had planned for this too, though she'd hoped they wouldn't have to talk to anyone.

She grabbed a foil wrapper from a cleaning kit and started crinkling it in front of the microphone, hoping it sounded enough like static to pass. Argent cleared his throat, then said, "Malfunction . . . sending . . . investigate. Stay . . . patrol."

They waited breathlessly for a reply and heaved a sigh of relief when the voice came over the radio again, this time sounding bored. "Really? Didn't they just work on that?"

Of course, now they had to come up with a response. Ista had no idea whether or not they'd done work on the gate and had to think for a moment. She whispered an idea to Argent, and they repeated the process.

"Don't . . . me . . . deal . . . morning."

"Roger that. Have them check on the mic too. You're cutting in and out again."

"Roger . . . "

The two gladiators looked at each other and then nodded. They quickly stripped the guards and pulled on the uniforms. They didn't fit well, but it was dark and if someone was expecting a guard and was bored, they might not give them a second glance.

Counting to herself, she estimated how many minutes had passed; Ista held up two fingers. She wasn't as confident in this area, as she'd only been near here total for a few hours ever, but there should only be two guards patrolling. And now that they had a gun, they could take them out long-range, if necessary to risk the noise.

Within five minutes, they hit the first guard patrolling, and Ista took him down with her dagger, which Argent had returned.

The pile of bones from earlier was still weighing heavily on her mind. Deciding to test her suspicions, she sliced open the guard's tunic, ignoring Argent's whispered question. Sure enough, the guard had a gladiator tattoo on the small of his back.

Shaking her head, she stood up and continued on their route. How could former gladiators be so disgusting . . . acting as captors for their own kind? Had their love of human meat overtaken them so much?

Argent asked what was wrong, so she explained her theory. He looked at her in surprise. "You didn't know that already?"

She shook her head. Well, she had only been a gladiator for a few years. Maybe that was something you learned later, as the gladiators you'd known transitioned into your captors.

But there was no time to dwell on it, as they could see the looming gate ahead. There must've only been one guard in the area, not two. They passed through the gate and headed for the transports. Sure enough, an emergency pilot was sitting in the break room, watching a film. Ista was going to kill him, sure that she could fly the transport well enough on her own, but Argent protested.

"What if it takes a retinal scan to fly the transport?" he said. "Are you going to haul his severed head along with you the entire way?"

She shrugged. "If I have to."

But given they were acting as a team, she agreed to take him hostage instead. Soon enough, they were aboard the transport, the young pilot visibly shaken as he tried to start it up. Ista sighed. She'd known this was a bad idea.

Still, information was good, so she carefully tracked which buttons and switches he hit in which order. She'd flown a light-flyer once before, and the controls seemed similar enough, though admittedly there were far more unfamiliar controls for larger vehicles.

"Where to?" the pilot asked nervously.

"The southern port. As fast as possible," Ista said. Once they made it off the continent, they should be able to make it to one of the anti-slave colonies.

But then she felt her weapon belt slip from around her waist and the gun was ripped out of her hands. An arm wrapped around her, keeping her from moving.

"Head for Duke Orin's estate," Argent ordered.

"What the hell are you doing?" she demanded.

She felt him shrug. "I get promoted to a guard if I bring you back to Duke Orin's estates, alive."

"Traitor," she hissed. "We could both be free. Why do you want to continue to live in a horrible place like this?"

"I'm too old to start a new life. Besides, do you really think we can escape? They fingerprint everyone going through the ports. They'll see that we're registered as gladiators and stop us there."

The transport lifted into the air and Ista seethed, her mind scrambling for a way out. As the daughter of Duke Terence, she had been fingerprinted and issued an ID, so she could accompany him and her mother on trips. Logically, nothing in the system should have been altered, as she'd never been taken through the ports for a competition. So that was one problem solved.

But there was still the traitor holding her captive. Since he'd deceived her, it seemed only fair to do the same to him.

"Damn you, asshole," she spat angrily. "But if you're gonna do this, the least you can do is give me the rest of your rats. I'm still hungry. I knew I should have killed you when I had the chance . . . "

He stepped back, training the gun on her, and shook his head. "Don't even think about it. I know you're just waiting for the chance to jump me. You'll get fed when we arrive."

She glared at him, then slumped down in a seat. A glance at the navigational screen and she was ready. When the transport turned, angling up on one wing, Argent took a quick step to catch his balance. She whipped the sharpened, decorative pin out of her hair and lunged. It went into his eye and through brain tissue, rendering him dead within moments. Of course, he still managed to pull the trigger, but a single hole in the side of the transport wasn't likely to be that big of a deal for a low altitude hop to the port.

The pilot shrieked and the transport jerked around for a moment. He risked a glance backward and his jaw dropped.

"Back to the original plan," she announced. "We're heading to the southern port."

He just stared at her until she bared her teeth, and then he jumped and started keying things into the navigational system. She watched to make sure that he entered the right coordinates, then turned back to the corpse at her feet.

After all, Ista was hungry . . . and Argent *had* promised she'd be fed.

She grabbed her knife and got to work.

The Trial of Ms. White

NORA B. PEEVY

For all of us who are broken, a little bit sad, a little bit angry, and a whole lot mad.

"Ms. White, are the allegations against you true? Did you kill seven men?"

Snow White's defense lawyer, the infamous Lilith, shielded her client with an umbrella from the cold October rain. Snow White pulled her black pleather raincoat over her head, sheltering herself from the tsunami of flashbulbs and the tirade of protestors penned behind bike-racks on either side of the walk leading to the courthouse steps.

Police in riot gear faced the angry mobs.

Some brandished pitchforks or tiki torches, chanting, chanting.

"Lock her up! Lock her up!" The motley gang thrust hand-painted signs at Snow White as she rushed past.

They read: *God hates dykes! Off with her head! The bitch is guilty!*

The crowd on the left held a six-foot banner with Snow White's face. A group of nuns held "Me too!" signs. Women: black, white, Muslim, young, old, and pregnant, dressed in black military gear or pink shirts stating, "Love is love" as they held white tapers in paper cups, singing Amazing Grace. Some held "End the death penalty!" signs.

The air crackled with tension.

As Snow White and her legal team climbed the steps of the Rhinelander Courthouse, a reporter dressed in pink, with a stylish matching tam, flitted back and forth on the steps, her wings flashing like stained glass against the camera crew's lighting.

"Rose? Rose, we're ready in five, four, three, two, one!" The main camera operator pointed at her.

"I'm Rose, your fairy godmother reporting live, from the steps of the courthouse in Rhinelander, Wisconsin where in an unprecedented move, The Fae Court is allowing reporting from inside the proceedings of one of the most shocking crimes of the century. Charged with seven counts of premeditated murder, Snow White faces the death penalty if convicted."

The camera followed Rose as she flew past a gaggle of reporters, toward the White Rabbit, who was dressed in a stylish blue double-breasted blazer, holding an oversized gold pocket watch.

His nose twitched as he side-hopped around Rose. "I'm late for a very important date. Excuse me."

Rose fluttered after him, keeping pace. "Mr. White Rabbit, do you have a statement you'd like to make, being the lead prosecutor on the case?"

He hopped up the stairs, his bedraggled and bewildered assistant at his side, balancing a mountain of banker's boxes while trying to keep his ridiculous purple top hat firmly planted on a mop of curls with the other hand.

"No comment."

"'Do you think she's guilty?"

"I s-said, nooo comment." The White Rabbit's voice echoed as he hopped down the long marble hallway.

❦

"The defense calls The Wicked Stepmother to the stand." Lilith, a buxom beauty, tried to project her voice, which could barely be heard above the crunching of beetle shells from the Fae. Titania and Oberon perched nonplussed in thrones carved from oak; decorated with feathers, pelts, crystals, flowers, berries, and insect shells, as was the custom. Titania and Oberon were attended to by a human size, golden elephant beetle with a hooked nose, and a green locust decked out in splendid servant's livery spun from the finest spider's silk.

"Objection!"

"And what is your objection, White Rabbit?" Oberon picked his teeth with a beetle's spiny leg.

"On the grounds of ch-character, my king." The White Rabbit rubbed his pocket watch.

"Adalwolfa's character has not been proven evil. This is highly prejudicial and draws sympathy for the defense's client."

"Noted. Proceed without referring to the stepmother as 'wicked.' We shall disregard this remark in our decision since Ms. White has waived her right to a jury. Continue." Oberon stifled a yawn as he leaned over and whispered something in Titania's ear—to which she twittered in delight.

The White Rabbit consulted his file as Adalwolfa sashayed to the witness box, wearing six-inch stilettos. Flashbulbs erupted in the courtroom.

"Ms. Huntsman. May I call you 'Adalwolfa?'" Lilith leaned against the witness stand, constructed entirely of small animal bones.

"Yes."

"Adalwolfa, is it true you were jealous of your stepdaughter's looks?"

"Objection! Relevancy?" The White Rabbit rubbed his pocket watch . . . again.

"If the prosecution would stop interrupting any time a girl opens her mouth, I would get to my point," Lilith growled deep in her throat, before casually tossing her long red locks over her shoulder.

"Continue, Lilith." Oberon waved his hand at her.

"Is it true you wished to be as beautiful as your stepdaughter?"

"No."

"Did you not try to have a hit put out on her?"

"That's preposterous! I only sent the huntsman after Snow White when I discovered the heinous crimes my stepdaughter had committed."

"Objection!"

"Yes, Lilith?" Titania twirled a black widow on a balloon line of silk like a top.

"My client is innocent of all crimes until proven guilty."

"This is ridiculous, Lilith! You c-called the witness!" The White Rabbit glared at his opponent. "Side bar, your honor?"

"Will the lawyers please approach the bench?" Oberon watched Titania kiss her pet spider and arrange it in her voluminous waterfall of curls like a jewel.

"Your Highness." The White Rabbit's nose twitched as if he was a junkie. "The bar where the defendant's defense client worked was recently raided by the police. There is video evidence from all the local networks and networks around the nation reporting what was found in that bar and if the defendant's lawyer would just allow me a little time to establish my case . . . "

"Oh, so now we're just assuming all women are guilty . . . until proven innocent.?" Lilith's nostrils flared.

"Well, if the broomstick fits."

"You condescending, mansplaining, self-righteous asshole!" The White Rabbit and Lilith were practically nose to nose.

"Silence!" Oberon snapped his fingers and zippers appeared over both Lilith's and the White Rabbit's lips. "We don't have time for this fiddle-faddle, and all the fanfare and cameras of mere mortals, do we darling?" He glanced over at Titania.

"Hmm?" She looked up from the game of cat's cradle she'd been playing with The Cheshire Cat. "I'm sorry dear. This is all so droll and I'm beginning to get a teensy bit of a headache."

"Someone get my queen a headache powder!" Oberon snapped his fingers at the elephant beetle servant who scuttled off for the powder. "Both of you return to your clients and cease the bickering at once. You're giving my dear queen a headache." Oberon snapped his fingers again and the zippers disappeared from the lawyers' mouths.

Lilith rolled her eyes as she walked back to her client.

"Your honor, if I may at this time introduce Exhibit A: a recording of the client's work establishment from the local news network?"

Lilith glared again at the White Rabbit. "Objection. Relevancy?"

"It's relevant because it shows how many innocent men have been murdered. The exact same number as your client is charged with. And your client worked at this bar. A bar many men from her father's paper mill frequented. Ms. White dearly wanted to hurt Adalwolfa in any way possible, including financially."

"Objection! Speculation!"

Oberon yawned. "I'll allow the prosecution leniency for the moment, but my patience is beginning to wear thin."

"I assure you, my King, we have witnesses to b-back up these statements and evidence.

The video please." All heads swiveled towards the screen projected on the wall. You could hear a teacup shatter in the silence. "Ahem. Mr. Dormouse?"

The grasshopper in the livery leaned into the dormouse's large ear. "Mr. Dormouse!"

"Augh!" He jumped and wiped a bit of drool from his mouth with his tie. "Mmm . . . yes?" He blinked, quivering as he stared into the sea of faces, staring back at him from the benches. Flashbulbs sprang to life.

"The video Mr. Dormouse. Now." The White Rabbit fiddled with his pocket watch and thumped his foot.

"Oh! Y-yes. My apologies. I had a spot of tea with breakfast and that's the last thing I remember." He scratched his head and searched his laptop for the file. "Isn't that the way it always goes? Ha. I should know by now not to drink the tea. Oh, here it is!"

On the large screen, police wearing blue gloves carried out plastic barrels. A young man in a blue windbreaker with a WISN6 logo held a microphone in front of his bulbous nose. "I'm standing here outside 'The Bucking Rose,' where authorities were alerted to a suspicious smell early Sunday morning. Upon arrival, police discovered the bodies of seven men—disposed of in barrels in the bar's walk-in refrigeration unit. Authorities will not comment on the cause of death or release the names of the victims until next of kin has been contacted, but we have it on good authority that all seven men worked for the late Mr. Albert Huntsman at the paper mill here in Rhinelander. In an interesting twist, his daughter Snow White has been working at 'The Bucking Rose' for the past six months, but she is unavailable to comment at this time, as is the owner," the reporter paused to check his tiny notebook. "A Ms. Rose Lovely."

"Boy, you can't make these names up, can you Dwight?"

"No, you certainly can't, Chuck. You certainly can't. I'll stay on the scene with more updates. They're expecting Chief Wilkinson to give a press conference sometime after lunch.

Until then, this is Dwight Mighty signing off for WISN6."

The screen went black. A loud slurping noise filled the silence. The entire courtroom, including Oberon, turned to Titania and The Cheshire Cat who floated beside her, drinking tea in great, loud sips with mock bougie pinkies up—though in The Cheshire Cat's defense, he had no pinkies, so made do with an exaggerated pouring technique which took forever and splashed tea onto the marble floor, sending the elephant beetle servant scuttling, struggling to balance a fresh tray of fried beetle backs while wiping up the mess with a piece of finely woven gold.

"My dear." Oberon blinked at Titania.

"Yes, bunnykins?"

"The trial."

"Yes, bunnykins. I think it is going just smashingly, don't you?" Titania slurped more tea and giggled.

"Continue." Oberon rolled his eyes.

"I'm s-sorry, Your Highness. I seem to have lost my train of thought." The White Rabbit rubbed his paws together.

"Is this it?" The Cheshire Cat conjured a toy conductor's engine above his head, complete with puffing smoke and a tiny waving conductor.

"Oh, poppycock!" The White Rabbit hopped up and down while the courtroom erupted in a storm of laughter.

"It appears the prosecution can't pull a rabbit out of a hat to save his client's life." Lilith smirked and wiggled her luscious hips, conscious of the cameras on her curvaceous behind.

"Objection! Lilith is pandering to the audience!"

"Make sure you get my good side, boys." Lilith bent over, her suit jacket rising to reveal her skintight, pencil skirt as she retrieved a file from her briefcase, leaving more than a few mouths hanging slack-jawed.

"This is ridiculous! Roll the next video. Dormouse. Dormouse!" The White Rabbit obviously agitated, pounded on the conference table.

"Hmmm? Was I napping again?"

"Roll video."

"Yessir."

The camera zoomed in on a closeup of a tearstained Snow White's face, her signature ruby-red lipstick smudged across her cheeks, trails of thick, black eyeliner running from her lashes. She looked paler than her namesake in a fluorescent orange jumper.

A fat detective sat across from Snow White. "Ms. Huntsman."

"Please don't call me by my father's last name. It's too painful."

"I'm sorry. Ms. White, do you understand the charges brought against you?"

"Yes."

"Do you wish for legal counsel?"

"No. I did it and I would do it all over again if I had to."

The courtroom gasped and the dormouse leapt to stop the tape. "Objection!"

"Yes, Lilith?" Oberon stared at the ceiling.

"My client was under duress when she made this false confession. She'd been at the station for over ten hours! I'd like to call a witness for her defense, at this time."

"Why not? Proceed." Oberon waved his hand at her.

The White Rabbit hopped up and down, muttering to himself over being interrupted.

"The court calls Mr. Mirror to the stand."

"W-what? He wasn't on the list of witnesses!" The White Rabbit shook his fist in the air. "This is preposterous!"

"No, this is what's called a surprise witness." Lilith turned and winked for the cameras.

"Your Highness, may I approach the bench?"

"Counselors, please approach the bench." Oberon picked up a beetle and crunched, legs sticking out from his mouth.

"Your Highness, Lilith's witness cannot be allowed. This 'Mr. Mirror' did not appear anywhere on our prepared list of witnesses."

Lilith handed a piece of paper to The White Rabbit, and another one to Oberon. "Here is a list of questions I will be asking. If Your Highness has any objections, I will refrain from questioning my witness, but I feel that would be prejudicial and in favor of the prosecution's case. Mr. Mirror clearly establishes the motive of Adalwolfa . . . to frame Snow White for the murders of those seven men, as we will prove in our line of questioning."

"Poppycock! My witness is not on t-trial for these murders." The White Rabbit jumped up and down.

Oberon glanced at the paper while twirling a greasy beetle leg. "You may not proceed."

Lilith grimaced at The White Rabbit. "So, I see The Old Boys' Club is still running hot around here." She fixed Oberon with a heated stare, and he raised one eyebrow at her.

"The prosecution will refrain from continuing to use the word 'poppycock,' as my queen is not fond of poppies." Oberon frowned at The White Rabbit.

"Piss water!" The White Rabbit made a note on a piece of paper.

Lilith stalked back to the defense table. "Your Highness, at this time, my client wishes to make a statement."

"Lilith, what could your client possibly say now that would help her case? And why haven't you informed the prosecution of this?" The White Rabbit twitched his nose, the whites of his eyes beginning to glow red. His cheeks started to blush pink under his thin white fur. "You're making a mockery of the legal system! Look at you! All of you! Playing cat's cradle, sipping tea like s-simpering sycophants, using your beguiling looks to win over the court of public opinion!" The White Rabbit hopped up and down. "And you!" He pointed at the dormouse. "Y-you're snookered! You can't even stay awake!"

"Enough!" Oberon's frosty, blue-eyed gaze froze The White Rabbit in the middle of his temper tantrum. "The court will allow the defense's statement to be accepted into evidence."

"Thank you, your Highness." Lilith dropped her pen beside her desk and turned to give the cameras a flash of cleavage. "Oops! I'm all thumbs today, boys." She grinned and licked her lips.

Snow White approached the witness box and arranged her skirt so just a hint of a red satin garter peeked out as she crossed her ankles in her white bobby socks and kitten heels.

"Your majesties, I did it. It's true. I killed those men. And I'm not sorry . . . "

"Your honors, could I have a moment with my client? The stress of preparing for trial has clearly addled her poor, sweet mind." Lilith glanced back and forth between Oberon and Titania.

"Oh, there's nothing wrong with my mind, you air-filled twat. I killed those assholes and I'd kill them again, or any other man alive like them, given the chance. You would too, if all your life you were put on display for your beauty and not your brains. And then, one day that wicked cunt of a whore-mother put a hit out on me, and I was forced to bargain with my beauty. I begged the hitman she sent after me in Central Park to not kill me, and he agreed to spare my life, but only if I paid with my virginity. I couldn't live with myself after that disgusting act, so I ran away to my father's hometown, to his paper mill here in Rhinelander. I figured it would be the last place a city princess like Adalwolfa would look for someone like me. I got a job at 'The Bucking Rose' and things were okay for a while. I fell in love with a sweet gal named Betty Lou and things were going swell until I got a stupid parking ticket and was summoned to traffic court. Betty Lou intercepted my mail, and after discovering my true identity, she contacted my whore of a stepmother in New York, at Trump Tower. The two of them became lovers. and then hatched a plan to have me killed and split the insurance payout, along with my father's inheritance. And that's when I decided, if I can't beat 'em, I might as well join 'em, so I hatched my own little plan to sabotage my father's paper mill any way I could. Yes, I killed those disgusting pigs that came into 'The Bucking Rose' night after night from the paper mill, catcalling and pinching my bottom when I bent over to get their beers, actually offering me money to blow them on the vomit-stained floor of the shit-stained head in back. I gutted them like fish and then after bar closing, I'd stay late to clean by myself and dispose of the evidence in a few barrels. I hid them in the back of the refrigeration unit. A girl that knows how to use a meat grinder, a mop, a box cutter, and a pallet jack can do anything. My momma, my real one, always said I could be whatever I wanted to be." She stopped talking, eyes glistening with unshed tears.

Lilith sashayed to the front of the courtroom, gesturing to The White Rabbit to join her. "In light of my client's confession, the defense wishes to move to the sentencing phase of the trial and rest our case."

"The prosecution has no objection." The White Rabbit straightened his bowtie and wiggled his ears, satisfied with his victory.

"Very well. Dear?" Oberon put a hand on Titania's shoulder. She sat with her head bowed, snoring louder than a hippopotamus.

"Mmm?"

"Shall we go to the sentencing?"

"Oh, yes. This is my favorite part!" Titania picked up a snoozing, veiled chameleon by the tail, turned him upside down, and banged his head on the arm of her throne like a gavel three times. "Guilty, guilty, guilty!" Titania laughed, as did the rest of the courtroom.

"And that's how I got here boys," Snow White said in a husky voice. She wore a 1950's reproduction of Marilyn Monroe's cocktail dress from 'A Seven Year Itch.' "Giovanni's Grand Guignol" flashed in glam Broadway bulbs above her head on stage, as she smiled and posed on a windy subway grate, just like in the movie.

"But that Titania has a bit of sass in her, that ole' gal. She decided to pardon me, even though she knew I was guilty, so I could share my story with you for all eternity, and murder all you mortals, until Titania's had her fill. Wasn't it Oscar Wilde who said, ***"Life imitates Art far more than Art imitates Life?"*** Eat your heart out, boys."

Another gust of staged wind from a fan below the stage rustled Snow White's dress as she leaned seductively into the audience filled with men who paid to see her act, hoping to be asked onstage. She pulled a pair of steel chompers, with diamond chiseled points, from thin air and popped them between her ruby red lips.

"Or I'll eat it for you," Snow White's eyes darkled as a gurney rolled itself onstage. A lumberjack lay strapped to the black leather table, his traditional red flannel ripped open, exposing white flesh as he screamed and screamed . . . while dainty Snow White, in her glittering kitten heels approached her meal.

The Woman in the Woods

SARAH JANE HUNTINGTON

I'd like to dedicate my story to Ida Ward, my grandmother. The strongest and kindest woman I've ever known.

Seventy-eight-year-old Alice Elizabeth Willshaw pressed her good ear against the door and listened carefully. She knew it was out there; sensed it—the knowledge it was stalking her—felt deep inside her very bones.

Besides, she could smell the beast from the awful, rancid stench it carried.

It was a strange feeling . . . the thought that only a single wooden layer stood between her and possible death.

"If it decides on tryin' to get me tonight, what'm I gonna do?" Alice asked herself, shaking her head to chase away the fear gripping her. "All I got's Levi's 39-year-old shotgun, may you rest in peace, my darlin'." A single tear slid down her cheek as she stared at her hands, now rigid from that damned arthritis.

Would she even be able to hold it properly, let alone pull the trigger?

For nearly two months she'd been plagued by odd noises outside. At first shuffling. Then it sounded as if something was rummaging around.

When the banging and scraping and growling had begun, more fervent every night, she'd called that useless town sheriff.

He'd come and looked around, assuring her it must've been raccoons.

220

"Ya' know, Alice . . . Living out here alone like this, a person can be prone to an overactive imagination."

Irritated, she slammed down her cane. "I'm tellin' ya'! Ain't no raccoons. Sounds like . . . like a Bigfoot!"

He'd stared at her as if she was delusional, irritating her further when he'd stood and patted her on the shoulder, then, as if speaking to a child, had said, "That's nonsense. You must've been dreaming. Bigfoot doesn't exist, Alice."

Oh, but they do.

"You know, we have a place in town called Shady Pines—" he'd begun.

She'd cut him off before he could finish, otherwise, she'd have been cussin' him out. "Thank you for your time, Sheriff. You have a good afternoon."

"Think about it, Alice."

She'd stood slowly, her eyes never deviating from his beady gaze. "Please call me Mrs. Willshaw."

"Yes, ma'am," he'd said, tipping his hat.

Good riddance.

"What in tarnation do ya' want," she whispered, feeling afraid as she gripped her walking stick tightly and backed away from the door. She could hear it, rummaging in the trash bins, most likely looking for any leftover food scraps. Well, money was too tight, so it wouldn't be findin' any. She only had one cooked chicken, and maybe a potato or two, to last the whole week.

Outside, the night was dark; as if a black blanket was thrown across the rural area after the sun descended. At least, it felt that way. The moon was nothin' more than a shard, not big enough to offer light to see the intruder clearly.

Alice lived alone in her small cabin, surrounded by thick woodlands, miles away from anyone who maybe would help her. Her husband had been her only company for over thirty-five years, and now he'd been dead for six. Levi had been a vibrant, happy man . . . now, all that was left of him sat on her mantlepiece. She often shook her head in disbelief that a man of his considerable size, who'd been so chock-full of life, now dwelled within the vessel above the fireplace.

Just ash inside a pretty urn.

Still, her wrinkled hand lovingly caressed all she had left now, in this world. Oh, how she missed him! They were never blessed with children, and now she was all alone.

So now what?

For a brief moment, her mind pondered on that infernal sheriff's suggestion the other day—*no!*

Maybe she was scared, but she was also strong-willed. She swapped her walking stick for her husband's old shotgun and pointed it at the door, her arms shaking uncontrollably.

"Don't you dare get in," she whispered. Then, raising her voice she yelled, "Get on outta here! This is my house! Mine . . . "

Her voice trailed off as her thought turned to the truth in those words. She and her husband had built this home with their own two hands. She'd helped fasten every nail and screw. Her blood, sweat, memories, and tears were in the essence of her cabin, and she would not leave it. She wasn't going to be driven out by any wicked beasts or monsters.

Or any smart-ass sheriff.

Would it leave, once it understood there were no food scraps? Or would that be the turnin' point, when it decided to catch fresh *human* meat and come shred her to pieces? She didn't know the monster's intentions, but she'd deal with the situation herself.

She heard it again! Alice gave a raspy chuckle. "Ain't enough out there to feed a sparrow. Food's getting too dear to throw any of it away."

Despite her bravado, the night was thick, the darkness closing in on her.

She was *all alone now, wasn't she?*

Alice's mind turned back to thoughts of what was outside. If it didn't find anything to eat—would it decide on a human meal, just for variety's sake?

Maybe it would leave, once it understood there were no food scraps . . . or maybe it would change its mind and decide to catch fresh human meat by shredding her bag of bones to pieces? She shuddered at the thought and cursed herself for being so skittish.

She heard the trash bin get angrily kicked over. Now it would prowl around the perimeter, stalking, staying far enough away that she'd only caught glimpses of its enormous form from the shadows cast on the wall. She knew what it would do, how it would behave.

It was the same most nights.

Tonight, however, the thing outside scratched insistently on her kitchen door, before drawing out a single, menacing rake down the wood. It made her heart jolt.

"Wretched brute," she muttered.

It wouldn't dare go near town unless it wanted that sheriff and his posse on its trail.

That only left a poor old widow to harass and scare.

She placed the rifle carefully on the table and grabbed her walking stick, stumbling slightly as she stood. Her knees and bones weren't what they used to be; movement some days was an epic struggle.

Into her living room, she walked: stick, step, stick, step. There, there it was, passing by the big front window.

It must be seven feet tall, or more. She wouldn't stand a chance against it.

Her mind fizzed and popped, and for a moment she questioned her own sanity. Then another raking sound snapped her out of it, and she imagined the huge claws it must possess to create such a noise. Who knew what that thing might be capable of?

Alice remembered glimpsing it . . . once. *How could she have forgotten that?* It had given her nightmares for weeks.

The doors and windows were locked, as always, so unless it smashed its way in, it couldn't get to her.

Could it?

There was a thump, and then she heard something new . . . whimpering. A more muffled noise, as if distressed.

What was it doing?

Ordinarily, it growled, and banged on her walls, in a show of strength. It never . . . cried.

Alice couldn't stand the new sound. The tone it carried seemed filled with pain and sorrow.

Could it be injured? Or was this some sort of trick?

"Animals can't think like that," she reasoned aloud.

Alice had always loved animals, nature, and everything the woodlands entailed. That's why she wanted to live out here, in such an isolated area. She adored feeding the birds, and all the other little wild creatures that came to visit. She hadn't been able to walk through the woodlands for nearly a decade, but years before, she did so every day. She'd known all the wild pathways by heart. This land belonged to her, and she belonged to the land. Life had always been peaceful and wonderful . . . until this intruder came along.

The creature, the thing outside, whimpered again.

Should she try and help it?

No, it had to be a trick, a way to lure her outside.
But what if it wasn't?
The sorrowful sound was pitiful and had a familiar ring to it. She had been lonely and alone, two very different things, but both painful in their own way. She was certain what she heard . . . was pain.

The only people she ever saw were her food delivery woman from the town store, and that idiotic sheriff, who felt it was his duty to check on her once a month.

She had wondered more and more lately, if something happened to her, how long would it be until someone found her? Would it be weeks until her death was even noticed?

Despite the trepidation gripping her, she wobbled forward and peeked through the window. All she could see was a heap of hairy darkness, curled up next to the sole chair on her porch. And there was that sound again—that awful, gut-wrenching sound, filled with misery.

Alice couldn't just listen.

Do something! Her mind screamed at her unforgivingly. "Alright, alright," she said.

The thought struck her that if the beast had truly wanted to hurt her, it could have smashed her windows, could've found a way to break in. Yet all it had done was knocked and scratched and made a lot of noise. Alice wondered now, and not for the first time if violence and savagery had never really been its agenda. Perhaps . . . perhaps she had allowed her fear to misinterpret the situation.

Miscommunication, mixed messages, assumptions, and expectations—it's what Alice had always hated about people; it was the main reason she had preferred living away from the flock. Now, was she doing the exact same thing . . . making assumptions?

What if she had it all wrong?

She'd never considered the possibility that perhaps *she* was the trespasser on *its* land. Maybe she'd been the invader.

Three light taps on her window broke the silence. She could see it was the creature's hand, then it fell away and she heard whimpering.

To Alice, it sounded like a desperate plea for help.

Be brave, be strong.

"No fool like an old dang fool," she mumbled as she hobbled into the kitchen. She needed her first aid kit, and perhaps the roast chicken she had in the fridge as a peace offering. Maybe a bribe not to eat her.

The night was cool on her skin as she stepped outside. She sucked in a deep lungful of the woodland air surrounding her.

Alice thought back to the time she helped those tiny baby birds—how she'd loved them and fed them, cared for them as if they were her own children—until one morning, they'd flown away.

The sight had left her heart filled with joy.

Then there was that raccoon with an injured paw that she'd helped heal. He had never tried to hurt her. Animals were smarter than most people gave them credit for; they had an intuitive sense about them.

Wild didn't always equal dangerous.

She knew what it was, despite the disbelief that filled her head. She'd heard rumors.

The folks in town thought she was crass and foolish, living out in the woods all by herself, but Alice was neither of those . . . never had been. Underneath her rough exterior, kindness, bravery, and compassion for all living things dwelled inside.

Swallowing her apprehension, Alice decided that if she was about to join Levi in the afterlife, then dang it, at least she would die on her own porch, trying to do some good.

Stick, walk, stick, walk. The sound echoed as she rounded the side of her house, and sure enough there it was.

A Bigfoot!

Its huge body jolted upright when it spotted her, and then using its large feet, scooched back some. In the wide brown eyes, she saw exactly what she'd been feeling. It was wounded and vulnerable, wary of her intentions. Closer, she realized its face had humanistic features, and she was witnessing intelligence, pain, and fear. The noise from her stick hitting the wood was making its body jerk in panic.

"Hush now," she said, using her most soothing voice. "I'm going to help you."

A few more slow, shuffling steps and she was near enough to touch the tangled fur that covered its body. She took the chicken out of the bag. The creature sniffed the air, clearly interested.

"Yes, yes, this is for you. I'm giving you my supper, so you behave now." She wondered about the possibility it had seen her helping other animals, and that's why it came.

"There's nothing to fear from this old woman. You ain't got no cause to be afraid of me." She chuckled softly and said, "Here, fill your belly, nibble on this." With shaking hands, she passed the chicken over. The creature snatched it and immediately began eating.

With the light from the inside of her house, she noticed a small pool of blood dripping steadily onto her wooden porch. A nasty cut was visible through matted hairs on its calf.

"Well," she began, "you been botherin' me for nearly two months now, then you come here lookin' for help. Seems kinda back to front, if'n you ask me."

The creature responded with a chattering noise, as if trying to apologize or explain, then tilted its head to the side, the way a dog does when you speak to one nicely.

She carefully sat down in her rocking chair, by its side, and watched—both curious and amused—as the behemoth practically inhaled the chicken, bones and all.

A real-life Bigfoot on her porch.

Alice knew the folklore and indigenous legends and had always guessed there was a kernel of truth in them. Now, here was one in flesh and blood, and the enormous one beside her looked intimidating, no doubt able to rip her limb from limb if it wanted.

It ate despite its injury, but then turned those big eyes back to her, using a moaning sound to plead for assistance.

"I can't bend, not at my age, so you best show me the damage." She pointed to the injury, then to her lap.

It seemed to understand and raised its thick leg high, resting it lightly against her.

She assessed the wound; it wasn't as horrific as she'd first guessed, but it was deep enough. Nothing that some care and time couldn't fix. She took the items she needed out of the first aid kit, holding each one up.

"Now, this might sting," she said. "But don't you holler at me none, 'cause it needs fixing." She poured Mercurochrome over the cut—she still kept some around—and cringed when the creature growled deep. She quickly applied antibiotic ointment on the area, the good stuff that helped with the pain.

She patted its knee gently as she wrapped a simple ace bandage around the calf. It only wound around the meaty calf twice, but it would have to do. "There, there," she soothed. It huffed, as if satisfied, before crunching a stray chicken bone as it regarded her carefully.

"You ought to be more careful out there," she warned. "Other people aren't as likely to help as I am. They might capture you, or—" As she looked her new friend over, she couldn't say what was in her head. "So, I s'pose you did right, by comin' here."

They sat quietly together for a few moments until whistling and banging erupted from the dark, thick, impenetrable woods. Communication by means of loud noises.

There were more of 'em out there, alright. The creature beside her instantly became alert.

"Get gone then," she said. "Back to your friends, and no more frightnin' me. I'm old." Before she could blink, it limped off into the night, moving away far faster than she'd have thought possible. He . . . or she, looked fierce and majestic, full of power, yet with a quiet and strong grace.

How she envied the ability to move like that.

She'd been wrong. That poor creature was no monster. It seemed more human than many of those townsfolk.

"Hmph. What a night," she mumbled to herself. "I figger, maybe I'll finally get a good night's sleep." She picked up her first aid kit but left the few scraps of chicken for whatever possum was brave enough to come this close to the house, then hobbled back inside to retire for the night.

The next day brought two surprises.

As soon as she woke to bright sunlight streaming through her bedroom curtain, she forced her creaking body to move. She went and opened her door, wondering if she'd dreamt the incident last night, only to find a huge Musky and a Channel Catfish lying near her doorstep.

She knew the fish were a gift of gratitude and laughed with glee. A full-bellied laugh . . . Alice was sure she hadn't felt this happy since before Levi had passed. She looked forward to a decent supper since she had given away her chicken.

The second surprise she was not so pleased with. The sheriff pulled up near her house, put his big hat on, and hitched up his trousers, in a manner that made her think he musta believed himself to be John Wayne.

Ha! As if!

Alice rolled her eyes over his theatrics, then put on her best fake smile, and waved.

"Just checking in," he told her.

"Don't worry, I ain't dead yet," she said. "A visit twice in one month; I'm flattered, much obliged."

She really wasn't, though.

The sheriff let out a humorless chuckle, then wiped his face and looked at her with a grim expression.

Oh, how she despised this man . . .

"Some hikers nearby reckon they saw a Bigfoot in these parts. I'm thinkin' it's some kind of crazy fellow, dressed up in a fancy Halloween costume. I'm wonderin' if maybe you saw anything unusual, since you mentioned seeing some kinda monster before. I decided it best to come out here, to see if you needed rescuing."

Alice frowned. "I don't need no rescuin' Sheriff. And I don't recall seeing your Bigfoot."

"No?" he asked, raising an eyebrow.

"Nope, I ain't seen nothin'. It's been just as quiet as weeds growin' in a graveyard around here, for some time now."

"Strange . . . last week you were telling me all about them," he said smugly.

"All due respect, Sheriff." *Smug bastard certainly hadn't earned any in her book.* "You said yourself, bigfoots don't exist. Remember? You told me so, your own self, so it must be like you said. Just some crazy fool dressin' up and playin' tricks. But lately, I ain't seen 'em."

"Yeah, yeah . . . gotta be it, some kind of prank," he said. Seemed like he was trying to convince himself more than Alice. "Well, if you're sure you don't need me, I'll be on my way."

"Mind how you go, now." Occasionally, what she was thinking slipped out.

"Say now, Alice, you'd tell me, wouldn't you, if something . . . or someone was hanging around and making mischief?"

Oh, but she had tried to tell that fool before, tried to explain. At the time, he hadn't given a rat's ass about her distress or her safety . . . not one bit.

"I reckon so," she fibbed, making a mental note to check her porch for any blood or leftover chicken bones. "Got a deep respect for the law, Sheriff. You know that."

The sheriff tipped his hat and got back into his car, backing up and driving away, down the long dirt track.

Good riddance. Alice thought to herself and smiled. It was kinda fun for her, to have a secret friend. No one in town ever cared enough about her before, to drive out and check on how she was managing, not even after her Levi had died. No doubt the sheriff was only doing his duty. Such was life.

For her, things had taken a strange yet wonderful turn. For once, she wasn't as alone as she thought and the woodland, her land, was still as wild and magical as ever—maybe even more so.

Alice sat outside most of the day, watching and waiting, but it was almost nightfall when her newfound friend finally came by. She saw the big shadow prowling the tree line first. The limp was already less, and she was glad to see the bandage had held.

"Come on out, then," she called. "I saved you some."

She raised a dish with the fish she'd cooked. She had been tempted to eat both, but one was filling enough, and she wanted to share.

The Bigfoot padded over, the ground vibrating underneath its gait. Quite a sight to behold, real power in every movement it made. This time though, she had no fear, only awe.

To her shock, she noticed a little one following—lighter in color and half her own size.

A child!

The youngster dashed straight to her vegetable patch and dug at the potatoes she'd been growing. Alice didn't mind one bit. She felt about as giddy as a schoolgirl, as she watched the little one's antics.

Such a wonderful sight!

How beautiful the scene was, how otherworldly.

The big creature sat on the porch beside her, and grunted towards the youngster, chomping happily on a potato. It was then that Alice realized this creature . . . this, Bigfoot . . . was a she! A mama.

She happily slid the dish toward her and smiled a big, genuine smile. As she watched her eat it with massive, human-like hands, she felt awestruck. Motioning to her child, the mama Bigfoot tore off a good-sized section of meat for her little one.

It seemed to her, that they had more humanity than many a human she'd known.

She was choked up, watching her pat the young one on the head. The child purred underneath its mama's loving touch, and watching the tender moment brought a tear to Alice's eye.

"That's a mighty fine youngster ya' got there," she said. With the birth of her new friendship, between them, a bond was forged.

The words of the sheriff came to mind. *"I came out to see if you needed rescuing."*

Rescuin' indeed. Alice had never needed such a thing. And besides, now she realized she was among friends.

And she thought to herself that she best practice holdin' Levi's shotgun . . . just in case that fool sheriff decided to come 'round at the wrong time. Because Alice understood that she would never be lonely again, not in this life or the next.

Mergers and Acquisitions

Elaine Pascale

This is dedicated to the women still struggling to be heard. Blast your words as if they were made of fire.

It was not unusual for Sara to sip her latte angrily while staring at the framed photo of the founder of **Azendolie**. She held no animosity toward him directly; he had simply become the symbol of her frustration at work. Despite her degrees, connections, and stellar track record, she felt she never received the same credit as her male colleagues. She was one of the few women in a decision-making role in the company yet was never included in the fishing and golfing excursions that were designed to promote 'bonding experiences' amongst the executives. The portraits and photos that celebrated the company's various successes decorated the walls of the hallways and conference rooms: *all male faces.* Sara felt like the men at **Azendolie** were respected and well-liked, while the women were always an afterthought.

Case in point: the founder's secretary had stopped coming to work shortly after his death over a year ago, and not even a mention of her had been made. No one bothered to find out why, or what had happened to her. If the poor woman was in trouble, there should've been some offer of help, considering she'd given twenty-five years of her life to the company. Sara knew it wasn't unusual for secretaries not to have their portraits on display at major corporations, but if she had died . . . *Why hadn't there been a memorial service?*

Sara also knew that in her role as a junior executive, she made sixteen to eighteen percent less than her male counterparts . . . But that wasn't what was preoccupying her thoughts now—it was the fact that the *Provident acquisition* had been *her* project.

Sara considered the Provident acquisition to be an independent deal; while representing the company, all decisions had been made with full agency approval, just as she made all business decisions. She had conducted the research, finalized the planning, and performed extensive financial and risk analyses. She had handled the major negotiations; then, her *senior* junior executive, Tim O'Leary had inserted himself into the closing and integration strategy and had talked right over Sara during the **Azendolie** finalization meeting. Despite her stressing that over ninety percent of the project had been hers and hers alone, the executives in the meeting favored Tim. Ignoring Sara's contributions, they had leaned over her as if she were an empty chair, to shake Tim's hand and pat his shoulder. Sara stood, forcing her hand into the round of handshakes. Her hand was received limply . . . as if it were contaminated, as if her very femininity was contagious.

A man with a slight lisp turned to both Tim and Sara but addressed only Tim.

"The CRC account is up for renegotiation. I think we can increase our percentage there."

"We may want to risk that percentage and aim for the recognition they could bring us in the Malaysian market. They are a name there, and we aren't."

Sara had stepped closer to the executive, positioning herself in front of Tim. "The return would be so much greater than measly percentages."

The man stroked his chin before nodding to Tim. "You two get on that."

Despite the edict that they collaborate on *CRC*, and despite Sara's repeated mentions of her work on *Provident*, both projects were listed beside a picture of Tim on the company webpage. He was smiling and looking slightly over one shoulder, in the same manner that the deceased **Azendolie** founder did in his portrait. Tim's bio and contact information were provided to clients. Sara knew she was being edged out of any important communication, but she refused to let her imprint vanish; she would not simply disappear like the founder's secretary had.

"Revenge is in order," Sara's friend, Trisha announced when she tired of listening to the constant complaints about Tim, and the *Provident acquisition*. Trisha's personality type prioritized action over words.

"Tim is an odd duck; I don't know that he would even recognize revenge," Sara lamented, stirring her after-work latte in agitation.

Trisha considered this. "He might not, but his wife, on the other hand—"

Sara feigned clutching invisible pearls. "We do not go after other women, remember? We adjust each other's crowns or some such bullshit."

"Fuck her. It's the price you pay for marrying an asshat."

Both Sara and Trisha had sworn off men months ago. They had reasoned that no man knew how to respond to them correctly, or how to clean up after himself; none understood that decorative pillows needed to be removed from the bed before putting their sweaty heads down.

"I guess she might have to be collateral damage," Sara conceded. "What are you thinking?"

Trisha smiled, eyes bright with mischief. "We hire a prostitute to go to his door and say he never paid her after their intense pegging session."

Sara's eyes widened. "Honestly, I love it. It just doesn't feel . . . like me."

"But it feels like me, right?" Trisha wiggled her eyebrows. "I got friends in low places, you know. I could make things happen." She laughed. "Plant drugs, falsify documents. I am still partial to the prostitute idea, though."

Sara sipped her latte thoughtfully. "Hmm, what if we hired a prostitute to come to the office? Embarrass him in front of everyone?"

"Girl, you don't need to embarrass him to look good. Honestly, you have brought more money and resources into that office than anyone."

"I wouldn't say anyone—"

"You wouldn't? Cause that is what I have been hearing. You

work like a dog. You barely take any time for yourself, and you are knocking contracts out at an unheard-of pace."

"Keep talking," Sara teased.

"I don't have to. You know what you bring to the table."

"No one else seems to."

Trisha frowned. "They will. Just keep being that 'squeaky wheel.' Force them to notice you."

Sara tilted her cup toward her friend. "Next time, the drink is on me. Thanks for listening to me vent. And you are right—I'm going to take Tim head-on. The men in the suits will realize who their MVP is."

"*CRC* is merging their brand with ours for international marketing." Sara passed the poster boards across the table to Tim. She had scheduled one of the meeting rooms for their work, making sure her name was listed as the person leading the meeting in the company's notes. "Legal has approved the new images and insignia." She traced a finger along the emblem. "Both corporations remain distinct, but the blending of missions is evident in the color scheme."

Tim nodded. "It is important to remain an individual . . . "

"I wouldn't call a company an individual, but it *is* important to retain identification. As **Azendolie** makes headway—"

"—you have to keep your head and not be absorbed by . . . " Tim was muttering and tapping the table nervously.

"You ok?" Sara noticed the dark bags beneath Tim's eyes; they had not been visible in the photo taken for the website. His skin appeared pale and damp, and he seemed jittery.

"Just a migraine." He looked at the poster boards. "This is nice work Sara, a truly strong campaign. It makes me . . . " He glanced at the ceiling of the small meeting room.

"Makes you what?" She found her hands reflexively squeezing into fists. She knew he would find fault or find a way to sabotage her work.

"Worried. You are doing so well—"

"You afraid of a little competition?" she asked, cutting him off.

"No. That is not it at all. You aren't listening to me. My god, Sara—*I have seen things*—you don't understand everything that happens behind the scenes."

"Now you are acting as if I am some naïve ingenue. I have degrees in both management and business law, you know!"

Tim glanced over his shoulder. "Not just behind the scenes, Sara. I am talking about the foundation, the *very foundation*. You aren't understanding . . . I am talking about what is happening at the *ground level*." Tim punctuated his final words by pounding his fist on the table in front of him.

"You are sadly mistaken if you think you are going to scare me off this project. I do not get easily overwhelmed, nor have I ever quit."

Looking deeply into her eyes, he said, in a voice that sounded sincere, "I recommend that you do."

Heat climbed up her neck and her face grew red with anger. "You want me to quit the project?"

Tim hung his head. "The company. Quit the company. *Quit everything, while you still can.*"

⁂

"That guy is such a . . . there are no words. It sounds like he threatened you!" Trisha huffed as they left the restaurant. Sara had paid for dinner, as compensation for her friend having to sit through yet another bitch session about her work. They strolled toward the center of town, where Trisha would hop on the subway and Sara would continue her walk home.

"I still can't believe it. The audacity. Apparently, I put some sort of fear into him with my business prowess."

"Well, you certainly are scary. Especially without makeup."

They chuckled together before passing a group of women, who plied their trade by the abandoned stores that were reproducing at an alarming rate. Businesses were folding regularly; it was nothing short of miraculous that **Azendolie** consistently stayed flush.

"You up for more trouble?" A tiny brunette asked, and Sara realized she was talking to Trisha.

"You really don't put much stock into discretion or confidentiality, do you?"

"I didn't realize it was a secret," the woman retorted.

"Bachelor party," Trisha explained to Sara.

"Do you go to those often?"

Trisha rolled her eyes. "It was for Justin."

"But he's gay."

"That was the joke."

The brunette pointed to Trisha. "This one likes her jokes."

"Pay me enough and I will laugh at all your jokes," a blonde interrupted.

"Actually—" Trisha began.

"Oh no you don't. We aren't doing *that*." Sara grabbed her friend's arm and pulled her along. "Thank you, but we are all set," she called back to the women. Trisha had her head turned and was mouthing something, yet Sara managed a stronger tug to disengage the woman.

"He deserves it, Sara."

"I am going to handle things my way."

"And how has that been working for you?"

Sara stopped walking. "What you want to do won't change anything. The 'boys' club' will just pat him on the back. I need the spotlight on *me* and away from *him*."

Trisha seemed to be mulling this over. "It would make him look like a douche."

"He does a good enough job of that on his own."

"I just hate to see you—"

Sara stopped further conversation by pointing up the street. "I am heading home. I am going to take a long bath and eat some chocolate. I will wage war again tomorrow."

Trisha nodded. "I see your chocolate and raise you a few shots." She gave Sara a quick hug before turning to get on the subway. "And maybe an edible to even things out," she said, laughing.

"Be careful," Sara called, knowing her caution would be ignored . . . as it usually was.

❧❧❧❧❧

Sara entered the office with a renewed resolve and began crafting the documents for *CRC*. All documents had her signature first, with Tim's beneath. She was copying contracts using the new merger template when she spotted a woman getting off the elevator. Sara recognized her immediately—the small brunette that Trisha had hired for Justin's bachelor party. Sara cursed herself silently for not taking the time the night before to ensure her friend had boarded the subway, but realized that the transaction probably happened after Trisha had filled herself with liquid and herbal courage.

"I can't believe she went ahead with this, even after I told her not to." Sara bristled, not truly shocked that her wishes had been ignored. Trisha thought she knew best, and it was impossible to stand in her way when she wanted to have "a good time." Sara's stomach dropped; this was the opposite of a good time. This could completely backfire, and HR could have her packing her things before the hour was up. Sara dropped her papers on her desk and moved to intervene, but she was not quick enough. The woman had reached the secretary's desk and was already asking for directions. The brunette gave Sara a nod before heading to the closed mahogany doors of the main conference room.

Once the woman disappeared into the conference room, Sara texted Trisha. "Are you out of your mind?"

Trisha texted back. "Usually, yes."

"You know what I am talking about."

"Oh, did catering arrive?"

"Not funny. I am pissed."

"You are innocent, my dear. You did nothing wrong. In fact, I would pretend like I knew absolutely nothing if I were you."

"She nodded at me. What if someone saw?"

"I thought you were basically invisible there?"

Sara groaned and slid her phone to the end of her desk. She had to ignore everything and keep working. Now, not only did she need to make certain she was in the spotlight of the *CRC* deal, but she would look suspicious if she kept glancing at the conference room door.

A few moments later, her phone vibrated, and she checked it to see Trisha's message: "Let me know what happens. Don't be afraid to film it, if it gets explosive."

But Trisha would have to wait, as would Sara, as the conference room doors remained shut for hours.

"What could be happening?" Sara texted Trisha.

"No idea. I didn't pay for them all to take a turn, though."

Sara continued waiting, even after most of her co-workers had left for the day. When the cleaning staff arrived, Sara followed them into the conference room.

It was empty.

"I don't know when or how everyone left, but they did," she

texted Trisha, who reminded her to delete the message thread but then asked her to follow up the next morning.

The following day started as any other. Tim was already there, initially looking none the worse for wear. Sara regarded him differently when she noticed the blood beneath his fingernails, as he handed her a sealed envelope.

The envelope contained a glowing performance evaluation and an updated contract with a substantial raise. There were signatures on the contracts of names she did not recognize, but assumed they belonged to additional uniformly suited gentlemen.

"Is this because of *CRC*?" she asked Tim, who didn't answer, choosing instead to look down at his shoes.

"Sara and Tim . . . we will be ready in just a few moments," a man said before disappearing behind the doors of the conference room.

"Who is that?" Sara asked, following Tim to the small foyer outside the conference room.

Tim continued looking at his feet, so Sara decided to end the awkwardness by helping herself to a latte from the machine tucked inside the foyer. She normally didn't use that machine; it was understood that it was reserved for the higher-ups, but she figured that if she had been called to go inside, then she could partake of the benefits outside.

Several types of dark roast coffee could be inserted into the machine, but Sara did not see any of the milk cups to make the foam. There was a cabinet beneath where she found the milk cups and stirrers and packets of sugar. As she knelt to scrutinize the offerings, she spied a tiny sock trapped beneath one of the wheels of the cabinet.

Sara pulled the sock free and examined it. It had lace around the cuff and a tiny pink bow at the ankle. It was small, and while Sara was unfamiliar with children's clothing, she estimated it would fit a large baby or petite toddler.

She was ignoring her latte for the sock when Tim approached her from behind. "You can still leave," he said.

"And pass up this opportunity? You'd like that; less competition for you."

He shook his head sadly. "There is still time . . . to save yourself. I told you to quit. I wish you would have listened. I wish you would have run away from all of this." His eyes welled with tears as he looked at the sock. "I know you will never believe this, but that was my wife's idea. She wanted me to have the salary and perks. She wanted to change our lives. I said no . . . no way . . . but she—"

They were interrupted by the doors to the conference room opening. Five men in suits waved them in. The room was dark, but Sara was able to make out a naked man suspended from the ceiling by a thick rope, tied beneath his armpits. His hands were bound behind his back and his ankles were lashed together. The tables had been separated beneath him and there was an opening in the floor. Sara had never visited the floor below and could not remember anyone having offices there; she had no idea where this opening ended.

The man was gagged, and his eyes darted wildly around the room. He paused on Sara, looking at her pleadingly.

A tall man with a barrel chest motioned for everyone to sit while a short blond man lit candles.

"What the fuck?" Sara breathed, once the shock lifted, and she found her voice. She looked at Tim, whose head was in his hands. His bloodstained fingertips were grasping his hair as if trying to prevent his sanity from escaping.

"Sara." A man with a thick mustache opened his hands in an expression of welcome. "We didn't know you had it in you."

"You showed us another way," Barrel-chest agreed.

Tim had begun chewing on a fingernail and sucking out the blood from beneath it.

A dark-skinned man in a pinstripe suit frowned. "Maybe show him out?" He nodded in Tim's direction. "This new information—what we have learned from Sara—is apparently too much for him."

"We don't need him?" Blond-man asked.

Pinstripe sighed. "Not anymore."

A large man with slicked-back hair pulled Tim to his feet and helped him walk to the door. Sara could see Tim, visibly crumbling as the door closed behind him.

"We hadn't thought of bringing in *other* offerings," Pinstripe explained. "We hadn't thought it was even possible to use replacements. We thought **Azendolie** only fed on its own. This is a new level of freedom."

Mustache-man chuckled in the cool way that accompanies excessive confidence. "We had actually planned to use you. You were top of the list for the next feeding, back when we thought it had to be an insider, or relative of an insider." He shook his head, as if amazed, then winked at Sara, "Congrats on your survival instincts."

"Feeding?" Sara looked at the man suspended from the ceiling.

"It's not that it happens often," Barrel-chest said, in a consoling manner.

"But in times of great trouble, it can be necessary to . . . feed the beast frequently," Mustache-man added, "and with *CRC* looming, we need all the sacrifices we can get."

"We all had to make contributions . . . of a more personal nature . . . to get here. It is not easy to keep **Azendolie** . . . happy. Our investments keep the system replenished, and Tim . . . " Blond-man pointed to the sock she was still holding. "He gave the ultimate investment."

"But now we know." Pinstripe gestured to the man struggling to loosen the binds that held him aloft. "We can just take to the streets for feeding time. **Azendolie** will accept those sacrifices." He smiled at Barrel-man's chest. "It's the ultimate merger that keeps us all afloat."

Blond-man stood up and pushed a button on the wall, which had been hidden behind a painting of a sailboat. Sara thought those types of contraptions only existed in movies. Several shelves containing business trophies separated, exposing a recessed cabinet that contained trophies of a different kind.

Human heads.

There was the woman Trisha had hired. There were also other heads Sara recognized: a cafeteria worker and a cleaning person, both of whom she had assumed left the job. Sara did not let her eyes inform her brain of the head of the child who was part of the lineup. At the far end of the row was the head of the secretary who had disappeared.

"The big guy told us," Mustache-man said as he pointed to yet another portrait of the deceased founder, "that the only way to keep the company going was through sacrifice. He had sacrificed time, so much time, and at first, we thought that was what he meant. But on his deathbed, he told us that the very foundation needed to be fed." He stomped on the floor beneath him. "The very foundation."

Blond-man pushed another button that caused the suspended man to be lowered into the hole feet first. He was submerged up to his neck, twisting on the rope as he tried to spin himself free. The men in suits nodded to each other and Blond-man pushed the button again, causing the sides of the steel top to slam shut, decapitating the man instantly. The sacrifice's head rolled to the side, and as the gag came free, Sara could have sworn she heard a groan escape his lips following the detachment.

A rumbling came from under the floor, where the body had disappeared.

"Hungry," Blond-man said, nodding to the floor as if he were talking about a stray puppy that he had just put a bowl of food in front of.

Sara felt vomit rising to the back of her throat.

"But now we know. You are one of us." Pinstripe made a wide, sweeping motion, managing to only include the parts of the room that were above the displaced head.

Sara thought of Tim and the way he had weakly lumbered out of the room. She was still there. Sick, but there. "Yes, I am," she mumbled, feeling that was the safest response.

"Your instincts are brilliant," Mustache-man said, widening his eyes in a way he probably considered attractive. "The acquisition you brought us, the girl . . . that was just perfect."

Blond-man laughed, "That was some acquisition."

"And we would like more acquisitions; we *need* more acquisitions," Barrel-chest told her sincerely. He picked up the head from the floor and wiped away some blood with the pocket square from his suit. He placed the head next to the prostitute and then turned the heads, so they were looking at each other. Blond-man smiled and murmured, "That's nice."

"That promotion." Pinstripe pointed to the envelope that was sticking out of Sara's blazer pocket. "Puts you in charge of the acquisitions for this ceremony. You are a true closer, a boardroom killer in the best possible way."

Sara began to understand his words. She shook her head. Her heart was racing, and she was sure that everyone in the room could hear it. Even the severed heads seemed to be looking at her with disapproval, except the brown-haired woman and the recent sacrifice, as they were looking at each other.

Barrel-chest patted the space at the end of the row of *Azendolie* trophies, next to the secretary. "I'm sure you wouldn't . . . But if you were to decide to turn down our offer, there are other ways you can serve the company." The other men smiled and nodded, seeming to prefer this option. "We would just make a different offer for you . . . one that leads right here."

I Won't Die Alone

NACHING T. KASSA

To Marty, with much love.

We were on our way home when night overtook us. It began in a riot of crimson, purpled softly into twilight, and then crept into inky blackness. Bear and I had not spoken to one another since the sun had abandoned the wide Montana sky.

I glanced at Bear. His handsome face, revealed in the dim light of the Honda's instrument panel, bore a grim expression. Dark hair hung loosely around his shoulders. Large hands clutched the steering wheel as he gazed out the windshield. The car would eat up another mile before I finally spoke.

"Bear, I'm going to Helena for three months, not forever. Don't you understand? Lionel's my boss. I have to do what he says, or I'll lose my job."

"Who cares what Hopkins says? The girl I married never backed down to anything or anyone. She was Little Wolverine and did what needed to be done. Why are you so afraid?"

"I'm not afraid. I grew up, learned to compromise. Lionel Hopkins says—"

"You don't need Lionel Hopkins. Get your own legal practice. Help the people here on the rez. Hopkins sends you on the shit jobs. He won't make you a partner in the firm. You don't owe him."

"He took me in when no one else would. You know damn well no one wanted a Blackfoot woman on their staff."

"Is that why you stopped wearing your beadwork? Why you cut your hair?"

"There's a dress code."

242

"Ha! You're ashamed of who you are and where you're from."

"I am not!"

Bear turned and glared into my face. "Why do you make me wait in the car when I come to pick you up? Why won't you introduce me to your white friends? Tonight, at the party, you wouldn't come near me."

"It isn't—I'm not ashamed." I crossed my arms and leaned against the door. It shook beneath my weight.

"The door will fly open if you lean on it," Bear said.

"I don't care. And I'm not ashamed."

"You lie."

His words stung and I bit back. "Blackfoot don't lie! It's you who's afraid and ashamed. Ashamed of yourself and afraid of my success. You're the one who couldn't make it in the white man's world. The one who hides in the Reservation school, telling stories. Jesus, Bear. It's the 21st century and you won't even carry a cell phone."

"I'm saving our culture."

"You're hiding. You ask what happened to Little Wolverine? What happened to you? What happened to the boy who faced Laughing Man? The boy who stabbed the ghost?"

"Don't speak his name," Bear said.

"He's been gone twenty years, Bear. Twenty years! He wasn't some sort of supernatural being. He was just a sicko who liked kidnapping kids. Who thought it would be fun to impersonate a boogeyman. He can't hear you if you speak his name. You act like an old man, jumping at shadows. I married a coward."

The words flew before I could call them back.

I fell silent and turned toward the windshield, a numb sensation sweeping over me. I'd never spoken to Bear that way. Never revealed the deepest recesses of my heart. In one night, I'd inflicted wounds no apology could ever salve. My vision blurred. I wiped my eyes on the sleeve of my denim jacket.

"You think he's gone?" Bear said, his voice little more than a whisper. "You think he left the night I stabbed him in my bedroom? He didn't leave, Mary."

A deer suddenly leaped out of the trees on the right. It streaked across the road in a blur of brown and white.

Bear swerved. Tortured brakes squealed, gravel crunched beneath the right tire, and we slid. The force pinned me against the passenger side door. It sprang loose behind me, and I screamed when it gave way. Metal screeched. I hurtled into space.

⁂

When I came to, I found myself face down, the smell of summer grass and tar in my nostrils. My left shoulder throbbed.

Something crunched beneath me. It proved to be my cell phone, and I pulled it from my jacket pocket. The cracked screen remained blank when I touched it.

"Mary?"

Bear's voice seemed far away, strained.

"Mary? Where are you?"

I tossed the broken phone aside. My fingers dug into cool gravel as I forced myself up.

The car's left headlight had been extinguished by a thick tree trunk. Everything on that side lay cloaked in darkness. The right beam revealed the edge of the road. Covered in tall grass, it sloped down into a ditch and then into the tangled forest beyond.

"Mary?"

The passenger door hung open. I staggered through the grass and peered inside.

Bear lay crumpled over the steering wheel, his legs lost in the twisted metal below it. Shadows concealed his face.

"Can't get out," he said.

"Oh, God. Can you feel your legs? Can you move them?"

"Trapped. Can't get the door open."

His words spurred me on. I stumbled around the back of the car and over to the driver's side. The door had folded and, to a degree, resembled a crushed soda can. Flakes of blue paint filled the creases. I jerked on the door handle, pulling with all my might. Pain, sharp as razors, coursed through my shoulder.

"I can't . . . get the door open, Bear. It's mangled."

He stirred, facing me through the window. Blood glistened on his skin like a mask. He fell against the seat.

"Bear!" I cried. I rushed back to the passenger side and scrambled into the car.

A small and shallow cut marred his scalp. The blood had already congealed around it. The large swelling near his temple garnered more concern.

"Tired," he said.

"You can't sleep," I replied, mopping some of the blood from his face with my shirt sleeve. "You might have a concussion."

A breeze entered the car and swept around us, stirring my hair. It bore a sweet, cloying scent, something I recognized from childhood.

"You smell that?" Bear asked.

My body tensed and I studied the darkness beyond the glare of the single headlight. The odor continued to waft in through the open passenger door. I slid over to close it, but Bear caught me by the wrist and pulled me back.

"Almonds," Bear said. "I smell almonds."

Panic flooded over me, and threatened to drown me. I trembled. The scent wasn't real, it couldn't be.

My mind reeled back, back to my trailer bedroom, back to the nights I dreaded. Grandmother's words echoed in my mind.

Go to sleep, Mary. Go to sleep or Laughing Man will come.
What if I can't sleep, Grandma?
Pretend. If he finds you awake, he'll rip your heart out.
How will I know he's here?
By the smell. He smells like almonds.

And I smelled the almonds; the scent had drifted through my window, and he had come. Come while I was still awake . . .

Bear's grip on my wrist grew tighter, dragging me out of the past and into the present. Out in the darkness, beyond the glare of the single headlight, the trees whispered.

"It's him," he said. "He's—there! Right there!"

I pressed up against Bear and followed the direction he pointed, scanning for movement or a glimpse of eyeshine. The darkness refused to give up its secrets.

"I don't see anything," I said.

"It's Laughing Man," Bear replied. He released my wrist and his head lolled to the left. He grew quiet. Cold.

Death is no stranger. Nor is he a friend. For a moment, I believed he'd taken Bear from me. I patted his cheek. Bear's dark eyes opened and stared into mine.

"Bear, you've got to stay awake. Please."

"If he finds me awake, he'll rip my heart out."

My skin tingled as though a hundred ants had suddenly crossed my skin. The sensation flowed over me, culminating at the top of my head.

My husband fell silent, his breathing shallow.

Movement caught my eye. A strange figure crawled out of the darkness and into the glaring beam of the single headlight.

I glanced at the car's passenger door. No way to shut it.

Footsteps approached. I leaned back in the seat and shut my eyes as a harsh whisper sliced the silence. "Bear?"

Something moved around the door.

Unlike a living body, the one near me radiated frost instead of heat. Gooseflesh rose on my skin when he drew closer. His scent filled my nostrils as he entered the car and hovered over me.

"Are you asleep, Bear?" He paused. "Are you dead?"

Vicious laughter filled the car's interior, and something dripped on my cheek. Ice cold, it slid over my skin. A memory of weeping sores, infection, and diseased flesh jumped to mind. My breath quickened. I pushed the thoughts away.

The creature moved back. I waited, then peered at him through half-slit lids. He stood with his back toward me, head cocked as though listening. Then, he bolted and vanished into the blackness on the opposite side of the road.

I scrubbed the strange substance off my cheek with my shirttail.

"Bear?" I whispered.

He stirred. For a second, his eyelids fluttered open then closed. I took his wrist. The artery still pulsed beneath his skin.

The hum of an engine sounded in the distance. I stepped out of the car and hurried toward the road. Headlights twinkled. My heart lifted as I rushed down the center line.

The white sedan roared down the road toward me. I waved my arms in the air, my shoulder twinging with the effort. It slowed and a window slid down. I rushed to it.

"Thank God you stopped," I said.

"What's going on here?" the woman asked. She wore her blonde hair short. Her wide eyes stared into mine.

"There's been an accident. My husband needs help."

"Where? I don't see anybody."

"It's up ahead. A deer ran across the road, and we hit a tree."

In the woods behind me, someone laughed. The sound grew louder.

"Please, hurry," I said. "There's someone out there. He wants to hurt us. He—"

"Back away from the window," the woman cried.

"What?"

"Back away!" The woman's hand shook as she grasped the wheel. "I don't have any money."

"I don't want your money. My husband is hurt."

The window slid up. I lunged forward.

"Wait, no!"

I would've stepped in front of the car, but she hit the gas. It accelerated and, as it sped away, the taillights glowed. They continued down the road, shrank into the distance, and winked out altogether.

"We need help!" I cried.

The woods resonated with laughter. It grew fainter, moving back up the road toward our car and Bear.

I found no one when I returned to the car. Bear peered at me; his face ashen.

"Was worried," he said. "Heard you scream. Thought he got you."

"I tried to flag a car down, but the driver wouldn't help. He's coming. I heard him. We've got to get out of here."

Bear shrugged. "Can't move."

"Is there a tire iron in the trunk? Maybe, I could pry the door open."

"Mary, listen."

"The keys are still in the ignition. Give them to me. I'll search and see."

"He doesn't want you. Leave."

"No," I cried. I bent forward and snatched the keys away.

"Mary, you can't stop him."

"You stopped him before. You stabbed him right in front of me, the night he found me awake in my bedroom. You jumped in through my window. I'll never forget it. He never bothered me—"

"Mary, he came back the next night. He came to my room."

"What?"

"He comes at night, while you're asleep, and he whispers my name. I've fought him many times, but the knife never stops him. It just keeps him . . . away for a while. He knew he . . . couldn't get me . . . not when I'm strong. He'll take me now. He can't be killed."

"Do you have a knife with you? Any knife?"

Bear paused. For a moment, I thought he'd dropped off again. "I was wrong," he said at last.

"Bear—"

"You be who you are. Don't let anyone, not even me, decide for you."

"We'll talk about this later. Just tell me you have a knife."

"It's on my belt. Next to the door. Can't reach it. But . . . there is another . . ."

"Where?"

"In the trunk. A . . . present for you. Saving it for your . . . birthday."

I turned to go. He spoke again, and I carried some of the words with me.

"Love you."

Darkness shrouded the rear of the car and without a light, I couldn't illuminate the keyhole. I fumbled with the keys for several minutes before the lid opened.

A silver and red flashlight lay just inside the trunk. I clicked it on.

The knife was in the back, under a blanket, and wrapped in buckskin. The blade was wide and about five or six inches long. Heavy but not unwieldy, it ended in a polished bone handle. A Scrimshaw carving decorated the hilt and the perfect semblance of a wolverine stared up at me.

I took the knife, blanket, and flashlight back to Bear.

"I got it."

He held out his hand.

"Give it to me."

"Why? You're in no shape to fight him."

"I have to. I'm the one who's going to die."

"No. You're not."

Bear shook his head. "If I fall asleep, I may never wake up. If he catches me awake . . . I'll be dead, and you'll be next. You have to live."

"I have a way."

"This is the only way."

"You're talking suicide and you're giving up. Blackfoot never give up."

His voice slurred once more. "Little Wolverine, you know me

better than that. If I die, it will be with a knife in my hand. I won't die alone."

Truth can be as sharp as any blade. When it cuts, you're never the same. Bear stared at me, the shadow of death in his face. I slipped into the car beside him and placed the weapon in his hand. His fingers closed around it.

"I swear . . . I won't let you die," I said.

His lids drooped and a faint smile touched his lips. "You can't fight death, Little Wolverine."

I threw the blanket over him and pressed my lips to his ear. "Watch me."

He didn't wake up when I took the knife. As the smooth handle filled my hand, thoughts filled my head. They tumbled unbidden, one after another.

I'm Mary Nighteagle, Blackfoot woman.
My husband calls me Little Wolverine.
I am a Child of the Real People.
Descended from warriors.
I won't quit. Won't lie. Won't shame my blood.
Death is my enemy. Let him become my friend.
If I fail, I won't die alone.

Sweet and sickening, the almond scent entered in on the breeze. I glanced out of the windshield, past the glow of the headlight. Then, out the side and back windows.

He was out there, somewhere.

I dropped the flashlight on the floor and hid the knife behind my right thigh. I lay with my back against Bear.

The smell grew stronger. I closed my eyes and affected the deep breath of sleep. He had seen me awake. Would he believe I had fallen asleep now?

Moments passed.

No sound had accompanied his arrival. The only warning I'd received was the prickling of chilled skin.

"I'm back," he said.

I clutched the knife. If Laughing Man touched Bear, I would bury the blade in his diseased throat.

"Are you awake?"

He crept closer and laid a hand on my leg.

"I know you're awake . . . Mary."

Before I could move, he caught me by the throat and dragged me from the car.

The left hand of Laughing Man squeezed my windpipe as he pulled me against him. Pinpoints of light, like stars, rose before me.

Wicked laughter filled my ears. Black eyes glittered in a face covered in festering sores. A broad grin displayed sharp, gleaming teeth.

"You're turning blue," he said, pressing his palm against my chest. My nerveless fingers began to uncurl. The knife almost slipped from my hand.

"No, no. Can't let you die the easy way."

He loosened his grasp on my throat. I took a deep shuddering breath.

"I've waited a long while for this. I have to make it last."

A blood-red haze misted my vision as my fingers tightened back on the bone handle. Pain, burning and sharp, coursed through my left shoulder. I whimpered.

"Yes, little girl. Cry. When I'm done with you, I'll hang your heart from the rearview mirror. Bear will wake and scream. Scream like the coward he is."

The pressure on my heart increased as did his laughter.

With all my strength, I drove the knife into the creature's side.

His laughter became a howl. I withdrew the blade and stabbed again. When I withdrew the second time, a mournful wail filled the air, accompanied by distant and flashing lights. When another siren joined the first, the monster turned. He fled toward the road.

I pursued.

He moved fast across the pavement and into what proved to be tall grass. In my haste, I forgot the flashlight and plunged into the darkness after him.

His feet pounded the earth ahead of me. I slashed and connected. Laughing Man screeched.

I raised the knife again and the ground beneath my feet betrayed me. I tumbled into the grass and the knife went flying. It landed with a soft *thump* a few feet away.

The footsteps ceased. I scrambled to my knees and crawled forward; hand outstretched. My fingers quested through the dirt and grass.

The sirens had stopped, and bursts of light now lit the field. Laughing Man still lurked nearby. His scent filled the air.

Something swished through the grass toward my left. I froze and waited as flashes of red and blue light strobed the spot. Laughing Man stood a few yards away, his manic grin widening.

Death's tenuous friendship had ended. He'd rejoined the monster. Laughing Man grinned and moved forward.

My fingers touched bone, then. They slid over the lines which formed the wolverine. I pulled the blade into my hand and, before Laughing Man could take another step, charged.

The grin faded. He spun around and our chase resumed.

Laughing Man poured on the speed and soon outdistanced me. No matter how fast I ran, I couldn't gain ground. At last, his footsteps receded. I halted and, panting, brandished the knife in the air.

"If I ever see you again, I'll make you sorry you survived. Your heart won't be the last thing I cut out!"

My words echoed in the dark.

This time, no one laughed.

Red Lipstick

VALERIE B. WILLIAMS

This story is dedicated to Moaner Lawrence, founder and leader of Moanaria's Fright Club, the best online generative horror writing workshop ever! "Red Lipstick" was born in Fright Club.

Eleanor turned the brass key in the lock and pushed open the bright blue employee entrance door for *"The Mane Event."* A strong gust of wind nearly tore the open door from her hand, so she had to struggle to pull it firmly shut before securing it with the deadbolt. A potpourri of faint but familiar scents greeted her: perm chemicals, floral shampoos, and hairspray, all overlaid by the mustiness of unused space. She'd bought the salon before ever setting foot inside, relying solely on the description provided by the realtor, along with a handful of outdated photographs.

Across from her, on the right side of the small shop, sat two black styling chairs—each facing large, wall-mounted mirrors as if admiring their own reflections. Two shampoo bowls hung from the back wall, only one paired with a reclining chair. A 1950s-vintage pale blue Naugahyde chair, complete with an attached, hard plastic dryer hood lurked in the corner just past the mirrors, with splits in the seat covered with peeling duct tape. Did it even work? Eleanor made the mistake of flipping the switch and jumped back at the sound, before quickly switching it off. She'd heard quieter jet engines.

Turning, she spotted a door in the opposite corner, marked with a makeshift sign that stated "Supplies." She pushed it open to find the room mostly empty, except for some dusty boxes on metal shelves and a stacked washer and dryer, which thankfully looked fairly new. Eleanor sneezed, then cracked the window on the far wall before turning her attention back to the main room.

She walked towards the front to inspect the small reception space, finding a desk with an attached cash register partially hidden behind a free-standing, mass-produced Oriental screen, and a waiting area that sported a matching loveseat and chair—in such a loud floral print that it made her eyes ache. A cheap, lopsided coffee table held a sprawling stack of dusty magazines and an ash-crusted glass ashtray. She groaned over her inability to immediately replace the dated décor.

At the far end of the reception area, Eleanor spotted the restroom. Like everything else in the shop, it needed a good cleaning. But the toilet flushed, and the faucets worked, so she wasn't going to complain.

The sharp smell of smoke greeted her as she left the bathroom. A new crushed cigarette lay in the glass ashtray, red lipstick smears covering the filter. Frowning, she bent down for a closer look. *Was that still lit?* She shook her head and blinked. No, of course not . . . no cherry burning. She picked up the ashtray and felt the bottom to reassure herself. Cold.

Hmmm. She must've missed the butt the first time she'd passed by.

⁂

Over the next three weeks, Eleanor cleaned, scrubbed, painted, and redecorated as best she could within her tight budget. Each night she returned to her small apartment and X-ed out the day on the kitchen calendar. She could never have imagined moving to a rural town in the mountains of Pennsylvania, nor could she have imagined, years before, that her very life would depend upon it.

October 31st bore a large green circle on the calendar. Halloween would've marked her sixth anniversary, and when that day arrived this year, she planned to breathe a sigh of relief and celebrate her newfound anonymity, alone and safe.

⁂

Prior to opening day in early autumn, Eleanor had added a roll-around set of drawers, the dryer hood was serviced, she'd bought a nice coffee table second hand, and restocked the supply shelves. Getting a new chair dryer would be next, followed by replacing the hideous reception furniture, once she had money coming in instead of going out. *"Elegance by Eleanor"* now decorated the front door in gold, flowing script.

When the shop closed abruptly last year, the ladies from Milesburg had been forced to drive twenty miles to the nearest salon, so they seemed happy to have her and willing to give her a chance. By the time October 1st arrived, she was already booked solid. Her first appointment arrived early, before she even had a chance to unlock the front door. The woman knocked loudly and "hallooed," her hands framing her face as she pressed it against the front window, fogging the glass.

"I'm so glad you're here, honey," Dottie Reynolds said as she came inside and plunked herself into a styling chair. She ruffled her limp gray curls. "I'm way overdue for a cut and perm." She barked a phlegmy laugh, then coughed violently.

"I'll get you fixed right up, Mrs. Reynolds." The aroma of cigarettes clung to the older woman like a barroom perfume.

"Call me Dottie. If you're gonna hear all my secrets, we'll need to be on a first-name basis."

"Dottie it is then." As Eleanor rolled swatches of gray hair around small perm rods, she found that Dottie had been serious about sharing secrets. She was also inclined to gossip, albeit not in a mean way. She mentioned that the women in the area had speculated the salon might remain empty after what had happened to "poor Velma."

"I heard the previous owner died suddenly. That must have been hard . . . didn't anyone in her family want to take over running the shop?"

Dottie's gaze met Eleanor's in the mirror; her eyes were wide, glistening with moisture. "You didn't know? Oh, honey. Velma's only family was her husband. And he's doing life in the state pen for killing her, that son-of-a—"

Eleanor missed most of what Dottie said next, because her knees went weak, and her ears began ringing.

"Oh, dear, not *here*." Dottie noticed her distress and waved a dismissive hand. "At their house. Stabbed her. Then wrote nasty things about her on the mirror. The Sheriff thought it was blood at first, but it was lipstick! Never saw Velma without her lipstick.

Revlon Fire & Ice. Kinda her trademark." Dottie shook her head sadly, coughed again, and a perm rod slipped from Eleanor's suddenly sweaty hand when she added, "Poor girl had already become an old soul . . . and she was only 36."

Eleanor took a deep, steadying breath before responding. "How horrible." She had celebrated her 38th birthday last week, hundreds of miles from her former life in Baltimore.

"I'm surprised Stan didn't tell you when you bought the place," Dottie harrumphed.

"Legally, he only had to disclose any deaths on the property," said Eleanor. No wonder the shop had been such a deal. But he could have, *should* have, told her as a courtesy. Then again, how could he have known . . . ?

Besides Dottie Reynolds, a surprising number of women in town smoked—even some of the younger ones. While Eleanor couldn't allow it in the salon, she wanted to be accommodating to her customers. There was a bench outside the front door, so every morning she put the big glass ashtray on the ground next to it. The ladies could step outside while their hair was processing to feed their habit. Each evening, she emptied and cleaned the ashtray and returned it to the storage room.

Exactly one week after learning about Velma, she entered the storage room and smelled smoke again. This time, there was a freshly extinguished cigarette in the ashtray, smoke still swirling around it. The same red lipstick she'd noticed before encircled the filter.

Instantly on edge, she checked the back door. Locked. She turned and gazed cautiously into the empty air. There was no logical explanation.

That led to the illogical. "Velma?" she said aloud, feeling a bit foolish.

Eleanor always left the radio playing after closing, otherwise, any unexpected sound startled her. Abruptly, the pop station she'd been listening to went staticky, and then Aretha Franklin's "Sisters Are Doing It for Themselves" began to play.

Eleanor started, letting out a nervous giggle. Her grandmother had been a firm believer in ghosts, and the rest of the family had humored her. But what if she'd been right? From what Dottie (source of all gossip in town) had told her, the salon had been Velma's pride and joy. It wasn't unreasonable that her spirit would linger where she'd been the happiest.

Over the course of the next few days, Velma made herself known. When Eleanor went to mix hair color, she found the small bowls already prepared. After collapsing on the loveseat at the end of a long day to rest for a few minutes, she would drag herself up to sweep the floor, only to find it spotless. Used towels she'd left lying next to the washer would be not only washed but dried and folded when she arrived in the morning. Eleanor had thought about hiring an assistant, but it turned out one came with the salon.

Being new and on her own, she hadn't made any close friends in town, so Eleanor found herself talking to Velma when she was alone, spilling all the ugly truths about her life in Baltimore. Maybe some would've thought it crazy, but although she couldn't see or hear Velma, Eleanor believed she was there . . . and that she listened. One evening, a couple of weeks into Velma's otherworldly help, she found a fresh tube of Revlon Fire & Ice on the edge of the sink in the salon restroom.

"Velma? A present?" Eleanor mused.

Leaning toward the mirror, she applied the lipstick and smiled at her reflection. Surprisingly, she liked the bold color, unlike anything she'd ever worn before; she began to wear it daily and received many compliments from her clients.

Eleanor enjoyed Velma's presence, and was even comforted by it . . . but try as she might, she couldn't break her ghost of a daily smoke in the storage room. Numerous entreaties to the empty room were ignored. Oh well, one cigarette a day was a small thing to tolerate for free help and an even smaller price to pay for peace of mind.

❧❧❧❧❧

Time flew for Eleanor since leaving Baltimore for her new life. Soon, the small shopping center surrounding the salon was brimming with witches, pumpkins, and scarecrows.

Halloween was only three days away. She'd always loved decorating for it, and although approaching the holiday with mixed emotions this year, it had still been fun to hang the paper chain of black cats with arched backs, alternated with grinning pumpkins, across the large front window. But no one knew how extra-special Halloween would be for her this year. Well, no one except her and Velma.

The paper chain in the window rustled as she rushed past, shooing the last customer out the door with a cheery "See you next time, gotta get this," before walking quickly toward the ringing phone. She grabbed the landline, smiling at the black roses from the dollar store she'd arranged in an inexpensive vase.

"Elegance by Eleanor, how may I help you?" she chirped into the receiver. All she could hear were traffic noises and static. Cell service was sketchy in the mountains, so Eleanor assumed a customer was calling from one. "Hello?"

The line clicked and went dead.

Eleanor shrugged it off as a wrong number.

She received a similar call the next day, Friday, just after lunch. The caller still didn't speak over the noisy background of cars and trucks.

Far more noise than was typical for a small town.

On Saturday, a call came as she opened the shop that chilled her to her core. This time there was barely any background noise, only breathing. The caller chuckled before hanging up—*a familiar chuckle.* Her pulse roared in her ears like ocean waves, and she lowered herself shakily into a chair.

He'd found her.

Saturday was normally her busiest day, and with the holiday she was fully booked. What could she do? Close the salon and run to the sheriff? What could she tell him, anyway . . . ? That she had some hang-up phone calls?

But she knew.

Rob had tracked her down. Her soon-to-be-ex was under a restraining order, for all the good that did. A jumble of thoughts assailed her as she absently rubbed her right wrist, over the area of a prior, healed break.

A knock on the front door startled her. Eleanor saw Jessica Mason peering through the window, grinning and waving at her. Relief flooded through her as she unlocked the door to welcome her in. The one fact that kept her going on October 31st was that Rob had never touched her in public. As long as the shop was busy, she would be safe.

The day rushed by at a dizzying pace; Eleanor could almost see the clock hands spinning. The only other calls she received were from customers making or rescheduling appointments. When she finished her last haircut, it was seven o'clock and dusk had fallen. She locked the front door and threw a load of towels in the washer, then swept the floor and wiped down the surfaces to prepare for Monday—tasks Velma would have taken care of, but tonight, Eleanor was afraid to leave the shop.

The last time she'd seen Rob, he'd come back to the house, using a copy of the key he had "returned," and broken her nose. She moved to the women's shelter the next day, staying for only a week before taking the little sum of money she'd managed to squirrel away and walking out into what she'd hoped would be obscurity.

Those traumatic memories were interrupted by a crash from the storage room. The back window! Eleanor ran for the front door, fingers trembling as she fumbled with the keys, but before she could unlock it, a hand grabbed the back of her neck, shoving her to the floor. Rob stood over her, leering.

"I thought we should celebrate our anniversary *together*," he drawled in a voice calm and silky, the tone he'd often used when acting charming. His eyes searched her face, and then his smirk dissipated. "What is that shit on your lips?! You look like a whore!" Rob hadn't allowed her to wear any bold make-up, let alone red lipstick.

Perhaps that was why she'd grown to love it.

Eleanor crab-walked backwards and pulled herself up with one of the styling chairs.

"You're not supposed to be near me," she croaked.

"But you *belong* to me. We took vows, remember?"

He chuckled and took a step toward her, striking with snake-like precision. She didn't even see his fist coming. Her right eye exploded with pain, and her head crashed against the mirror. She groped blindly on top of the supply drawers, finding a pair of scissors, newly sharpened.

Her fingers tightened around them, gripping them in her fist. When Rob lunged at her again, she drove the blades into his shoulder. He roared with pain, then quickly recovered to grab her by the throat, slowly squeezing her windpipe as he lifted her off her feet. Black dots swirled in her vision as she kicked her feet helplessly. She tugged at his hands, but they were like iron vises as he laughed maniacally.

Rob's laughter was abruptly cut off, replaced by choking noises. Eleanor dropped to the floor, gagging and clawing at her throat as her vision cleared. Through watery eyes, she watched as the cord of a curling iron wrapped around her husband's throat, seemingly under its own power. His eyes bulged as he fought; his fingers dug under the immovable cord as he staggered backward. The underside of his knees met the edge of the dryer chair, and he went down with a thump. The hood slammed over his head, covering his face as the dryer roared to life. The curling iron released its hold on his throat and whipped around his body, binding him to the chair.

A gust of superheated air blasted from the dryer; the see-through hood revealed his reddening face and wild, terror-filled eyes. The stench of burning hair and cooking flesh filled the air, along with her husband's screams.

Horrified, Eleanor staggered to the dryer chair and flipped the 'Off' switch. Nothing. Rob's body jittered.

Realization dawned. "Velma, no! Stop!"

Instead of stopping, the dryer whirred louder. Rob's eyeballs popped and vitreous fluid streamed down his charred cheeks, the wails of agony ceasing as his body went limp in the chair. The dryer finally shut off, smoke seeping from underneath the hood. The curling iron loosened its grip and dropped into his lap.

Eleanor put her head between her knees, fighting against the bile rising in her throat as she gasped for breath. When she was sure she wouldn't pass out or throw up, she wobbled over to Rob's motionless form and felt his wrist. A feeble pulse remained—he was still alive. Her legs gave out and she collapsed against the wall, closing her eyes. When she opened them, the misty shape of a woman hovered in front of the dryer chair.

"You need to get out." The strange, ethereal voice echoed all around her. "I'll finish this."

"Velma, why? He . . . he was a bastard, but nobody deserves . . . this." She gestured at Rob's burnt, limp body.

"He deserved that and more," Velma howled. "He wouldn't have stopped! Don't you understand . . . ? I'm giving you the chance I never had." The ghostly shape that was surely Velma quivered with unbridled rage. "Now leave!"

Eleanor shook her head, unable to wake from this nightmare. She pushed herself to her feet and picked up the phone. Dead. She stumbled to the door, intending to flag down the nearest person to get help for her husband. All the other shops in the small downtown area were closed, and the streets were deserted. Everyone was busy, either handing out Halloween candy or escorting their kids trick-or-treating. A lone car approached the town square and she flung herself into the street, waving her arms. The last thing Eleanor remembered was a loud explosion and a blast of heat slamming her face-first onto the pavement.

⁓⁂⁓

"Ma'am, wake up." A hand patted Eleanor softly on her uninjured cheek. She pried open her eyes to see a young paramedic kneeling over her. Sirens sounded and lights flashed. The air was thick with smoke. Her mouth held the metallic taste of blood. She remembered Rob and tried to sit up. The paramedic pressed her gently, but firmly back.

"My . . . my shop. What happened?" she croaked in confusion.

"I'm afraid there was an explosion and a fire. You probably have a concussion. Please lie back and let me examine you, ma'am."

Explosion? Fire? thought Eleanor. *Velma, what have you done?*

"B-but my husband was still in there!"

The paramedic nodded and spoke urgently into his radio. Eleanor closed her eyes and drifted into a peaceful darkness.

When she awakened, it was to a stark white hospital room and a brown-uniformed sheriff sitting next to her bed.

"Miss Clark?" He leaned forward. "How are you feeling?"

Eleanor stared at him blankly for a moment before remembering her new name. "Lucky, I guess. Please call me Eleanor." Memories of Rob rushed back. Should she mention him? How could she explain that a ghost killed him? No one would believe her. She wondered if it had truly even happened . . .

The sheriff seemed to take her silence as a cue. "We found a man's body in the storage room, but I'm afraid the fire was so intense we were unable to identify him."

Tears dribbled down her cheeks. Tears of relief, not grief. But all tears look the same from the outside.

Eleanor scrutinized the sincerity displayed in the older man's eyes. It was difficult to trust, but she had to try. The kindness she saw caused a rush of emotion, and she broke down. She told the sheriff everything; the restraining order, her escape from Baltimore to Milesburg, and how her abusive ex-husband had tracked her down. She explained how he'd attacked her, and how she managed to grab a pair of scissors . . . *she didn't know if the fire would have melted them.*

Then she recalled the heavy glass ashtray and said she had hit him on the head with it, allowing her enough time to run out the door for help. The more she talked, the easier her version of the story flowed. Her blackened eye and the marks on her throat lent credence to her claims, supporting the parts that were fabricated. No one would believe what really happened anyway. She finished by giving him Rob's address, so they could track down his dentist and formally identify the body.

Eleanor was released from the hospital the next day. The fire marshal's report blamed the fatal combustion on faulty old electrical wiring that had met with an unextinguished cigarette.

Two weeks after the explosion, Eleanor stood in front of the hole where the salon had been. She raised the hood of her heavy coat against the increasing snow, pushing her hands further into her pockets to keep them warm. Despite the explosion and intensity of the fire, the buildings on either side had, thankfully, sustained minimal damage.

The salon was a total loss. Today she would finish mourning her business but would also celebrate her freedom from fear. Time had offered perspective. She could, and would, begin again.

"Thank you, Velma," she murmured softly. "You were right. He did deserve it."

She turned to leave, but a glint at the edge of the charred wreckage caught her eye. She crouched, reached into a pile of ashes, and pulled out a familiar, shiny gold lipstick tube. Smiling as she stood, Eleanor tucked "Fire and Ice" into her pocket, walked away . . . and never looked back.

Farm Wife

NANCY KILPATRICK

*"Farm Wife" is dedicated to Don Hutchison who edited Northern Frights,
the first book in which this story appeared. Don's enthusiastic responses to
my work which he published in six anthologies over the years have created
a special place in my memory. He was one of the talented editors whose
encouragement and praise helped me to feel confident and to move
forward in my career.*

Noma stationed herself at the back porch and propped the screen
door open with her left foot. The sun hadn't set but one hour ago
and already the Napanee sky was the color of ashes from the wood
burner. Out past the pale tripod fencing and across the dying rye
fields she saw Bert shuffling, Dog by his side. The sickness drained
him. And left him hungry. Hungry all the time.

Lord knows she fed that man a baker's dozen meals a day, but
it was never enough. The more he ate, the thinner he got. Wasted.
Just this morning she noticed he barely cast a shadow.

A mosquito trying to sneak into the house paused on her meaty
upper arm. Yard was swarming with the last of 'em. She watched
the bloodsucker poke its snout into a pore.

"Want blood you'll get blood," she promised. Her skin began
to itch bad, but she made herself wait. Easy now. Ball the fist and
knot the shoulder like her daddy had showed her. Noma's work-
developed muscles tensed. She believed she could feel the strong
blood forced up that chute.

The sucker went rigid.

Swelled to triple size.

Probably didn't even think about getting away.

She flicked the bloody corpse into the coming night and scratched her wound.

Noma shut the screen door but continued watching Bert make his way slowly toward the house.

Sure is a stubborn man, she thought. Had been the forty-odd years she'd known him. Her daddy'd warned her, said it ran in Bert's family, but she wouldn't listen.

When Bert first came down with the sickness, she tried getting him over to the hospital. But he didn't trust city-trained doctors, didn't trust doctors at all, especially since his sister. Noma couldn't blame him, though. Seeing Ruby lying like milkweed fluff on those crisp sheets, the color of white flour and brittle as dead leaves, eyes shot with blood and sunk back into her head, breath rank, gums shrunk up from the teeth like that . . . God, what a waste.

The doctors claimed it was some fancy kind of anemia. Gave her stuff but it didn't make the slightest bit of difference that Noma could see. Bert did the right thing in bringing her home. Ruby stayed upstairs in the room next to them, fading day by day, withering to less than nothing, just like Bert was now, until one morning when Noma took up eggs and bacon and found that Ruby had departed.

"Best that way," Bert said. Noma had to agree.

And now it's him, she thought. As he reached the vegetable garden, even in the poor light she could see his bones pressuring the skin to set them free. His face wasn't more than a skull, with hardly any flesh for that pale hide to stretch across, and just a tuft of red on top. He lifted an arm and waved—she knew how hard that was for him.

As Bert reached the porch, Noma stepped out, ready to give him a hand up the steps, but he shrugged her off. *You old curmudgeon!* she thought. Even now, when he can use it most, he won't take no help. Well, that's just like a farmer, isn't it?

By the time she'd latched the screen door and closed and locked the inside one, he was at the refrigerator, dragging out the apple pie she'd baked this afternoon. He got a dessert plate from the cupboard and placed a hearty slice of pie on it. That slice went right back into the refrigerator. Out came the cheddar, and pure cream she'd whipped. He plunked himself down in front of the bulk of the pie, helped himself to a wedge of cheese the size of Idaho and scooped seven or eight kitchen spoons of milk fat onto the whole mess.

She figured by eating so much, he fooled himself he wasn't sick. "Cuppa coffee?" she asked.

He grunted and nodded but didn't pause.

Noma plugged in the kettle, but before the water got a chance to boil the pie tin was empty and he was back for that abandoned slice.

She measured freeze-dried coffee into two mugs—one twice the size of the other—and glanced out the window while she poured water over it. Gonna be cool tonight—October tended to be like that. Leaves on the willow'd been gone over a week; branches swayed in the breeze like a woman's hair. Might be a harvest moon come up, if the sky stayed clear. Low on the horizon. And full. She checked the calendar. Nope. Full moon tomorrow night. Be plenty to do come sunrise.

When Bert finished the pie, he leaned his skinny self back in the chair and belched loudly, then patted his stomach, or what used to be a stomach but had become so bloated he looked like he swallowed a whole watermelon.

"Waste not want not," he said, and she agreed. She handed him his coffee and he took it to the living room. She heard the television; sounded like a sports show.

About eleven Noma put Dog out, and then they both went upstairs.

Bert tossed and turned, keeping her awake for a time, but she must have dozed off because she woke when she heard the stairs creak as he stumbled down. The refrigerator door opened and closed. Opened and closed again. Then the back door. She heard the screen door slam. Turning onto her side, Noma pulled the feather pillow over her ear and went back to sleep.

⁂

Up with the sun and down in the kitchen, Noma cleaned up the mess Bert had left. She opened the back door to let Dog in and fed him the scraps. The sky was packed with clouds the color of cow's brains, the air snappy. Farmer's Almanac promised frost tonight.

When breakfast was out of the way and she'd fed the chickens and pigs and milked the cows and turned them out to pasture, Noma harvested as much of the Swiss chard from the garden as she could—two and a half bushel baskets worth. She washed and blanched the iron-rich greens then stuffed them into airtight plastic bags that she sealed for the freezer. Bert hated chard, hated vegetables on principle, he said, but Noma couldn't get enough.

There was bed making, washing to do, some mending, lunch to get ready and eat, vacuuming, and a call to the feed store to see if that new corn and soya mix for the pigs was in yet.

It wasn't.

Around four Noma began supper. Hadn't seen Bert all day.

Didn't expect to. Still, she cooked up a mess of chard, and a ton of beef stew, the way she'd made a big lunch and breakfast, just in case.

Around six the cows came back. She locked them up in the barn and on her way to the house, looked across the rye. The fields had faded to the color of dry bone. No sign of Bert. Not surprising.

Still.

Noma watched reruns of that show with the fat woman but it wasn't very funny this week. She crawled into bed early, not quite ten-thirty. She'd done all she could, all anybody could, but sleep wasn't about to help her out tonight.

The eaves creaked. The wind picked up and howled the way it can. The house her daddy left her was old but solid. Noma grew up here, married here, had her kids, buried her folks.

Through every season, lean and plenty, she was used to the sounds.

But when Dog howled at the moon, well; Bert always looked after Dog. She went to the window at the back and was about to warn the mutt to settle himself or else, but stopped. Dog wasn't making a peep now. He stood quivering, scruffy tail between his legs, ears back, about to bolt.

And staring at Bert.

A cloud lifted from the bloated moon and Bert turned his face up. The sickness was all over him. Eyes flecked with red like the blood that spurts from a leghorn when you chop the head off. He'd turned into a skeleton and what flesh he had left, the moon showed, was a kind of whitewashed blue.

"Noma," was all he said. He grinned at her and she saw his gums had receded; his teeth reminded her of the sharp teeth on the combine. But the worst of all was his shadow. It was gone.

"Ain't letting you in!" she told him firmly.

His eyes got hard and fiery red like Sumach fruit. He stepped up onto the porch, out of her sight. She heard him rattling the back door.

"Noma," he called again, so pathetic it got to her.

Despite her better judgment, she went down to the kitchen and opened just the inside, keeping the screen door between them.

"Best you be off," she told him. He cocked his head to one side—that always softened her up. The yellow kitchen light gave him some color.

"Noma," he whispered, like they were in bed together.

She shook her head but opened the screen door.

He was on her in a second, pitchfork teeth tearing into her throat. Noma'd always been a big strong woman, but he was stronger—she'd discovered that early in their marriage. This was more so. He stank like the compost heap and his skin rivaled the frosty air. It was plain enough: he was starving, she was supper.

He held her against the kitchen table. She felt the iron-blood being drawn from her like milk from a cow. Wasn't but one thing to be done, what her daddy had taught her.

Noma worked slow, tensing the muscles up from her legs, through her privates and stomach, her arms, chest, and back. When that was done, she eased up a second. One final overall squeeze did the trick.

Bert looked like he'd been slammed by a bale of hay.

Blood gushed from his mouth, nose, and ears. His eyes popped wide. He swelled fast, the way the skin does when you're frying up chicken. A funny sound, kind of a cross between her name and a goose hissing, started to rise out of him but didn't get much of a chance.

Noma shook for a while but figured there wasn't much point to that. The clock over the stove read two-thirty. She glanced out the window. Frost had taken the last of the chard. The waste of it troubled her.

The walls and ceiling were splattered, the floor slime.

She cleaned up what she could of the gory mess, then opened the door. Dog bounded in, happy to gobble the scraps.

Noma dabbed alcohol on her neck and checked the clock again. Time to get herself to bed. Sunrise wasn't far off.

Tomorrow there'd be plenty to do. Always is for a farm wife.

The God of Sea and Land

CHRISTINA SNG

For my daughter, the builder.

With clay, the girl molds them
One limb at a time,
Each a replica of the other.

This is not the making of sand.
In creatures, symmetry is necessary.
They move faster, synchronized.

Each addition strengthens them,
Makes them agile, adaptable,
An army so resilient

Even her father,
The Great Neptune
Will not be able to defeat them.

When they are gathered,
She challenges her father
For his crown

To free her mother and sisters
From his unbending will
And iron fists.

Christina Sng

He summons his army to face her,
Charging the sea with electricity,
Driving them out of the water.

The creatures do not die.
They spasm as their bodies
Take in the charge,

Fueling their rage as they surface,
Breathless, pounding the waves,
Bringing down the sky.

They fly—
Dodging Neptune's attacks,
Each bolt closer than the other.

Neptune surfaces,
Bringing his army with him.
He orders them to charge.

The creatures dive,
Plunging their hands
Deep into Neptune's chest

Before ripping him in half,
Throwing one piece to another,
Devouring his flesh

Before his horrified army.
They surrender.
The battle is over.

The girl takes the throne,
Placing her mother as queen
And her sisters as commanders.

She and her creatures
Depart the land of their birth
To find new worlds to conquer.

The God of Sea and Land

They return to the surface
And take their first steps onto shore
With the feet she made for them.

There, she molds a piece of clay
With forked tongues
And curved horns.

She names it demon
And gives it the power
To wield fire.

She makes another.
And another
Till there are enough

To conquer the land.

Endra—from memory

CHELSEA QUINN YARBRO

From the memoirs of Melizan kem Gishcar-Shwy

It was a bright chilly day when the ship came into the harbor, turned gracefully as her sails were lowered while she slid into the end of the dock, her floatation nudging up to the tarred wood; the gangplank was lowered and its crew of six disembarked at the base of the ramp of the dock's loading crane. The grand ship flew the colors of the Taksteppe Empire, and everyone was excited to see the ship so far to the north and the east of her home port. Men and women from nine other ships crowded around the dock where this splendid vessel was secured, for the ships of the Taksteppe Empire were among the most admired on earth, and were not often found in this quarter of the globe.

No one who saw it will ever forget the impression Endra YuiduJin made as she stepped from her deck onto the gangplank; I haven't forgotten, although it is more than fifty years since she first arrived here; no other arrivals have eclipsed the splendor of her first introduction to Lavrant City. She came to the top of the gangplank and stood, the wind snapping at her while she smiled; unlike her crewmen, her clothes were made of Taksteppe silks, and they glowed as if lit from within. Like many foreign Captains, she had a lightning gun and a small image recorder in her hands. I came to the foot of the gangplank since it was my duty to monitor all new arrivals; she slipped the gun into her wide belt of gilded leather scales and faced me. "What ship?" I asked in Coigne, the language used by nautical people the world over.

Endra—from memory

"The *Empress FahrenDier*. Out of Sui-Kan-below-the-Dam. Captain Endra YuiduJin asks for the haven of your harbor and access to your markets. If you'll tell me what I owe for the privilege of tying up here, I would be most appreciative." She made a sweeping kind of bow and came down to the dock, apparently unaware of the sensation she had created.

I found it impossible to speak, so captivated was I—I'm afraid I goggled at her, and I hoped none of my assistants saw.

Her eyes glistened with amusement. "Will you give me permission to land? Or tell me what I must do to acquire permission?"

"I will," I said, and would have said the same thing if she had asked permission to take off and fly. "First you must come to me."

"You're the Harbormaster," she said, regarding me with mild but approving curiosity. "Or a newsmonger?"

"Harbormaster isn't quite the function, not the way we do things here, but I have the authority to admit you to the trading zone of Lavrant City. I am the Trading Monitor." I smiled at her, not wanting to cause her any alarm. "How is it that you are so far from the usual trade routes of the Taksteppe Empire? We see few of your ships."

She looked at me and laughed. "Happenstance, and perhaps luck."

I put her age at thirty, though she had an air about her that seemed older; I knew that the sea pulled the youth from the faces of those who earned their living on the water, and made allowances for that as I studied her. Yet thirty, or even thirty-five seemed young for a Captain. "Is this your first command, or are you on a mission?"

"It is not, and yes, I am," she said emphatically. "I am trying to circle the world west to east and north to south. My mother tried it, twenty years ago, and failed at the south pole as the weather turned hard. I've been at sea for almost two years. There were eight in my crew when we started out. One stayed in Bhandi, the other was injured and died." She pointed to the four windmills attached to the outrigger rails amidship that ran the generators which powered the lights and machines of the ship, and when the wind failed, kept the vessel moving. "We need to replace the windmill on the foredeck. It was damaged in a storm, nine days ago. The rest need inspecting and retuning. We have a long way to go; we're a long way from home."

"Eight crew," I mused, regarding the grand ship that was being secured by lines to the high metal cleats on the edge of the dock. "A small crew for such a long voyage, and such a large vessel."

"But a loyal one, and very experienced," she said, and held out her hand for the thin sheet of stiffened cotton that I would use to record her arrival, her cargo bought and sold, and her departure. "What do I owe you and where do I put my sign?"

"You owe the city six ounces of gold or twenty-one standard blocks of first-grade plastic for seven days dockage. You sign here. And here," I said to her as I held out the record book, smiling at her as if no one were near us. "Do you have an invoice on your cargo?"

"In total or for trade or sale?" She regarded me steadily, and then she laughed. "I haven't made up my mind about what I want from here. When I've decided I'll let you know what cargo I'm offering here in Lavrant City. In the meantime, I'll order the plastic blocks delivered to—"

"—to my office. It's at the end of the main dock, where the freight yard begins. The office has three gold stars over the door." I tried not to look too eager to have her come to my cramped wooden cabin.

"Then it's settled," said Endra, about to depart. "You'll have your plastic by sunset, top quality, don't worry. Any newsmonger who wants to find me can seek me out where I lodge." She made a show of pondering, and though I knew it was a ploy, I was still captivated by her. "Perhaps I should mention that I have a guard belowdecks, and only I can disarm it."

I cleared my throat. "That may be a problem. Here in Lavrant City, we ask to know what all the cargo is, whether or not you offer it in the market."

She had already taken a step away from me, but she stopped and regarded me as if I had deliberately offended her. "Why is that?"

I could see many in the crowd around us watching with anticipation as if they wondered how she would react. "Not long ago there were pirates in these northern waters, and they would steal from our merchants and merchants in other cities, and the goods would be sold far away. Since that time, we have required a complete inventory of cargo upon arrival, a comparison inspection before you depart, and records kept so that the stolen goods may be traced." I had explained this many times before, but this was the first time I had felt apologetic about it. "Our coasting courier-ships carry information to all the main ports within three days' sail."

"I see," she said, her brows rising. "Well, you give me something to think about."

I could not allow her to walk away yet. "If it will ease your mind, I'll attend to the inspection myself. You may have your guard monitor all I do. But it must be done, or dockage will have to be rescinded."

She made a show of considering my offer. "All right. I'll have my recorder prepare a copy of the current inventory, and you may check it out tomorrow. I'll give it to you in the morning, and arrange for your inspection then, if you don't mind."

It was highly irregular, so I said, "The custom is for the inspection to occur within an hour of arrival, but as you are unfamiliar with our laws, we will station a guard at the base of your gangplank from now until morning, one that cannot be disarmed without sounding a loud warning. You may join us for the inspection, if you like." I motioned to Skeimir, my first assistant, and said, "See that this is done."

"If it is your custom, then do what you must." As she moved away from me, she looked back at me in a manner that I thought might be flirtatious—although I had long since learned that the customs of others are often misunderstood. "Not to impose, but can you tell me where I can get a drink and a bed for the night? Something stronger than wine, and among sailors and others used to the sea? I don't like to drink alone in a strange port."

I thought for a moment. "The Blue Pelican has been a favorite of sea-goers for three generations. It's one street over, and along on your right. You can see the sign easily from the corner." Glowmosses were sealed in the sign, the image of the bird shining by their light as they consumed the thin smudge of bacteria that outlined the pelican; the smudge was renewed daily. I pointed it out to her. "With the sky-blue door. Ask for Thenemor."

"Thanks. You can find me there, then. I need a bath, a meal, a drink, and a bed. I trust they'll provide them?"

"Certainly," I said. "At a reasonable price."

The assembled people on the dock parted to let her through. She was almost to the edge of them when she halted and called back to me, still in Coigne, and asked, "What language do you speak here?"

"Candish, and some Nirikal," I replied.

"I'd best stick to Coigne, then; I don't know the other two at all." She waved and went on toward the Blue Pelican.

I watched her go, my thoughts disordered and excited. Never before had I been so captivated, and never had I encountered such a remarkable woman. I should not permit myself to be so engaged by a visitor to Lavrant City, but I couldn't help it: I was fascinated, and I knew I would have to find an excuse to seek her out by the end of the day. The afternoon would be an endless wait for an opportunity to visit the Blue Pelican.

From the desk journal of Ogmar kem Zrol, keeper of the Blue Pelican

Guest 14 today, arrived early afternoon—Endra YuiduJin, Captain of Taksteppe Empire merchant ship the Empress FahrenDier, home port Sui-Kan-below-the-Dam. Assigned Room 41, paid for a week in gold. Ordered an hour in the bath, and said she may want more later in the week, for she contemplated a stay of four or five days. I dispatched Ringrif to bring her things from her ship; strict instructions for him to stay above decks since the ship's guard is set below. She bespoke six rooms for her crew and paid for their lodging, then she ordered a meal for herself to be served in two hours, and took my recommendation for the pork-and-lentils, claiming she was tired of fish; then she asked if Temui HeimunWei had been in this city of late, and I said I did not know this Temui HeimunWei. She offered me a standard block of plastic to improve my memory, and I told her once more that I didn't know the person in question, much as I would have liked the plastic.

From the report of Volai kir Achdoer, ledgermaker of Lavrant City

The Empress FahrenDier has two long floatation out-riggers which contain no cargo or other supplies. Like all Taksteppe Empire vessels, the ship has a flexible frame and is made to withstand severe storms without breaking apart; the sails are battened at regular intervals and fold up like old-fashioned blinds; from their arrangement, the ship is best designed to reach and run, although its outriggers would allow it to point into the wind fairly closely. There are some signs of recent repair on the starboard prow, which appear to be in good order. The galley is amidships, the Captain's cabin aft, the crew's quarters forward. Generators are at the mid-fore and mid-aft decks, in ceramo-plastic housings. There are six cargo holds, four of which are full. Most of the cargo is fairly standard: plastic cubes for currency, long cheese, textiles, copper and gold wire from Ormud, wine and distilled wine from Karpat, some objects said to be from sunken cities like Venz and Myam and Riod, to choose the deepest. Two waterproof chests contain bulletins and broadsheets from many ports, and may be copied, I am told, for a fee. There are stores of foodstuffs in a preservation unit, which serves the Captain and crew, and stored clothing for weather of all sorts, and some foods that can be sold as well as eaten. But the most astounding thing in the cargo holds is wood—three different varieties, all in standardized lengths and widths, cut with precision and ready for use. This ship carries a fortune in lumber, and all of it is marked with seals to show its legality. There must be more than enough to build a large house, entirely of wood. Where are they willing to cut down so many trees and then sell them? I know of no city or nation that is profligate with its trees.

The recorder shows the route the ship has followed, and where trade has taken place, with whom, and what profit has accrued from such negotiation. The personal log of the Captain confirms what is recorded. It is truly a great journey the Captain has undertaken. I can only guess at which port they traded for all the wood—and what they must have paid for it. I have added copies of the inventory and of the itinerary and made an entry in the recorder that I have done this on my own authority.

From the memoirs of Melizan kem Gishcar-Shwy

I spent half that evening at the Blue Pelican, listening to Endra YuiduJin tell stories of her voyages and all she had seen in her travels, which, if even half of it was true, was enough to compel all her listeners to regard her with the same respect that an officer of the Fleet is held. Mard Compatel, the main newsmonger, sat at the end of her table and scribbled while Endra spoke. She told of departing from the Taksteppe Empire and proceeding eastward past the Nimo Archipelago to the Three Chains Islands and the port of Yash-Cu, then north to the Great Sandras Sea, which she entered and where she traded at three ports before returning to the ocean and headed northward where she docked at Scade Mountain before going northward again; she said she encountered many large icebergs but little pack-ice, over the crest of the world and down to Lavrant City. I told her pack-ice was quite rare in this part of the ocean, even though it is to the north a goodly way. Endra was curious about the lack of pack-ice, but she wouldn't say why, and when I pressed her on the matter, she changed the subject: she spoke of many storms in the warm parts of the ocean, and humid air at the midpoint of the world that was more water than not; she said she had called at fourteen ports and had encountered a total of fifty-three ships at sea since the voyage began; one of those sighted she said was flying a plague flag, and so steered away from it. Her intention, she said, was to go down the coast all the way to the Bulge, then cross to the eastern side of the ocean and continue to the south end of the world, then pass through the Southern Atolls, and finally to return to the Taksteppe Empire at last. She said her recorder had corrected the charts for the area northwest of here, where one of the passages had been changed by a massive landslide. "Keeping charts current is a constant labor. I will leave a copy of the revisions we have for you."

"Thank you." My appreciation was genuine, for charts often went out of date quickly, and I longed to have something of her after she departed.

"It is my duty as a Captain to provide current information to other seafarers." She said it by rote, but with a shine in her eyes that made me hesitate to ask her anything more on the matter.

At one point in the conversation, I said, "You are planning to trade everywhere you go, I suppose."

"I have to do something to make the voyage worthwhile. Trading is the purpose of the journey, officially." She smiled again, more beguilingly than before. "It isn't just my advantage I'm serving: you can profit from a larger trading zone. If I bring a good report, there will be more traders coming from the Taksteppe Empire to Lavrant City, and other ports."

"Very likely," I allowed. "And no doubt we will have cause to thank you in time for your travels."

She laughed once. "Why do you dislike the ocean so much?"

"It is a devourer of land and of lives," I said before I had actually considered my answer. "It encroaches constantly."

Endra laughed again. "And what does not? At least the sea brings freedom; it gives us its bounty. You curse the rising water, but you forget that when the floods were at their worst, how would any of us have lived without the fish of the ocean to feed us." She took her cup and drained it, then held it up for more. "It is good to be ashore and in pleasant company."

Casting a wary eye upon her and convinced he had gained all the information he could use, the newsmonger rose and bowed himself out of the taproom.

"It continues to rise—the sea does," I said. "More slowly, but it rises. In the last hundred years, it has risen by more than the length of my leg, and there is no sign of abatement."

"And one day it will fall, according to all the scholars of Pideng. The sunken cities around the world were once above the water, all of them. The great teachers say they will be so again, in time." She tossed a coin to the barman as he refilled her cup. "And if the water rises until there is no land left, then it will be as well to be on good terms with the ocean, wouldn't it?" She drank, a little of the distilled wine sliding down her cheek.

"It would have to rise a very long way," I said.

"And people would have to crowd onto fewer and fewer islands," she said, a morose note in her voice. "That, or drown as so many have, they say. The analysts on Ropea say that in all the world there are less than half a billion people now, and the numbers continue to fall. In Tit'clan, they say that there are less than a quarter million residents, where legend says there were once ten times that number." She leaned back, looking up at the ceiling while balancing on the rear legs of her chair. "The marshes of N'Da—you know where they are, in the south-southeast? Once they were vast plains and creatures we have only seen in ancient pictures roamed there in their thousands upon thousands. As the water rises, many things are lost, not just drowned cities."

"So, all the records agree," I said somberly, wishing the unhappiness in her face would vanish, and not knowing how to make that happen.

She continued to drink, finally looking at me over the rim of her cup before she hoisted it for another refill. "Now that we're alone, shall I tell you a secret?"

I considered her bibulous state and knew it was an imposition to ask her anything more. "If you like," I said, making a sop to my conscience that I had not actually encouraged her to tell me anything. I wondered if I should simply postpone our discussion, but I couldn't make myself leave her.

"I have a bet. With Temui HeimunWei." She giggled and drank some more from her newly full cup. "We're looking for Simoon. Whoever finds it first gets the other's ship. I'm looking forward to being Captain of the *Wave Flyer*." Her eyes shone with excitement at the thought. "Last year, when he and I met in Bongar, he said he had come upon a map to the Six Inland Seas. They're south of you, according to the map, and to the west, and Simoon is at the far end of the central sea." She wagged a finger at me. "Now don't tell anyone. Don't say a word. Not to anyone. But if you see Temui HeimunWei, then tell him—only him, mind—that I'm going to try to find the entrance to the Six Inland Seas."

How I managed to maintain a calm face, I can't begin to remember. But I couldn't keep from saying, "Isn't Simoon just a legend?"

"Most people think so," she said, "which is why no one's ever found it."

"What do you mean?"

She gave me all her owlish attention. "If everyone thinks it doesn't exist, no one will ever find it, because they won't bother looking. But the legends say it is located at the far end of the third of the Six Inland Seas. Once the passage to the Six Inland Seas is found, then it shouldn't be difficult to go and look for Simoon."

"Aren't you asking for a lot of disappointment?" I asked, trying to be gentle with her, and arousing her ire.

"How could I be disappointed?" She slapped her palm on the table. "It's *Simoon!*" She looked around the taproom and lowered her voice. "Oh, I don't expect to find all the treasures lost to the rising water, and all the delights of the ancient times, but I believe that Simoon has managed to keep more of those treasures than the rest of us have, and maintained a way of life that is more pleasant than most of the cities of the world can boast. They say that the people of Simoon love knowledge more than all other pursuits, and uphold justice. They have banished hunger and strife. If nothing else, they would have a great many things to teach us."

I tried not to be too skeptical—she had been at sea for many months, and she was giddy from drink—but I had to say, "Do you truly think they would want to be found, if they exist at all? If they have achieved so fine a society, why would they disrupt it with strangers?"

"Well, wouldn't you?" She challenged me. "Don't you think they'd want to know they aren't the only ones left?" She let this question hang in the air before she said, "I know I would."

"If they have a peaceful, just society, as it's said they do, where sadness is unknown, they might not want anything to change it, and admitting those from beyond Simoon would bring changes," I said, not because I believed this, but because she was so caught up in her pursuit of the place.

"How cynical you are," she said as she pushed herself to her feet, then leaned over and kissed me full on the mouth before teetering off toward Room 41.

As I watched her go, I tried to think of all the things I should have said, and all the things I might have done, but I knew they were useless, and I wondered how I could bear to see her every one of the days she would remain here.

From the records of the Lavrant City Trading Authority

The trading of the Empress FahrenDier has concluded with the following exchanges with registered merchants of the Lavrant City Trading Authority:

To the merchants of the city, ten planks of oak, for fifty-nine standard blocks of first-grade plastic and fourteen barrels of purified water.

To the merchants of the city, ten bolts of silk, for ten full bundles of musk-ox yarn and a crate of cured otter-skins.

To the merchants of the city, two full spools of copper wire, for a newly restored generator and windmill for the Empress FahrenDier.

To the merchants of Eijmor, nine full bolts of Theopic linen, for sixteen casks of Gasbin resin, and two casks of dried figs.

<h1 style="text-align:center">Chelsea Quinn Yarbro</h1>

From the memoirs of Melizan kam Gishcar-Shwy

I hated to see her leave, but I was also relieved. The *Empress FahrenDier* stood out to sea with half her sails unfurled and battened, as fine a vessel as any I have ever seen. I wished Endra YuiduJin well on her fruitless search, and I hoped that she would come to her senses and return to Lavrant City, and to me, even as I knew that she was a madness in my blood. I chided myself for such a selfish idea—how could she give up the sea just because I adored her? —but I could not banish it entirely from my thoughts; it nagged me unceasingly for two years, until at last she came back.

That was another windy day, the bay afroth with spume, the sea twisting and coiling like a serpent; the sky lowered under heavy clouds and the wharf was seething with crews looking for safe mooring for their ships since a storm was coming. The *Empress FahrenDier* glided up to the dock as if the deteriorating weather meant nothing, snuggling up to the berth as if she had been a rowboat on calm waters; as I hurried toward the ship, I saw Endra YuiduJin standing at the steering console, a roguish grin on her face. She turned to look at me and waved. All the perils of the gathering tempest faded from my mind as I waited for her gangplank to descend.

"Did you miss me?" she asked as she came down to the dock; she looked more tired than she had two years ago, but there was the same glint in her eyes that revealed so much of her nature that I found myself once again almost holding my breath.

"Did you find Simoon?" I countered, and wished as soon as I said it that I had bit my tongue out instead.

"Not yet," she said with the same determination she had expressed before, her unhumorous decision to find this mythic place stronger in her than it had been before. "But I've found more good information to help me in my search. It's out there—I can smell it." She squinted out at the bay as if expecting to find information there on the spume-frosted water.

"What does Temui HeimunWei think?" I asked, trying not to flounder.

"Our paths haven't crossed since I left here last time. I was told that he wintered in Dyskin, far to the south this last year, where it was summer, but I haven't learned where he was bound. I've asked about him in every port, and so far, nothing." She held out her plastic-imbued cloth. "Here is the information you want; your inspector may go aboard to make his report as soon as you like." She lifted her chin as if expecting me to argue with her. "I'm going along to the Blue Pelican."

I knew I should remain with her ship to supervise the monitoring of the inventory, but once again I called my assistant, Skeimir, and ordered him to take over the monitoring. "I have something I need to ask Captain YuiduJin."

"I'll send to the Blue Pelican if there are any questions." Skeimir tromped toward the gangplank as if he felt he had to carry the sum of the inventory on and off the ship in his own arms.

Endra was already well into her first tankard of strong brandy when I went into the taproom and found her seated on the bench by the fire. She was grinning as she drank. "Kem Gishcar-Shwy," she called out, waving her hand and motioning me to sit across from her. "You'll have hot brandy, too. Two comrades, sharing a drink." She very nearly winked at me but strove for a little more decorum.

The barmaid regarded me dubiously but poured out the drink as she had been ordered.

"Have you had a profitable voyage, Endra?" I asked as I sat down across from her; the light from the window was on her face, and I drank in the sight of her.

"Enough, enough," she said. "I was afraid we'd lose all to raiders, but we outran them, and that meant we saved our cargo and our lives. They had impressive guns, but their seamanship failed them in a following sea, and they paid the price." She set her tankard down with a satisfying bang, then called out, "What do you have cooking?"

"Shrimp-stuffed salmon and roasted goose; duck eggs and salt-cheese," said the barmaid. "We're supposed to get some upland goat tomorrow."

"I'm hungry tonight," said Endra, and winked at me. "For a lot of things."

I tried to keep myself from feeling encouraged by her innuendo, but I could feel my pulse increase and a tightness in my loins that was not answerable to reason. "I hope all your wants are satisfied."

"So do I," she said, and licked her lips.

"What about the newsmonger? He'll be here shortly."

"I've left word that I'll see him tomorrow afternoon. Tonight, I want only your company."

Had it been anyone but her, I would have thought her blatant display unwelcome, but it was Endra, and I had dreamed about her too long to disapprove of anything she did. I drank with her, ate with her, and slept next to her while she tossed and mumbled through the night, and in the morning, I went to the dock with her, for the joy of her company. Along the way, I did what I could to persuade her that she belonged ashore, with me, safe and protected. I knew as I spoke that I was losing her, that all my closely reasoned arguments were nonsense, but I could not keep from saying that "The sea is a demanding life, one that belongs to younger men and women. You have succeeded where your mother failed, and have twice circumnavigated the planet, and your reputation is assured. From the Taksteppe Empire to Riton to the ends of the earth, you are known as the finest of all the Captains. Can't you be content with that?" It was too much; I knew it as soon as the words passed my lips. I can still recall the look she gave me, reproachful and recalcitrant at once. "I know you love the oceans, and you needn't give them up, but think of all you could do coasting. We need more regular inspections of the coasts, captains for our couriers, and with your background, your contribution would be incredibly valuable."

"Make the sea my hobby," she said in a tone so strange that I couldn't sort out her meaning.

"More than a hobby," I said in what I thought was a helpful manner, "but not as laden with risks as what you have done."

She was about to say something when we rounded the end of the wharf and saw her ship tied up along the dock. Endra shaded her eyes and gave a little cry of dismay and hurried toward her ship.

Besq SoVirth, Endra's First Officer, was pacing up and down the gangplank, his manner agitated. "Captain! Finally!"

"What is it?" In spite of her hard drinking, enthusiastic eating, and nightmares, she appeared fresh and capable as she stepped onto the gangplank.

SoVirth pointed to the orotund hull of a Ritonic merchant vessel that was tied up farther down the dock, swaying on the boisterous water. "They arrived not two hours ago. The Watchman said that two days out they encountered the *Wave Flyer* bound to the south and the Maithen Channel."

Endra leaned close to SoVirth. "And Temui HeimunWei—he was aboard the *Wave Flyer*."

"According to the Watchman. I can send for him, if you like?"

I wanted to say something, to encourage doubts in Endra's mind, but I could see already that I would lose any attempt to discourage her. "You're paid for four days," I pointed out, an act of futility.

"Keep it," she said, and addressed SoVirth. "Go and round up the others. Tell them we sail within the hour."

"You'll go against the tide," I warned.

"Our windmills make enough power to get us to the open sea, and we should be able to make good time." She made a wave of impatience and almost hurled SoVirth from the gangplank. "Hurry. We need to be off now. And Melizan," she went on, pointing to me. "Expedite our departure."

"But Endra—"

"Do it for me. Please. Simoon, Melizan. Think. The country that is good and just, and where the treasures of the past haven't been lost." She came and took my arm, looking into my face with such an open display of supplication that all my stalwart intentions faded and I said, "I'll arrange full credit for you. For next time."

This time her smile was genuine. "Yes. For next time." She watched SoVirth jogging toward the street. "That will be the third time—don't the heroes of seafaring always return three times to their home ports?" She offered me a jaunty little bow. "Next time, Melizan. Truly."

I took a deep breath, prepared to pledge my life to her return, but she was already on the deck, checking the windmills and starting them turning. I had stepped away when she called out to me.

"Wait for me, Melizan. I'll come back to Lavrant City, and to you." She waved as she hurried about, making ready for her departure.

I couldn't bear to stay and watch.

From the report of Volai kir Achdoer, ledgermaker of Lavrant City

On order of the Trading Monitor, Melizan kem Gishcar-Shwy, the overage of dockage payment received from Captain Endra YuiduJin of the Empress FahrenDier is to be held in trust against dockage charges upon her return.

From the memoirs of Melizan kem Gishcar-Shwy

But, of course, she didn't return. For years I railed at myself for not being able to entice her to stay, blaming myself that I had not had the courage to speak to her while I had the chance. Ten years after her last visit, someone said that she and the *Empress FahrenDier* had gone down off the Shallow Sea in the south. Later I heard that she had been seen in the Riton Islands, fighting off the raiders who frequent those waters. Perhaps thirty years ago it was reported that she had become a recluse, living on the isolated peaks of the volcanic island of Jiya, and had given up the sea for a life of contemplation. Two decades ago, after a particularly hard winter, a sailor from Hatp on the Great Sandras Sea said he had seen the wreckage of her ship on the Eastward Isles. And not so many years ago a traveler said he had heard that she had finally caught up with Temui HeimunWei and together they found Simoon, and were made welcome there.

Gradually Endra YuiduJin passed from speculation to rumor, and then into legend, so that now half the sailors on the boats that call in at the harbor believe she never existed at all, and is only a myth of the oceans, like the Ship of Light. Others, less kindly, say age has distorted my memory, so that what I report is only of dreams and fancies, there never was such a real person as Endra, that I have built this passion on the tales I have heard through the years. But you have seen my proofs, from the inn, from the harbor records, from the Trading Authority, preserved here with my recollections, and you know that she was at Lavrant City in her ship the *Empress FahrenDier*, that flew the colors of the Taksteppe Empire—that Endra is real.

I have passed my seventieth year, well beyond what most people attain, and I don't think I will last another decade; in the long time I have thought about Endra, I have gone from yearning for her return to accepting this would not happen, and mourning her absence. Yet recently I have begun to hope that she did indeed find Temui HeimunWei, and that they reached Simoon, where all the treasures lost to the rising waters remain, pristine and perfect; where all men love knowledge and peace; where there is no hunger, no injustice, no cruelty, and sadness has been forgotten.

The Final Girl

MIA DALIA

For Chelsea—here's to a world that makes sense.

She could hear his voice in the wind, guttural and sibilant at once, calling, calling her name. Harsh consonants kept getting tangled up in the tree branches that whipped her body, heavy vowels that got caught in the forest floor beneath her feet, tripping her up.

"The duff" was what the man used to call it, all that dead vegetation on the ground. He seemed to have a word for everything. All the things she never gave much thought to, all the things she hadn't needed to know in her life before this one.

It was difficult to think about that life now; impossible. It simply didn't seem real. This—these trees, this wind, even the man's voice—all felt perfectly, vividly, viscerally real.

The voice couldn't be, though, she knew. Flashes of her memory, sharp as lightning, brought back the man as she had left him, with a knife stuck in his neck up to the hilt, arterial blood from the slashed carotid, bright red surrounding him like a grotesque halo.

Bright red. She remembered. Like the afterimage of the sun the moment you close your eyes after sky gazing. All that oxygenated hemoglobin. Another thing the man taught her. Before.

She was getting winded; this had to be the most running she'd done since high school track. But she wouldn't dare stop. Not now. Not when she was so close.

She could hear the highway, the familiar swoosh of passing cars. It felt comforting, almost like a distant childhood memory—

funnel cake sugar dust at the amusement park—but she knew it couldn't have been that long since she heard it last.

At the man's cabin, she had lost track of time. There was no calendar, no newspapers, no TV; even her period had stopped . . . owing to the stress and the new sparse diet, but by her best reckoning it must've been months, four or five months.

The highway seemed to be below her, down the steep hill crisscrossed with shrubbery and small trees. She plowed through it, barely noticing the new cuts and wounds being added to the old ones. The feeling in her feet was lost a while back, now she was afraid to even look.

There were no shoes; the man took hers away and his were too giant to move in. She tried them on before leaving, they were like crudely made boats. No tightening of shoelaces would be enough.

The hill sped up her descent so much that she had to arrest her velocity by falling to her hands and knees onto the highway asphalt when she reached it. A passing car swerved to avoid her with a loud honk. Did they think she was doing this for fun? Being merely careless?

There were no more cars coming, that she could see.

She scrambled to the lip of the road and let her body be overtaken by gravity, plopping into a sort of sit/crouch position. Braved a look at her feet.

The sodden, bloody, torn mess of them would have made her weep—had she any tears left. It must have been pure adrenaline that carried her this far because the horror show below her ankles certainly couldn't have done the job alone.

She dreaded to imagine what the rest of her might look like. There were no mirrors in the cabin—the man abhorred vanity and was too cunning to leave around something that could easily be weaponized. Sometimes he let her bathe, in an old-fashioned tarnished metal tub that made her think of a watering trough. First, he made her boil water and pour it in, then mix it with the rain runoff from the outside barrel. About a month into this, she tried to throw the pot of boiling water at him. She missed. He got angry, so angry . . . she shuddered to remember. After that, there were no hot, lukewarm, or even tepid baths. There were barely any baths at all.

She was filthy now, she could feel the dirt, sweat, and spilled blood congealed around her skin like a gruesome carapace. Her hair—naturally blonde and lustrous, once upon a time she thought it to be her best feature—was now matted, unbrushed, untended for much too long.

She wore a t-shirt the man gave her a while back, one of his own, worn so thin it could be considered see-through, the logo on it long ago faded into illegibility.

The man was a giant, or at least that's how she came to think of him, for it seemed to her that he had always towered over her. His t-shirt came down nearly to her knees, a makeshift dress, of sorts. Ripped now by the sharp branches, bloodied by both of them, the old owner and the new.

There was a car at a distance, the sound of it approaching—a Doppler effect in practice—was as beautiful as music to her ears. She unfolded her protesting limbs, coached them into verticality once more, and suppressing a scream into a whimper held her arms up.

The car skirted her so closely she could feel the heat of the exhaust on her wounds. Classic rock blasting through their open windows and not a care in the world. Nor did they want any.

She didn't have the energy to scream at them, to cuss them out. The carelessness, the casual comfort with which they moved through life, she too had known it once.

She'd like to believe she would have stopped for herself or someone like her, but she couldn't be sure. That version of her seemed so far away, almost unreachable through the bloody fog of the recent months.

Remade, she knew she'd been remade by the man, broken and put together again, a close but incomplete approximation. All she felt was the missing parts, all he talked about were the added features. He told her he was making her stronger, smarter, more adaptable to the lawless wilderness he perceived the world to be. In her weakest moments, she believed him too. He could be so convincing. As convincing as the jailer with all the keys. As the hand that's feeding you.

For so long, the man and their shared nightmare had been the only game in town.

What was she now? A victim? A survivor? Was she stronger indeed? Strong enough to slay her dragon? Strong enough to get away? Or was it merely desperation that drove her, a primal instinct she had no control over, no say in?

Something was poking at the back of her mind, some phrase acquired long ago and never used, never given the opportunity to be used. A college roommate obsessed with horror . . . what did she call the last one left standing in her beloved slasher movies? Oh yes! *The final girl.*

That's what she was then. The final girl. She smiled. It probably didn't look like a smile. Too calculated, too bitter. In the animal kingdom, such things were displays of aggression, the man taught her. Well, then, be it, she thought, better to be an aggressor, a predator instead of the prey.

The final girl straightened out her spine, brushed down her ragged shirt. Folded her hands into fists to feel the jagged nails bite into her palms, then unfolded them, put them over her head to wave.

The next car stopped.

⁂

Afterwards, there were questions. So many questions. Monochrome walls, an overpowering smell of Lysol and bleach, and good intentions.

She had been cleaned, fed, hydrated. Examined through and through and found to be in a mostly satisfactory condition. Her cuts were bandaged, her bruises left to heal.

The journalists weren't allowed near her, but the police were more than enough. The cops were worst of all. Detective Jennings and Clay were a pairing straight out of Cervantes, one tall and skinny, one short and chubby. They tried the official approach with their notepads out and serious expressions on; they tried the friendly one: Call me John, call me Stacy. Nothing took.

She didn't want to talk to them, didn't want to relive her nightmare, didn't want to satisfy their curiosity, which to her felt increasingly more prurient.

What did it matter? The man was dead. She did her best to give them directions to his house. Justice, if such a concept still existed, had been served. All she wanted now was to be left alone.

She was never good at meditating, no matter how enthusiastically her mother had recommended it, but at the man's house, she found a way to sort of zone out, find a dark quiet place within herself, and go there. It was a self-defense mechanism, a coping strategy. A fragile thing—a single angry shout from the man could rip right through it. But sometimes, there was silence. Beautiful, welcoming silence. Hers only whenever he left to go attend to whatever business he might have had in the outside world. Not the city sort of silence she was used to from her life before—the cacophonous symphony of sirens, passersby's conversations, car honks, crying babies, and yapping dogs—but a pure perfect middle of nowhere silence where the loudest thing was her own breath.

She learned to crave it, need it. Now she missed it terribly. Nowhere was quiet anymore.

Most conversations forced upon her she ended by simply turning her head away, toward the window, as if desperately looking for something.

Trauma, they said. PTSD. They didn't understand that she was merely disassociating the only way she knew how, the only way she could, trying, trying to tune out.

Her parents came all the way from Wisconsin. Mortified, relieved, stunned. With tears and questions of their own.

They looked older, greyer, with new thinness to their skin. A far cry from the chatty, relentlessly upbeat Midwesterners she left behind in her conquest of adulthood, relegating them to holidays and Zoom calls.

This version of her parents wore their concern heavily, and she could see it was wearing them out. She could feel it, the oppressing cloud of it; hear it in the things they said and, especially, in the things they didn't say.

In their almost-but-not-quite-teary eyes, all the unasked questions swam like piranhas. She thought they could leap up to the surface and attack her at any time. The loudest scariest of them all . . . what did this monster do to our daughter?

What would she say to that? What *could* she say to that? Perhaps she was a monster now in her own right, monstrous by association.

Whenever they offered her a mirror, she turned away. Even asked to cover the one small industrial one above the bathroom sink. She didn't want to see herself, but in her parents' kind, exhaustingly kind faces, she could, and she hated it. Knew she must have changed, so much. Too much, maybe.

For the first month or two of her time with the man, she missed seeing her face, in reflective surfaces, mirrors, selfies. But vanity must have been the sin easiest erased because, after a while, she found she didn't miss it at all.

Her parents insisted. They wanted photos, tangible proof of their daughter's return. She acquiesced, reluctantly. Then asked to have her hair cut short.

Shorn, she felt a certain relief, a certain freedom. Fresh, clean. Combined with sharp, privation-diet-cheekbones, and a newfound steeliness of her seen-too-much eyes, the new look was striking. Slick, icy, sharp—she looked like a blade's edge and loved it.

The inherited softness of her features and the mild expression were gone, she no longer looked like her parents. The photos made it blatantly obvious. The contrast was strange, strong; they stopped with the camera.

'Why do you look so old?' she wanted to ask. 'It's only been a few months. All you had to do was worry. Sit on your comfortable reclining couch in your comfortable suburban home and worry. That's nothing. Nothing compared to what I'd been through. Nothing at all.'

Eventually, she did ask. Well, not all of it, just the main question.

"But honey," her mother said, the look of consternation wrinkling her forehead, "it's been three years."

They let her go, after a while. There was, after all, nothing wrong with her that time, good food, and an army of shrinks couldn't fix.

Her apartment in the city was gone. Well, it was still there, but long since taken over by a stranger. Her parents at some point had closed out her lease, packed up her belongings, and taken them back to Wisconsin.

Normally, she would have bristled at this invasion of privacy—imagining her parents going through her things—but now it didn't seem to matter. She went through boxes of her clothes, books, and knick-knacks and felt nothing, no emotional tug, nothing at all. It was as if they were owned by another person, in another life.

Her childhood room welcomed her, complete with the pink-comforter-covered twin bed. It was a 10x12 space struck in time; preserved by her parents for her infrequent visits with the assiduousness one normally reserves for museums.

She didn't feel welcome. Didn't care for the way her parents tiptoed around her like she was made of glass. Didn't want to reconnect with any old friends or visit old haunts.

She ate what she could at family meals and pretended to watch TV with them, her thoughts miles away.

Nothing felt real.

Whenever she was outside, she scanned crowds for predators, the man taught her to recognize them—something around the eyes. All her survivalist training remained tightly coiled inside, just waiting to spring free. Nowhere was safe and people who acted otherwise were fools. Life just hadn't gotten to them yet, hadn't broken them yet.

Their conversations were meaningless and built upon small talk. Their experiences . . . well, just stupid. The edgiest of all talked dreamily of the make-believe dangers of being mock-locked-in somewhere to solve a puzzle or going bungee-jumping.

It was as if none of them had realized that life was dangerous enough as is. That just getting through the day in one piece was enough. That you mustn't chance it or tempt it.

She hadn't in the past. Well, she barely did. A drunken romp through the city at a late hour now and again, sure, but nothing crazy. And he *still* found her.

Still took her.

She barely remembered that night. Everyone presumed it would be etched into her memory, chiseled into her psyche, but no—it was a Friday night like so many others. Tequila shots at El Chupacabra with the girls, another tedious work week dished over and erased, and then a stumble home. Her Uber was late, and she got tired of waiting; it wasn't that far of a walk.

The man grabbed her right off the street; her clearest recollection was the strength of his arms, the way his giant frame obliterated the night sky behind him.

Then a long, impossibly long drive. Then a new life.

A life she hated every moment of but one that felt real in a way nothing else ever had. It wasn't anything she could explain.

Shrink after shrink now, one pair of sympathetic eyes after another behind the designer frames. Tastefully understated offices that screamed 'strategically-designed comfort'. Chairs that were soft but not too soft. They all wanted to understand. They all offered her labels, PTSD, Stockholm Syndrome.

But surely not. Surely not. There was no trust, no affection between her and the man. She'd hated him. She'd *killed* him.

She'd do it again, too.

He was vicious, violent, vile. He did terrible things to her, things she could still feel on her skin like aftereffects, still see when she closed her eyes, like afterimages.

But he had never lied to her. Never made promises. Everything he taught her was practical. In his mind, he was preparing her for the world to come.

There was no apocalypse scenario in which she wouldn't fare well now, she knew. Unlike her parents, their neighbors, her former coworkers, and old friends, she would have a real fighting chance, come war, zombies, or aliens.

Was the end of the world on its way, as the man had been so convinced it was? Difficult to say. She read the news and thought so; saw the destructive patterns behind the events, read between the lines.

On the other hand, the world wasn't a particularly dynamic place—it cherished its status quo. No matter how crappy things got a certain balance was still maintained. The madmen postured but retreated. Muscles were flexed then relaxed. Nobody, it seemed, wanted to be the one to upset the intricately crafted equilibrium. And so, they perpetuated. The mad carousel of the world going round and round.

Now that she'd been taken from it, yanked off so rudely, so irrevocably, she couldn't get back on. Couldn't imagine doing so. Didn't think she wanted it.

There were no jobs she saw herself performing; going back to marketing seemed absurdly unfeasible. Her parents pushed and prodded ever so gently, and she smiled and nodded and pretended to peruse employment opportunity websites.

She lied to them that she was applying for positions. They lied and told her to take her time.

They were happy, so happy to have her back, but they didn't seem to know what to do with her now that they got her back. She wasn't the daughter they remembered, merely a ghost of her. A difficult and distant presence, all sharp edges and unfathomable thoughts. A stranger who shared their DNA and last name, someone they loved dearly and couldn't understand at all.

For years, all they ever wanted was for her to return. After a while, their hopes began waning, but they never stopped wishing for, at least, closure.

Their lives had been so simple, so scripted until now, that the tragedy of her disappearance had hit them like a tornado, in a place where a tornado had never been seen. They didn't have the fortitude, the mental stamina, to endure the uncertainty of their only child's fate. The world had always been so kind to them . . . until that Friday years ago.

Now they'd become a local center of attention—something neither of them relished. In their church, at their respective jobs, at the swim club—their only stab at luxury—supermarkets, the post office. A town small enough that a scandal, any scandal, reverberated for years to come. Everyone wanted to know the ugly, salacious details, the how, and the whys. Things they barely knew themselves because their daughter didn't talk about them. Not to them, anyway.

Maybe to the dangerously expensive psychologists they had to move funds around to afford. Maybe to them.

Truth be told, as happy as they were to have their daughter back, they also desperately wanted their lives returned to normal. It was a monstrously selfish thought for either of them, so much so that they didn't dare voice it, even to each other—but privately they craved it all the same—the restoration of their comfortable, predictable, easy lives . . . with their daughter safely and happily back in the city and seen on holidays and Zoom calls. The way things were once upon a time. The way things worked best.

They didn't dare push her though. They told each other it would happen. She'd change, find a way back to her old self, reconnect with friends, get a job. They buoyed themselves with these thoughts and floated on this current of wishful thinking through their days.

Their hopes took on dreamlike aspects, waiting to feel real.

✷✷✷✷✷

She walked out of the movie midway through, unable to stand any more stupidity. At the rate the main heroine was carrying on, she could have killed the girl herself. Weak, pathetic. The movie crowd cheered for the blonde on screen, though. Would they have cheered for her? Would they have cheered when fear is real, and blood isn't corn syrup-based? When the final girl isn't wearing makeup and designer clothes?

The villain on screen was a joke, too. A caricature of a man in a torn clown suit with a lachrymose backstory about childhood abuse. The menace he projected was a joke. Overdone, over-the-top, telegraphed from miles away.

In real life, or rather in the only life that felt real to her now, the man was perfectly normal looking, if oversized. He told her in his rough, serious voice that he'd had a nice childhood, good parents, that he had never murdered an animal he didn't plan on eating.

People, well . . . people, of course, were a different story.

She knew there had been girls before her; she saw the graves. Evenly spaced out, simply marked with a flat rock. No crosses, no initials.

She knew he remembered them, though. He didn't believe in taking photos or writing things down, he believed in the power and strength of memory. Said it took care of sorting the wheat from chaff, important things from trash.

Whenever he talked about it, she thought of her perfectly photographed and curated life before, social media presence strong, tagged, followed, liked. Insta-beloved if not Insta-famous. She had kept a journal too.

Recently, while going through the boxes of things her parents brought from her old apartment, she came across it again. She idly wondered if her parents had read it. She bet her mom would have been at least tempted.

Looking at it now, it was just page after page of nothing meaningful; it disgusted her. She made a fire in a metal barrel in the backyard and burned it that night. Which felt nice, cathartic. She brought some more of her old things and did the same, until her parents stopped her, sensibly offering to take them to Goodwill instead. Tax credits were mentioned. She relented. Let them have their way.

Going to the movies had been a stupid idea. Something her old self would enjoy. Something her new self found too fake.

In the man's house, there were books. Heavy serious tomes on history, biology, physics. A telescope out back, along with shooting ranges set up for both guns and bow and arrows. A gym's worth of exercise equipment, old, battered, and duct taped.

He watched the skies. Read the news. Prepared.

He was fit, strong, powerful. A mountain of a man. She hated him and hated how she felt around him, simultaneously unsafe and perfectly safe. He was the main source of danger and her main protector, all in one. A maddening combination. She depended on him, and she wanted him dead.

She wondered if he knew how she felt. If he had always known. There was a look in his eyes when she buried the knife in his neck, a look she couldn't forget. Recognition and something else . . . respect? Pride? That he had, after all, after all the years of failures and murders, fashioned a proper predator.

She could still feel his blood on her skin, the burning heat of it. There weren't enough showers to wash it away.

They'd found the man's house since. Her directions worked. They found the graves, brought closure to grieving families, or rather, introduced them to a new kind of grief. They celebrated her, talked about her. She was a hero. She was newsworthy.

She didn't follow any of that noise. Tried to avoid even her parents' mentions of it. Refused the journalists, refused the interviews. All that money, all those opportunities "to tell her own story." She was offered mid-six figures for a tell-all book. More than that for the rights and participation in a six-part dramatization for a prime network.

Her story resonated. People wanted to hear it. She was the one who got away. Who served up justice old-Western style, by winning the standoff. A proper American heroine. Awash in blood.

She wanted nothing to do with any of it. Had no interest in correcting them. None of it felt real.

It took her a while to convince her parents to let her go to the movies by herself. The situation brought flashbacks to high school. They'd become so overprotective. And who could blame them? Though statistically speaking the odds of her getting kidnapped again . . .

They didn't know she had a weapon on her, that she never went anywhere without it. So many things could be fashioned into weapons if you knew what to do, and most importantly, if, when the time came, you wouldn't hesitate to use them.

She had been taught every weak point in the human body, every easily snappable bone. The man provided extensive training, optimized for her size.

She thought about it often. In retrospect, it almost seemed like he was building his own killer. Someone to make him proud and then take him away from this mad and hostile world.

Perhaps he was tired of it all, exhausted from the weight of his bleak expectations, his personal darkness. Perhaps his final act was engineering his own death.

It didn't make her feel manipulated, on the contrary, it spoke to her of purpose.

She had been many things in her life before: a loving but not overly attentive daughter, a good and cheerful friend, a performer of meaningless tasks, a partier, a planner, a tenant, an employee. None of it compared in potency and resolve to be simply this—a weapon.

The streets gave in to the night easily this time of the year. She still sometimes forgot what month she was in, but the pumpkins on the stoops declared it, unmistakably, to be October. The veil between the worlds would be thin in the upcoming days; ghouls, ghosts, and goblins coming thorough, to play and wreak havoc. People would dress up in silly costumes and pretend their world was something they were so sure it wasn't. Man-made dangers, manufactured fears.

She smiled a mirthless smile. Shook her head.

A pumpkin grinned at her from its newel post pedestal outside of someone's house. Something about its crudely carved face reminded her of the man. She took out her knife and refeatured it. There. Better.

The pumpkin's leftover innards were sticky on her hand as she walked away.

People were never as quiet as they thought they were—she heard the footsteps following her for blocks now. Tentative at first, then gaining confidence. It would be any moment now . . .

"Hey, you. You, pretty lady. You got a light?"

She didn't stop. Didn't slow down.

"Hey, I'm talking to you." The indignation in his voice now. And what a voice, grating, unpleasant. With undertones of cigarettes and alcohol, and beneath it all, a whine. A weakness.

She stopped without turning around and allowed him to catch

up to her. When she heard him near, she spun on her heels to face him; a movement so sudden that it threw him off balance.

He staggered before finding his footing.

5'10" or so, a once-decent build gone to seed, a hairline receding from a sharp widow's peak, several days' worth of stubble, small too-close-together eyes full of low cunning. The man before her was a textbook picture next to the phrase, "Up to no good."

"I don't have a light," she said, evenly. "What else did you want to talk about?"

That threw him, if only for a moment.

"Well, you're all alone, and I'm all alone, and the night is young . . . "

She took a measure of him. Saw straight through the deceptively average exterior and down to his twisted dishwasher-grey soul. Saw all the terrible things he could do, would do, given a chance.

The knife went into his heart like it belonged there. The man had taught her well—

sharp weapons and precise hits. That way size didn't matter. That way, *you* were the predator.

The ugly man crumpled and expired at her feet.

She felt nothing.

No, she self-corrected, she did feel something. She was taught to never disregard her feelings, to take an estimation of them, learn from them. And right now, she felt righteous. Satisfied. Just.

There was blood on her hands, wind in her shorn hair, and a sense of satisfaction coursing through her veins. At long last, everything felt real.

The final girl walked away. Into the night. Into the world she could—she now saw—learn to understand and enjoy after all.

Death Warmed Over

RACHEL CAINE

A tribute to the late Rachel Caine. Thanks to her husband, her agent, and her assistant for allowing me to print her fantastic story again . . .

I hate raising the dead on a work night.

My booker, Sam Twist knows that, and so it was a surprise when I got the email on a Monday—telling me he would need a full resurrection on Thursday.

"Short turnaround, genius," I muttered. It took days to brew the necessary potions, and I'd have to set aside the entire Thursday from dusk until dawn for the resurrection itself. Not good, because I knew I couldn't exactly blow off Friday. I had meetings at my day job.

Sam, who ran the local booking service for witches, was usually somewhat sympathetic to my day/night job balancing act, mostly because I was the best resurrection witch he had—not that being the best in the business exactly paid the bills. It was a little like being the best piccolo player in the orchestra—it took skill and specialty, and not a lot of people could do it, but it didn't exactly present a lot of major money-making opportunities.

Then again, at least resurrections were a fairly steady business. Some of the other types of witches—and we were all very specialized—got a whole lot less. It was a funny thing, but so far as I could tell, there had never been witches who could do what the folklore claimed; those of us who were real worked with potions, not words. We couldn't sling spells *and* lightning. Our jobs—whatever our particular focus—took time and patience, not to mention a high tolerance for nasty ingredients.

I contemplated Sam's message. If I'd wanted to, I *could* have turned down the job; I wasn't hurting for money at the moment. Still. There was something in the terse way he'd phrased it that made me wonder.

So, was I taking the job, or not? If I said yes, prep needed to start immediately after work. Part of my mind ran through the things I was going to need and matched it against the mental stock list I always kept in my brain. The bowls were clean and ready, I'd put them through the dishwasher and a good ritual scrub with sacred herbs just a week ago. I'd need to put a fresh blessing on the athame. I had most of the other things: rock salt, Sulphur, attar of roses, ambergris, and a whole bunch of slimier ingredients. I might be running low on bottled semen, but the truth was, you could always get more of that.

I fidgeted in my chair as I stared at the message. Sam wasn't telling me much—just timing and dollar amount, which while considerable, wasn't enough to pay my mortgage. On their own, my fingers typed my reply. *I might be interested. Who's the client?*

I rarely asked, because most of the time that fell under need-to-know, and I didn't. So long as the client paid Sam, and Sam paid me, we were all good. But this time . . . this time I felt like it was worth the question.

I went back to my regular work. Tonight, that meant straightening out a worksheet the experts in accounting had completely trashed—and I was a little surprised when Sam's emailed reply came so quickly. Then again, it was a short answer.

P.D. Police Department.

My hackles went way up. The police didn't part with their money willingly for resurrections. The testimony of the resurrected had been thrown out as inadmissible five years ago, and the land-office rush for witches to bring back the dead had dried up just as fast. Some of the richer cities still managed one or two resurrections a year for particularly cold cases, just to generate leads, but I hadn't seen one in Austin for quite a while.

So, if the Thin Blue Line was knocking, something was up, and it was big. Very big.

Why? I wrote back and hit SEND.

It didn't take long to get my answer. Four minutes, to be exact, give or take a few seconds, until my cheery little *you have mail* chime dinged.

They need a disposable, he wrote, and this time, I sat all the way back in my chair. And rolled my chair back from the computer. *Tried to talk them out of it. Told them you wouldn't want in. You can pass on it, H.*

In technical terms, a disposable is a long-term resurrection—counterintuitive, but that's police parlance for you. Most resurrections last no more than a few minutes, maybe an hour—you really don't need that much time to do whatever needs to be done. It's mainly finding out the name of their killer, where they stashed the family silver, or where the bodies are buried if your deceased soul is the one who buried them in the first place. Holding them longer is brutally hard, and gets harder the longer it goes on. When a police department requests a long-term resurrection, it's almost always specific; there's a situation that requires a particular person to resolve, or a particular skill. When cops ask for a disposable resurrection . . . well, you know it's going to be bad.

I knew it better than anyone.

I typed my reply back in words as terse as Sam's had been to me. *Bet your ass I'm passing.*

I hit send, feeling only a little wistful twinge of regret at all that virtual money disappearing from my future, and began to shut my computer down.

I'd just picked up my purse when my cell phone rang, and I wasn't too surprised when the screen's display told me it was Sam.

"Hey," I said, shouldered my bag, and headed for the elevators. "Don't try to talk me out of it. I don't do disposables. Not anymore."

"I know that" Sam said. He had a deep, smoky voice, the kind that implied a cigarette-and-whiskey lifestyle. I didn't know that for sure; for all I knew, Sam might have lived prim as a preacher. Sam and I didn't exactly hang out; he kept to himself, mostly. "Not trying to talk you out of it, H., believe me. I'm glad you turned it down."

"Shut up," said a third voice, male, grim, and completely unfamiliar.

"Who the hell is *that*?" I blurted. "Sam—"

"Detective Daniel Prieto."

"Sam, you *conferenced* me?" He'd never put me on the spot before.

"Hey, they're cops. I got no choice!"

"Hear me out." Prieto's voice rode right over Sam's. "I'm told you're the best there is, and I need the best. Besides, you have a prior relationship with the . . . subject."

My mouth dried up, and I stopped in mid-stride to lean against the wall. A few coworkers passed by and gave me curious looks; I couldn't imagine what was on my face, but it must have been both alarming and off-putting. Nobody stopped. I tried to speak, but nothing was coming out of my mouth.

"Holly? You there?" That was Sam. I could still hear Prieto breathing.

"Yeah," I finally managed to say. "Who?" Not that there was really much of a question. I only had a *relationship* with one dead man.

And Prieto, right on cue, said, "Andrew Toland."

I felt hot and sick, and I needed to sit down. Never a chair around when you need one. I continued walking, slowly, one shoulder gliding against the wall for balance. "Sam, you can't agree to this. You can't let them do it again. Not to *him*."

"What can I say? I'm just the dispatcher, H. You don't want to take it on, that's just fine." The words sounded apologetic, but Sam didn't do empathy. None of us did. It didn't serve us well in this line of work.

Cops had the same problem. "I have to tell you, if you don't agree, we're still bringing him back. We'll ask Ms. Flores; right Mr. Twist? She's the one who recommended this particular guy be brought back, right?"

"*Lottie*?" I blurted it out before I could stop myself. *No. Oh, no.* Carlotta Flores and I went back a long time, and not one minute of it was pleasant. In resurrections, we prided ourselves on detachment, but Lottie took pleasure in the pain that her resurrected souls felt; she *enjoyed* keeping them chained into their flesh. I'd reported her dozens of times to the review board, but there was never any real evidence. Only my word for what I'd seen.

The dead can't testify.

It was her fondest wish to run a disposable, and it was the very last thing she should ever do. *God, no.* The idea of letting her handle Andrew's resurrection was more than I could take.

Detective Prieto somehow knew that, but then again, I supposed he'd done his homework. He'd probably gotten it from Sam, the chatty bastard.

"That a yes, Miss Caldwell?" Prieto asked. Sam was distinctly silent.

"Yes," I gritted out. "Dammit to hell."

"Right. Let's get to business. City Morgue, Thursday at dusk, you know the drill. Come loaded, H." Sam was back to brisk and rough again, his brief moment of empathy blown away like feathers in a hurricane.

"Send me the details." I sounded resigned. I didn't feel resigned. I felt manipulated, defeated, enraged.

"Will do," Sam said. I heard a click. Detective Prieto had signed off without bothering to say goodbye. "Better you than Lottie, I guess. Though look, if you just don't show up, what're they going to do, arrest you?"

"They'll let Lottie do it instead. You know I can't let that happen, Sam."

"Kind of guessed, yeah."

"Why *him*? God, Sam—"

"Don't know. Lottie had some kind of chat with Prieto. Next thing I know, he's telling me it's Toland he needs. Maybe Lottie told him about how tough the son of a bitch was. *Is.*"

Maybe Lottie just wanted to yank my chain. Equally possible.

"Holly? Sorry about—"

"Yeah, whatever. See you." I folded up the phone. I couldn't take any more of Sam's vaguely false apology. He knew my agreement was final. You don't become a witch making false promises.

The stakes were far too high.

I must have punched the elevator buttons properly, because the next thing I knew I was in the lobby, walking toward the parking garage. I couldn't feel my feet, and wherever my head was, it wasn't a good place.

I got inside my vehicle and bent over to rest my aching, sweaty forehead on the steering wheel.

My name is Holly Anne Caldwell, and I'm a licensed seventh-generation witch, with a specialty in raising the dead.

And I wished, right at that moment, I wasn't one of them.

I buried myself deep in prep work. It took up most of my nights, and I sleepwalked through my day job until Thursday.

Late Thursday afternoon, I went to raise the dead.

I knew the way to the morgue all too well. I had a parking pass, and the guard at the door knew me by sight. He still checked me against the list and opened my heavy case to check the contents. All above board, along with my certification papers from the State of Texas. I'd dressed professionally—a nice dark suit, very funeral home-friendly, with sensibly heeled shoes. Moderate makeup. Light perfume.

It helps, because I do run into the odd person who still believed witches came with green, cackling faces, and cauldrons.

The guard hooked me up with a temporary ID badge and escorted me back to the—excuse the phrase—guts for the morgue, which always reminded me of a large-scale industrial kitchen, with all the chrome work surfaces and sharp instruments neatly arrayed on racks. Once there, he checked with the coroner's assistant, then backtracked me to a room that was normally used for family viewings. Nobody had bothered to 'dress it up' for the occasion, so it had a certain creepy sterility to it that unsettled me.

Detective Prieto unsettled me, too. He was about my father's age, stern, and possessed only one stony expression as far as I could tell. He didn't like me, and he didn't like what I was doing. He gave me the paperwork, I read and signed, and he checked all of my credentials again before leaving the room to stand in the viewing area.

I pulled the sheet back on the corpse and there, lying pale and still in front of me, was Andrew Toland.

He looked damn good, for having been born in 1843, and especially since he'd died in 1875. By rights, I should have been looking at a skeleton, not a fresh corpse—like the last time we'd been through this. Another witch had produced a copy from his genetic template. It was known as a homunculus, within the trade. How such things were made was a closely guarded secret, although I knew the body would contain some kind of tissue or bone from the original corpse to hold the link. I wouldn't have known how to begin to conduct that kind of operation, but then again, the witch who'd made the mortal clay couldn't have breathed life into it, either.

Specialists.

I'd been here before, in this very room, with Andrew. One year ago, almost to the day—my first disposable. I'd been nervous and excited and thrilled at the prospect of meeting the man who'd made history. I hadn't been prepared then, for the idea that I would *like* him.

And that I would mourn him when it was time to let go.

I didn't want to do this. It had hurt too much, been too intimate. I wanted to walk away from all of it . . . but if I did, someone else would be standing here within the hour. Someone like Lottie, who would turn something wonderful into something horrible.

I had no choice.

Andrew Toland looked peaceful, frozen at that moment of death. He no longer had the wounds that had killed him; the last witch had repaired that as part of the reconstruction. He was just . . . dead. All I had to do was bring him back.

And once again, I had to wonder: *why him?* Lottie had wanted him, specifically. It could have simply been her one-two punch of hating me and wanting the prestige of running a disposable, but I couldn't believe that. There were easier ways to hurt me, and Andrew Toland was nobody she'd want to mess with. She knew his story, just as I did.

Andrew had lived a hard, interesting life, and earned himself a reputation, in his thirty-two short years, of being one of the toughest men during a rough and ready period of American history. A resurrection witch, like me, he'd gone down fighting during one of the worst zombie wars ever conducted in the Southwest. From time to time, a resurrectionist goes bad, and when that happens, the results are massively dangerous. Get three or four of the bad ones together, and you have the makings of an unstoppable army of the dead.

Andrew Toland had gone up against that and earned himself a broken neck. Then, by prior agreement with his friends, he'd had himself resurrected to fight again.

He'd won. Most of his allies had been taken out, and in the end, he'd carried on by himself—a gritty two-week campaign of attrition against the toughest opponents imaginable. And even when his own resurrection witch had been killed in the last critical moments, he'd still managed to stay alive long enough to take out the enemy. It had been unheard of then, and it was still without parallel, and in the textbooks that apprentices studied, he had an entire chapter all on his own.

You just don't get more badass than that.

I knew Prieto was watching, and the last thing I needed was to lose my objectivity at a time like this. I put all my feelings away in a lockbox, bent down, and opened Andrew Toland's death-filmed eyes.

I parted his clay-cold lips and poured in the first massive dose of the potion. It pooled in his mouth, liquid silver, and then I performed the part that nobody else could do.

I kissed him, very gently, on the lips, and completed the last step of the preset spell. I felt a line of power spooling out of me, traveling through the dark and connecting, with a jolting snap to the spirit of Andrew Toland.

The last time I'd done this, Andrew's power and strength had overwhelmed me. This time, it felt oddly soothing. Like being folded in warmth and light.

Andrew coughed, swallowed, and blinked. His skin remained pasty white for a few seconds. The cataracts on his eyes faded first, fainter with each blink, and then his skin took on color.

He wasn't back, but he was breathing.

I took his hands and poured more power into him, raw and wild. It was sweaty work, bringing back the dead, and it required me to be vulnerable in ways that most witches weren't willing to attempt. I had to touch his soul and let him touch mine. I had to not just taste death, but drink it down—accept it as a lover.

He gasped when I made contact, and the shine in his eyes shifted from mere existence to real life. Real consciousness.

I heard the first slow thud of his heartbeat, then the second. Then the steady rhythm falling into place.

And despite all the drugs cushioning his fall, I saw the agony hit him—I felt it, too, dim but strong, through our link, and had to breathe deeply to control the pain. He didn't scream. Some did, but not Andrew; he hadn't screamed when I'd revived him last year, either. His hands tightened on mine, brutally strong, and I tried not to wince. *It'll pass* I told myself. *Breathe. Breathe, dammit.*

I was doing fine until he met my eyes, and he whispered, "Holly. Wasn't it finished? Didn't we get him?"

Holy hell. He remembered.

For a frozen second, I couldn't think what to say, but training came back to me in a rush. *Establish control. Guide the dialogue.*

"Andrew," I said, keeping my voice low, gentle, and soothing, entirely steady. "Andrew Tolland. Do you hear me?"

He nodded. He hadn't blinked since focusing on me.

"I need you to sit up now," I said. "Can you do that?"

He could, and he did. He swung his legs over the edge of the cold morgue table and came upright, and I stopped him long enough to adjust the sheet over his lap. I wasn't usually so fussy, but Andrew had thrown me off; I couldn't see him as a tool. He was a man: a living, vital *man*.

He hadn't looked away at all from my face. There was something very unusual about him. I'd brought back hundreds of dead, and I couldn't think of a single one who'd begun the process with a question like that. It takes time for the personality to reassert itself, for memories to become clear.

He had been crystal-clear from the moment our souls touched.

"Holly, you must tell me the truth," Andrew said. "Did we kill that bastard?"

How could he possibly *remember who I was*? I'd had one other soul I'd brought back twice, the CEO of a major corporation who'd forgotten to pass along the passwords to some vital corporate accounts. I'd had to do it twice because the Board of Directors wanted to be sure they had everything from him, and that man, young and fit as he'd been, hadn't recognized me at all. Hadn't remembered a thing from one resurrection to the next.

"Holly!" His tone was sharp with concern. *He* was concerned. About *me*. I pulled my focus from about a thousand miles away and realized that he was frowning, totally focused on me. "Can you hear me?"

I laughed. I couldn't help it. It came out a strained, strangled gasp. "Yes," I managed to say, "I heard you, Andrew. We stopped him."

"Then I expect there's a tale to be told about why I'm back here." He released me from his stare to turn it on the room around us. "Well, this place don't get any prettier."

He remembered that, too? Unbelievable. "How do you feel?"

"Feel?" His gaze came back to me, electric and warm, and his lips curved into a smile. "Alive, would say "fine". But I'm not alive, I know that. You've brought me back again. Why?"

I turned away to pick up a stack of clothes from the pile nearby. Hospital scrubs, for now, nothing fancy. I handed them to him, and he frowned down at them for a few seconds.

"Clothes," I said. It was unnecessary; he clearly knew what they were, but I was rattled. I was all too aware of Detective Prieto at the viewing window, seeing me lose my cool.

That earned me another faint smile from Andrew. He had a nice face—a little sharp, with a pointed chin. In certain lights, in certain moods, he could look sinister, except for the humor in his eyes. "I know we're well acquainted, but a bit of privacy . . . ?"

I turned my back. I heard the faint sound of his bare feet slapping the cold floor as he stood, and the rustle of fabric moving over skin.

He was way, way too fast. Too well adjusted, for any newly revived corpse. He had *continuity*, and that meant he remembered all the trauma of the first resurrection.

"How long?" he asked. "How long have I been away this time?"

I cast a look over my shoulder and found he was adjusting the fit of the pants on his hips. Except for the slight, indefinable distance in his eyes, he could have been any hospital attendant. He looked completely . . . alive.

"About a year," I said. "Andrew—"

"Feels like yesterday," he said and looked down at his hands. He flexed them, frowning. "Awful strange, not knowing that."

"We have work for you," I said. I was sticking to my script, even though Andrew had lost his. "I'll help you understand what you need to do. How do you feel?"

"Holly, my sweet, I'm annoyed you're not listening to how I feel." He frowned, and I was right, he could look menacing. Which shouldn't be true, I think. No corpse revives so quickly as to be annoyed over such minor things. Andrew should know. He'd been a better witch than I ever could be.

"You're no ordinary person," I said. My heart was pounding, my palms were sweating, but I sounded as cool and soothing as any clinical practitioner. "Are you in any pain?"

"No."

"None at all?"

"Miss Holly, I've been in your shoes." His gaze moved to focus on them for a second, smiling. "Never ones so dainty, maybe. But there's no need to treat me like an invalid. I'll let you know when I start feeling it."

I stared at him. He stared back, challenge in those bright blue eyes. He was an average-looking guy in a lot of ways—pleasant features, except for that sharp, aggressive chin; sandy brown hair that had grown into a style that seemed both modern and antique— shaggy, certainly. He had a sharp ridge and a twist of his nose as if he'd broken it early in life.

I tried to get my mind back to business. "If you start feeling anxious or drifting, tell me. I don't know what the police need you for, or how long it will take, but you need a dose–"

"Each hour. Yes, Miss Holly. I'm the one who wrote up the damn rules. Police, you say?" That seemed to give him pause for thought. "Why us again?" *Us*, not just him. Andrew assumed instantly that we were a team.

I didn't want to be a team. It had hurt so much the last time around, I couldn't imagine how bad it would be this time, when I knew him. When I cared.

I opted for neutral topics. "Detective Prieto is waiting to brief us."

Detective Prieto entered the room, and both of us turned to look at him. "Mr. Toland," he said and nodded stiffly. "I won't say thanks, since I know you didn't really have a choice in coming . . . here," Nice way to avoid the whole death/life conundrum. "But I'm giving you a choice for the job. If you don't want to do it, we'll end this right now."

Andrew had lost his smile. His eyes were narrowed, hard-focused. That was how he looked when he fought, I thought. And yes, he could be intimidating.

"It's no small matter if you picked me," he said. "I slept a hundred thirty-some-odd years before Miss Holly here brought me back the first time, and I'll allow, as how that job was worth the trouble. I expect this one's just as raw."

"Yes," Prieto said. Now that he was face to face with the soul he was about to send into torment, possible horrible death, he seemed deeply uncomfortable. "I need you to help us save lives."

"Didn't expect you brought me back for a pony ride, mister. Fine. I'll do it."

"Andrew," I said quietly. "Hear him out before you agree to anything."

"Don't need to. Like I said, I wouldn't be back here if it wasn't bad."

"All right," Prieto said. "We have a credible terrorist threat against a protected group of individuals here in Austin. Four are already missing, and we've got intel about the next one to be abducted. We think these people are being killed, but we haven't found remains yet."

Andrew studied him for a moment in silence, then said, "I

understood little of that, 'cept you have four missing and some dead. I ain't equipped to solve your crimes, so I don't think that's what you need me for, is it?"

"We need you to protect one of the people on the list of potential victims."

"Wait a minute!" I blurted, horrified. The resurrected—even disposables—weren't bodyguards, they were weapons—point them directly at a clearly defined objective, and let them go achieve it no matter what the damage. Disposables didn't have a self-preservation instinct, so they were perfect for sending in on suicide runs.

Bodyguarding was completely different. For one thing, it was likely to be long-term, much longer than a disposable ever lasted. Days. Weeks. Months, even.

"Wait a minute," I repeated. My voice was loud enough to ring off the morgue steel. "What the hell? Since when did the resurrected join the force? This is something that any cop in Kevlar could do, right?"

Prieto gave me another look. This one was blank and cool. "We've tried that," he said. "Didn't go so well, which is why we decided to go with somebody with nothing to lose, like your friend here. Our intel says the attack's going to come in the next few days. The fact is, when we booked the job in the first place, we were planning to protect a completely different person. While you've been *preparing*, we lost two more of the targets, *and* the teams of cops assigned for protection. So I don't give a shit about your problems, lady. I lost four of my own police officers protecting these—people. The least you can do is your job."

"But you can't—"

Andy interrupted me. "Who'd I be protecting?"

Prieto had been waiting for the question, and he seemed to take a special kind of pleasure in saying, "It's her. Holly Anne Caldwell. These fucking freaks are taking out witches."

We left the viewing room to go down the hall to a small, airless conference room, where Prieto had set up shop for the night. He had folders.

He had a *lot* of folders.

I knew every one of the victims. Shayle Gallagher had been the first—he'd been taken right out of his flower shop (like me, he only moonlighted at the resurrection business), and there had been signs of a vicious struggle. Could have been robbery or a hate crime, so that hadn't raised too many unusual red flags at first, especially with no body found.

Two weeks ago, though, Harrison Wright had failed to show up to work at his medical practice, and his multi-million-dollar estate showed signs of the same brutal attack as at Gallagher's store.

Lottie Flores had been the next victim, and she'd disappeared the day after I'd taken the case from Sam.

"We kept it out of the news," Prieto said. "Wasn't easy. Oh, and Sam agreed we shouldn't interrupt you while you were working."

Sam agreed? I was going to have a talk with Sam. One involving a punch in the mouth.

"You said there were dead police officers," Andy said. Prieto nodded.

"My officers had missed a scheduled check-in. When backup arrived, their car was empty. They were found in the Flores house.

"Why not bring one of them back, find out just what went on?"

Prieto looked grim. "We thought about it, but the families wouldn't sign off, and by then, we were knee-deep in missing resurrection witches. Didn't think we should waste valuable time trying to convince anybody."

I looked at the photos of the two dead police officers and felt my stomach twist. They'd been beaten to death. That wasn't easy to do with any officer, but you could at least see how the five-foot-five, petite woman could have been overpowered. Not her partner, six-foot-four and big enough to intimidate pretty much anyone. He looked like he'd chewed nails as vitamins.

"Neither one got a shot off," Prieto said. "No sign of Flores in the house, but we found blood and the same smash-up, indicating a struggle. Blood in the bedroom turned out to be hers."

Lottie's house was neatly kept. Most of the damage was confined to her bedroom—bed pulled sideways, covers wrenched half off, blood smeared on sheets and floor, leading down the hall. She'd been dragged out.

I hated Lottie. I had good reason; I'd been her apprentice for three resurrections before I'd transferred to Marvin Jones, my permanent instructor. I'd hated every filthy second of being around Lottie and watching her work. I'd lodged a complaint against her with the Board of Review; nothing had come of it, of course. There weren't so many resurrection witches running around that they could afford to turf one just because she was—let's face it—a psychopath.

Even with all that, it still made me cringe to think about what that had been like . . . and what might still be happening to her.

The next file was even worse because I had no reason at all to dislike Monica Heitmeyer; she was a nice older lady specializing, like me and Lottie, in resurrections, but she mainly did family gigs, reconciling loved ones. As far as I knew, she'd never done any work with the police. She was in the feel-good business.

Two more dead officers at her house, these two killed in the backyard. One had a snapped neck. The other looked like a sack of raw meat. Someone had used him for punching practice. Monica, like Lottie, was missing and she'd left behind a lot of blood.

Andrew hadn't said anything. His eyes had gone dark and cold, and whatever he was thinking, he kept it to himself.

"What makes you think I'm next on the list?" I asked.

"Not a hell of a lot of witches in your line of work in Austin," Prieto said. "Most of them are already gone. It's down to you and the other one—"

"Annika," I said. "Annika Berwick." I knew her slightly, not well enough to have much of a feeling for how well she'd handle something like this. Annika was frail, nearly seventy, a sweet only grandmother of a witch who'd informally retired from practice last year. "You're protecting her, right?"

"Sure they are," Andy said softly, although his hardened gaze hadn't left Prieto at all. "They leave you open, you're the next target. That the idea, Detective? Holly's your damn stalking horse?"

Prieto didn't answer. The truth was that he probably had strike teams ready to roll, and full surveillance, but he wanted it to look like he wasn't coming anywhere near us.

He wanted everyone to think that we were all on our own.

"Have you talked to Annika?"

Prietro nodded. "She's good."

I didn't know about Annika, but I knew how I felt about it, and "good" didn't exactly ring true. I desperately needed a shower and a gallon of Ben & Jerry's ice cream to deal with this.

All of this explained why the police department was willing to spend the exorbitant cost to have Andrew Toland brought back.

Resurrection witches were a rare breed, and valuable. Six in a city of more than 600,000; there were even fewer in Dallas, only a couple hanging tough against a storm of fundamentalist persecution. Austin remained the home of the weird.

Didn't feel like home right now.

I turned to Andrew. "You don't have to do this," I said. "I can release you. I *should* release you. This isn't your fight, it's mine."

He gave me a look that drilled right into my core. "No, it's not. They were right to bring me into it, Holly. This is how the war starts—put down those who might fight and do it early. Nobody left to fight when the evil comes calling." His blue eyes took on a distance and a chill. "I've seen it done." It had, in fact, been done to him.

"It's still not your problem."

"True enough," he said, and there came that slow, warm smile again, breaking my heart. "Still. I think *you're* my problem."

We didn't speak on the drive back. I heard the jingle of the bottles in my case in the back seat; I'd been watching Andy for any sign that he needed a booster, but he seemed fine. Better than fine, actually. The spell that bound him here also bound us together. I knew I'd feel some sense from him if—when—he began to feel pain or drift.

So far, nothing. It was like being with anyone. Any *living* person, that is.

"The last time," Andy said. "I know we got the killer. What about the girl? Did I get her out?"

I shuddered. I couldn't help it, and I couldn't hide it. All of a sudden, the realities of it crashed down on me, and the lockbox of feelings blew open, and I was shaking like a leaf in a storm.

I dimly heard Andy asking me what was wrong, but I couldn't tell him. I pulled the car over into a vacant parking lot, threw it into park, and stumbled out with my arms wrapped around myself for comfort. The warm, humid air didn't help. I was shaking apart.

I heard Andy's passenger side door slam, and quick footsteps on the gravel, and then his arms wrapped around me fast and hard. "Hush," he murmured, with his lips against my hair. "Hush, now, Holly. It's not so bad as that."

But it was, oh, it was. His questions had opened up Pandora's Box, and I couldn't keep any of it under lock and key anymore. "She . . . she . . . oh, Andy, I'm sorry—"

"She died," he finished, and pushed me back far enough that he could look into my eyes. His were dark, all pupils, even under the streetlight. "Feared she would. Couldn't get to her before he cut her. All I could do was try to get her to you before it was too late."

My heart just broke. He remembered, but he didn't *know*. I'd resurrected Andrew last year to deal with a witch out of Chicago who'd been on the run, who'd taken to abducting girls he fancied, killing them, and reviving them over and over for his fun.

Andy had gone to stop the witch and save the last girl before it was too late.

He'd accomplished part of it—the witch was dead, and Andy had made damn certain the bastard couldn't come back. The girls he'd enslaved were gone as well.

But that last child, all of sixteen . . . she'd died in Andy's arms, as he used the last of his strength to try and get her to safety. It had felt like it was all for nothing, because of that. It wasn't—that witch wouldn't be hurting anyone else—but it had felt hollow. Horrible empty.

I hadn't realized until just now why it had felt so awful. It had been the tragedy of that girl, yes, but it had been *Andy*. Andy's stunning courage.

I felt him let go, and it felt like losing someone I loved.

I burst into tears and buried my face in his hospital-style shirt. He smelled sterile, astringent, not living at all, but it didn't matter. He felt *real*.

And I could *not* be in love with a dead man. I just could not. No matter how close we'd gotten before. No matter how good this felt now.

And he smoothed my hair with gentle strokes, not speaking. I felt him touch his lips gently to the top of my head.

"I remember, you know," he said at last. "You were there all the time, Holly. You were all that kept me moving, at the last. You were the light."

That only made me cry harder. I was thinking about him wounded and dying, struggling to save that girl. About how I'd kept him alive, alive, alive through all the pain and agony.

Until I hadn't.

It hadn't been Andy who faltered . . . it had been me. I hadn't been strong enough for him, in the end.

"She was dying before I ever got to her," he said. "And she's peaceful now, Holly. So let it be."

I couldn't stop crying. His hand rubbed my back in slow, gentle circles.

"I don't think you understand what it was like waking up today, seeing you," His fingers touched my chin and tipped it up. "If I need to die for you, I will. But let's not spend the time in tears."

I could feel his heartbeat. See the fast pulse moving under his skin. I could feel our souls touching, intimate in ways that mere living people couldn't achieve, and I understood just how deep this went between us.

I pressed my hand over his heart, feeling the strong, steady pace. "You can't stay with me," I said. My voice, normally so steady, sounded soft and uncertain. "We don't get second chances, Andy."

He smiled. "Sure we do," he said. "What's this, if it ain't a second chance? Or, more proper for me, a third?"

And he kissed me. Warm lips, blood-warm, tasting of the potion I'd given him. *Toxic,* something in me warned, but I didn't care.

Andy's thumbs stroked my cheekbones, and his big hands seemed so certain about what they were doing.

I was kissing a dead man, and I didn't care a bit. I wanted to keep on kissing him until the sun burned out.

The memory of the harsh, bloodstained photographs Prieto had shown us flashed across my eyes, and I pulled free with a gasp, stepping back.

"What?" he asked. He took my hand but didn't try to pull me into his arms.

"It's not safe," I said. "We're not safe. We need to get inside."

Andy smiled—a real, full smile. "You think I can't protect you, Holly?"

"I don't want you to have to."

He nodded out into the dark. "Ain't the only one. Prieto sent a couple of fellas on our tail. They're parked over there, watching us."

I shuddered. Somehow, that made it even worse: that there were eyes on us, and that I was putting Prieto's men at risk just by being such an easy target. "Let's go home."

We got back in the car, and I broke every speed limit on the way.

Andy was all business when we pulled into the drive. Although he'd never worked as a bodyguard, at least not that I knew of, he made me stay in the car with the motor running and the garage door open as he went into the house and checked it out. I waited tensely, imagining every second that I would feel an echo of *something* through the bond . . . I'd lived through the sickening spiral of his torment and death once already, and I knew what it would feel like.

I nearly screamed when he popped up next to the car and motioned for me to get out. I closed the garage door, shut off the motor, and followed him into the house.

"Locks?" he asked. I turned them, and then set the security alarm for instant alarm. If any door or window opened, we'd know, and so would the police. My heart was hammering. I thought about Lottie, evidently surprised in her sleep. And before, Monica, taken in the evening as she was getting ready for bed, bath water cold in the tub. "They come at night," I said. "Don't open any doors or windows. The alarm will go off."

"Fancy."

I smiled faintly. "Normal, these days. We live in scary times."

"Ain't nobody ever lived any other time," Andy, not content with the electronic alarm, was roaming around and testing doors and windows, engaging all locks. "You set this magic watchdog when you left today?"

"I didn't know I was being *stalked*."

Andy stopped and looked at me, hands gone still on a windowsill. "They didn't tell you."

I shook my head.

"Why not?"

"People all that fond of resurrection witches back in your day?"

That question earned me a full crooked grin. "Not enough so you'd blush. Stay here, I'll check the other floor."

I watched him take the stairs, then went to the kitchen and put away the ritual pots I'd washed. I fixed myself a sandwich. Spellcasting took a lot out of me, and despite everything, I was feeling a small, significant drain of energy through the bond with Andy. Needed to keep my strength up, through the magic of carbs and protein.

I was just swallowing the last bite when Andy walked into the kitchen. "Never got to see your house the last time," Andy said. He sat down at the kitchen table and looked around. "Big place. Warm. You live here all on your own? What about your family?"

"My parents and my sister live in New England. You going to tell me a woman can't live on her own?"

"I'd never dare," Andy said. "'Specially not one who holds the keys to life and death. Then again, that's pretty much any woman, so I'll just keep my peace about it. Besides, I don't know your world all that much, 'cept it's about as full of villains, same as the time I knew. Could be women tell men what's for now, strange as that would seem."

"Andy—"

His blue eyes stopped surveying the granite countertops and focused on me, and *wow*, that packed voltage. "I'm not sorry," he said. "Stupid for a man to fall in love once he's dead, but I've done it, and there it is. But at least you know I'll do everything in my power to keep you alive, Holly Anne."

I couldn't even speak. What do you say to that? A dead man falls in love with you, and there's no chance for a future together. I knew that every minute, every *second* of this was limited. I wanted to take him straight to bed, but I didn't know—I didn't know for certain how that worked. Or even *if* it did. The subject of sexual performance of dead men had never been included in my apprenticeship—probably deliberately. The potential for abuse of resurrections was huge, and our limits were strict. It was part of why we maintained such emotional distance.

Andy sensed my internal struggle, and he brought out his gentlest smile. It did great things to his face, putting a devastating sparkle in his eyes.

I stood up, barely able to feel my legs. "I'm—going to bed. Do you want—" My throat closed up, and I had to clear it. Embarrassing. "Do you want me to make up the spare bed?"

Andy kept smiling. "No. I ain't sleeping, am I?"

He had a point. Bodyguards didn't, and neither did the dead. I felt flushed, awkward, and out of control.

"Okay, then," I said. "Good night."

He nodded and watched me as I left the kitchen.

A hot shower and a pair of silk pajamas later, I retreated to my soft, lonely bed and tried to sleep. It was getting on toward the wee hours of the morning, but I didn't feel tired. I felt anxious and achy, and relentlessly squirmy.

I could hear Andy roaming around downstairs. I wondered what he was doing—looking over my bookshelves? Examining my pictures? Getting intimate with me in ways that didn't involve climbing into bed with me?

Shut up, I told myself, when my brain started to run wild with images. *The man is dead. He's here to do a job, and then he's gone. And that's it.*

Except it wasn't, and Andy had said he loved me, and I knew I loved him. No getting around that. Bringing him back a second time—no, for him it was the third—had been cruel, unnecessary, and wrong . . . and if I'd known what Prieto wanted him for, I'd have said no, even at the cost of my own life.

I didn't want Andy dying for me.

I'd drifted off into an uneasy half-slumber when something woke me up. I felt a tingle inside and opened my eyes to stare at the ceiling. I knew that feeling all too well. No chance of sleeping now.

I slipped out of bed, wrapped myself in a silk robe, and went downstairs.

Andy was standing at the windows, looking out. He didn't wait for me to ask. "I'm fine," he said.

"You're not." I'd carried my black case in from the car, and now I flipped it open and reached for the second vial of the stepped dose.

It felt light.

The bottle was empty.

I stared at it in stupefied horror for a few seconds, then dropped it back into the holder and pulled the third. The fourth.

The bottles were *all* empty. I began yanking the rest out to check. *Empty, empty, empty!*

Andy turned at the sound of my labored breathing and the rattle of glass. He frowned. "What?"

"It's not—someone sabotaged my case." *Breathe*, I told myself. Come on. Think. The case had been with me, and completely full, at the morgue. All the time? No. I'd set it in the corner of the viewing room and we'd both gone with Detective Prieto to look over files. The case had been left unattended. "The potions. They're gone."

Andy took a step toward me, then stopped. His blue eyes widened, just a little. "All of it?"

"Everything."

I abandoned the case and raced into the kitchen. I opened the refrigerator.

The four doses I kept on hand for emergencies were gone. I found the bottles in the trash, empty.

"Oh *Christ*," I whispered. Andy's hands touched my shoulders, and I felt him behind me, solid and real.

"It's all right," he said. "I don't need it yet."

"It's not alright. It takes hours to brew, and—" A terrible thought struck me. I opened the pantry where I kept my supplies.

Gone. I'd been cleaned out.

A numbing horror ran through me. "There's nothing. I can't even get the ingredients until tomorrow morning at the earliest, then it takes all day to brew the base—"

"It will be alright," Andy repeated.

I turned on him, suddenly furious. "It's not! Don't you get it? I know you're in pain already! It's only going to get worse, Andy, and if I don't let you go—"

His hands closed around my face. "Pain, I can handle. I ain't leaving you alone. They've been here. They were in your house."

"Who?"

"Somebody who knows you," he said. "Somebody who knows what you're afraid of."

I was afraid of hurting him. Again.

He smoothed back my hair and kissed me. It was soft and cool and gentle, but I sensed how much restraint it took for him to keep it that way.

"I can handle this," he said firmly. "I *will*. You believe me now, Holly?"

I gulped and nodded convulsively. "Okay."

I didn't, and it wasn't. But he wasn't finished.

"Get dressed and pack a bag," he said. "We're leaving."

No matter how tough you are, nobody takes pain well when it comes on slow and cold, with nothing to cushion it.

I kept dialing phone numbers, trying to get *somebody* on the phone who could help as we drove. Sam Twist wasn't answering—not his phone, his cell, or his secret emergency number. I tried Annika. No answer there, either. I tried Detective Prieto, but it rang directly to his voicemail.

I thought about calling 911, but what was I going to say? *I have a dead man here who needs his medicine.*

I had no idea what to do. I could feel Andy's pain, black and constant and growing, and I was helpless to prevent it from getting worse.

"Holly?"

"I took my eyes off the steering wheel for just a second. His eyes shone silver, unreal, in the dashboard lights.

"Why'd you bring me back?"

Of all the questions I'd expected, that had to be last on the list. I held his stare for a long few seconds, then blinked. "Lottie," I said. "They were going to do it anyway, and they were going to let Lottie—I couldn't let that happen. I thought maybe it would be better for you if it was me, that's all."

"That's all."

"Yes."

"You're a liar. Pretty one, but a liar all the same."

And he was right. I was lying not just to him, but to myself.

I loved him. I'd grown to love him during that first resurrection, and I'd lost him, and it had hurt me. Having him back was a painful, barbed-wire ball of a miracle because it contained the seeds of its own destruction.

One hand left the steering wheel and touched his, and his fingers closed warm and strong over mine.

"Where are we going?" he asked.

There was only one place, really. The other witches had been abducted, dragged out without warning, which meant that their supplies would have remained intact.

I needed to make him some potion.

Lottie's house was the closest.

Before we'd left the house, I pulled a suitcase from under my bed and took out a pair of pants, a dark shirt, underwear, shoes, and socks.

His own clothes, from the last time I'd brought him back. Somehow, I'd never been able to get rid of them. I'd put them on the bed, and he had given me a long, measuring look that told me he understood why I'd kept them. Why they'd been so close at hand.

As soon as he changed into the clothes, we'd left.

"The cops," I said. "Are they following us?"

Andrew had shut his eyes—fighting back pain, I could feel it— but he opened them as I turned the car out of the driveway and scanned the street. "Don't see 'em," he'd said. "Don't mean they ain't around, though. Since we're bait in the trap, they'd like your killer to have room to breathe, seems to me."

I'd hoped the police would follow us, but I couldn't wait to find out. Time was running out.

On the way, I remembered to call in sick to work—not that keeping my day job was the most important thing in my world, but it was normal life, and I desperately wanted to believe that there would still be a normal life, after today.

The sun was on the rise as we navigated morning rush hour, heading for Lottie's neighborhood. She had a place in an upscale area, one story but sprawling. It was the kind of place that was deserted by day—working families out from seven to seven. The only sign of life along the street was a lawn service truck in the distance, and a couple of guys on riding mowers.

Lottie's driveway was empty, so I turned in and parked in the back. Yellow police tape fluttered here and there, but they'd finished their work in the yard. An official-looking seal was on the back door and a newly installed padlock.

Andy opened the trunk of the car, took out a rusty tire iron, and popped the padlock with a single wrench. He had to stop for a moment and brace himself, and I felt the swirl of darkness between us as the inevitable tide rolled over him.

"Andy," I said. He shook his head.

"Let's just get it done," he said. "This ain't nothing yet."

He was right. It would get a lot worse. That didn't mean it wasn't bad, though; bad enough to drive most men to their knees.

The death-tide was pulling him back. Pulling him away from me.

I ripped open the seal on the door and stepped into Lottie's kitchen.

There were few signs of violence here—neatly racked pots and pans, shelves of supplies. I quickly rummaged through them, breathing easier with every single thing I found. Yes, yes, yes . . .

I opened the refrigerator door and saw inside not just a few bottles, but a gallon jar of swirling silver liquid.

A gallon jar.

Andy joined me, alerted by my expression. "Why'd she make so much?" he asked. I shook my head. There was absolutely no reason for Lottie to do a thing like that—the expense was enormous. Unless she'd found an effective way to really store the stuff—no, when I wrestled the gallon jar out of the refrigerator and onto the counter, I could tell that it was at least a week old, probably two. Not bad, but not fresh, either.

In another week, it would be useless. It was a foolish waste. Why the hell had Lottie brewed it like this?

"She's been up to something," Andy said. He might have been reading my mind. "Makes you wonder why she wanted me back, don't it?"

I dipped up a cup of the potion, sniffed it again, and tilted it this way and that in the mug. "I don't trust this," I said. "It doesn't feel right, Andy. I just—"

He held up a hand to silence me.

"What?" I whispered."

"I think maybe someone's here," he said quietly.

I sealed up the jar and hefted it. We'd take it with us. It would have to serve until I could brew my own.

Andy turned his eyes back toward me, and something was dawning in his expression, something grim and terrible.

He lifted the mug I'd filled and poured it into the sink.

"What are you doing?"

"Somebody's been studying up." Andy didn't bother to keep his voice down. "Used this same trick myself, long ago. Made up a batch of poisoned brew, left it for the revenants to drink when they came looking. Did for quite a few that way, back during the wars."

Poison. I looked down at the jar and let it slide out of my hands back to the counter.

"Come out," Andy said. "Face to face. You want us dead; you better do it barefaced."

"All right," said a smoke-strained, whiskey-rough voice from the hall, and a big, red-headed man stepped into the light. A gun was in his hand, pointed not at Andy, but at me. "How's this?"

Sam Twist. *I'm just the dispatcher.* "Sam—" I wet my lips. Andy stepped between me and the gun, and I heard three loud pops in quick succession.

Andy just stood there and took the bullets, shook himself, and said in a voice I didn't even recognize, "You all done, Irish, or do you want to reload?"

I slid slowly along the counter, angling for a view of Sam. He was calmly holding the gun at his side.

"No, need," he said. "I was just softening you up a little. No question, you're one hell of an opponent. That's why I tried to get Holly to take a pass on bringing you back again.

"Mine," scraped another voice, and the thing shuffled into view next to Sam . . . if it had been born human, it hadn't stayed that way. Misshapen, malformed as a dropped lump of clay, but roped with muscle. Dead gray eyes. Pointed teeth displayed by lips that had been cut or ripped away. Sam was a big man, and this—creature—topped him by a foot or more. Its shoulders were broader than the doorway.

I remembered the photographs of the cops. Beaten to death. Necks snapped.

Andy had never looked fragile to me until that moment.

If he was worried, or even startled, it didn't show. He bounced lightly on the balls of his feet, eyes fixed on Sam's monster. "Well, ain't you pretty?" he said, cool and quiet. "Your momma must be real proud."

The thing swayed but didn't move. Its blind-looking gaze strayed from Andy . . . to me.

A low growl started in its throat, a diesel engine running rough, and I felt Andy's entire body tense. "Get behind me," he said. "Holly, dammit, do that right now."

I did, but not before I got a glimpse at the blood soaking the front of his shirt, and the tattered flesh beneath. Dead men could die, and they could feel pain, and no matter how focused and tough Andy was, he couldn't overcome this monster.

Not alone.

"Who is he?" I whispered. Sam couldn't have brought this creature back, not on his own.

"He was my brother, Donal," Sam Twist said. "Before Lottie got hold of him."

He was *Lottie's*. But Lottie was dead. Wasn't she? "She—brought him back?"

"He got knifed in a bar fight," Sam said. "Strongest man I ever knew. I begged her to help, and she did. She brought him back. But I didn't know what she'd *do* with him."

Sam moved over to the side, edging to where he could once again see my face, and line up a clear shot. Andy didn't move. He clearly thought it was better to stand between me and Donal.

"What did she do?" I was acutely aware now of the blood pooling at Andy's feet, of the waves of darkness vibrating in the air between us. Death was coming, and coming no matter how hard he pushed against it.

"What does it *look* like she did, you bitch?" Sam spat, and the sudden raw fury in him exploded like nitro. "She used him. My own brother. She told me she put him back to sleep, but she didn't. She set him to fighting other dead men like some trained bear, and brought him back, kept dragging him back until there was nothing left. She took *bets*." Sam swallowed hard. "But he remembered. He heard my voice on the phone, and he remembered."

Sam's face was red, distorted with anguish, and his eyes were glittering with tears. I swallowed hard to clear the lump from my throat. "He came to find you," I said. "Oh, Sam, I'm truly sorry."

He sneered at me. There was no more sanity in his eyes at that moment than in his brother's. "Keep your pity," he said. "I don't want it. I'm putting you down, bitch. I'm putting all of you *down*."

Lottie wasn't dead. Lottie couldn't be dead if Donal was still alive. Sam had her somewhere, under lock and key, maybe drugged or worse, but still breathing.

She was Donal's only vulnerability.

I was still partly blocked from Sam's view. With my right hand, I dug my cell phone from my pocket, flipped it open, and hit the speed dial number I'd assigned to Detective Prieto. I had to hope he'd answer, or at worst, that his voicemail would give him the clues he needed after the fact to put it all together. "You kept Lottie alive," I said. "Right, Sam? To suffer."

"Damn straight," he said. "When I'm done with you, I'll take out Annika, and we can move on to the next town. You have to be stopped, all of you."

"You're using Donal just as much as Lottie did," I said. "Let him go, Sam. God—please let him *go!*"

"No," he snapped. "Not until every single one of you is dead. Don't move, Holly. I want you to watch what happens next."

He knew. He knew about Andrew; he'd heard how traumatized I was when I'd lost him before.

He wanted me to watch him die again.

Donal was fast, but Andy was faster. Even wounded, he was as lithe as a cat. He dodged Donal's roaring charge, tripped the twisted giant, and bashed Donal's skull hard into the marble counter. I backed away, dodged behind the fighting men, and screamed into the phone, "Prieto, it's Sam Twist! Find Lottie; Lottie's the key—"

Donal's hand slapped the phone away from me, and it bounced and broke into scattered pieces against the far wall. A bone snapped in my hand, and I choked back a scream, then another as I felt Andy's torment surge stronger. He was feeling my pain, too.

He'd do anything to stop it, and that was so dangerous.

I needed the gun Sam held.

I settled for grabbing a cleaver from the block next to the stove. Lottie, like all good cooks and witches, kept her tools in order; the cleaver had a wicked fine edge, a silky deadliness that vibrated the air.

I kept Donal between me and Sam as he sought a clear shot. And slipped in his own blood; his strike at Donal's massive throat lost its strength, and Donal's huge gray hands closed on his shoulders.

I felt Andy's arm being wrenched out of its socket. I screamed. He grunted and pulled halfway free, But Donal bunched up a fist and drew back.

I threw myself to the floor and swiped the cleaver through Donal's Achilles' tendons, and he toppled, howling, like a tree. The table collapsed under his impact.

Andy squirmed free, panting, and I felt the tide coming faster, deeper, all that darkness swirling and clouding the air between us as he tried to get to me . . .

Sam fired twice. One shot hit Donal's flailing arm and kicked a fist-sized chunk of flesh out of it. The second shot . . .

The second shot took Andy in the chest as he lunged to cover me.

"No!" I shrieked and took his weight in my arms as he collapsed against me.

There was no fighting the emptiness that rolled over me now, the call of endless peace, and I felt Andy slipping away.

I felt him find some small, impossible anchor in that tide, and his body shuddered against mine, holding me tight against him. *He can't. He can't make it.* Even the dead had to die.

But Andy refused to go.

He pulled back, and his eyes were liquid silver, the color of the potion I'd dosed him with at the morgue. His skin was as pale as paper. Most of his blood was poured out on the floor, an offering to harsher gods than I could ever worship.

But he *stayed standing*.

He took a deep breath and closed his eyes. "Potion," he whispered. "Give it to me."

The jar behind me on the counter.

Poisoned.

"No," I said. "No, Andy."

Another shot struck him. I screamed something at Sam, I don't even know what, and he bared his teeth in response. Donal was crawling toward us across the floor. He couldn't stand, but he wouldn't give up. He wanted me dead as much as Sam.

Andy reached behind me, fumbled the gallon jar of silver liquid, and looked at me with the most heartbreaking plea. "Help," he whispered. I felt the tide roaring in again. Stronger this time. He couldn't resist that, not even for me.

I helped him lift the jar.

One swallow.

Two.

Sam's next bullet hit the jar and it exploded into a shower of glass. The potion coated us both and swirled in silvery streams as it mingled with the blood on the floor.

But it worked.

I felt the black surging inside of Andy fall away, and the sudden, pulsing beat of life took over. For just an instant, his eyes locked with mine, and I saw a promise there.

An acceptance, too.

Donal's huge hand swiped at his feet, but Andy sidestepped and waltzed me with him. He put me gently out of the way and turned to Sam Twist.

"You got plenty of cause to hate," Andy said. "Your brother's been used hard. But you took it too far, mister. You got no quarrel with Holly."

"She's a witch."

Andy's smile turned wolfish. "So am I, mister. And now you got a quarrel with me."

Sam had reloaded and fired, hitting Andy again. The bullet wounds didn't seem to matter at all. With a bellow of rage, Sam rushed forward, gun pointed.

Andy moved like a bullfighter, avoiding the attack, and swung his arm around Sam's throat from behind. He threw his weight into the motion. Sam's feet slipped in the blood, and his neck snapped with a muffled, dry crackle. It happened too fast for me to really take in, and then the life was leaving Sam's blue eyes and his body falling, in that utterly empty way that only the dead can fall, as Andy let him go.

Donal howled, and it hurt me to hear it. Andy turned toward me, and our gazes met again.

He'd taken two steps toward me when Lottie's poison took hold. Andy's fearsome strength of will might be able to deny bullet wounds, but this was different. Very different.

His legs folded, and he fell to his side, panting. His pupils grew huge, no longer silver but black, black as the death that was coming for him.

"Next time," he whispered.

I dropped to my knees beside him and put my hand on his forehead as he began to convulse.

I tasted poison on his lips, and I wondered in a black, desolate fury if it would be enough to finish me. It wasn't.

The universe wasn't quite that merciful.

"Miss Caldwell," Detective Prieto said. I raised my head slowly, every muscle aching and hot. Part of it was Lottie's poisonous mixture; the other part was a collection of injuries I hadn't realized I'd accumulated until the heat of battle had passed. I was back in the hospital. They'd taken Donal away in a massive steel prison truck, still fighting. They'd taken Andy away in the coroner's wagon, along with Sam. I'd screamed about the two of them riding together, but the cops thought I was out of my mind.

Maybe I was.

I looked at Detective Prieto wearily, too exhausted to care about the pity in his eyes. "Did you find her?"

"We did," he said. "She was drugged. Chained up in a room underneath Sam Twist's house.

I nodded. "And the others?"

He just looked at me. Sam hadn't needed the others, of course. He'd only needed Lottie to keep Donal alive.

Perversely, Lottie still lived, like the cockroach surviving nuclear winter. And so did Donal, for all the good it did him.

"You okay?" Prieto asked. It was my turn to stare, and he turned away from what he saw in my expression. "Lottie's down the hall, I hear. They say she'll make a full recovery."

With that, he pushed open the door to the grim little hospital room and left. It hurt too much to stand up, but I did it anyway and shuffled to follow.

Prieto was getting into the elevator when I emerged, but he caught my eye and jerked his chin down the hall. "Four down," he said.

The doors shut.

Carlotta was a lovely woman with the soul of a pig. I'd always known that, but I'd never really *known*.

I'd never seen the depths. Now I couldn't get out of them. Not without climbing over someone else.

She'd do.

Carlotta was asleep. She was an older woman, with black hair threaded with silver and lines on her face. Could have been someone's mother, someone's grandmother. Asleep, you couldn't see the real person.

Her eyes opened when I dragged a chair up next to her bed—dark brown, as confused as any soul dragged back from the dark. Except she'd been drugged, not dead, and the softness cleared from her in seconds.

"Holly." She nearly spat my name. "I should have known he'd spare you. Sam always liked *you*."

I didn't answer her. Somewhere, in the coldest part of me, I was seeing the agony of Andy's last moments, and I was realizing how much Lottie would have enjoyed it.

"The others?"

"Dead," I said. My voice sounded soft and distant. "How long have you been doing this?"

"Doing what?"

"Bringing back the dead and fighting them like dogs. For *money*."

Lottie's bitter brown eyes narrowed. "Don't you judge me, you narrow little bitch. We all bring them back for profit." She smiled slowly. "I'm just more creative."

The room appeared red for a few seconds, and I had trouble controlling my breathing. My hands ached, and I realized I'd clenched them into tight, shaking fists.

"Creative," I repeated. "Why'd you ask Prieto for Andy?"

"I knew somebody was stalking us," she said. "If anybody could stop it, Toland would have been the one. Besides—" she was still smiling, and it had a sharp, cutting edge to it, "he'd have made me a lot of money, after. A *lot* of money."

I shuddered. It was hard to stay in the chair. Hard not to put my hands around her throat and squeeze.

"You're done," I said. "I'm going to make it my personal mission to see that you're finished."

"How?" Lottie's laugh broke on the air like ice. "You're a stupid girl. I'm the *victim*. You counting on the Review Board? Better not. So many resurrection witches are gone. They might give me a fine, but they need me. Now more than ever."

She was probably right, at that. Resurrection witches were a rare breed, and she and I were the only ones left in the city. The Review Board would blame Sam. Lottie would get away with a slap on the wrist.

Lottie would do it again, and I wouldn't be able to stop her. The police wouldn't act.

The dead didn't have legal rights.

I stood up. Lottie's dark gaze followed me as I crossed to the door. There was a thumb lock on the inside, and I flipped it over.

Lottie laughed. "You going to kill me, Holly? You going to spend the rest of your life in prison over a dead man?"

"No," I said. "Funny thing about comas, Lottie. You can slip back into them without warning. It's tragic, really."

A flash of something in her eyes that might have been fear. Her hand reached for the call button.

I got there first.

I held her down. She struggled and snarled, but when my lips touched hers, it was all over.

I was the best resurrection witch in Austin. One thing about being able to give life to the dead . . . you can take it from the living. It's forbidden, but it can be done.

I didn't take all her life. Just enough.

Just enough to leave her wandering in the dark, screaming, trapped inside her own head. Her body would live, mute and unresponsive, for as long as modern science could maintain it; but Lottie Flores would never, ever bring back the dead again.

Not even herself.

Andy was in the morgue downstairs, two drawers away from Sam. I had to see him. What I'd done to Lottie had hurt me in ways I knew might never be right again, but somehow seeing his face, even in death, would give me peace.

I had no potion. I had nothing but what was left inside of me. Darkness and passion and need, so much need it seemed to bleed silver from my pores.

He was so lovely. And he was at peace, the way I knew he should be.

I kissed him lightly. No potion and no spell behind it; it was just a kiss, just the brush of our lips.

But the *emotion* behind it—that felt like magic.

I felt him reaching for me, in the dark, and I couldn't help but respond. It wasn't my own magic. I wasn't this strong.

I felt the connection snap clean between us, silver and hot, vibrating like a plucked string.

His eyes opened, and he smiled.

"You came back," I murmured.

"Course I did, Holly," he said. I'll always come for you."

"I didn't—there's no potion—"

"Don't need it," Andy said. He stirred, and the sheet across his bare chest slipped down, revealing raw bullet holes that were, before my eyes, sealing themselves closed. "Got myself some skills, you know. More than most."

I kissed him again, tasting potions and poisons and my own tears. "How long can you stay?" I asked.

"Long as you want me."

Forever.

The End?

Not if you want to dive into more of Crystal Lake Publishing's Tales from the Darkest Depths!

Check out our amazing website and online store
or download our latest catalog here.
https://geni.us/CLPCatalog

Looking for award-winning Dark Fiction?
Download our latest catalog.

Includes our anthologies, novels, novellas, collections,
poetry, non-fiction, and specialty projects.

WHERE STORIES COME ALIVE!

We always have great new projects and content on the website to dive into, as well as a newsletter, behind the scenes options, social media platforms, our own dark fiction shared-world series and our very own webstore. Our webstore even has categories specifically for KU books, non-fiction, anthologies, and of course more novels and novellas.

About the Authors

Rose Blackthorn lives in the desert but longs for the sea. She is a writer, dog-mom, jewelry-maker, avowed coffee drinker, and photographer. Her short fiction and poetry have appeared online and in print with a varied list of anthologies and magazines including the collection Beautiful, Broken Things.
More info can be found at:
http://roseblackthorn.wordpress.com/
http://www.facebook.com/RoseBlackthorn.Author
http://amazon.com/author/roseblackthorn
https://twitter.com/rose_blackthorn

H.R. Boldwood, author of the Corpse Whisperer series, countless short stories, and two-time Imadjinn Award finalist, is a writer of horror and speculative fiction. In another incarnation, Boldwood was a Pushcart Prize nominee and winner of the Thomas More College Bilbo Award for creative writing. Boldwood's characters are often disreputable and not to be trusted. They are kicked to the curb at every conceivable opportunity. No responsibility is taken by this author for the dastardly and sometimes criminal acts committed by this ragtag group of miscreants.

Boldwood's work can be purchased on Kindle, Nook, and in print wherever quality books are sold.

To contact H.R. or to learn more about her work, visit:
www.hrboldwood.com
hrboldwood@gmail.com
https://www.facebook.com/hrboldwood
https://twitter.com/BoldwoodH
https://www.amazon.com/H.-R.-Boldwood/e/B01LWY22MD

Mia Dalia is an internationally published, CWA-nominated author of all things fantastic, thrilling, scary, and strange. Her short fiction has been published online by *Night Terror Novels, 50-word stories, Flash Fiction Magazine, Pyre Magazine, Tales from the Moonlit Path, carte blanche magazine, Jaded Ibis Press, Weird Wide Web;* in print anthologies by Sunbury Press, HellBound Press, Black Ink Fiction, Dragon Roost Press, Unsettling Reads, Phobica Books, PsychoToxin Press, Wandering Wave Press, rebellionLIT Press, Bullet Points Vol. 3, Critical Blast, Off-Topic Publishing, Exploding Head Press, Sinister Smile Press, DraculaBeyondStoker Magazine, Mystery Magazine, Headshot Press, Nightshade Press, WonderBird Press; and featured in narrative podcasts such as Zoetic Press' Alphanumeric, Sudden Fictions, and Tales to Terrify.

More stories coming soon in the upcoming anthologies by Grendel Press, Dragon Roost Press, WriteHive, Crystal Lake Publishing, Dark Matter INK, and more.

Mia's work has been selected as Tales to Terrify's top ten best stories of 2023 and shortlisted for the Crime Writers Association's Daggers Award 2024.

She is the author of the novels *Estate Sale* and *Haven*, novellas *Tell Me a Story, Discordant,* and *Arrokoth,* and the collection *Smile So Red and Other Tales of Madness.*

Find her at

Official website: https://daliaverse.wixsite.com/author

Twitter: @ Dalia_Verse

FB: DaliaVerse

Instagram: daliaverse

https://linktr.ee/daliaverse

L. E. Daniels is a Bram Stoker Awards® nominee for short fiction and an American author, poet, and editor of over 130 titles living in Australia. Lauren edited Aiki Flinthart's *Relics, Wrecks and Ruins* (CAT) with Geneve Flynn, winning the 2021 Aurealis Award. With Christa Carmen, she edited *We are Providence: Tales of Horror from the Ocean State* (Weird House Press), a 2022 Aurealis finalist, and *Monsters in the Mills* (Interactive Publications) in 2024. Her novel, *Serpent's Wake: A Tale for the Bitten* (Interactive Publications) is a Notable Work with the HWA's Mental Health Initiative.

Recent publications include "Silk" in *Hush, Don't Wake the Monster* (Twisted Wing Productions) and "Hangman's Coming"

in *Where the Silent Ones Watch* (Hippocampus Press). Lauren's personal essays appear in *Holistic Horror, Quick Bites,* and *34 Orchard.* Her recent poetry is published in *The Cozy Cosmic* (Underland Press), *Under Her Eye,* and *Mother Knows Best* (Black Spot Books), with "Night Terrors" *(Of Horror and Hope,* HWA) a finalist for the 2022 Australian Shadows Award. Lauren runs Brisbane Writers Workshop.
Website: https://www.brisbanewriters.com
Facebook: https://www.facebook.com/laurenelisedaniels/
Instagram: https://www.instagram.com/lauren_elise_daniels/

Claire Davon is a USA Today Bestselling author who has written for most of her life, starting with fan fiction when she was very young. She writes across a wide range of genres and does not consider any of it off limits. Her novels can be found in the paranormal romance and contemporary romance sections, while her short stories run the gamut. If a story calls to her, she will write it. She currently lives in Los Angeles and spends her free time writing novels and short stories, as well as doing animal rescue and enjoying the sunshine. Claire's website is www.clairedavon.com.

Aelth Faye lives on the east coast near her vast collection of siblings and niblings and enjoys handicrafts and computer games when she's not reading a book. Her primary series, "Fairytale Hour" can be found on Amazon and she also has published sci-fi and fantasy stories for Raconteur Press, Kindle Vella, and multiple online magazines. You can find her at https://aelthfaye.com/

Mary Genevieve Fortier
Multi Award-Winning Author of Poetry/Prose
Deemed, "The Modern Day Poe" by her esteemed Peers.
Columnist (Written and Audio Versions), "Nighty Nightmare" –http://www.nightynightmare.net
Editor: JWK Fiction; Nocturnicorn Books; Black Bedsheet Books
Reviewer: Hellnotes; Dark Regions Press
"Terror Train Podcast" Co-Producer, Character/Creator /Performer/Dialogue Writer, "Terror, the Disembodied Voice;" author of opening/closing poems.
Audio Performer (All Better Audio/The 4077th Productions)
Narrator (Fortier-Schütz/Wooden Box MediaWorks).
Featured guest: "Whispers in the Dark;" "Zombiepalooza

Radio;" "Deadman's Tome;" "A Knife and a Quill."

Reviewed by "Ghoul Guides;" "Hellnotes;" "The Parlor of Horror;" "FEAR Magazine"

Featured Poem (audio advertisement) "Floppy Shoes Apocalypse."

Listed in the "HWA's Reading List 2016;" "Ellen Datlow's List of Honorable Mentions,

Volume 8."

Interviewed by Marge Simon, HWA Newsletter 2017

Co-Founder, "The Greater Saint Louis Area Horror Writers Society."

Named, "Woman in Horror" by "Blaze McRob's Tales of Horror/Blazing Owl Press," 2014-2021.

Featured twice on "The Wicked Library" and "Hellnotes, Horror in a Hundred."

Facebook: https://www.facebook.com/MaryGenevieveFortierWriter

Amazon: https://www.amazon.com/stores/Mary-Genevieve-Fortier/author/B00GQCYXWM

Rowan Hill is an author of horror and sci-fi with a heart firmly stuck in the 80s listening to its own synth soundtrack. She loves a flawed woman who occasionally murders and a plot twist within a plot twist. She has several short story credits of such things and her debut novella, *In The Arctic Sun*, was released in 2022 with D&T Publishing. She can be found online or her website, writerrowanhill.com.

Nancy Holder is a New York Times bestselling author. She has received seven Bram Stoker awards including the Lifetime Achievement Award from the Horror Writers Association, and was awarded the "Faust" Grand Master Award by the International Association of Media Tie-In Writers in 2019. She is a Baker Street Irregular. She has written and edited dozens of novels and book projects; hundreds of short stories, essays, and articles; two online games; and comic books and graphic novels. She is currently working on pulp fiction as well as and two comic book series, Johnny Fade (Moonstone Books) and They Call Me Midnight (IPI Comics) with her writing partner, Alan Philipson.
@nancyholder
www.nancyholder.com

Sarah Jane Huntington is the author of several horror novels and collections. She has a new horror collection out this year with Velox books and recently released a science fiction horror with 3-B publishing.

Rue Karney lives in Meanjin/Brisbane (on the unceded lands of the Turrbal and Juggera peoples) and loves to read and write stories that are strange, unsettling, bizarre and weird. Karney's work has appeared in the anthologies *Hauntings, In Sunshine Bright and Darkness Deep, Monsters Amongst Us, Pacific Monsters and Nothing* as well as the magazines *SQ Mag, Midnight Echo* and Hinnom Magazine. Her Australian Horror Writers Association winning short story, "Brother", was translated into Italian and published in Collana Mondi Incantati as Fratello.

When not exhuming the strange places and people from her head to create stories, Karney enjoys learning French and reading about psychopaths.

Naching T. Kassa is a wife, mother, horror writer and Talent Relations Manager at Crystal Lake Entertainment. She is a proud member of the Horror Writers Association, Mystery Writers of America and The Science Fiction and Fantasy Writers Association.

Award-winning author ***Nancy Kilpatrick*** is a writer and editor in the horror/dark fantasy genre but has also written mysteries, science fiction, fantasy, and erotica. Her 23 novels include her current series Thrones of Blood, recently optioned for film and television. She has published over 220 short stories, 7 collections of her stories, and 1 non-fiction book. She is also an editor with 15 anthologies to her credit. Nancy has just finished a science fiction/horror novel. Currently she is working on the 6th and final Thrones of Blood volume, Imperilment of the Hybrids. You can connect with her on Facebook, Twitter and Instagram. Check out her website where you can subscribe to her once-a-month, pithy newsletter: http://www.nancykilpatrick.com

Gerri Leen lives in Northern Virginia and originally hails from Seattle. In addition to being an avid reader, she's passionate about horse racing, tea, and collecting encaustic art and raku pottery. She has work in *The Magazine of Fantasy & Science Fiction, Nature, Strange Horizons, Galaxy's Edge, Dark Matter, Daily Science Fiction,* and others. She's edited several anthologies for independent presses, is finishing some longer projects, and is a member of SFWA and HWA. See more at gerrileen.com.

Since learning to write at the age of five, *Yvonne Mason* has wanted to be an author. She wrote her first novel Stan's Story beginning in 1974 and completed it in 2006. Publication seemed impossible as rejections grew to 10 years. Determined, she continued adding to the story until her dream came true in 2006.

Yvonne's brother Stan has been her inspiration and hero in every facet of her life. He was stricken with Encephalitis at the tender age of nine months. He has defied every roadblock placed in his way and has been the driving force in every one of her accomplishments. He is the one who taught her never to give up

Yvonne is currently the author of several novels, including:

Stan's Story—the true story of her brother's accomplishments, it has been compared to the style of Capote, and is currently being rewritten with new information for re-release.

Tangled Minds—a riveting story about a young girl's bad decision and how it taints everyone's life around her yet still manages to show that hope is always possible. This novel has been compared to the writing of Steinbeck and is currently being written as a screenplay. This novel will be re-released by Kerlak Publishing in 2009

Brilliant Insanity—released by Kerlak Publishing October 2008

Silent Scream—Released by Lulu.com October 2008- Slated to be made into a movie -Listed at #5 in Mainstream Novels for 2008 In Predators and Editors Poll.

Patricia Miller is a member of SFWA and writes science fiction, fantasy, and horror. Publications include short fiction in numerous anthologies, *Metastellar, Zooscape, Stupefying Stories,* and *Cinnabar Moth Literary Collections.* Her most current publications include stories in *99 Fleeting Fantasies* edited by Jennifer Brozek and *The Horror That Represents You* coming in December 2024 by Brigids Gate Publishing.

Donna J. W. Munro teaches high schoolers the slippery truths of government and history at her day job. Her students are her greatest inspiration. She lives with five cats, a cute curly haired dog, a fur covered husband, a sassy septuagenarian Mama, and an encyclopedia son. Her daughter is off saving the world.

Donna's pieces are published in Corvid Queen, *Enter the Apocalypse, It Calls from the Forest, Apparition Lit, Pseudopod 752, Shakespeare Unleashed, Novus Monstrum, ParABnormal, and many more. Check out her novels, Revelation: Poppet Cycle Book 1, Runaway: PCB2, and Revolution: PCB3.* Her website has a complete list of works at https://www.donnajwmunro.net/.

Elaine Pascale is the author of *The Blood Lights; If Nothing Else, Eve, We've Enjoyed the Fruit; and* the soon-to-be-released *The Language of Crows.* She is the editor of *Dancing in the Shadows: A tribute to Anne Rice.* She is a regular contributor to Pen of the Damned and the Ladies of Horror Picture-Prompt Challenge and is part of the Strong Women, Strange Worlds marketing group.

She is also a reviewer for Hellnotes. She would never take revenge on someone in real life due to a fear of karma, but those that irk her may find themselves in one of her stories. Elaine is happy to engage with readers at:
Website: elainepascale.com
Amazon:
https://www.amazon.com/Elaine-Pascale/e/B003MRXUCS/ref=ntt_dp_epwbk_0,
Facebook: elaine.pascale
Twitter and Instagram: @doclaney
TikTok: @elainepascale

Nora B. Peevy is a cat trapped in a human's body. She's traveled around the sun forty-five times. Nora is a member of HAG and the HWA and has been published more times than she has fingers. She's also a submissions reader for various presses, and the newest team editor for *Alien Sun Press.*

Nora is a stock photographer for Getty Images. Her hobbies include breathing, sleeping, hanging out in cemeteries, and avoiding taking pencils in the eye. She hails from Wisconsin, the land of cheese, living with two wily cats and her turtle, Bradbury. His own writing career has not taken off, yet.

Rosalind Place has been writing since childhood: her first work was a 5-page book carefully printed on coloured paper in grade school. After growing up, she first became a poet and went on to publish several literary stories in magazines and anthologies. She is a member of The Mesdames of Mayhem, a collective of Canadian

crime fiction writers. Her stories appear in four of their anthologies including the soon-to-be-published "The Thirteenth Letter". She has recently completed her first novel.
https://mesdamesofmayhem.com/

Alisha Rath is an author based in Kelowna, BC, Canada. Drawing from her background in community support work and the film industry, she brings a unique perspective to her writing. Alisha's works have been featured in publications spanning academic, memoir, and fiction genres. Her primary focus lies in crafting compelling thriller and horror narratives that resonate with readers.

Suzanne Reynolds-Alpert writes short fiction and poetry in the horror, sci-fi, and dark fantasy genres. Her short stories have appeared in the anthologies *Wicked Women, The Final Summons, Killing It Softly (Vol.1),* and *The Deep Dark Woods.* Read her poetry in the *HWA Poetry Showcase Vol. VI,* the anthologies *Beneath Strange Stars* and *Wicked Witches,* the websites Tales of the Zombie Wa and Eternal Haunted Summer; and in *The Wayfarer: A Journal of Contemplative Literature.*

She published a short collection of poetry, *Interview with the Faerie (Part One) and Other Poems of Darkness and Light* in 2013. Suzanne is a technical services librarian, freelance writer and editor, and has been exploring mixed media art. When she's not working, reading, or arting, she's busy meeting the incessant demands of her feline overlords.

Rie Sheridan Rose's prose appears in numerous anthologies, including *Killing It Softly Vol. 1 & 2, Hides the Dark Tower, Dark Divinations,* and *Startling Stories.* In addition, she has authored twelve novels in multiple genres, six poetry chapbooks, and dozens of song lyrics. Her newest work is a poetry collection entitled *Two Dozen Stars.* She is a native of Texas and lives there with her husband and several spoiled cats. When not writing or editing, she is usually walking—being a Virtual Race addict. Member of the HWA and SFWA, she X's irregularly as @RieSheridanRose. Her website is www.riewriter.com, or find her on Facebook at https://www.facebook.com/RieSheridanRoseAuthorPage/.

Alex T. Singer lives in coastal Connecticut with her wife, daughter, and more sci fi/fantasy novels than she can count. She is the author of the graphic novel MIRRORVERSE: BELLE (Viz

Media). Her short stories have appeared in *Lunar Station Quarterly*, *Apparition Literature,* and *Pseudopod.* Her short story, "Nothing But The Gods On Their Backs" (Metaphorosis Magazine) was a finalist in the 2024 WSFA Small Press Award category for short fiction. Samples of her work can be found at: http://littlefoolery.com/.

Christina Sng is the three-time Bram Stoker Award-winning author of *A Collection of Nightmares, A Collection of Dreamscapes,* and *Tortured Willows: Bent. Bowed. Unbroken.* Her poetry, fiction, essays, and art appear in numerous venues worldwide, including Interstellar Flight Magazine, New Myths, Penumbric, Southwest Review, and The Washington Post.

Valerie B. Williams' short fiction has been published by Flame Tree Press, Dark Recesses Press, Grendel Press, and Death Knell Press, among others. Her most recent published story, "An Echo of Murder," appeared in Issue 3 (July 2024) of the Carnage House E-zine.

Her debut novel, a story of supernatural suspense titled *The Vanishing Twin;* will be released by Crossroad Press on October 1, 2024.

Valerie spins twisty tales from her home in central Virginia, which she shares with her very patient husband and equally patient Golden Retriever. When not writing, she can be found reading and drinking either tea or wine, depending on the time of day.

Website: Valerie B. Williams (valeriebwilliams.com)

Amazon: Amazon.com: Valerie B. Williams: books, biography, latest update

Facebook: https://www.facebook.com/valerie.b.williams.2

BlueSky: Valerie B. Williams (@valwillwrite.bsky.social)

Jezzy Wolfe is a poet and author who has appeared in numerous anthologies and publications, such as Smart Rhino's Zippered Flesh trilogy, *Insidious Assassins,* and *Asinine Assassins* Anthologies, Crystal Lake's Shallow Waters anthology, Western Legends' *Unnatural Tales Of The Jackalope,* ZombieWorks' Unwelcomed: Stories Of Hauntings And Possessions anthology, and magazines such as Siren's Call, Space & Time Magazine, and Weird Tales. Her debut poetry collection, *Monstrum Poetica,* is now available from Raw Dog Screaming Press. When she is not being chased by her ferrets or tripping over hiking trails, you can find her on her blog at jezzywolfe.wordpress.com, on Facebook at www.facebook.com/jezzywolfeauthor, and on Twitter at @JezzyWolfe.

Nemma Wollenfang is a speculative fiction writer who lives in Northern England. Her work has appeared in several venues, including: *Beyond the Stars, Cossmass Infinities, Third Flatiron, Abyss & Apex, Speculatively Queer, Broken Eye Books,* and Flame Tree Publishing's Gothic Fantasy series. She is a recipient of the Speculative Literature Foundation's Working Class Writers Grant and a participant of Writers on the Moon. She can be found on Facebook and Amazon.

Chelsea Quinn Yarbro has been a professional writer for more than forty years, Yarbro has sold over eighty books, more than seventy works of short fiction, and more than three dozen essays, introductions, and reviews. She also composes serious music. Her first professional writing—in 1961-2—was as a playwright for a now long-defunct children's theater company. By the mid-60s she had switched to writing stories and hasn't stopped yet.

After leaving college in 1963 and until she became a full-time writer in 1970, she worked as a demographic cartographer, and still often drafts maps for her books, and occasionally for the books of other writers.

She has a large reference library with books on a wide range of subjects, everything from food and fashion to weapons and trade routes to religion and law. She is constantly adding to it as part of her on-going fascination with history and culture; she reads incessantly, searching for interesting people and places that might provide fodder for stories.

In 1997 the Transylvanian Society of Dracula bestowed a literary knighthood on Yarbro, and in 2003 the World Horror Association presented her with a Grand Master award. In 2006 the International Horror Guild enrolled her among their Living Legends, the first woman to be so honored; the Horror Writers Association gave her a Life Achievement Award in 2009.

A skeptical occultist for forty years, she has studied everything from alchemy to zoomancy, and in the late 1970s worked occasionally as a professional tarot card reader and palmist at the Magic Cellar in San Francisco.

She has two domestic accomplishments: she is a good cook and an experienced seamstress. The rest is catch-as-catch-can.

Divorced, she lives in the San Francisco Bay Area—with two cats: the irrepressible Butterscotch and Crumpet, the Gang of Two. When not busy writing, she enjoys the symphony or opera.

Katie Young is the author of Moth Girl, a previously unpublished story. She is a writer of dark fiction and poetry, with work appearing in various publications, including anthologies from Flame Tree Press, Shortwave Publishing, Brigids Gate Press, Dark Dispatch, Scott J. Moses, Nyx Publishing, Ghost Orchid Press, and Fox Spirit Books. Her story, Lavender Tea, was selected by Zoe Gilbert for inclusion in the Mechanic Institute Review's Summer Folk Festival 2019. She lives in west London with her partner and an angry cat.

Editors

Marianne Halbert is an author from central Indiana. Her quiet horror stories have been described as "whimsical and terrifying" as well as "elegant and macabre". Her latest collection is *Cold Comforts* (Crossroad Press, 2019) and is full of slow-burn horror stories. Marianne is a member of the HWA and has a story on PseudoPod (Ep. 776). You can follow her on social media @HalbertFiction or learn more about her work at https://www.halbertfiction.com/

Over a decade ago, ***Suzie Lockhart*** finally gave in to the gnawing urge to write. Her first story was published in 2011, and she's never looked back. Since then, she's had numerous short stories published in a variety of genres.

Suzie has also edited over a half dozen anthologies, including the award-winning *Killing It Softly Vols. 1 & 2*. She is an Associate Member of the HWA

Readers . . .

Thank you for reading *Dastardly Damsels*. We hope you enjoyed this anthology

If you have a moment, please review *Dastardly Damsels* at the store where you bought it.

Help other readers by telling them why you enjoyed this book. No need to write an in-depth discussion. Even a single sentence will be greatly appreciated. Reviews go a long way to helping a book sell, and is great for an author's career. It'll also help us to continue publishing quality books.

Thank you again for taking the time to journey with Crystal Lake Publishing.

Visit our Linktree page for a list of our social media platforms. https://linktr.ee/CrystalLakePublishing

Follow us on Amazon:

Our Mission Statement:

Since its founding in August 2012, Crystal Lake Publishing has quickly become one of the world's leading publishers of Dark Fiction and Horror books. In 2023, Crystal Lake Publishing formed a part of Crystal Lake Entertainment, joining several other divisions, including Torrid Waters, Crystal Lake Comics, Crystal Lake Kids, and many more.

While we strive to present only the highest quality fiction and entertainment, we also endeavour to support authors along their writing journey. We offer our time and experience in non-fiction projects, as well as author mentoring and services, at competitive prices.

With several Bram Stoker Award wins and many other wins and nominations (including the HWA's Specialty Press Award), Crystal Lake Publishing puts integrity, honor, and respect at the forefront of our publishing operations.

We strive for each book and outreach program we spearhead to not only entertain and touch or comment on issues that affect our readers, but also to strengthen and support the Dark Fiction field and its authors.

Not only do we find and publish authors we believe are destined for greatness, but we strive to work with men and women who endeavour to be decent human beings who care more for others than themselves, while still being hard working, driven, and passionate artists and storytellers.

Crystal Lake Publishing is and will always be a beacon of what passion and dedication, combined with overwhelming teamwork and respect, can accomplish. We endeavour to know each and every one of our readers, while building personal relationships with our authors, reviewers, bloggers, podcasters, bookstores, and libraries.

We will be as trustworthy, forthright, and transparent as any business can be, while also keeping most of the headaches away from our authors, since it's our job to solve the problems so they can stay in a creative mind. Which of course also means paying our authors.

We do not just publish books, we present to you worlds within your world, doors within your mind, from talented authors who sacrifice so much for a moment of your time.

There are some amazing small presses out there, and through collaboration and open forums we will continue to support other presses in the goal of helping authors and showing the world what quality small presses are capable of accomplishing. No one wins when a small press goes down, so we will always be there to support hardworking, legitimate presses and their authors. We don't see Crystal Lake as the best press out there, but we will always strive to be the best, strive to be the most interactive and grateful, and even blessed press around. No matter what happens over time, we will also take our mission very seriously while appreciating where we are and enjoying the journey.

What do we offer our authors that they can't do for themselves through self-publishing?

We are big supporters of self-publishing (especially hybrid publishing), if done with care, patience, and planning. However, not every author has the time or inclination to do market research, advertise, and set up book launch strategies. Although a lot of authors are successful in doing it all, strong small presses will always be there for the authors who just want to do what they do best: write.

What we offer is experience, industry knowledge, contacts and trust built up over years. And due to our strong brand and trusting fanbase, every Crystal Lake Publishing book comes with weight of respect. In time our fans begin to trust our judgment and will try a new author purely based on our support of said author.

With each launch we strive to fine-tune our approach, learn from our mistakes, and increase our reach. We continue to assure our authors that we're here for them and that we'll carry the weight of the launch and dealing with third parties while they focus on their strengths—be it writing, interviews, blogs, signings, etc.

We also offer several mentoring packages to authors that include knowledge and skills they can use in both traditional and self-publishing endeavours.

We look forward to launching many new careers.

This is what we believe in. What we stand for. This will be our legacy.

Welcome to Crystal Lake Publishing— Tales from the Darkest Depths.